China Court

CHINA COURT 1840

b. 1801–*d.* 1889   Eustace, *m.* Adza   *b.* 1817–*d.* 1874

THE BROOD

[1ST GENERATION]

Mary	Eliza	Anne	Little	Mcleod	Lucy	Marion
1841	1844–94	1845	Eustace	the 2nd	1850 *d.*	1849–50
			1846–59	1848		

Jared,   *m.*   Lady   Damaris, *m.* Mr. King Lee
1851–98   Patrick   1853–71   in 1870
             1857–1904

[2ND GENERATION]

Borowis, *m.* Isabel   John Henry, *m.* Ripsie
1876–1900   1878–1930   1879–1960

[3RD GENERATION]

Stace, *m.* Barbara   Bella, *m.* Walter   1904 1905 1907
1900–44   1902   The Three Graces

Tracy 1939

Polly came to China Court 1841, *b.* 1806–*d.* 1895
Cecily came to China Court 1909, aged 14
Groundsel came in 1906 as garden boy
Minna came 1912, *m.* Groundsel in 1913

China Court

The Hours of a Country House

Rumer Godden

WILLIAM MORROW and COMPANY, INC.

NEW YORK

A serial version of this book appeared in the *Ladies' Home Journal*

Library of Congress Cataloging-in-Publication Data

Godden, Rumer, 1907–
    China Court : the hours of a country house / by Rumer Godden.
        p.   cm.
    "A serial version of this book appeared in the Ladies' home journal"—T.p. verso.
    ISBN 0-688-11722-8
    I. Title.
PR6013.O2C48   1993
823'.912—dc20   92-20702
                                                                      CIP

Printed in the United States of America

First U.S. Edition

1 2 3 4 5 6 7 8 9 10

BOOK DESIGN BY BARBARA BACHMAN

FOR

John Betjeman

Preface

I n   r e a l   l i f e   when one meets a large family, with all its ramifications of uncles, aunts, and cousins, as well as grandfathers and grandmothers, grandchildren, and great-grandchildren, their friends, servants, and pet animals, it takes time to distinguish them; one does not expect to remember straight away that it is Jane who is married to Bertram, Jack who was born with a club foot, Aunt Margaret who had the unfortunate love affair. One has to get to know them.

China Court is a novel about five generations of a family, so that, as in real life, there are many names and personalities, but I believe if the reader is a little patient—and can bear not to skip—they will soon become distinct and he will have no need to look at the family tree on the frontispiece.

Life, Chaucer says, is a "thinne subtil knittinge of thinges"; naturally it is difficult to understand.

R. G.

Contents

China Court

Lauds

Nox praecéssit, dies autem appropinquavit. . . .

THE NIGHT IS FAR ON ITS COURSE; DAY DRAWS NEAR.

LITTLE CHAPTER FOR LAUDS FROM MRS. QUIN'S
Day Hours

T *h e* V *i s i t a t i o n* · The scene takes place in a walled garden. The Virgin holds the half-kneeling Elizabeth in her arms and raises her to her feet. Zacharias stands by with bowed head. On the right-hand side is part of the house with the door open giving the spectator a glimpse of a charming interior. A woman is watching the scene through an open upper window.

Full border of flowers, harebells, and strawberries and ivy leaves, painted in colors and heightened with gold. Figure of a monkey making a long nose with both hands at the woman watching the scene from the window.

MINIATURE FACING THE OPENING OF LAUDS
IN THE HORAE BEATAE VIRGINIS MARIAE, FROM THE
HOURS OF ROBERT BONNEFOY

O *l d* **M** *r s* . **Q** *u i n* died in her sleep in the early hours of an August morning.

The sound of the bell came into the house, but did not disturb it; it was quite used to death, and birth, and life.

The usual house sounds went on, but muted: footsteps, upstairs, Dr. Taft's, though he did not stay long— "Cause of death, stopped living," wrote Dr. Taft on the certificate and said he would call in at Mrs. Abel's on his way home; then Mrs. Abel's steps as, quietly, she did what she had to do and, downstairs, Cecily's as she carried in the coal and made up the kitchen fire, hers and Bumble's, the old spaniel's, padding as he followed her backward and forward, forward and backward; Bumble was uneasy, while August, the young poodle, rushed to the front door, back door, upstairs and down, barking, anguished by he knew not what. The fire made a warm fanning sound; a tap ran; the post-van came and the postman dropped letters into the letter box. Trill, the canary, sang. Moses, the cat, meowed for his morning milk and rabbit as, in their turn, Toby, the tabby, Minerva, the stately white cat, and the naughty small one

like a sprite, Cuckoo, meowed too. Groundsel had come
at eight o'clock as usual and left his pasty on the kitchen
windowsill for Cecily to take in and warm for his lunch.
Now the sound of his shears as he clipped a box hedge
came in from outside, with the calls of blackbirds and
robins and the throbbing of an engine from the farm
where they were threshing. With all these other sounds,
mingling with them, came the bell: "In the midst of life
we are in death" was the message of the bell; the house
seemed to answer, "In the midst of death we are in life."

"Shouldn' us pull the blinds down?" asked Mrs. Abel.

"She wouldn't like it," said Cecily. "She always says,
'Don't shut out the garden.' That's why Groundsel
thought he ought to work, even today."

"There now!" said Mrs. Abel, vexed with herself. "I
purty near forgot! Didn' I promise to bring her a root
o' me rose piony."

Neither Cecily nor Mrs. Abel whispered, nor did they
speak of Mrs. Quin as if she were not there, but all the
same, things were muted; there was no early-morning
firing of explosives from the quarry, which had stopped
work when the news was heard and the men had been
sent home as a mark of respect, "But the news will be in
the village before the men," said Cecily.

Of course; Dr. Taft's car would have been seen, then
Mrs. Abel coming down, and Cecily knew the vicar
would be here at any moment. "No one goes in or out
of China Court who isn't seen," complained Cecily often,
"seen and talked about." The village was not kind:
proudly inbred, it kept for strangers the spirit of its
wrecker forebears, though where it respected it was
staunch and for Mrs. Quin there would be genuine feeling. "Mrs. Quin gone!" It would be a blank that would
leave St. Probus for once dumb and the whole village

would listen, Cecily knew, with respectful silence to the bell. "Eighty-one strokes," said Cecily as she bent down to push in the damper of the range. "You have enough hot water, haven't you?" she called to Mrs. Abel. "I must get the oven hot."

It is an Eagle range, blackleaded, with shining steel hinges and handles. "Everything in this house is hopelessly old-fashioned," Mrs. Quin's eldest daughter, Bella, always cries when she has to come to stay; when Mrs. Quin breaks her ankle, for instance, and when Cecily has influenza so badly that it turns to bronchitis. The Eagle has flues that Bella cannot wrestle with but Cecily understands it: "I ought to, I have known it for nearly fifty years," ever since, at fourteen years old, she comes— "as kitchen maid then," says Cecily—from Wales. It is the same great old range and now it burned red. "I shall have to bake," said Cecily. "Eighty-one strokes," and as she straightened herself a tear sizzled across the iron plate.

"It seems so dreadful, on'y the two on us," said Mrs. Abel but, if Mrs. Quin could have been asked, this was as she would have preferred it. Cecily was her long familiar and neither of them could remember the time when they had not known Mrs. Abel, who was the unofficial nurse of the village and its layer-out of the dead. If there had to be someone to touch her so intimately, Mrs. Quin would have said, let it be Mrs. Abel with her capable work-rough hands. Mrs. Abel's ways were simple: clean linen and bandages, camphor and carbolic, soap and hot water; the eyes closed, the feet laid decently together, hands folded on the breast, chin firmly tied up; simple ways but decent, dignified, "and time-honored," Mrs. Quin would have said. In the village Mrs. Abel would have had certain other duties, even rights:

to help with the funeral tea; to arrange the family
wreaths; if there were thirteen mourners to walk or
drive in the funeral procession and make a fourteenth,
but this was China Court and when the time came Mrs.
Abel would keep in the background.

She and Cecily conferred together. "The best linen
sheets?"

"Certainly," said Cecily.

"One pillow?"

"She always had one."

Cecily helped to make the bed and when they moved
the pillow they found a book tucked under it. "Her
prayer book," said Mrs. Abel approvingly, then, as she
looked more closely at it, "It id'n' a prayer book."

"It is," said Cecily and had to resist an impulse to
snatch it out of Mrs. Abel's hand.

All these last years the book had been kept by Mrs.
Quin's bed, on the table with "Mother's old clutter," as
Bella calls it. There is certainly a clutter on the table and
most of Mrs. Quin's possessions are old: her clock has a
battered silver case and loses ten minutes a day; there is
a bottle of pills prescribed three years ago and letters,
turned yellow. Though books nowadays are sold with
their pages cut, she still keeps a paper knife in the shape
of a sword on the table, the hilt damascened in black
and gold; John Henry, her husband, gives it to her,
long ago in Toledo. There is another knife, a silver
penknife—"Stace's," says Bella, always jealous of her
brother—and a miniature tea set, held in a painted
apple that Tracy leaves behind. "Mother doesn't like
photographs, she likes relics," says Bella.

There are, too, always flowers, not often a vaseful
but a bouquet of the smallest wild ones in a miniature
Venetian glass, sharp at one side where it has been

dropped and chipped; or else there is a rose or a single flower in a specimen glass. A candlestick, matches, another bottle of heart-shaped indigestion pills, are part of the clutter with, usually, a paper-bound detective novel and the two books that never change, the one in Mrs. Abel's hand, shabby now and bound in black leather, the other, to Cecily its companion because for so long she has seen them together, a very old and dumpy book, almost clumsy, bound in rubbed pink velvet with a silver clasp, and always carefully wrapped in a silk handkerchief, itself so old that it is nearly rotten.

"*The Day Hours,*" said Mrs. Abel, reading the title of the black book, "Day Hours, whatever be they?"

"Prayers for the hours of the day," said Cecily.

"I didn' knaw Mrs. Quin was religious."

"She wasn't," said Cecily, but when the bed was made and Mrs. Abel had carried her basins out of the room, Cecily put the book back under Mrs. Quin's pillow; the pillow lay unevenly and to level it Cecily tucked the handkerchief-wrapped book under the other side. Then she smoothed the bed and began to clean the room.

"I always know when Cecily has cleaned a room," Mrs. Quin says often. "It smells of well-being." Cecily cleaned with her usual thoroughness now, polishing the floor and rubbing up the furniture. When she had finished, she carried in a vase of the small pink Damascus roses Mrs. Quin had loved the best and, clearing a space, put them on the bedside table; she set the window a little open and came out and, as gently as if Mrs. Quin could have heard it, closed the door.

"Shouldn' us watch?" asked Mrs. Abel. "Some of the women 'ud be glad to come."

Cecily shook her head. "She always liked to be alone," but in an old house, a family house, one is never alone.

The motes of dust that Cecily had disturbed glittered and spun in the sun that came through the window. A tiny fly whirred in the roses. As they grew warm, their scent filled the room, mingling with Mrs. Abel's camphor and carbolic. The bell had stopped but, as if like the dust they had been disturbed, the house voices seemed to rise: "You can have my egg collection."

"Hester will show you the different rooms."

"Oh, not those sickly sweet-pea colors, Mother! I want scarlet or amber."

"I thought Latin was battles, Roman wars."

"Tracy, if you poke that fire again I swear I shall hit you."

"You will be grown up. Then you can come back."

"That whacking great allowance . . ."

"We have no asparagus tongs."

"I could use a gin."

"It is Papa's place, my dear," and, like a cry, a single name:

"Boro! Borowis!"

Tracy, Mrs. Quin's grandchild, immediately fixes on that name. Perhaps it is its oddness; "but so many are odd," says Tracy. She loves to go back from herself through the family tree that Eustace, the first Quin at China Court, starts long ago for his children. It is written in india ink and gold at the beginning of the big Bible that has a table to itself in the hall and, "Funny names," says Tracy, creasing her forehead as she tries to spell them out, "Eustace; Adza; Jared; Borowis. I have never heard of them."

"You have heard of Eustace," says Mrs. Quin.

Tracy has heard of Eustace because his name is like her father's, Stace, and her own, Tracy. Eustace's name is the first on the family tree, hers is the last. Some of the names are ordinary, names everybody knows: Eliza, Anne, John Henry, Mary, but there is a Lady Mary. "Why *Lady* Mary?" asks Tracy.

"She wasn't called that. She was always called Lady Patrick."

This is more confusing still. "Patrick is a boy's name."

"She was called Lady Patrick because she came from Ireland. Irish people are sometimes called Patricks," and, "Poor tragic exaggerated silly Lady Patrick," says Mrs. Quin.

Tragic and *exaggerated* are too difficult for Tracy but, "Why was she silly?" she asks. She likes Mrs. Quin to tell these stories over and over again and Mrs. Quin is willing, "as far as I know them," says Mrs. Quin. Stories, she knows, can never be really told, so much of them is hidden and she often says that when they are told they sound like fairy tales, as if, with time, truth leaks out of them; only the house and the hours spent in it—"and the garden of course," says Mrs. Quin—seem real to her now, but the people are very real to Tracy. "Damaris is another funny name," she says.

"Quite a number of girls were called Damaris then," says Mrs. Quin.

"But they are funny names," argues Tracy.

"Not when you get to know them," says Mrs. Quin. "You will get to know them." She closes the book up but Borowis's name stays in Tracy's mind and she asks, perhaps for the twentieth time, "Who was Borowis?"

It is odd how Tracy asks that question again and again. Perhaps it is a difference in her grandmother's voice when she answers that arrests her; it is not what Mrs. Quin says because she always gives the same answer: "Borowis? He was a boy."

"A Quin boy?"

"Yes."

"You knew him?"

"Yes." There is sharpness in that, then Mrs. Quin's voice quiets and Tracy immediately grows still, for she knows her grandmother is remembering. "I came up the valley path," says Mrs. Quin, "and looked over the wall and he was there. *They* were there," she corrects herself.

"Borowis and John Henry?"

"Yes."

"That was when you were Ripsie?"

"When I was Ripsie," that thin neglected shabby little girl.

"Was Ripsie long before me?" asks Tracy. It is not really a question because she knows the answer perfectly well. "Before me?"

"Long before you."

The valley path is the children's path; it comes from Penbarrow by way of the river and woods to a gap in the China Court boundary wall which is built, as most Cornish walls are, of loose stones, big-sized, covered with moss. It and the clapper stones of the footbridge over the river have been here "for hundreds of years," says Tracy. By the wall two great beech trees stand in a dell where the wood flowers have seeded over the wall and, in spring, make drifts of snowdrops, then violets and anemones. From the dell, through a wicket gate, a path leads across a sloping field to the kitchen garden, bounded by another lower granite wall; in summer a hedge of sweet peas separates the kitchen garden from the flower beds and terraces of the garden proper. The garden is of little account when Ripsie first sees it— "hideous," says Mrs. Quin—but it has a flagpole which impresses her very much; the creepers up the house front are there and the two elms at the side. The house faces west, and as the time is sunset, every window has such a brilliance of light that the house seems lit with gold.

As she watches, a maid comes out on the terrace and begins to put away the garden chairs. Ripsie has not seen a parlormaid before and she leans on the wall entranced; the maid is Pringle, who is often to shoo her away from the front hall, and even at this distance Ripsie can see how importantly befrilled Pringle is in black with a large white apron, pinafore-frilled over the shoulders. Her sleeves are puffed at the top, she has white cuffs, and her cap is shaped like a Scots soldier's, but with white streamers behind. Ripsie watches fascinated, until a sound makes her turn. Near her, in the dell, is a boy.

"Your John Henry?" asks Tracy's mother, Barbara, who is unfailingly romantic—even after all those affairs, thinks Mrs. Quin unkindly. "Your John Henry?"

"No, it was Borowis," but Mrs. Quin does not say that aloud, not to Barbara. "He invited me in," she says slowly. Barbara thinks she is speaking of John Henry, but Tracy knows better. Her grandmother is speaking of Borowis; a different look has come into her harsh old face. "He invited me in," says Mrs. Quin. "I never went away again."

Hers is a long span, stretching from Tracy back to Eustace, "for I can remember him," says Mrs. Quin. Eustace, the boys' grandfather, is paralyzed after a stroke so that he cannot move out of the Yellow Room which he insists on taking as his bedroom when his son, Jared, marries Lady Patrick and brings her home. Though the Yellow Room is sunny the old man always sits by the fire, a rug over his knees. "We used to go in to him," says Mrs. Quin. "His beard was most beautifully combed and he had a complexion like an Ophelia rose."

"Ophelia rose?" asks Tracy.

"Those roses by the sundial, pink with brownish cream. They are old-fashioned now. It's not easy to get them. On Sundays—and he always knew it was Sunday—he used to spread a silk handkerchief on his lap and cut our nails, yes, even Boro's. Mine were often dirty and bitten and he used to say, 'Those are not nails for a little lady.' He was the only person who ever called me a little lady and I loved him for it," says Mrs. Quin, "but I think he was confusing us with the Brood."

"The Brood?"

"That's what he called his own children. There were so many of them."

Tracy to Eustace, or Eustace to Tracy: It is a long span, and toward its end for Mrs. Quin as for Eustace, names and times often became one but the people and their stories are distinct. "Of course. They are each themselves, and I am not yet an imbecile," says Mrs. Quin. It is only that the edges as it were, the differences, no longer matter. Like the dust motes Cecily disturbed, they rise and settle, "anywhere," says Mrs. Quin.

When Barbara, the daughter-in-law, takes Tracy back to America and Mrs. Quin and Cecily are left alone, the girls do their best to make her leave China Court: Bella and her husband Walter, and Mrs. Quin's three other daughters and their Toms, Dicks, and Harrys, as she calls their husbands for she cannot keep up with them any more than with Barbara's, they all try to make her give up the house. "It has had its day," says Walter. "It's time it went."

"Yes. It's ridiculous, Mother, you living all alone in that great house."

"It isn't a great house. It's only big."

"But all alone," they say.

"I'm not alone. I have Cecily, Bumble, August, Moses, Trill."

"But it has no amenities."

"I don't want amenities."

"If you sold it, even as it is now, you could have a much bigger income and a comfortable little flat."

"I don't like comfortable little flats."

"You would be far more free," says Bella.

"I don't wish to be free. Even in this generation," says Mrs. Quin, her voice disagreeable, "a few people do not wish to be free of their house."

"If they can afford to keep it," says Walter. "Seriously, in rates and taxes alone—"

"The farm rent pays the rates and taxes."

"When, and if, you get it." That is a thrust and Mrs. Quin knows it; the farm, Penbarrow, is let to Peter St. Omer and, "that young man has got hold of Mother," says Bella darkly.

Penbarrow is all that is left of the China Court estate; John Henry has to sell the quarry to pay off the debts he inherits, and after Stace is killed, Mrs. Quin sells the china-clay works and makes a settlement on each of her daughters. It is they who insist she keep Penbarrow, "and a lot of good it's been," says Walter. To begin with, she will not turn out the old tenant farmer who has been there for sixty years and is long past farming. "Let him die in peace," says Mrs. Quin.

"And kill the farm," says Walter. Over the next tenant he prefers to gloss, "because it was his mistake, not mine," says Mrs. Quin with asperity. Walter persuades her to put in an up-to-date farmer, "thoroughly go-ahead," says Walter. "A college man," who spends so much on what Mrs. Quin calls gadgets that he goes bankrupt. She refuses after this to lease Penbarrow to the rich gentleman-farmer Walter has patiently found again. "Lease it or, better, sell," urges Walter, but Mrs. Quin will not listen. "It would have helped him with his income tax," mourns Walter, "so that he could have afforded a decent price, which Peter St. Omer certainly can't."

"No. Peter doesn't pay any tax because he hasn't any income," says Mrs. Quin calmly. She is calm about Peter; she believes in him.

From her bedroom window she can look over the garden and valley, with its hidden river, to the farm which is so much on the skyline of the opposite hill that its animals often seem to be grazing against the sky. She can look and "mark carefully," says Mrs. Quin. She has marked very carefully, but she does not tell Bella and Walter her findings: that for these four years Peter has worked five hours a day every day for the old farmer at Glentyre, "to learn," says Peter; that she has heard the tractor working at dawn and again by its headlamp or moonlight far into the night. She has watched Peter build up his stock of chickens and pigs; now that at last he has been able to rebuild the old cowsheds, she has seen the beginning of his herd and, all this summer, as soon as she wakes, and she wakes early, she hears him calling his cows.

The cows have proper cow names: Clover, Buttercup, Daisy, Poppy, Parsley, which strangely satisfies Mrs. Quin, but, "If Peter has no income, how did he buy those valuable cows?" asks Walter.

Mrs. Quin pretends not to hear, but Walter asks it again. "Perhaps his father helped him," she suggests innocently.

"Nonsense. St. Omer hasn't a penny," says Walter.

The St. Omers are scattered now, their town house sold and all their cottages and farms, while Tremellen, their Cornish seat, is leased as a girls' school. Tremellen is the one great house of the district; Bella is exaggerating when she calls China Court "great"; it is a family house, ample and plain.

It must have looked very plain, quite uncompromising, when it is first built. It is a granite house; naturally, granite is the local stone; only the rich landed families, the St. Omers as they once were, can afford to have bricks carried inland to build the turreted hideousness of a new Tremellen in 1850, and China Court's granite has the added advantage of being cut in Eustace Quin's own quarry.

The house stands square to the valley; behind it, the quarry hill rises steeply to the village that lies along the spine of the hill, its houses built low against the moor wind. The hill shelters the China Court garden from those same winds when they whistle over the moor, though it is open to the west and the Atlantic gales.

The hill is steep and a steep lane runs down it, dividing China Court in two: its orchards and stable block are on the far side and there too is the waterfall, a fall of perhaps twenty feet, its pool choked with rubbish from the quarry above. The stream runs on beneath the land and comes out under the China Court gate making, when the rain swells the water, a loud rushing sound in the darkness below. There is a grating over it so that the gardeners can get down to clear the channel when it is blocked with leaves; the youngest ones of the Brood—

that first batch of China Court children—will never go over the grating alone. They quake and wait for their nurse, Polly.

"Why are you so silly?" asks their mother. "What is there to be afraid of?"

"The zeal," they say, their eyes round.

"The zeal? What zeal?" but Polly has diagnosed it. "Eliza has been frightening them again," she says.

Eliza has been frightening them, "deliberately," says Polly. Eliza, second eldest of the Brood and far older than any of them in cleverness, has been learning the Psalms and, "The zeal of mine house has eaten them up. Eaten them up. Eaten *you* up," chants Eliza, terrifying her small brothers and sisters.

The hill is steep and the garden, willy-nilly, is steep too, sloping above and below the house. "I'm always grateful," says Mrs. Quin, "that there is nowhere level that is large enough to hold the village fête."

"You could have it on the drive." Bella is more civic-minded than her mother. "If you did away with the rhododendrons there would be room."

The drive runs from the gate to make a loop round an island of rhododendrons. "Not an island, a fort," says Mrs. Quin and indeed, when they are in flower, red, white, and pink, the clumps look like battlemented walls, bristling. "Rhododendrons are always militant," says Mrs. Quin.

At the side of the house, and standing there long before it, the elms, rook-inhabited, rise higher than the slates; when the wind is from the west, that Atlantic wind, the elms make a sound in the house like the sound of the sea.

The rooms are ample, too; the drawing room runs the width of the house from front to back and needs two fireplaces to warm it. "Central heating," says Bella longingly, but there is no money for that. A great deal of money has been spent; Eustace, for instance, builds on a conservatory that does not match the house at all; Mrs. Quin pulls it down. Eustace adds the nursery wing; Lady Patrick makes new stables, but now, for years, little even of repairs and painting has been done. "It's too expensive," insists Bella. "Too big."

Even the hall is spacious, flagstoned, with a stone fireplace and granite curb. The stairs are wide and also of stone. A passage leads past morning and dining rooms to the big kitchen wing, from which the back stairs go up to the nurseries with, at their top, a white gate that has a catch too high to be reached by adventurous toddlers. A comfortable smell of cooking, of wet wool drying, of hot starched linen always hangs about those stairs.

A green baize door shuts off the kitchen wing and its noise from the main house, but, before it is reached and opposite the dining room, is a small arched door opening into the office, which has another outside door so that Jeremy Baxter, Eustace's clerk, and later Mr. Fitzgibbon, his works manager, can come and go without disturbing the house. It is a real office, overflowing with files, papers, and deed-boxes, and has a safe and a copying machine; in 1850 Eustace buys, in one lot from a Penzance sale, a great bookcase with more than four hundred books and for a little while the office becomes the library, but nobody in the family ever sits or reads there and it soon becomes the office again. It was here that Mr. Alabaster had been installed the week before Mrs. Quin died, "and very glad I am that he was," said Cecily. "He sent all the telegrams."

"Perhaps I should go," Mr. Alabaster said. "Yet, under

the circumstances, I might be doubly useful. Perhaps I had better stay."

The best rooms upstairs look over the garden; the big bedroom, where Mrs. Quin lies now, is first Eustace's and his bride, Adza's; in the dressing room beside it are his wardrobes, shoe stand, and mahogany shaving mirror, but Adza's furniture is gone. The spare room with two brass-knobbed beds is next door and there are lesser rooms named in colors, the Yellow, the Red, the smaller Brown, and the White, and a room known as the Porch because it is over the front door, though that has no porch. The one bathroom is big and inconvenient, with a mahogany-edged bathtub set into the floor. The nursery bathes in a tin tub shaped like a flowerpot saucer but with a lip; it is painted white inside once a year by the knife-boy—when there is a knife-boy—and a favorite nursery bath pastime is to peel bits of the white enamel off when it has become softened in hot water.

In the time of the Brood, Polly carries all that hot water up herself, for seven children. It is Lady Patrick who insists on the bathroom. The bath, then, is filled with cold water overnight and every morning the boys, her sons, Borowis and John Henry, have to plunge in. "Damned cruelty," says Borowis. He cheats, but John Henry faithfully goes through with it.

Until John Henry's time there is no downstairs cloakroom except in the servants' wing, and apart from that only one lavatory, dark and big with a wide mahogany seat and willow-pattern pan; when its plug is pulled the noise echoes through the house.

The maids sleep two by two in attic rooms, excepting the cook, who always has a room to herself. Now the attics are shut; for a long time Cecily has occupied the

Brown Room. Kitchen and laundry maids have always come in daily from the village, but the knife-boy sleeps in a cubbyhole in what was a cupboard below the pantry; his trestle bed is still there, folded up. "Then someone slept *here?*" said Tracy as a grown-up, appalled.

The house is so much on the slope of the hill that below the kitchen is plenty of space for a big larder with slated shelves, a storeroom, the laundry, and coal and wine cellars.

There is neither gas nor electricity, but the drains are well laid; the water, soft and sometimes brown, comes from the moors and is heated by the Eagle range which, as Bella says, eats coal; indeed Eustace arranges for a ton of coal to be delivered from the works each Saturday morning and the custom stays for years; since the war Mrs. Quin has only one fire in the morning room, an oil stove in her bedroom, another in the hall. The drawing room is too big to heat at all in winter but in summer she goes back to it again; she loves the long room, with its cabinets of famille rose porcelain, jade, and family bric-a-brac, its pale darned chintzes, split damask, and paintings, "two Benjamin Wests and a Winterhalter," says Mrs. Quin.

The Winterhalter is over one fireplace, the mantel kept bare; but on the other is a French clock in gilt with an enameled cupid, holding blue ribbons. Each side of it is a Chelsea figure, a shepherd and shepherdess that the child Tracy loves; she calls them the Pale Blue Girl and the Little Pink Boy and pretends they are hers. One window looks down the drive onto the rhododendrons; the other over the garden to the west; it is by this one that Mrs. Quin likes to sit.

It is an unruly Cornish garden, sloped, with granite rocks and steep paths dark with yews, its beds tangled with flowers. Cornish gardens are famous for their flowers—half Mrs. Quin's neighbors in the big houses live by selling theirs, specializing in Parma violets, arum lilies, mimosa, rhododendrons, "but not your mother," says Walter to Bella sarcastically. "Nothing half as useful."

"A garden isn't meant to be useful. It's for joy," says Mrs. Quin. To watch her among her flowers is, as John Henry her husband says, like watching a scholar in his library who, as he talks, goes to one shelf or another, pulling out a book to show, to brood over, or to read from. Mrs. Quin, each time she comes in from the garden, has a leaf, a flower, or a bud in her hand: a berry with a spider's web, seeds that she will put in saucers on the windowsills, a spray of bergamot to smell, or a new African day lily of which someone has sent her a root that autumn; sometimes it is an especially well-formed rose, or a tendril of bryony. "You are like the householder in the Bible," says Cecily.

"The householder?" asks Mrs. Quin puzzled, but Cecily, being chapel, is well versed in texts and cannot be shaken. "The householder which bringeth forth out of his treasure things old and new."

Mrs. Quin likes that; her garden is her treasure; she refuses to commercialize it and at China Court the azaleas, unexploited, are left to shimmer on their banks with the tree peonies, with roses, iris, lilies, and poppies bursting their buds; delphiniums, larkspurs, lilacs, while along the drive edge to the gate are hydrangeas, deep blue and as tall as trees.

The house date is under the passionflower that has ramped over the front door as other creepers have done over the garden front and side walls, softening their outline and weathering the granite, while lichen and house leek—and rook droppings—have colored, or discolored, the roof.

To how many children has Mrs. Quin explained the passionflower? Breaking one off and, because she knows very well the added value given to things by having to wait for them—"I waited years," she could have said— she keeps the flower in her own hand as she tells the story. "The passionflower stays open for three days, because it was three days before Christ rose again; its whiteness is for purity, its blue for heaven. See here"— and she points to the leaf—"is the spear, and here, the five anthers are the five wounds." The tendrils are the whips and cords; the stamens, hammer-shaped, are the hammers; the three styles, the nails. "And here"— she touches the threads—"is the wreath of thorns, and the fringe, so gaudy on the calyx, is the glory of the nimbus." Then she gives the flower to the child.

To how many children does she tell that? She never knows, but always, below the creeper, she seems to see children's heads.

The last child at China Court is Tracy, not counting the evacuees from London in the war. Mrs. Quin has a fellow feeling with the evacuees—she was once Ripsie— but they do not stay long. There is little modern drainage in St. Probus; the school has only one room and the evacuees are taken away. Nor does she count her other grandchildren: "They are not Quins," says Mrs. Quin. To her Tracy is the only grandchild, the last child at China Court, "as far as I know," says Mrs. Quin.

"I'm not interested in girls." She has always said that. Indeed, John Henry has a story that each time he goes in to ask his wife what the newest girl baby is to be called,

she absently answers "Grace." The story is not true, but
Bella's younger sisters are always known as the Three
Little Graces.

Long long ago, Borowis decides to pencil Ripsie's
name into the tree in the family Bible. "But what's your
real name?" he asks her.

"Ripsie."

"That's not a real name. The name you were christened."

"Christened?" asks Ripsie, mystified.

"Oh, ask your mother," says Borowis, bored.

Ripsie asks and it appears she was not christened.
"Mother says it's twaddle," she reports cheerfully, but
Borowis and John Henry are shocked, especially John
Henry. Then Borowis solves it. "I will take her up to the
church and christen her at once."

"*You* will?" asks John Henry.

"Yes."

"In the *church*?"

"Yes."

"From the *font*?"

"Why not?" But John Henry is so plainly horrified
that Borowis, who now and then listens to his younger
brother, remembers that he has not yet fed his ferrets
and Ripsie's christening is put off. Her real name proves
to be Deborah, but "Ripsie" stays, in pencil, in the family
tree.

It is not noticed because for years nobody opens the
Bible and then nobody bothers to rub the name out.
When Tracy is born Mrs. Quin pencils in "Tracy," meaning later to put the baby's full name in the india ink she
needs to match it with the others; but the months and
years slip away and the name is still in pencil when Tracy
finds it: "Ripsie," "Tracy," the penciling seems to make

them kin, apart from the others. "We were truly kin," says Mrs. Quin, and it is true that Tracy is like her grandmother in many ways: For instance both, from the moment they first see it, are enslaved by China Court. "Absolute fanatics," says Walter.

The small Tracy is not as interested in the story of the passionflower as she is in the date over the front door, when Mrs. Quin pushes aside the creeper to show it to her. "Eighteen forty. That is more than a hundred years ago," she says.

"Yes," says Mrs. Quin.

"And we have been here all that time?"

"The house has never changed hands."

"Hands?" asks Tracy, startled.

"Yes, hands." Hands to direct, to sign letters and write checks for bills, to put a latchkey in the lock and bolt the doors at night. Other hands that hold keys too, but household keys; write notes that are dispatched, make pothooks in the top lines of copybooks, and pencil verses on canvas for samplers. These hands often write recipes: "Our apple jelly with lavender and rosemary flavoring." "Our duck with cherries." "Our velvet cream." The recipe book is still in the kitchen and Tracy's Great-great-grandmother Adza's velvet cream is still made on rare and especial occasions. These ladylike hands sew and knit; garden—but in gloves—play whist, leave cards, rub ointment on bruises; smooth hair back from hot foreheads, spank. There are younger, slimmer hands that embroider, and do the flowers, play the piano, cut the pages of novels, sketch—"and twiddle their thumbs," says Eliza. There are small hands, very often dirty, that pry and poke, into cupboards, work baskets, jam pots; make mud pies and cut out paper dolls; play cat's cradle and conkers, marbles, spillikins, Snap,

Happy Families, and Monopoly—no, not Monopoly, for no one has played games in China Court for a long time and Monopoly is almost modern. There are humbler deft hands that sweep and dust, wash china and clothes and linen; iron, mend, sew, cook, bake, make fires and beds, sound gongs, carry trays; and rougher hands still that chop wood, clean shoes, groom, dig, wash the motorcar, mow the lawn, "but all our hands," says Mrs. Quin.

"All belonging." And Tracy gives a sigh of content.

In her short life she has been rattled around "unmercifully," says Mrs. Quin, first in the wake of her father, Stace, in the army, which means India, Egypt, back to England; then in the war when Barbara takes Tracy swiftly to America and Connecticut, her home state; Barbara divorces Stace and gets her first part in films and grows ambitious; she and Tracy go to Beverly Hills, with changes to hotels or rooms in Bel Air, Santa Monica, or Los Angeles as their fortunes vary. "Sleeping in so many different beds," says Tracy, getting to know people, friends, and servants, and then losing them; leaving pets behind, gardens, schools. Tracy is proud of the memory of her father and of her elegant gay mother, but if a little girl can be world-weary, she is and, at China Court, she sinks with bliss into an ordinary humdrum child life, but three years later Barbara comes to England with a stranger man; Tracy knows what that means, "and he lives in America," she says in horror. It is not that she does not like America, but it is not China Court.

Tracy, like Ripsie, is wary of grown people, but she has learned that Mrs. Quin is safe and she decides to sound her. "Can I have another father?"

The question jolts Mrs. Quin. Stace seems to have

been dead such a little while, but, *It is nearly four years, and anyway, they were divorced*, thinks Mrs. Quin and she answers evenly, "You can have stepfathers, but only one real father and mother."

"And one grandmother?"

"You can have two." With a pang Mrs. Quin has to acknowledge that other and American grandmother. "Two, but you can't change them either."

"Not whatever they say?"

"Not whatever they say."

Tracy gives another sigh. "I shall stay here forever," she says, but she is a child and children can be taken away.

When, that last day, the time comes for Barbara to take Tracy from her grandmother, Tracy clings to her with eyes shut. It is Mrs. Quin who bends down and gently unloosens her hands. "Listen," she says and Tracy—who on countless occasions these last three years has listened to story after story, all the tales and happenings "and wisdom," says Tracy afterward—opens her eyes and listens.

"You will come back," says Mrs. Quin.

Tracy nods—she trusts her grandmother—but her eyes still stream with tears and her face is white and swollen with grief.

Mrs. Quin takes one of the pair of big front-door keys from its place on the hook by the front door and puts it into Tracy's hand. "Here is the key."

Her voice is so matter-of-fact that it seems as if Tracy were coming back tomorrow, but the years pass and the gap between America and China Court widens. Soon, for Mrs. Quin, Tracy, Stace, and Borowis slide into one, and it begins all to get misty and confused.

Is it Borowis or Stace who has the glossy little hunter,

Mirabelle? She seems to remember John Henry's complaint: "I never had a hunter," but did he say it of Stace or of Borowis? And that small figure, flying up the drive above the scudding legs in blue dungarees, is Tracy? asks Mrs. Quin. It must be Tracy and yet it could be one of Tracy's children, "Because I believe it goes on," says Mrs. Quin.

No one else believes that. "It has had its day," pronounces Walter. "It is time it went," until Mrs. Quin is driven to answer, "Walter, I think you should remember the apricot tree."

When Bella marries Walter as a young captain he has, as a hobby, just completed a correspondence course in agriculture and fruit-growing. "When he finishes his service we shall go in for apples," says Bella. "He's really quite an expert," and she brings him to China Court to advise on the orchard. "I don't need advice," says Mrs. Quin. "I understand the orchard," but Bella brings him.

The young Walter spends the morning appraising the trees and then takes Mrs. Quin around, telling her of his findings: This apple has canker, he tells her, this pear, pear midge; "diplosis pyrivora" says Walter, and Mrs. Quin listens in a silence that even Bella begins to sense is ominous. Finally they come to the apricot on the south wall, an espaliered tree, mottled, and spreading thirty feet wide, buttressed with iron hoops. "One of the oldest in the county," says Mrs. Quin.

"Kept for sentimental reasons?" suggests Walter.

"Kept for fruit," says Mrs. Quin. She says nothing more, but listens while Walter tells her what is wrong with it. "It is time it went," says Walter of the tree as he has said of the house. "It's diseased." And he shows her. "It has mildew," says Walter. "It might even be silver leaf, stereum purpureum," he says solemnly.

"I thought that attacked plums, not apricots," says Mrs. Quin, but Walter sweeps on. "The wood here"— he taps the trunk—"is wormy. Yes, it has had its day. It's a mistake," says Walter, "to keep these old trees; the yield grows less, the fruit gets bitter and small."

That is twenty years ago. Mrs. Quin still says nothing but every year she sends Walter a basket of large sweet apricots.

"What be 'ee goin' do now?" Mrs. Abel asked Cecily.

"Make cakes," and presently, through the house crept the warm and living smell of baking: of Cecily's drop scones; of yeast in a bowl set in the fender with a cloth over it for the yeast to prove; and presently, a smell of hot fruit bread and, pungent, of saffron cake.

"They will expect that," said Cecily. "Saffron cake and clotted cream. They don't have time to make homemade things, poor souls."

"Will 'em all come?" asked Mrs. Abel as she and Cecily were drinking tea at the kitchen table. Cecily nodded, but the nod was short.

"If Miss Bella and Mr. Walter takes over th' house I suppose you'ud be stayin'?" said Mrs. Abel for mischief.

"Not for all the tea in China," said Cecily. "Bella's all right," she added. "Her bark's worse than her bite, but Mr. Walter!" Then Cecily's face hardened, which was the only way she could contain her grief. "The house won't be taken over. It will be sold."

"Not for all the tea in China" is one of Cecily's favorite expressions and it is odd that she should use it, for it is, in a way, the tea in China that builds China Court. Great-Uncle Mcleod, "who began it all," says Mrs. Quin, makes a fortune in the China tea run and, though Eustace is only his nephew, the St. Probus quarry is bought for him; it amuses Mcleod to buy property in the village where he began—he buys land as well and builds China Court as a wedding present for Eustace and Adza.

The portrait over the fireplace in the hall is of Great-Uncle Mcleod. "Your great-great-great-great-uncle," Mrs. Quin tells Tracy. There has always been a rumor in the village that he has Gypsy blood and this, with the gossip that he is in reality Eustace's father, might explain the magnificent and unexpected darkness of the two youngest of Eustace's brood, Jared and Damaris, though they do not look Gypsy, but as if there were a strain, from some sailor perhaps, darker than Cornish, a Venetian or Spaniard. It is only a rumor and certainly the middle-aged man in the portrait is very much an Englishman, portly, with pale-brown hair, paler blue eyes, a long nose, and such a floridly red complexion that Mrs. Quin's irreverent children call the portrait "The Prawn."

The water-colors on the stairs are Great-Uncle Mcleod's too, his clippers, the *Foundling* and the *Mary Bazon*. "His wife was Mary Bazon and he was a foundling in this village," Mrs. Quin tells Tracy. "That was why he took the name Quin." The village is full of Quins, to Eliza's chagrin.

The house is not named for the tea clippers, nor for the collection of famille rose porcelain—reputed to be authentic—sent home by Mcleod the Second when he goes out to his great-uncle's business in Canton when it has settled down again after the Opium War. Though these reasons for China Court's name are invariably given by the village, it is from neither of them, but from the more mundane fact that the day the roof goes on, with beer for the workmen and a green bough in a chimney, is also the day Eustace—following in his uncle's footsteps in making money—buys over the china-clay works at Canverisk. "Better call it China House," he says, but to Adza, his little bride, plump even then as a pigeon and as simple as a bud, the house is more impressive than any she has ever imagined and, "Not China House, China *Court*," says Adza.

It has a courtyard, where the kitchen and nursery wing makes an L, but the house is decidedly not a court: it is middle-sized "and middle-class," says Eliza, but the name suits a house built on the edge of the Cornish moors that have a strange foreign flavor as they roll to the skyline, with their tors and the pale-colored Chinese coolie-hat shapes of the sand dumps at the different china-clay works breaking the dark landscape: Stannon, Hawks Tor, Temple, and Canverisk. The house is quiet, domestic, but one has only to hear the wind in the chimneys to know how near and rough the moor wildness is. "Quite a lot of us that were brought up here are a little wild," says Mrs. Quin. "A little queer."

"Believe me," said Cecily to Mrs. Abel now, putting down her cup. "She knew something was going to happen."

"Mrs. Quin?"

"Mrs. Quin." Cecily was solemn. The tea was so black and strong that it gave the drinker a knockback almost like spirits; this was the fourth pot Cecily and Mrs. Abel had drunk since the morning and, with it and her tiredness and shock, Cecily felt what she called "out of herself." "I have been turning it over in my mind," said Cecily. "Yesterday she was excited."

"Mrs. Quin was?"

"Yes, and glad." Glad in a way Cecily had not known her to be glad for years, "though she was always con-

tented," said Cecily. "When she walked she was—quick."
Cecily searched for words. "I have never known her
more alive," and Cecily's eyes filled again. Cecily's big
body was worn; though it was heavy, it had the thin
knotted legs and overlarge hands of a woman who has
worked too hard, but her black eyes were still young,
and innocently responsive. "It was as if somebody was
coming," whispered Cecily.

"Do 'ee think her knawed her was goin' die? That her
foresaw it?" asked Mrs. Abel. "Some folks do y'knaw. I
mind—" but Cecily cut her short.

"It wasn't dying she was thinking about, it was living.
She was at me to spit and polish the house. She did all
the flowers. Somebody's coming. I'm sure of it," but
nobody came. "Except the ones who would come," said
Cecily.

There were many of them. August was kept busy,
frantically barking and running first to one door, then
another; he had not learned the wisdom of Bumble,
who knew that most comers to China Court were
friends; besides August's nerves were on edge. Dr. Taft
came again; then the vicar, who, though Cecily was
strong chapel, was still her good friend. He sent Hoskins
the builder, who was also the undertaker, while all day
there was a trickle of people to the back door: women
carrying a basket, or a plate covered with a napkin. "Just
slipped down with a bit of my lardy cake," ". . . saffron
buns," ". . . a Lyons Swiss Roll," ". . . half a dozen eggs,"
". . . thought you would be needing extra with all the
family coming." Most often it was a bunch of flowers:
"Cottage flowers, the only kind I want"—Cecily could
hear Mrs. Quin saying it. "But don't pick all the Michaelmas daisies," she would have said. "I don't want to spoil
the harvest festival."

It was odd that Mrs. Quin, who has done less in the village than any other lady of China Court—Adza with her soups and visits, or conscientious Anne, or Bella with her Red Cross lectures and Workers' Adult Education courses—should be the one St. Probus loves, perhaps the first it really accepts; though Great-Uncle Mcleod is village-born, the Eustace Quins when they come from Devonshire are reckoned as foreigners in St. Probus, foreigners from England. "Well, isn't Cornwall England?" Barbara asks puzzled, but in Cornwall people speak of "going to England" as if it were another country and St. Probus is Cornish unalloyed, encouraging no outsiders. "Well, nobody would live here unless they had to," says sharp-tongued Eliza. "There is nothing here, nothing," she cries passionately.

"Only everything," says Damaris, her sister.

The flowers began to heap up in the tubs Cecily put for them on the larder floor and in the afternoon telegrams began to come, "but no one will be here until tomorrow," she told Mrs. Abel. "Bella and Walter have to come down from Worcestershire—he will be in a fine old state, having to leave just when apple-picking starts. The others are on holiday in Oban," said Cecily looking at the telegram, "that's Scotland, isn't it?" The second Grace was working in London, and could not get away until tomorrow. "They will all bring their husbands. That means getting all the rooms ready," said Cecily. "Just as well Mrs. Quin did make me have a real clean."

Mrs. Abel helped her with the beds. The sheets were linen but old now and thin—some of them come with Adza when she marries, some are turned sides to middle during the war. The blankets were old too, washed thin, almost cottony, and some of the towels were rubbed through. For years there had not been so many rooms used and Cecily had to send Groundsel up to the shop for cakes of soap to put in the soap dishes on the old-fashioned marble-topped washing stands. She filled the jugs with clean water, "and weren't they dusty inside," she told Mrs. Abel, ashamed.

" 'Ee couldn' do all th' work o' this gurt house," said Mrs. Abel.

It was late afternoon when they reached the White Room, "but I have done that," said Cecily. "It was got ready yesterday, before—" she broke off, not trusting her voice.

The White Room by tradition belongs to the girls of the family. "We even have to be bedded two by two," says Eliza. "I want, how I want, a room to myself." When she has one after Anne is gone, Eliza is no longer a girl but a "cantankerous secretive old spinster," says Eliza. After she dies, there are, for a long while, no girls. Borowis sleeps in the handsome Red Room, where no boy or girl has been allowed before; it is John Henry who has the boys' traditional room, the shabby Brown; as he and Borowis are the only two children where all the Brood have been, they can inhabit a room each.

Ripsie, of course, does not dream of sleeping at China Court, but she is condescendingly allowed to peep into the White Room when the boys' cousin, Isabel Loftus Kennedy, comes to stay. With its white-and-pink-dotted wallpaper, white muslin curtains, flowered rugs, and its low mahogany furniture, the White Room looks to Ripsie like a girl's bedroom in a book, and when her own daughters, Bella and the eldest Grace, come to sleep in it, she will not have it changed. No man or boy or married woman has ever slept in it, it is kept for girls, and now, when Cecily and Mrs. Abel went in, they saw some-

thing that was not there when Cecily cleaned it yesterday: a vase of pink Damascus roses, twin of the one she
had put by Mrs. Quin. "She put it there," whispered
Cecily.

Cecily always knows Mrs. Quin's rating of people by
the flowers she gives them. She gives plenty; no visitor
ever leaves China Court without a bouquet; flowers are
always put in Bella's or the Graces' rooms when any of
them come to visit, "but only the ordinary kinds of
roses," says Cecily, "or sweet peas or anemones or snowdrops." Mrs. Quin is careful of her pearls.

Once, when Cecily is ill, Mrs. Quin gives her a bunch
of these same roses and Cecily has known her to take
them up to the churchyard for Damaris, but they were
for nobody else, thought Cecily.

Now, for a moment she stayed looking at them; then
she pushed Mrs. Abel out and closed the door. The
room seemed suddenly private. "I can put a Grace and
her Tom into the night nursery," she said. "Or they can
split up and go into the Porch Room and the Yellow,
but I don't think they should come in here, especially
not Bella," she added. "No. I won't let Bella and her
questions in here."

"Would 'ee like me to stay th' night?" asked Mrs. Abel.
But Cecily shook her head.

"Don't bother. I shall sleep."

"Sleep?" Cecily felt Mrs. Abel's look of surprise, but
it was better that Mrs. Abel should disapprove than have
hurt feelings. "No one shall watch by Mrs. Quin but I,
Cecily Morgan," that was what Cecily wanted to say but,
"I'm sure I shall sleep," she said instead and presently,

under the eyes, surprised too, of the village, Mrs. Abel went home. Soon dusk settled over China Court.

It was late when Peter came from the farm, down through its field to the river, across the bridge and up the valley path. He stopped by the wall to look, as Ripsie stops more than seventy years before.

He had been threshing since dawn—"and two men short on the thresher," said Peter. It was booked to go on to Glentyre so that Penbarrow had had to finish in one day. Peter's clothes smelled of oil and dust; there was chaff in his hair and down his neck; its dust was stuck to his sweaty body and his eyelids were swollen with it. The throbbing noise of the thresher and the worry of its cost seemed locked into his head; he ached with tiredness and such sadness as he had never known for his old friend, Mrs. Quin.

"I have no father and mother now, thank you," says Peter when he first meets Mrs. Quin again and she talks of Lord and Lady St. Omer. "No relations, thank you, no friends," but he and Mrs. Quin grow steadily through all the stages he condemns: friends, then curiously intimate relations, until it is almost "mother and another son," says Mrs. Quin.

Peter comes up the drive one summer day to try and buy the famille rose. "I used to come here and see you sometimes when we lived at Tremellen," he says.

"I remember," says Mrs. Quin.

"And sometimes when you didn't see me," says Peter. "I was poaching." He has a smile that he has been told is charming. It does not charm Mrs. Quin.

"I remember that too," she says. "You tried to sell me a salmon out of your own father's river, you and that old rogue Jim Neot. How did you get caught up with him?"

"I liked him better than my father," says Peter.

"So did I," says Mrs. Quin. She and Borowis, with John Henry as an uneasy accessory, often poach with Jim Neot—a boy Jim in those days—trespass and poach Lord St. Omer's rivers. Not this Lord St. Omer, the one before, Lord Harry, Mrs. Quin reminds herself. "And now you want to poach my china," she says aloud.

"Yes." Peter tries to be unabashed, but he is working for the kind of firm that makes Mr. Alabaster—of Truscott, Alabaster and Grice, Valuers and Assessors—purse his lips and Peter does not say it with zest. "I thought you had some pretty nice things," he says. "And I'm down here poaching. I hoped the natives might not know the values."

"Including this native," says Mrs. Quin.

"You scallywag!" explodes Walter when he hears. "Trying to get round an old woman," but Peter does not get round Mrs. Quin.

She raps out, "We're Cornish. If anyone is done it won't be us."

"I'm Cornish too," says Peter.

"Then what are you thinking of?"

"It is no use thinking," says Peter severely.

Mrs. Quin is normally not much interested in people and it is only the severity that makes her look at this young man with more attention. *Why does he fence himself in with these barricades?* asks Mrs. Quin silently, and an odd thought comes into her mind, that if her farm, Penbarrow, has been allowed to run down, this young St. Omer is more run-down still. Why has Penbarrow come into her mind just at that moment? She does not know—then, says Mrs. Quin. Peter's face is more than thin, it is haggard; surely young people ought not to be haggard? She can see no reason for it; there is no depression now, no war. His fingers are yellow from cigarettes, his skin yellow too, but yellow-white; too much fug, too little air, she thinks, and his breath smells of drink; his red hair is dull and broken-ended, while his clothes are worn thin, even frayed—she glances at his cuffs. His shoes are cheap, and with certainty she knows how much he hates them to be that, and again Penbarrow, with its good soil given over to thistles and nettles, its tumbledown sheds and vanished stock, is in her mind. "When you used to come here, you were going to be a farmer. Why weren't you?" she demands.

At once there is another look in his eyes, then it is promptly throttled, thinks Mrs. Quin, and his voice is as carefully light as before as he says, "Why wasn't I? Laziness? Propinquity. All my tribe are in London, haunting the more dubious professions. We are broke, you see. Really broke, even our consciences and our guts."

"I'm sorry," says Mrs. Quin.

"Don't be. It's quite peaceful; more, it's miraculous. What do we do for a living?" His voice mocks. "Almost nothing, yet we still live."

"Nonsense," says Mrs. Quin.

"There wasn't any money for training," he says quietly. "None of us has any brains. And we were brought up to be useless. The old man is wise in his ugly fashion. He has quarreled with us all so that he is quite justified in keeping what he has for himself, or perhaps he's keeping it for Harold. Poor old Harold. He's worse off than any of us; one day he will have to wear the family crown and it's cardboard now, not even made of tin." Then Peter says, as if in spite of himself, "I did farm a bit, at Tremellen, on the home farm, but Father wouldn't let me keep it to try; probably he couldn't let me. We were thick in mortgages fallen due, like a melodrama." He mocks and the light voice comes back. "I had to let it go. Everything went." He shrugs.

"You could have tried somewhere else."

"Where?" asks Peter. "We left a nice little trail behind us: bills not paid, repairs not done, cottages falling to pieces, cases against us. Ask your Walter. He will tell you and he's always right. No one in their senses would trust one of us with a dog kennel, let alone a farm."

"No one in their senses," agrees Mrs. Quin and she offers him Penbarrow.

"Good God in Heaven," says Walter when he hears what she has done. "Good God!"

"He is good; I believe that," says Mrs. Quin, "and, you know, Walter, I thank Him that I am a sinner. At least it prevents me from judging."

"Evidently," says Walter. "That scallywag and Penbarrow."

"Why not?" asks Mrs. Quin.

"Quite apart from being a St. Omer—"

"He has quarreled with them," says Mrs. Quin serenely.

"There you are. It makes it even more unsuitable. A St. Omer and he was trying to swindle antiques."

"He was never successful. His heart wasn't in it."

"Trying to swindle," says Walter firmly and, "I'm quite sure he knows nothing at all about farming."

It must be said now that Walter had cause for alarm. It did not seem likely that any young man, notoriously lazy and irresponsible, with a town weediness, and stamped with all the St. Omer characteristics, the flaming-red hair, brown eyes that respected no one and the casual manners that never failed to nettle Walter, could take over a run-down farm and make it pay. "Well I didn't believe it either," said Peter. "It hasn't paid yet, but it will," and, "How could you die?" he wanted to cry now to Mrs. Quin. It seemed to him unpardonable. "I was going to surprise you," said Peter. He had harvested his real crop, built his first hayricks, and at long last started his herd. Tonight or tomorrow—"Please God not tonight," said weary Peter—his first calf would be born: it would be the firstborn, first fruit, and, little heifer or bull, he had planned to give it to Mrs. Quin.

He looked across the garden to the house. He could see star-shine faint on the roof, catch a murmur of life from Cecily's guinea fowls in the tree in the kitchen garden where they roosted at night; but it was only the ghost of a murmur, the dark windows of the house gave their own message.

China Court will be sold, thought Peter. He could not imagine Bella or Walter living there, nor their echoes, the three Graces with their Toms, Dicks, and Harrys. There would be a sale; strangers would flood in as they had at Tremellen, to handle and pick over, assess furniture, pictures, and china. It would all go: the private things, the flowers, even the cat; then the house would be sold, though who would buy it he did not know. "People won't live in big houses now." Bella was always saying that, but, looking at China Court across the garden, it seemed to Peter exactly fit, for someone wanting a home, thought Peter. I would buy it tomorrow, thought Peter and had to laugh—though it was a hollow-sounding laugh. Buy China Court. He had, perhaps, forty pounds in the bank and, with a shock, he saw what he had not realized until this moment: He was finished too. With the house, the farm would be sold. Bella and

Walter would certainly not have him as a tenant. The knell that had rung for Mrs. Quin had run for them all: China Court, Penbarrow, Peter, "finished," said Peter and lifted his hands from the wall.

It was then that he saw the lamp. He had not noticed it before, it was so small, small but steady. It shone in one of the upper rooms, in—and for a moment Peter's heart leapt with shock—in Mrs. Quin's room. Then he knew the reason: Someone was watching.

Watching, not standing lamenting, and dreaming. *I never thought of watching,* thought Peter, and, if he had, it would have seemed to him something remote from himself, old-fashioned, superstitious; but now he knew it was like China Court itself, fitting and faithful.

He wondered if he should go in, take his turn. It was, of course, Cecily who watched but, like one of Mrs. Quin's raps, and over the knuckles this time, he remembered he was not free; there was, after all, another kind of watching, of keeping faith. That calf might be born tonight. Her calf, thought Peter.

For a moment he stayed, then absurdly heartened, absurdly because nothing was changed, he swung back down the path.

After he had gone, the light shone steadily through the night.

Prime

Jam lucis orto sidere Deum precémur sûpplices . . .
NOW DAYBREAK FLOODS THE EARTH WITH LIGHT.

HYMN FOR PRIME FROM MRS. QUIN'S *Day Hours*

T *h e*   N *a t i v i t y* · The scene takes place at night, the stable being lit by a single lantern hanging in one corner, the rays of which shine full on to the Virgin and Child. The Virgin is seated on a mound of straw and raises one hand to shade the sleeping Child's eyes from the light. Joseph is in a corner preparing a meal. In the shadows at the back of the stable the heads of three cows are visible.

Full border of conventional flowers, pimpernels, and fruit, mulberries, and ivy leaves, painted in colors and heightened with gold. Figures of stags, hounds, and hares. Grotesque archer, with the head of a man and the body of a bird, shooting at a stag.

MINIATURE FACING THE OPENING OF PRIME
IN THE HORAE BEATAE VIRGINIS MARIAE,
FROM THE HOURS OF ROBERT BONNEFOY

I *n   t h e* early morning, larks sing on the moors. Not
many humans hear them. It is too early yet for men to
go to work, or children to walk across the moor to school
or, nowadays, wait for the school bus; too early for the
farm carts or cars starting on their way to the market at
Bodmin, even for the postman's van or riders to the
meet. Only the milkers, like Peter, and one or two shepherds at lambing time, hear that first fine flush of song,
the trilling rise, the wings beating up and up until they
fold and, like a plummet, the lark drops into the grass
and heather; only milkers and shepherds and Damaris
and Mrs. Quin.

The villagers do not see Mrs. Quin go up the street
on those early mornings, as they do not, in her day, see
Damaris. The cottages are shut fast, every crack sealed
that might let in air, but, on the way back, the doors are
open, often a half-door to keep the children in; fires are
lit and lamps and candles; pasties and cans are put ready
for the men going out; there is the sound of voices, a
slap, a child's cry, or laughing. At half past seven the
quarry hooter goes and, farther away, the clay works
hooters, and then there is a sound of hobnailed boots

hurrying down the road. At half past seven the village is ready for work, but early as the lark is too early for St. Probus.

The village people seldom go on the moor; the most they do is to walk along the road to its edge on Sundays. For anyone to walk up there at dawn, and only to hear birds sing, St. Probus would call plainly "mazed"; indeed, it disturbs Adza for Damaris, and John Henry for Mrs. Quin.

The high moor is light first, then the village and hill, and the light comes slowly downward until it reaches China Court. It grew now in Mrs. Quin's room, picking out the white sheet, the looking-glasses in the wardrobe fronts. The white cloth glimmered on the table, the white marble in the fireplace, and the light caught Cecily's white hair, worn in a crown of plaits that had slid a little crooked as she slept. The circle thrown by the lamp was lost as the darkness went; the flame grew pale. "Now daybreak floods the earth with light."

It is at this time that Mrs. Quin still wakes, even after a wakeful night, for she sleeps now as the old sleep, lightly as breath; for the last years she has not been able to walk as far as the moor and it is now that she has taken to reading the black book of the *Day Hours*, moving the green ribbon marker through the week at Lauds, as she moves a peacock feather tip to mark Compline of the different days; it is these two of the Offices that she chiefly reads.

She owes this to Tracy because Tracy, in her short years at China Court, starts the habit of coming into Mrs. Quin's bed in the early morning and bringing the other Book of Hours with her, the velvet-bound one with its borders and paintings. "What's the story?" asks Tracy of each. "What does it say?" and for the first time

Mrs. Quin realizes that this is not simply a quaint picture book, but that the monk or nun who illuminated it with such delicate care was doing it for a purpose. She cannot make out a word of the Gothic script, the old Latin, but in the loneliness after Tracy is gone, she comes back to it again—it seems to bring Tracy close to her—and, one morning, *Do they have books of hours now?* she asks herself, *modern ones, in translation?* In a moment of inspiration she writes to the Abbey at Dozemary to find out.

Day Hours. The Hours of the Day. The Little Breviary. She is amazed at the list the nuns send. "Are they all different?" she writes to ask and the answer comes back: "There are different editions, but they are essentially the same." She buys the *Day Hours* as being the simplest name and, when she has succeeded in finding her way about in them, begins her habit of reading them.

She grows to value them. The Hours seem to thread the day and give it meaning; like the windows of China Court, they reflect the day: dawn, sunrise, morning, the passing of noon and afternoon, sunset, evening, dusk, and night until, "The night is past and the day is at hand. . . . Cast off the works of darkness . . . put on the armor of light. Let us walk honestly as in the day," and it is morning.

"But is this English?" Bella asks distrustfully after looking at the book. "I mean, does it belong here?" It is English of Cynewulf and Caedmon, of Sir Gawain and King Arthur, of Alfred and Chaucer, *The Canterbury Tales* "and Canterbury Cathedral and the Pilgrim's Way," Mrs. Quin would have said, as English as it is universal, which is perhaps why she finds it satisfying.

Great-Uncle Mcleod would have been even more distrustful than Bella; he would have been shocked. "Popish! A Papist book in my house!" China Court is lightly streaked with religion, no more than that, but its prejudices are strong. Adza and Eustace, temperately Church of England, are upset when Anne becomes chapel, "like a villager!" says Eliza scathingly, while Eustace is even more upset when Jared, marrying Lady Patrick, has to agree to their eldest son, Borowis, being christened a Roman Catholic. He is not brought up as one and there is no trouble when John Henry is born; by then Lady Patrick has closed her heart and mind to any faith at all.

Besides the family Bible and the Books of Hours, there are in the house prayer books, hymn books, Wesleyan as well as Ancient and Modern, Christmas carols, a *Child's Pictorial Gospel* and a *Peep of Day*. In the drawing-room cabinet is an ivory crucifix on the same shelf as bundles of joss sticks and a Chinese God of Plenty that the ignorant Quins always refer to as a Buddha. There is also a real Buddha, a head in green soapstone that the family fondly believes to be jade. Most of them only vaguely connect it with religion, but the peace of its face pervades the room.

Cecily had fallen asleep. She had meant to watch, but the constant stream of people, the baking, and getting the rooms ready—"and grief," she could have said— had made her more tired than she knew. "And Mrs. Quin would want me to sleep if I was tired." Toward dawn she had grown cold and crept out and fetched a blanket to put over her knees and feet. She put one over Mrs. Quin too. "Silly or not, I felt I had to," said Cecily. "I can take it off before they see it."

She could feel, under the sheet, how Mrs. Quin had stiffened. "You are not afraid to stay alone?" Mrs. Abel had asked, but no more than Mrs. Quin was Cecily alone.

The Quins have always been good faithful employers and they have good faithful servants—almost always; it could have been said, "There was Ann Sly."

Ann Sly is second housemaid in Lady Patrick's time. Lady Patrick quite genuinely does not notice servants; for her they are part of the necessary furniture of a house. She would be surprised to know that they have feelings and if she wants a handkerchief or a glass of water in the middle of the night, she rings but, as Ann Sly goes about her work, curiously Lady Patrick has to look at her, and Ann Sly looks back, her black eyes hard and bold as marbles. Lady Patrick seems to see that look again in Ripsie, though why she should it is hard to say, for Ripsie's eyes are green-gray. Perhaps, to Lady Patrick, they have the same bold interloping look.

Ann Sly is well named, but faithfulness is more usual. Polly, for instance, comes as nursemaid to Mary and Eliza, the first two of the Brood, and stays until she is nearly ninety. She is not Cornish but no one remembers where she came from or if she has a family of her own because she seems part of the Quins, and no one of them knows, least of all Polly, how much they love and depend upon her; all the Brood: Mary, Eliza, Anne, Little Eustace—until he dies—Mcleod the Second, Jared, and Damaris. Borowis and John Henry love Polly too, but she is not such a power with them, "and how I dreaded her," says Mrs. Quin. She dreads McCann too, when McCann comes to look after Stace. "My baby is my religion," says McCann and Mrs. Quin does not dare to contradict that "my"; McCann leaves when the third and youngest little Grace is five years old.

Among the servants there is, too, the elegant parlor-maid Pringle, who first forbids Ripsie the house, Pringle and after her, Paget; and long before either, when Adza is first married, the maid who is the first in China Court to be called by her surname instead of the homely Emmie or Patty; "a grand maid," says Adza trembling, the parlormaid Abbot—though Abbot is soon shortened to Abbie. There is Hester, the upper housemaid, unfairly dismissed; and the little Alice, Tracy's nursemaid, not very much older than Tracy herself. Alice comes from the village, and many other village girls and boys take service at China Court. "We had knife-boys then," says Cecily, "and stable boys and laundry maids. We used to be seven in the house," she says, "and two men and a boy outside"; it is nothing, of course, compared to the St. Omers, but it is respectable, even Eliza has to admit that.

There is one foreigner, the Swiss maid Minna. Mrs. Quin takes her over from the St. Omers when McCann leaves, to wait on the schoolroom, do the children's bedrooms, sew, wash, iron, and speak German with the little girls.

Minna never succeeds in getting the children to speak a word of German and she is most unhappy. She suffers in the long mild Cornish winter; at night, when she turns her face into her pillow, its stiff white slopes make her think of the mountains round her home where there are hundreds of fir trees hung with frost, and tracks of sleigh runners like railway lines over the snow. "We have snow, but it seldom lies," says Mrs. Quin and she adds, "Our winter is beautiful."

It is beautiful but, "No snow," says Minna. Even in December, the garden has scatterings of flowers that worry her, they seem to deny the winter. "It is not-so— to see the flowers in winter," says Minna. "They should not have came," but no one understands what she means.

That makes her feel more than ever a foreigner; but does anyone, she asks silently, even those who have breathed it all their lives, feel at home in this chill, damp, heavy Cornish air? They do not, to Minna, seem at home; they seem each apart, cold, private, even the children. They are so different, these English children, from any Minna has known; they live apart in rooms of their own; they are dressed in colorless clothes; they have very young pink faces and an elderly aloofness and they laugh unfeelingly at her halting English. Everyone laughs at that; even Mrs. Quin has a fleeting controlled expression that tells Minna at once that she has said something funny. "You will begin your work tomorrow, Minna."

"Yes, Madame, and I shall give you an extraordinary performance, I can promise you."

They all laugh at Minna so kindly, but to live she has to speak and that does not seem to occur to them. There is someone who does not laugh at her, Groundsel, who is the young gardener-handyman.

"Handyman" is a good description of Groundsel—he is handy and he is a man. He helps with the horses, stokes the boiler, and mends the lawnmower; on his hands there is always dirt or earth or grease, but they are good-looking hands. He is a black Cornishman, very swarthy, with dark and wavy hair. He has never been out of Cornwall in his life and yet he has sympathy with Minna. From the first day that she comes, he looks at her in an especial way "and doesn't laugh," says Minna.

As the light grew and the birds sang, not the larks but the garden birds, the house seemed to wait for its accustomed stir.

When Cecily first comes, at fourteen, she has to be downstairs before six to light the fire for the morning baths. On Wednesdays she has to black-lead the big range, polishing the steel, and every day, when she has carried in the coals, she goes down on her hands and knees and scrubs the stones around it. "Lily-white, they had to be," says Cecily often, telling of this. There had been no young kitchen maid to do that for years and yet the stones still showed whiter than the rest.

Now Cecily slept and nothing stirred. No windows were open, except Mrs. Quin's; the front and back doors were locked; Trill, the kitchen canary, was covered in his cage; Moses, the cat, slept in the kitchen armchair; Bumble was alone in his basket in the hall because Cecily had prevailed on Groundsel to take August home for the night. "He's driving me mad with his panics," she said.

There have always been dogs at China Court: Dreadnought, Eustace's bulldog, Jared's gun-dogs, and, in the stables in Lady Patrick's time, two brisk little Jack Russell terriers, often lent to the hunt—Borowis names them Nuts and May. In summer too, there is often a hound puppy being walked, but August, the big poodle, is like a living nerve in the house. He is called August because he is given to Mrs. Quin by the girls in August, just a year ago, "So that when Bumble goes there will be another dog with you," they say. Bumble is devoted, very much a dog, but August quivers with intelligence and is as clever as any human, with more than human antennae; his coat is black and his eyes are peat brown, the color of the deep pools in the moor rivers. When he is clipped, his head looks as if it wore a black perruque and he has moustaches, while below the fleecy cowboy chaps of his legs his paws are delicate and smooth with long black nails. At first Mrs. Quin looks at him in dismay. "But I'm used to spaniels."

"A poodle is a change," say the girls, but, "I'm not a change," say those poodle eyes. "I am forever. I am August."

It was Moses who lifted his head when he heard the sound of a car, then the steps on the drive. Bumble was too deaf, too dim and amiable to stir. The steps were so light that they did not wake Cecily, but they were walking certainly. They came up to the front door and there was the sound of a key put in the lock and turned, though slowly, as if it were not accustomed to being used. The door opened and Bumble woke, but, instead of growling, he too lifted his head for a moment, and then his tail thumped as if someone he recognized as belonging to the family had come home.

Come home: When one of Mcleod the Second's famille rose bowls or vases is rung it gives off a sound, clear, like a chime, the ring of true porcelain; so China Court gives off the ring of a house, a true home. That ring is in sight; the first sight of any house that has smoke going up from the chimneys or clothes alive in the wind on the line; in Adza's day the laundry maids come from the village, and sheets, pillowcases, towels, and huge white tablecloths are hung out as well as pinafores in dwindling sizes, dresses, shirts, nightgowns, frilly drawers, and socks. It is a long time till Alice slips Tracy's dungarees and shirts on the line and then when Mrs. Quin's nightgown, stockings, and vest, and Cecily's, wave there alone.

Home, too, is in the sight of curtains opened every morning, drawn at evening; in the light through windowpanes; light on polished doorknobs, on the letter box and knocker; it is in cuttings and seed-plots in the garden, and in cats. The China Court cats inherit, one after the other, the sunny windowsill outside the morning room. In spring, the bed below it is planted with wallflowers; the cats lie there half drugged by the heavy sweetness.

Home is very much in the smell of a house; at China Court the smell is always of smoke, peat and wood-smoke; of flowers, polish, wine, and lavender; of wet wool from the outdoor coats, the drab smell of gumboots and galoshes, and earlier, of dubbin rubbed into gaiters; and of gun oil and of paraffin for the lamps. On Mondays the prevailing smell is of soap and water, boiling and steam; on Wednesdays of baking. That is perhaps the best smell; when the bread-oven door is opened, the scent of hot loaves fills all the house. "But I like hot cherry pie best," says Borowis, for the ring of home is in taste as well. John Henry likes steak and onions. To Ripsie, in the emptiness of her inside, the smell of all food is so entrancing that she cannot choose. On Tuesdays the smell is of hot linen, sometimes of singeing from ironing, while always there are smaller special smells: the smell of the tortoiseshell tea caddy; of a bowl of dried rose leaves; of whitening from the hearthstones. Sometimes there is a slight smell of cat, for one of them, the black sprite called Cuckoo, prefers not to go outside when it is cold and she uses the basin in the servants' cloakroom.

Home is, too, in touch: feeling the fine grain of wood and the roughness of stone; the smoothness of starched linen and, to Damaris, youngest of the Brood, the horrible feel of the flannelette strips that have to be knitted into squares on thick wooden needles for the hospitals. What do the hospitals use them for? She is never told, but she knits, while her sisters, Mary, Eliza, and Anne, more patient and more capable than she, make samplers. Eliza's, as usual, is the best sampler, and one worked by her still hangs in Mrs. Quin's bedroom:

> *Give me O Lord thy early grace*
> *Nor let my soul complain*
> *That the young morning of my days*
> *Has all been spent in vain.*

Eliza is five years old then and very pious.

The ring of home is, too, in the feel of paper, of firelight warm on fingers, of ivory piano keys and cold housekeys, in the softness of a cat's fur stroked, a child's hair brushed, in kisses, but most of all, home is in sound.

The sound of bells pealed, of clocks all over the house, from the clock in the hall, a grandfather in a mahogany case, to the French clock with its painted cupid under the glass dome in the drawing room. The clocks tick and taps run; there is a sound of a twig broom, a besom, sweeping the paths; of a chopper as wood is split for kindling; of the lawnmower on sleepy afternoons and the rhythmic slap-slap-slap of a horse being groomed. There are dog barks and cat purrs; the sound of rooks and Cecily's guinea fowls—"horrid noisy pests," Bella calls them—and always there is the sound of footsteps, running up and down stairs, pacing the terrace, high heels tapping on polished floors or flagstones; the scuffling steps of boys kicking out their boots and children's steps and maids'; and there are voices, from the garden, the dining room, the kitchen, nursery, and stairs, so that it is difficult to tell who is speaking.

"It would be nice at Christmas . . . velvet . . . the bridesmaids could have small muffs."

"Twelve pounds of tapioca. *Twelve pounds!* It's impossible."

"A Baptist missionary, not even C.M.S."

"You walked straight into the lion's den, you little fool."

"*Ach,* yes! *Ach,* yes! I love."

"He is a professional charmer."

"That's a rare book. Touch it carefully."

"No more idea than a babe unborn."

"Mother says it's twaddle."

"He can't sell that. It was Mcleod's."

"Who said you could play here?"

Now the new light steps ceased, as if somebody stood in the hall and listened; there was a long pause, then lightly they ran up the stairs, crossed the landing, and knocked at Mrs. Quin's door.

That soft knock woke Cecily. Half asleep she mumbled, "Come in," then, like a dog on guard, in a flash she was wide awake. *There is no one in the house, no one!* Cecily remembered and all Mrs. Abel's tales woke in her mind. No one could get in. No one had the key. Her legs were suddenly cold, and her hands cold too as they gripped the chair; her hair felt as if it crept on her scalp.

The soft knock came again, but Cecily's throat was dry and she could not speak. She could only give a small choked croak. The handle turned and, slowly, the door opened.

There was another pause. Then startled, frightened

young eyes met hers. They looked and Cecily half rose from her chair. "So that was who . . ." began Cecily. "So that . . . It is . . . It is, isn't it?" She was still not certain. "Isn't it?" Then, "It is," more positively, and "Tracy!" cried Cecily. "Tracy!"

Tierce

Flammescat igne caritas accendat ardor proximos. . . .
MAY THE FIRE OF LOVE BURN EVER BRIGHT, ENKINDLING
OTHERS WITH ITS FLAME.

HYMN FOR TIERCE FROM MRS. QUIN'S *Day Hours*

T *h e   A n g e l   a n d   t h e   S h e p h e r d s* · The scene is set in a field in winter. The angel stretches out his hands to comfort the frightened shepherds, who are kneeling with their hats doffed. His presence seems to warm the bleak landscape. A few sheep are straying about.

Full border of conventional flowers, poppies, cornflowers, sheaves of wheat, and ivy leaves, painted in colors and heightened with gold. Grotesque of a bearded man's head without a body, but with arms and legs growing from it.

MINIATURE FACING THE OPENING OF TIERCE
IN THE HORAE BEATAE VIRGINIS MARIAE,
FROM THE HOURS OF ROBERT BONNEFOY

P e t e r b r o u g h t up the milk. He was still swollen-eyed and light-headed with tiredness and want of sleep, but he had bathed, shaved, and put on clean clothes. "I want to pay my respects," he might have said, "my very profound respects." On top of the milk can was a bunch of clover. He had picked it because the cow, Clover, had calved in the night. Night! Two o'clock this morning, thought Peter. Though he could not help feeling happiness and relief about the calf, in his heart was the same unbearable ache of loneliness.

As he and Mrs. Quin had hoped, it was a heifer calf. There would be seven in the herd now—*And this one looks a beauty,* thought Peter. That was not all—the threshing yesterday had yielded an average of one and a half tons of wheat for every acre. "Not bad," said Peter. He would have to sell his wheat, as he had no room to store it, but he would keep the straw. Yesterday at this time there was only promise; today this augmentation. *I must be more than two hundred pounds richer,* thought Peter, and again it was not only that: The corn and the calf were proof of his work and planning—*And I was quite wise,* thought Peter, surprised—the planning and the work of every day.

In spite of his sadness, of knowing what must happen, those two words *every day* seemed that morning to Peter the most beautiful in the world, heartlessly beautiful when he thought that for Mrs. Quin these were not every days but the last. *Tomorrow, or the next day perhaps, they will bury her,* thought Peter. He could not believe it. The marigolds along the kitchen-garden path brushed dew on his gaiters—he, as she did, liked boots and gaiters better than gumboots—the sun shone on the dew, drawing out sparkles, throwing long shadows; he had never seen the garden look more alive, heartlessly alive, thought Peter. It should have been gray, shrouded for this last day. That was written now in capitals in his mind: LAST DAY, but smoke was going up from one of the chimneys; the kitchen fire was lit. It was like a calm message from the house; last days too are every day, said the message.

Anyone walking up from the China Court kitchen garden to the house in high summer must come upon the sweet peas behind the low wall, a thick hedge of them making a confusion of colors: whites and creams, limpid pinks and mauves, queer hot-looking purples, magenta with white threads, salmon pink, deep-smelling wine. It is Mrs. Quin's habit to pick them in the evening when it is cool, and every night long, in August, a bunch sits in a pail on the path to catch the dew.

Now Peter stopped bewildered; the pail was in front of him. But—they have been *picked*, he thought.

"Haven't they always been picked?" He could almost hear Mrs. Quin saying it, but who had picked them? Cecily? Cecily would scarcely have had time but, *It must have been Cecily,* thought Peter reasonably.

He smelled them, going down on one knee; then he brushed the grains of granite dust from his breeches and went on up to the house and around to the kitchen, treading on the grass so as not to disturb the quiet, then stopped short in the doorway.

"If he had seen me at any other time, he would never have liked me," said Tracy afterward. "He wouldn't have let himself like me," and it was true that he would not have spoken to her if he had seen her as she had first appeared to Cecily that early morning; in her traveling suit and matching coat she would have been like any of the girls in the world he had run away from—St. Omerland he called it now—and instinctively, he would have run away from her too, but now she had tied one of Cecily's aprons around herself and was getting breakfast—"helping Cecily," as she would have said twelve years before. As he saw her now she was standing at the table slicing bread, too absorbed to see him. Behind her the range was well alight, making the gentle rushing sound of a fire drawing well up the chimney; the front was open and the glow filled the room. There was a smell of breakfast, and Peter felt almost faint remembering the mug of coffee, half warmed and full of grits, that he had snatched before milking; the mixture, that seemed nauseating now though he did not remember tasting it; of a slab of bread gone stale and oily sardine. When he brought up the milk he often stayed for a gossip with Cecily, "and to get a cup of good hot tea inside him," said Cecily, but the smell that assailed him now was of coffee, fresh and hot, of milk simmering, of bacon and fresh toast, of warmed china. "It wasn't fair," said Peter afterward.

To Bella, China Court's kitchen has no charm at all; it is simply old-fashioned, muddled, and deplorably cumbersome. "And there is the big pantry, and all those silver cupboards and linen presses, the cellars and storeroom down in the basement, the knife room and that enormous scullery, with *wooden* sinks!" cries Bella.

"A wooden sink never breaks or chips anything," says Mrs. Quin, but even she has to admit she would like some of the kitchen furniture a little smaller.

The Eagle range has an array of plates, a spit, and has two vast ovens, the second used for warming china and drying kindling; Cuckoo, the little cat, always tries to have her kittens there.

The dresser is on the same scale and holds sizes of dolphin-handled dish covers, copper molds, japanned trays, and china, while its drawers are always bursting with mysterious odds and ends, and there is an untidy pile of recipe books on its bottom shelf. The table, "big enough for three kitchens," says Bella, is scrubbed white and has a coffee-grinder fixed to one end. The kitchen chairs are wooden and there is a rocking chair with a blue cushion. The floor is flagstone with a rag rug on the hearth and there are always plants on the windowsills, geraniums now, but in winter, white chrysanthemums, and early bulbs in spring. On the sills too, the gardeners put their pasties to be warmed for their lunches; there is a great deal of warming, of cloths and bowls, of cream, of yeast and, usually, of a cat on the hearth rug or armchair. Altogether it is a warm, comfortable, spice-smelling place and now to Peter it seemed to emphasize his emptiness and loneliness—and the dirty little kitchen scullery at Penbarrow; he watched almost yearningly as Tracy put the fresh-cut bread ready for more toast and turned the bacon. *Who is she?* wondered Peter. *Someone I don't know from the village?* But she did not look like a village girl. A friend of one of the younger Quins come down? But then, stepping away from him she went to the dresser, opened a drawer and quite certainly took out a tablecloth—*As if she belongs here?* thought Peter.

She must have sensed that somebody was there and thought it was Cecily because she said, over her shoulder, "Shall we have breakfast here in the kitchen?" and before Peter had time to think, "Please," he had said, "Yes, please," and Tracy jumped and turned round.

Always, afterward, she remembered that first glimpse of Peter, a young man gazing at her with such warm approval that it warmed her too. He was smiling at her, but, as she smiled back, the gaze was abruptly withdrawn and, "I beg your pardon," he said stiffly. "Of course you were not speaking to me."

From the village! This unknown girl was looking at him with eyes that were completely familiar, that he had loved, the unmistakable gray-green eyes that were Mrs. Quin's, but looking at him now from a girl's face, young and wan as if it were tired—and shocked, thought Peter—dark-shadowed under the eyes and streaked with tearstains. The village! This girl was a Quin.

It was uncommon for Tracy to smile at strangers, however approving, but Peter was right: She was in a state of shock, a turmoil of unhappiness for Mrs. Quin, and happiness, because nothing could gainsay the fact that she was back at China Court, "but nothing was as I had imagined it," she said afterward. For her China Court and St. Probus had been halcyoned by distance— *and I suppose by how Americans think of England,* thought Tracy, *as mellowed, picturesque, cozy;* she had not been prepared for the wastes of moorland, bleak and gray in the early morning, nor for the harsh plainness of the village, "and the house and garden seem so small," said Tracy. "I had thought they were boundless." *It's all so matter-of-fact,* she had thought disappointed, and then, strangely, began to be glad—*because it makes it real,* thought Tracy. Altogether she, like Cecily, was quite out of herself; she had forgotten to put on the polite defensive mask she usually clamped over her too child- ish face, and now she smiled warmly at Peter and, "Are you the milk?" she asked.

He did not look like a milkman, this tall young man, lean to thinness, in the shabby whipcord breeches and checked shirt. He was looking at her as if he were dis- pleased—*Why should he be displeased?* wondered Tracy— and he said stiffly, even accusingly, "It was you who picked the sweet peas."

Tracy would normally have been routed at once but, when one defensive person meets another, they recog- nize each other, *like prisoners,* thought Tracy, and Peter's defensiveness only calmed her, so that it was without even the stammer which dogged her in moments of nervousness—and she was always nervous with young men—that she answered, "Yes, I picked them," and ex- plained, "I used to do that with Gran, and Cecily wanted them."

If I had stayed in St. Omerland, Peter was thinking, *I should have met girls like this on equal terms. It doesn't matter how rotten you are,* he thought savagely, *if you have the trimmings.* What trimmings had he? A few cows and stock, a crop of wheat, some silver cups and books in a tumbledown farmhouse—*that isn't even mine,* thought Peter. *I had better go,* he thought, *and put the can on the table.* "Yes, I'm the milk," he said abruptly.

"But you must have a name?" Tracy was still calm.

"Peter St. Omer."

"St. O—There was a Lord St. Omer here, I remember him. Then are you . . . ?"

"I'm the farmer at Penbarrow."

"But it was Mr. —" She broke off. "Of course, that was twelve years ago." She lifted her eyes to look at him again. "I'm Tracy Quin," she said.

"Tracy? *The* Tracy?" asked Peter, interested in spite of himself. "But you were a little girl."

"I was, twelve years ago," said Tracy sadly and she cried, "Oh! How could I have stayed away so long?"

"You seem to have managed it for twelve years." Peter was cold again but she did not appear to notice.

"I let them keep me, let them order me about," and she said, more to herself than to him, "I don't think it occurred to me that I could order myself. And all this time I was quite close, in Rome. Why, I have been there nearly two years." Her eyes were filling with tears again, but Peter refused to sympathize.

"You must speak Italian very nicely," he said coldly.

"No. I'm not good at talking to people. I think altogether I was wasting my time. Then Gran wrote to me, but to America; they sent the letter on, too late." She stopped, looking down at the table, trying to hold back her tears. "Oh! I came as fast as I could," cried Tracy. "I thought I would surprise her. I came straight on from London. I had to stay the night in Exeter, but I didn't leave the station and caught the first train." The words tumbled out pell-mell. "It was a funny little milk train to Camelford and the stationmaster there woke up a taximan."

"I heard a car come down the lane and wondered . . ." But Peter would not betray his interest and instead, "You needn't have done all that," he said. "There's a perfectly good night train from Paddington that puts you out at Liskeard."

Why was he so unsympathetic and terse? But Tracy

was often terse herself, and once again, it had the effect
of making her calm and she was able to lift her head
and look at him squarely. She had not seen coloring like
his before and the red hair, skin brown as a Mexican's,
made her feel like a wraith in her paleness; his eyes were
brown too, not easy eyes, and now, not friendly. "Please
tell Cecily," he said, "I brought three pints extra for the
Horde."

"The Horde?"

"I'm sorry, that was rude of me. It's my name for
Mrs. Scrymgeour, Bella, and the others, your uncles and
aunts."

"You know them?"

"I know them." He said no more than that, but his
briefness told Tracy what he did not say, and, *Did I like
Aunt Bella?* she thought. *I don't think I did.* "Tell me
about them," she wanted to say but she could hardly
ask questions about her own relatives from someone
so obviously hostile; instead she put out her hand and
touched the bunch of clover on the can. "You brought
these for Gran?"

The edge went out of his voice—and out of his face,
thought Tracy—as he said, "The cow she gave me, Clover, had a calf last night."

"A calf?" Tracy sounded as pleased and interested as
Mrs. Quin herself would have been, and, "It's our first,"
Peter volunteered. He had to tell somebody. "But you
have other cows as well?" She seemed really interested,
and, "We had Clover, Buttercup, and Daisy, Poppy,
Pimpernel, Parsley, the beginnings of a real Jersey
herd," said Peter; then the edge came back, abruptly.
"But that's no use now," he said.

"Why is it no use?"

"Because"—and Peter said it as lightly as he could—

"because tomorrow, or the next day, as soon as they read the will, my farm will probably belong to your Aunt Bella."

"To Aunt Bella?" Tracy looked startled. "And China Court, the house?" she asked anxiously.

"The house too, I expect."

"What will she do with it?"

Peter shrugged. "Sell it, I suppose. If she can."

"*Sell it*, but she can't." Tracy was incredulous.

"She can and she will. Bella and Walter or one of the others," said Peter, "it makes no difference. It will be sold, broken up. I'm sorry," he said as he saw the tears really spill over now. "I'm sorry but it will."

"Gran wouldn't have let them," Tracy whispered because she could not trust herself to speak. She bent her head so that the sides of her hair swung further and he could not see her face, but a sob shook her, then another. Peter did not go away as ten minutes ago he would have done at once. Instead he felt an answering uncomfortable tightening in his throat and, *Thank God Cecily came in then*, thought Peter.

Cecily came in and looked at them, but all she said was, "Peter, you had better have some breakfast," and, "Tracy! Are you letting that bacon burn?"

In Eustace's day, before there can be bacon there have to be family prayers. Mary and Eliza, the two eldest of the Brood, take it in turns to put out the books, "if you have learned your hymn verse, text, and Collect," says Adza.

"I have learned them," says Eliza. "I learned all three while Mary was learning her verse."

"Eliza, you must not boast."

"But I did."

"That will do, Eliza."

Eliza, at this time, is an exceedingly plain little girl of seven, dressed like Mary in a wide four-tiered skirt of triangular plaid in bilious blues and greens with a white bodice jacket, the vest and sleeves trimmed with white braid. The low neck shows Eliza's knobbly little shoulders, while her hair is strained tightly back on her head by a round tortoiseshell comb, so that her forehead is revealed as large and unmistakably bumpy, but, "Those are my brains," says Eliza.

"Eliza, you must not boast."

Eustace, who loves them very much, has drawn up a timetable for his children.

Eliza has no inkling yet that he never intends her to get far beyond it: "Solfeggio, needlework, drawing, accomplishments," mocks the grown-up Eliza, but now there is nothing to disturb her content. At the foot of the nursery stairs, five holland pinafores hang on hooks; only five because Jared is still a baby, and Damaris is not yet born. The pinafores vary only in size; after breakfast the Brood will put them on, boys and girls alike because there is no difference marked between them yet, except that little Eustace, being just five, learns less, while Mcleod the Second, who is two years old, does not learn at all. Eliza can still be proud; she has not yet understood that she is only a girl, plain and without money or distinction—the little Quins are not invited to the St. Omer parties, for instance—she only knows she is the best at copying, arithmetic, and reciting, though the younger Anne is gently best at music, while Mary, like Adza herself and years later, like Bella, has a voice like a flute. Little Eustace is not best at anything; Mcleod the Second does not count. The three girls in their plaid and white,

MARY	ELIZA		ANNE	EUSTACE
To be called ¼ to 7	To be called ¼ to 7	7	To be called ¼ to 7	
Rise	Rise		Rise	To be called ¼ past 7
Hymn, text, collect	Hymn, text, collect	8	Hymn, text	Rise
	Family *B R E A K -*	9	Prayers *F A S T*	
Practice	Write Copy		Learn Lessons	Write Copy
	Learn Lessons		Write Copy	
Write Copy	Practice	10	Draw	
Learn Lessons		11		
Read Bible and answer			questions thereon with Mamma	
Say Lessons	Say Lessons		Say Lessons	
General Reading or conversation			with Mamma	
Solfeggio	Solfeggio	12	Solfeggio	Solfeggio
Draw	Draw	1	Practice	
Gymnastics	Gymnastics	2	Gymnastics	
	D I N -		*N E R*	
New tune or song	Needlework	3	Exercises or ciphering	
Needle work	New tune or song	4		
Exercises or ciphering	Exercises or ciphering	5	New tune or song	
			Needle work	
Walk 〰〰〰	〰〰〰 *to* 〰〰〰	6	〰〰 *meet* 〰〰	〰〰 *me*
TEA	TEA	7	TEA	TEA
				Go to Bed
Go to Bed	Go to Bed	8	Go to Bed	

ranged before Adza, have each a private hassock to kneel on, their own prayer books to read from, while the mop-headed little boys have nothing at all and simply stand by their mother.

Abbie sounds the gong—Adza has forgotten she was ever in awe of her—the maids file in; only Cook is excused because she has to get breakfast, and the knife-boy because he is too dirty.

Eustace comes in, solid, almost square in his long buttoned-up frock coat and his fawn waistcoat with lapels that are always slightly crumpled because a child often hangs on to them when riding cockahorse on his knee. He has a chain that ends, as the children know, on one side with a seal and fob and on the other with a large gold watch which they are allowed to hold in their hands when they have a dose of medicine—Gregory powders, thinks Eliza with a shudder, or rhubarb.

Eustace and Adza, at this time, have grown to look very alike; the plump little bride has become solid and by the weight and width of her clothes—fourteen yards make a dress-length for Adza—she is even squarer than her husband, just as her brown hair is a deeper shade than his, her round eyes deeper blue than his pale-blue ones.

As Eustace comes in there is a respectful standing up and a hymn is sung. One of the little girls says the Collect of the week—Eliza loves this—and then there is a rustle as everybody sits for the chapter that Eustace reads from the big Bible carried in by Abbie from the hall. A longer, louder rustle follows, with creaks of whalebone—now and then even a crack—as they all kneel devoutly facing their chairs, while Eustace prays aloud, which makes the young maids inclined to giggle. The little girls kneel on their hassocks, the soles of their small cloth boots upturned to heaven, the ends of their embroidered long drawers showing above a gap of white stocking, and their heads so devoutly bent that their hair falls forward and Eustace can see the napes of their necks, so small and white and vulnerable that sometimes he loses his place.

The smell of bacon drifts across the Lord's Prayer—always for Eliza, the two are mingled, though she does not, at that age, get any of the bacon—and as the smell rises Eustace increases his pace. Adza deplores this—she knows what the maids must be thinking—but she is too tender-hearted to tell him of it, and it is, thinks Adza, a comforting thought that breakfast is waiting; the children, upstairs, have porridge and milk, white bread and the second-best butter; but for Eustace and Adza the morning-room table is laid with porridge in blue-and-white plates, cream, brown bread, muffins, honey and rolls, while the bacon keeps hot in a silver dish over a flame, with another dish of kidneys or sausages or sometimes kedgeree. A comforting thought, thinks Adza and gives a contented sigh; a good table, a clean and comfortable house, a full nursery, and a thriving business—what more could anyone want?

It is the year of the Great Exhibition. All England is humming with new inventions, new ideas; new horizons too, because foreigners have come from all parts of the world. "Those are mandarins!" squeals Eliza, finding engravings of them in the *Illustrated London News*, and she asks, "Does my great-uncle Mcleod look like *that*?"

"Don't be foolish, my dear. He is not a heathen Chinee!"

Eliza loves to unfold the diagrams and pictures. " 'The Transept looking north,' " she reads out reverently. " 'The view from Hyde Park East.' 'The Pavilion.' 'Her

Majesty the Queen opening the Exhibition on May the first, eighteen fifty-one.' 'The Prince of Wales in Highland dress,' " Eliza reads out; " 'The Princess Royal in white lace with a wreath of flowers.' " Adza likes to hear about the royal children's dresses, but Eliza is not interested in them but in herself and cries, "Oh, Mamma, when can *we* go? We are going, Mamma? Say we are."

"Papa may go," says Adza comfortably. "For us it is too far."

"But Mamma! We must go!"

"You may not say *'must'* to Mamma, Eliza."

London has never been so fashionable and gay. The small Eliza follows it almost breathlessly. " 'Court and Haut Ton,' " she spells out. "What is Haut Ton?"

"I don't really know, my dear."

" 'May tenth. The Queen gave a State Ball at Buckingham Palace to a most brilliant Court.' How lovely," breathes Eliza. " 'Covent Garden, Carlotta Grisi danced in the revived ballet of *Les Metamorphoses* as the sprite, assuming six different forms with the utmost grace and vivacity.' Who is she, Carlotta Grisi?"

"I don't know, my dear."

" 'Mr. Macready's last performance as Macbeth.' Who is Mr. Macready? Can I read *Macbeth*?"

"You must ask Papa," but it is no use asking Papa either; he doesn't know or care, "about *anything*," cries Eliza. Not about the hummingbirds in Mr. Gould's collection at the Zoological Society's Gardens in Regent's Park; nor that it takes only eleven hours now to get to Paris—"My dear, I am not likely to go to Paris"—nor about Mrs. Fanny Kemble's Shakespeare Readings, nor the ascent of Mr. Hampton's balloon. He does not care a pin about any of them.

All the same Eliza loves her father far more than her

mother and she finds his work as enthralling as she finds Adza's domesticity boring. Eliza has never wanted to help give out the stores, or make cowslip wine or jam or pickles, but she loves going to the quarry with Eustace. All the children have been there; it is next door, just up the hill. They have been shown—though Anne grows cold with terror because she knows a bang is coming—how the explosives are placed in the holes drilled in the granite hillside; "Ten minutes and that ull blaw up, my dears"; and seen the cutting of the granite while water squirts to prevent its getting too hot. Even the noise of the drilling is exciting to Eliza, when the deadly fine granite dust flies up—"It can kill a man if it gets into his lungs"—and she takes a real delight in the precision and finish of the polishing and letter-cutting and carving of headstones.

She has never been to Canverisk, though Little Eustace has, riding across the moor on the front of Eustace's saddle, but Eustace has made out a copy about the works for all the children to write and learn: "What is china clay? It is a high-grade white or nearly white clay, formed by the natural decomposition of mineral feldspar."

"What is this natural process called? This natural process is called kaolization."

"For what is china clay or kaolin used? It is used in the manufacture of paper, pottery, ceramics, and pigments."

Mary complains that the words are too difficult, but Eliza loves them. "Pigments, ceramics and pigments," she chants. "And our china clay, in England, is the best in the world, especially here on the moors. Papa says so," she boasts, but now the first buffets of being only a girl begin to be felt. A girl cannot ride cross-legged on the front of Eustace's saddle; she must stay at home with Mamma, which in Eliza's case is not comfortable for either of them.

"Mamma, why does Papa always read prayers? Why not you?"

"It's Papa's place, my dear."

"Why is it Papa's place?" or, "Mamma, does the lady have to wait until the gentleman asks her?"

"Asks her what, my love?"

"To marry her or can she ask him first?"

"Mamma, when we go up to the Exhibition"—and Eliza still cannot believe they are not to go—"shall I call the Queen 'Your Majesty' or just plain Victoria?"

It is a cuckoo voice—Adza cannot compete with it— and gentle little Anne when she says "no" can never be made to say "yes" and when Damaris, the youngest, is born and grows up, she is oddly shy, "like a little savage," says Polly, and will not speak to people or, even at five years old, go into anyone's house, "not even for the nicest party," says Adza, unless Polly holds her coat and hat in front of her the whole time so that she can see them and know she can go away. "But they were all so *sweet*," says Adza, "with their silky heads and their little hands joined together when they prayed; they were so sweet, but where are they now?"

"Once upon a time," she could have said, "the house was like a nest." Indeed, it is for that Eustace calls his children the Brood, but, "Where is everyone?" asks Eustace, looking around the empty morning room, and Adza echoes, "Where are they?"

Some are gone legitimately as it were: Mary marries, "the only available man," says Eliza. He is Dr. Smollett's new young assistant and, "Who would want to marry a man like that, no better than an apothecary?" says Eliza.

Little Eustace dies; Mcleod the Second has been pledged from his birth to go out to China to Great-Uncle Mcleod—Mcleod the Second, who sends home the famille rose. These absences Adza can understand; she can grieve over them, miss these children and mourn their empty places without bewilderment, but the grown-up Eliza will not get up in the mornings and lies in bed staring at the wall and has written "fuddy-duddy" across her prayer book, while Anne has suddenly begun going to the common Bethsaida chapel in the village and, "Goodness knows where Damaris is! Probably walking the moors, like a Gypsy, and all alone!" says Adza. Then Mary ceases to write, Mcleod the Second is in mysterious trouble in China while Jared, the adored, has been sent to this costly and dangerous place, Oxford, and, last time he is home, comes in at breakfast, still in evening clothes, his breath smelling, "of spirits," says Adza, horrified.

"Of course it smelled," says Jared. "I had been drinking." He laughs, but to Adza he is still the baby of her sons, the one who makes up to her for Little Eustace, and she cannot bear these signs of—"profligacy?" whispers Adza.

"Mother, *we* are not chapel even if Anne is," says Eliza. "Don't be narrow-minded." But "Must they all, always rebel?" asks Adza; it seems that almost always they must. The morning room feels empty with only Eustace, Adza, and the maids and presently Eustace decides to give up family prayers.

Eliza will not get up because she does not want to get up. "What is there to get up for?" asks Eliza.

Anne is up early to practice before breakfast. Her

piano playing—"never very good," says Eliza—is the solitary accomplishment left of all that Eliza and Anne bring back from school where, at Eliza's continual "worritting" as Polly calls it, they are sent for a year, to be "finished." "Finished, we haven't started yet!" says Eliza.

The school is Miss Manners's School for the Daughters of Gentlemen, at Truro, "not even out of the county," says Eliza in shame. She knows from village gossip that Helena St. Omer, whom she has never met, is being sent to Dresden. Miss Manners's is distressingly simple and humdrum, its curriculum only an amplification of Eustace's timetable. In the house, still, are a teapot stand in burnt-poker-work made by Eliza—some of the hollows impatiently burned too deep—and an afternoon tea cloth and dressing-table set embroidered in shadow-stitch by Anne, two sketchbooks covered in linen with a wide band of elastic, and filled with watercolor sketches of the moor, Mother Medlar's Bay and Penzance. "We learned some French, which we shall never speak, the use of the globes, for places we shall never see, and we brought it all home in a portmanteau of pride," says Eliza.

She cannot bear to think now, eight years later, of those silly—silly to hope—young creatures, herself and Anne, though it is not easy to know if Anne has any hopes or ambitions. Eliza, when she comes home, has hopes and excitements as swelling and unmentionable as the then rather clumsy breasts behind her new grownup dresses. The thought of those dresses makes Eliza wince; before she leaves Truro she buys a dress with money that her godmother, Great-uncle Mcleod's Mary Bazon, whom she has never seen, sends her for her eighteenth birthday.

It is a ball dress of salmon-pink *"poult-de-soie,"* as Eliza tells Adza, and it is not crinolined. "Crinolines are on their way *out*," says Eliza scornfully. It has the fullness swept around to the back in a pannier, which falls to a train ruched with lace and velvet bows. It makes Eliza's waist look becomingly slight though the bodice, fashionably low and right off the shoulders, gives her the same knobbly look that she had as a child. With the dress go two stars, mounted on velvet bows, for her hair. "Very pretty," says Adza doubtfully, "but when will you wear it?"

"The St. Omers give balls at Tremellen."

"They would hardly be likely to ask us," and as Adza looks at the dress, comprehension begins to cloud her china-blue eyes. Mcleod the Second is nearly fifteen, but what good is that to eighteen? and Jared is only a small schoolboy. Dr. Smollett has not replaced his young assistant, there is no curate and, *Where else are there any young men of our kind?* thinks Adza. "This is a country place," she says slowly. "Country and remote." The St. Omers are often at Tremellen—in fact Jared and Damaris for a while share lessons at the vicar's with Harry and Helena St. Omer, but only lessons, nothing else. The St. Omers are often down from London, but there is a firm demarcation. "Your father *could* ask them," says Adza doubtfully.

"It is they who should ask us," says Eliza.

Adza does her best. She takes Eliza and Anne to call on old Lady Merron, who is deaf and lives with a companion. They play pool and Pope Joan with the doctor's wife, the wife of the lawyer in the next village, and with the vicar's sister, Miss Perry, who has known them all their lives. Anne goes to stay with a school friend in London, with cousins in Bristol, and she has some chapel friends, whom Eliza despises, but she, sharp-tongued and critical Eliza, has never made friends easily and she is asked nowhere. They help one Christmas with a bazaar at St. Austell; that is an excitement, "but leads to nothing," says Eliza. The day when Mr. Fitzgibbon, Eustace's new manager, first comes to midday dinner is an excitement too, but one that speedily fizzles out; he is already middle-aged and, as they learn, he is bringing a wife.

Eustace has installed Mr. Fitzgibbon to help him with his expanding businesses, the quarry and the china-clay works. There is much to be done with the integration of two small pits, Canverisk and its neighbor Alex Tor, Eustace's latest purchase, into one: there are plans for pit development, another pump, new settling pits, a flat floor kiln with the latest hot-air drying, a second warehouse at Fowey. "I could do with two Fitzgibbons," says Eustace.

"Why not take me?" asks Eliza. "I could help you, Papa."

"You do help me, my dear, by looking after Mamma."

"She doesn't need looking after, and if she did, Anne and Damaris can do that."

"You are the eldest now."

"Then I should be with you. In the works."

"You are a girl, my dear."

"And girls can't learn. They have no brains," says Eliza bitterly.

"My dear, of course they have, only—"

"They must addle them all day long," says a voice.

They are in the office and the voice comes from behind the screen in the corner. It is a shabby old screen hiding the desk where the even shabbier old Jeremy Baxter does his work. Eliza, confronting Eustace at his desk, can just see the old clerk's wild white hair and

every now and then catch a whiff of him, for Jeremy
Baxter drinks brandy. Eustace keeps him because, "even
drunk," says Eustace, "he's twice as clever and quick as
any clerk in the district."

"And twice as cheap," says Jeremy Baxter and adds,
"Quin dearly loves a bargain." He persists in calling
Eustace "Quin" without the respectful "Mister" and
when he has been drinking he can be talkative. "Girls
are not respectable if they are not addled," he says now.

"But *why?*" Eliza cries out.

Jeremy Baxter shrugs. *"Consuetudo pro lege servatur."*

"I don't know what that means," says Eliza.

"Nor does Quin, do you, Quin?" asks Jeremy Baxter.

Eustace is the most sweet-natured of men, but his rare
temper is coming up. "I said that will do, Mr. Baxter."

"But I want to know what it means," says Eliza.

"Consuetudo pro lege servatur? Roughly, 'As it is the
custom, it must be the law.' At any rate in St. Probus.
No, there's no hope for you, Miss Eliza," says Jeremy
Baxter. "No hope at all. You must addle."

"But I can learn." Eliza's temper has risen too, though
that is not rare. "I could do accounts as well as Mr.
Fitzgibbon, better because I'm quicker."

"Which wouldn't be difficult," says Jeremy Baxter.

"I can give orders and take responsibility. Please,
Papa, oh, please!" but Eliza has not learned to conceal
herself; she still clamors and, "The men would not like
taking orders from a girl," says Eustace. He gets up,
closing the subject. "And you know the works are for
Jared."

"Who will probably ruin them," says Jeremy Baxter.

"Mr. Baxter, you will kindly attend to your ledgers."

"Not kindly," says Jeremy Baxter, "but I will."

It is of no use Eliza clamoring. Mr. Fitzgibbon stays,

keeping Jared's place ready for him while Eliza can arrange the flowers, write notes for Adza, pay calls, visit
the cottages, do needlework and sketch, and read all the
magazines and novels that come into the house.

"I shall go to London," she says daringly, but London
seems impossibly far off and she has no money, no
friends. "I could be one of those models for painters in
Paris," she says more daringly still, but she is too thin;
those tender young-girl curves have fined down to flat-
ness. "I'm ugly," says Eliza and no one contradicts her;
of all the Brood she is the one to inherit Great-uncle
Mcleod's long nose, her hair is even more colorless than
the others', and her eyes have a touch of green.

"You could work for poor people," says Anne. "That's
what I mean to do."

"Like Octavia Hill?" asks Eliza restlessly.

"More even than that," says Anne, her eyes shining,
but Eliza is not listening or looking.

"Octavia Hill only wants people with money," she says
which is, of course, not true, but she can hardly give her
real reason, which is that she does not want to work for
other people, she wants to work for herself. *I want to see,
touch, feel,* she cries, silently, but in a frenzy of frustra-
tion, and "That eldest girl of Eustace's," says Mr. Fitzgibbon to his wife, "has the eye of a bolting horse."

In the summer of 1870 Eliza is twenty-six, Anne twen-
ty-five, Damaris just seventeen. "Seventeen has a
chance," says Eliza and cannot trust herself to think of
Damaris.

"Hate your sister," says Polly to Eliza, "that's wicked."

"I don't hate her, I pity her," says Eliza loftily, but as
usual Polly has divined the truth. There are times when
Eliza does hate this younger sister who is so different

from herself, so beautiful, unashamedly big and free, and so content.

Damaris and Jared are like two towers among the stocky Quins. Where the others have fine straight mouse hair, excepting Anne who is flaxen, their hair is black and Damaris has falling curls, almost vulgarly abundant. They have the only dark eyes in the family, so dark a blue they are almost black, sloe-shaped and lashed "like an ox's," says Eliza. Everything about Damaris is big; when she is laced, in an attempt to give her a waist, her bust swells up almost embarrassingly high and firm. "It's all that walking," says Adza in despair. Damaris walks, Polly says, "like one of the quarrymen's wives," but it is more like a quarry boy, often barefoot and for miles. It is easy to believe that that faraway sailor must have been a peasant. There is no denying that Jared and Damaris are magnificent creatures, but in small society in the seventies, magnificent girl creatures are not thought polite; Jared is accepted as dashing, but Damaris is unmistakably vulgar and Eliza is sure that the reason why the Quins are not "accepted in the county," as she says, is not only because Eustace is in trade, and Adza homely, nor because Anne has reverted to chapel like a villager—"thank God only the village knows that"—but because, thinks Eliza, this ignorant young sister makes herself conspicuous traipsing over the whole county and running wild.

Adza has to let Damaris run wild. Away from the moors, she is like a caged animal and, like an animal, makes no protest, only wilts, "as if she were dumb," says Eliza impatiently; wilts and suffers. When Damaris at fifteen is sent to Miss Manners's, "to be tamed," as Eustace says, she accepts it, but she neither eats nor sleeps and becomes so thin and starved that she has to be brought home. It is odd to see her with a blanched sick skin and it frightens Adza. "But you shouldn't have brought her home," says Eliza. "She can't go on being a savage forever."

"Perhaps she would have grown used to school," says Adza, whom anyone can talk into anything, but Damaris says simply, "I should have died."

That August there is a three days' gale. It brings a lilac dawn with the wind still tearing at the sky. Though the gale is blowing itself out, the morning is dark and full of wind and the butcher boy has to force his way down against it from the village. At China Court the elm branches thresh as if they were going to fall, while up above, the wind howls and whistles past the village, where, they say, the sound of bells is blown out across the moor. It is the wind in the church belfry shaking the bells, something heard only on the roughest of days, "and Damaris is *out*!" moans Adza.

She comes in long after breakfast. "Damaris! You haven't been up on the moor!" but Damaris only laughs.

"You will get coarse and brown," says Eliza, but Damaris is, rather, ivory and red; her skirt and the disgraceful old purple cloak she wears are soaked, rain hangs on her hair. "You might be a Gypsy," scolds Adza.

"They thought I was," says Damaris and laughs again.

"They? Who?"

"Harry St. Omer and a man."

When, for that brief while as children, Jared and Damaris share those vicarage lessons with Harry St. Omer, they know one another well enough for Christian names before they are separated and the boys sent to school. "Harry St. Omer and a man," says Damaris.

"Then the St. Omers are back?"

"Yes," says Adza. "They arrived on Wednesday. Mrs. Tremayne told Cook. What man?" she asks Damaris.

"Just a man," says Damaris. After a moment she adds, "An American."

"How do you know he was an American?"

"They spoke to me. I was sitting on a wall to get my breath, and they rode up to me. I suppose they thought it odd to see a woman sitting in the rain."

"More than odd, mad," says Eliza.

"They rode up to me and I heard Harry say, 'Good God! It's Damaris Quin.' Then he rode closer and asked if they could help me." Damaris bursts out laughing, but even Anne, who never censures anybody, feels ashamed for her. "Damaris! They must really have thought it extraordinary!"

"Yes," says Damaris serenely. "Then Harry seemed to feel he needed something else to say. He asked when we expected Jared."

"What did you tell him?"

"I said, 'Never.'"

"You needn't have said that," says Eliza slowly. "They might have come over. Goodness knows we never see anyone. Then what did they do?" she asks.

"They hovered," says Damaris. "Perhaps they didn't like to ride away and leave me there. I said I didn't need any help, that I was walking, and the American asked, 'Is it by choice?' I thought he had a twinkle in his eye, rather like Papa and I wasn't afraid to speak. I said, 'By choice,' and then to help them to go, I jumped off the wall and wished them good day and walked away."

"What aged man?" asks Eliza suddenly. "You said like Papa."

"Oh! an old man," says Damaris. There is a pause. "Not very old," says Damaris uncertainly.

"It's love that makes the world go round," sings the little kitchen maid as she peels apples for Cook.

There are very many songs in the house, songs and ballads, hymns and nursery rhymes, and most of them are about love. Love, *Liebe, amour, amore,* in English, German, French, and Italian. Outside the drawing-room window on summer evenings when the white rhododendrons are out, the lamplight falls on the exquisite full-skirted flowers bunched on the dark-green leaves. At sunset, between the light from the windows and the light from the sky, they hold a mysterious pink fire. Inside the windows there is firelight as well as lamplight—even on summer evenings the big room is chilly. There are green coffee cups with silver edges and the Schubert song falls sweetly as honey—*"Röslein, Röslein, Röslein roth, Röslein auf der Heide,"* the young woman in the draped dress sings, cascades of lace falling from her sleeves as she lifts her hands.

The young woman's name is forgotten, but the song is still in the house, as is the moment when Lady Patrick catches sight of her husband's face, not listening to the song, but watching the singer with an eagerness that Lady Patrick knows. The eagerness is tempered for the moment by politeness, but Lady Patrick knows what will come later. She turns her head away and looks into the fire, not to hide tears—she has no tears left now—but because an old wound throbs as it feels the cold.

Love. *"Parlez moi d'amour,"* sings Bella. Even as a woman nearly thirty she has the fluting voice of a boy, and McWhirter, the fierce bachelor gardener, is equally contradictory—he who hates women sings as naturally as he breathes: "She is coming, my dove, my dear," and, "My love is like a red, red rose."

The Lieder are in Lady Patrick's time, but in Mrs.

Quin's and John Henry's, music is still brought to dinner parties and left in the hall, or upon the spare-room beds with the wraps, to be modestly fetched after dinner. Stace and Bella and the Three Little Graces sit hidden at the top of the stairs listening to: "I passed by your window," "The Rosary," and "Because." "Because God made thee mine," thunders the baritone, "I'll cherish thee-ee" which gives the girls sentimental shivers up their spines.

"Trink, trink, Brüderlein trink," sings Minna as she sits at her mending, or *"Ach du lieber Augustin."* She is to suffer for her German in the 1914–18 war; none of the St. Probus villagers then know the difference between German and German Swiss, but now she sings blithely. She knows that Groundsel makes it his business to rake the path below the kitchen window because of her singing. Raking up the old dead leaves from the elm trees, he pauses and looks at the window as if he would like to see inside, and the look on his dark face is thoughtful and gentle.

Effie, the impertinent little kitchen maid in Minna's time—Cecily has then just been promoted to under-housemaid—Effie leans across Minna, plucks the thimble off Minna's hand, and taps on the window with it. That seems an unpardonable liberty. Minna cannot bear it that her thimble should tap to Groundsel in that forward way and immediately she stops singing.

Songs are memories, "even when you don't want them to be," says Mrs. Quin. "They persist," she says in pain, and once she is betrayed into crying out to Bella, who has a passion for old tunes, "Don't play that. Don't."

Bella can never accept a request without knowing the reason and, "Why not?" asks Bella, playing on. "It's from some old thing called *Floradora*."

"I know."

"Then why do you mind?"

"It hurts," but Mrs. Quin does not say that to Bella or anyone else. "It sears" would be nearer the truth; each time Bella plays this tune, the silly lilting tune—"If you're in love with somebody, Happy and lucky somebody . . ."—she hears it again, not tinkled out on the piano or sung, but played by a band, "Yes, here at China Court a band, a dance when . . ." but Mrs. Quin refuses to think of it.

There are war songs that wound too: "Sergeant of the Line" and "The Girl I Left Behind Me" in the Boer War. Borowis is killed at Paardeberg, "but for me he had already gone," says Mrs. Quin. "It's a Long, Long Way to Tipperary" is played on a brass band as she watches John Henry marching away with his draft on the way to France; "There's a Long, Long Trail" and "Little Grey Home in the West" belong to that time too and in 1939 there is another band playing "Roll out the barrel . . ." with again the beginning of dread, this time for Stace.

Why is there so little of Stace in the house? Mrs. Quin's heart has always cried that. Why? "Because he was hardly ever here," she says. "He was always away." Is it John Henry's doing, or is it simply the pattern of a little boy of that time, of that kind? She never knows, but when she tries to think of Stace, remember him, John Henry is always in the way. Perhaps that is her punishment. Then does John Henry know? He never says and she never asks him, dares not ask, though she has always been able to say anything to John Henry; but it is he who, six months after Stace is born, plans the trip to Cape Town and Johannesburg to see the mines—St. Probus is a mining village—and Stace is handed over to trained starched McCann. "You will visit the nursery once a day, ma'am, and that at my time," and the round-headed rosy baby disappears. He comes back for a year or two as the enchanting small boy in the portrait in her room, but in a moment, it seems to Mrs. Quin, there is school, the dreadful system that snatches little boys away from their mothers and turns them into bony objectionable small monsters. "But you must not show feeling," says Mrs. Quin, "not even if he is unhappy at school, nor when public school takes him and changes him completely." She tries to be scrupulously fair; the girls are given as much as or more than Stace. Remembering Eliza, Mrs. Quin insists that they go to boarding schools, and finishing schools abroad, are trained, and have coming-out dances, yet there is no mistaking where her heart is. "But what is the use of having a heart?" she would have asked; for Stace, after school there is Sandhurst, then the army, then marriage, then death. He is killed on the beach at Anzio in 1944.

Sometimes, in February, come rare days warm and still enough for April, when primroses, celandines, and crocuses that have bent to batterings of rain and sleet stand up in shining and confident colors. The garden is full of birds, the first bees find the catkins and palm buds swell; Mrs. Quin is out all day, nor will she lose time by coming in so that Cecily follows her around with a tray. "I can't stop," says Mrs. Quin. "At this time of year it will be dark by five o'clock."

"Nine hours' gardening is too much at your age," says Cecily unmoved. "Sit down and eat," but on this February Tuesday of 1944, Cecily is away for the day and Mrs. Quin has been gardening unchecked when, in the afternoon, she looks up from the clump of Japanese anemone shoots she is weeding and sees the vicar and Mr. Throckmorton, the schoolmaster, walking up the drive.

The combination of vicar and schoolmaster tells her at once and without words what they have come to bring her. In the village they would know she is alone and the postmaster would not send a telegram like that by the postman or a boy. She would have preferred it to come as usual. "The envelope would have been enough," says Mrs. Quin.

For a moment she stays where she is, and slowly picks a snowdrop from where it has seeded itself among the stems of the young anemones. She has plenty of snowdrops picked already for there are hundreds out in the dell; she has put a bowl of them in the morning room, but she picks this solitary one now and smells it, her fingers trembling; it smells, very faintly, of honey, but more of cold wet earth and holly, from the old leaves that have blown over the clump.

Then she stands up. Her knees are stiff with kneeling in the cold, and, as Cecily has warned her often enough, rheumatic pains have started in them. Her tweed skirt bulges at the knees and she is wearing her disgraceful old jerkin—Bella says it is not fit to be seen—two scarves, woolen stockings, and leather boots caked with mud, while her old gardening gloves are two sizes too big. "Proper ol' scarecraw," Groundsel would have said, but Groundsel is not there that afternoon either; he is on Home Guard duty. No one familiar is near her and, quite alone, she waits for the vicar and Mr. Throckmorton to come up to her; she feels wisps of hair blowing across her face and cold gripping her heart.

As they tell her, she fixes her eyes on the snowdrop, minutely looking at the three green-edged petals, the tiny stamens. It is the schoolmaster who speaks; the vicar is the new young man she has not met yet and obviously it is only a sense of duty that has brought him. Well, duty can be very kind, thinks Mrs. Quin. As the words are spoken, though she is expecting them, the snowdrop seems to burn itself into her brain. The pain is so intense that she has to close her eyes against it, but it burns through the lids. Stace! She gives a strange little gasp and the young vicar puts his hand on her arm.

Mrs. Quin opens her eyes. The snowdrop has gone; she has dropped it; there is only the sun-filled day and the two faces regarding her anxiously. "Thank you," says Mrs. Quin politely, and because it is afternoon she asks, "Will you stay and have some tea?"

The faces look shocked. It is the young vicar who recovers first. "It is we who should make tea for you. Or perhaps you would like a little brandy."

Mrs. Quin is silent while they watch her; then she says abruptly—the vicar does not know yet that it is her way—"In that case I had better go on gardening."

She does not know how long they stay after that. She has no inkling that she has been unconventional, perhaps even ungrateful and rude; she simply gardens on, carefully freeing the suffocated anemones, clearing away the dead prickly leaves, snipping dead stems, picking out stones, which are always a nuisance in the China Court garden. She does not feel it when the sun goes down, though the garden grows very cold, and Sophonisba—the spaniel before Bumble—noses her to go in; Sophonisba likes her comforts, but Mrs. Quin takes no notice. At times the snowdrop comes back, and Mr. Throckmorton's words; she can feel them beating in her head.

Cecily finds her when it is almost dark. Without a

word, she takes away the gardening fork and helps Mrs. Quin to her feet, when her knees hurt so agonizingly that she cries out. Cecily helps her to the house and takes off her boots and gloves; and presently, when the fire is making its full noise in the kitchen, Mrs. Quin has tea, laced with brandy.

Afterward Cecily puts her to bed; she offers no sympathy; her face is as grim as Mrs. Quin's and they hardly talk, only, as Cecily brings the old stone hot-water bottle wrapped in flannel to put against Mrs. Quin's ice-cold feet, "I don't have a bottle," says Mrs. Quin.

"You will have one tonight," says Cecily and before she leaves the room she comes and stands by the bed. "I think you should ask Mrs. Barbara to send you the child," says Cecily.

It happens to suit Barbara well; she has been offered her first real part in a picture, "How did she get that?" asks Walter. "I can guess how," says Bella. The picture is to be made in Mexico and Tracy is getting too big to trundle around, and thin, nervous, and shamefully backward at her lessons. Tracy is sent over to China Court, "and to stay," says Mrs. Quin, but the picture is disappointing—"Disappointing! A disaster," says Bella —Barbara gets no more parts, and decides to marry again and wants Tracy back and, "That was the third time I was stricken," says Mrs. Quin.

"Memory is the only friend of grief"—Alice, the village girl who comes as maid-companion to Tracy, writes that on one of the tombstones she designs. Alice likes to draw tombstones for all the people she knows and Tracy colors them from her paintbox. "Memory is the only friend of grief," writes Alice. Tracy shows it to Mrs. Quin, who says it is not true.

Even when one is stricken, much remains—often creature things: drinking good tea from a thin porcelain cup; hot baths; the smell of a wood fire; the warmth of firelight and candlelight. The sound of a stream can be consolation, thinks Mrs. Quin, or the shape of a tree; even stricken, she can enjoy those. To hold a skeleton leaf, see its structure, can safely lift one away from grief for a moment, marveling; and sunrises help, she thinks, though sunsets are dangerous, and moon and stars; they stir too much. Shells are safe, and birds and most little animals, kittens or foals especially, for they are not sentimental. Dogs sometimes know too much, though it is then, after Tracy, that she gets a new puppy, Bumble. "I have been happy in food," Mrs. Quin is able to say. How ridiculous to find consolation in food, but it is true, and when one is taking those first steps back, bruised and wounded, one can read certain books: Hans Christian Andersen, and the Psalms, Jane Austen, a few other novels. Helped by those things, life reasserts itself, as it must, even when one knows one will be stricken again: Tracy, Stace, Borowis, those are her private deepest names.

"But what was Borowis like?" asks Tracy in one of her many times of asking.

"His hair was cut round in what they called a pudding-basin cut," says Mrs. Quin one day, but it cannot have been; Borowis is thirteen when she first sees him and boys of thirteen do not have their hair cut like that. It must be the "Boy with the Hoop" in the Benjamin West—one of Lady Patrick's family pictures—who has that pudding-basin cut, but Borowis? It is strange that Mrs. Quin cannot remember, although she can describe every line of John Henry, from the pale slow heavy little boy to the pale slow heavy young man, "unfailingly kind and steadfast, once he had made up his mind," says Mrs. Quin.

John Henry does not make it up quickly, not even as a small boy. Soon after they know her, Ripsie begs to be allowed to say she lives at China Court. "You can't, because you don't," says John Henry.

"She can if she wants." Borowis is grandly generous.

"Want or not, Mother would never allow it."

It is odd that it is John Henry, not Borowis, who has to fight that particular battle.

"But Borowis was the eldest. He should have had China Court," objects Barbara in her short time with Mrs. Quin.

"The eldest—technically." As soon as she has said that Mrs. Quin knows it is not the right word and sure enough Barbara pounces.

"What do you mean, *technically*?"

"He never grew up," says Mrs. Quin groping, and then, suddenly, she can exactly describe him. "He stayed young and cruel."

"You loved him," says Barbara at once.

Mrs. Quin looks up and sees that Barbara's eyes are filled with pity and—*liking*? asks Mrs. Quin surprised. Perhaps not liking but kinship; in this moment they are not the daughter-in-law who has wounded the son, the mother-in-law who sits in judgment, but two women who have loved and know how to love.

"You loved him, yet you married John Henry."

"Yes," says Mrs. Quin and she adds in justification, "John Henry had the house."

"I think that's sad," says Barbara.

"Sad and glad," says Mrs. Quin.

How can something be sad and glad at the same time?

For most of the Quin women, it has been like that. "All unhappiness," says Mrs. Quin, "as you live with it, becomes shot through with happiness; it cannot help it; and all happiness, I suppose, is shot through with unhappiness. But I was usually happy," says Mrs. Quin. "I had Stace and the garden. There were times when I didn't remember Borowis for years."

Adza is happy because it never occurs to her to be anything else, though she is troubled by the strange egretlike children that she has produced—not swans, egrets, those outlandish birds with the coveted feathers. Perhaps Adza is obtuse; it certainly never occurs to her that Eliza is sharp-tongued and restless because she is bitterly unhappy, but then Adza has never been bitter in her life.

Eliza, in the end, finds happiness of a peculiar, but to her, satisfactory, kind. No one knows what Anne finds, for Anne is always the same until she springs her surprise: To the end she is quiet and withdrawn as a shadow, if a shadow can be pale gold. Damaris is not happy at China Court, she is blissful. Jared, her dark brother, marries the happy young Lady Patrick and makes her unhappiest of all.

It is Mr. Fitzgibbon who sees the first signs. On the young couple's first morning at China Court, Jared takes Lady Patrick to look over the quarry, "and believe me, I have never seen anyone as lovely," says Mr. Fitzgibbon. It is beauty that no one can deny, as they cannot deny beauty to a tree in blossom, or to an April sky or a pearl. "Yes, a beautiful woman," says Mr. Fitzgibbon. "Now I have seen her I know I have never seen another," and, "No wonder her father was furious."

Beside her Jared's good looks seem flamboyant. "Well, she is another clay," as he says himself when he is penitent.

"An earl's daughter?" asks Adza when Jared's first letter comes. "How can Jared marry her?"

"An Irish earl," says Eustace, trying to keep his head level, but this is not the sort of Irishness Eustace, and most other Englishmen, think they know.

Jared pretends he knows. "My little Patrick," says Jared introducing her. He has called her that from the beginning and the name sticks. He thinks it is amusing; her family does not. "*Arragh!* They are a feckless lot, these Patricks," says Jared in what he thinks is Irish speech, whereas the Clonferts—the Clonferts of Clonfert and Brandan Abbey, Brandan with an *a*, not an *o*— are as aloof and rigidly cold as they are rich. "Narrow and noble," says Harry St. Omer. "And we do not say, '*Arragh*,'" they might have said, but Jared persists in saying they do. He is almost as obtuse as Adza. "*Why* did she marry Jared?" asks Eliza, amazed.

Jared has only to look in the glass to know the reason why. He is the youngest son and, after little Eustace dies and Mcleod the Second goes to China, the only son at China Court and he is quite amazingly spoiled. He goes to Rugby with Harry St. Omer, then to Oxford, where he is "very well breeched," says Jared, not in Lady Patrick's sense of the words, which means estates, even half a county, very well breeched for China Court. "But an earl's daughter!" says Adza dazed.

She does not live to see it, and Eustace has had a stroke and handed over the quarry and works to his son before she comes, because Jared has to wait for his Lady Patrick to grow up; she is still only eighteen when she

runs away with him. They are married before her father
and family can stop them.

"But they will forgive me." She is so happy and confident that she is sure no one can resist her. No one, "But
they did, damn them!" says Jared.

They write and the unkindness of those letters still
stings the air. "You have married out of your kind and
out of your faith. I do not think you can come here
again. . . ."

"You have put one of God's creatures before God."

"You have chosen your bed. You need not ask us to
help you out of it."

And Lady Patrick's quivering pride writes back:

"We shall never come."

"I love him better than I love God."

"I like my bed."

They are young phrases but she is very young. All
the younger and fresher, thinks Mr. Fitzgibbon, almost naïve because she has been cloistered and strictly
kept. She is as unspoiled as her complexion. "Like a
rose," says Mr. Fitzgibbon, who over Lady Patrick is
unashamedly sentimental. "Like a wild rose." Mrs. Quin
says that too.

In the summer of 1920, a mouse dies behind the
wardrobe in her and John Henry's bedroom. The
weather is so hot that Sam Quin from the village—a
village Quin—has to be sent for at once to unscrew
the big cupboard with its beveled looking glasses and
flowered china drawer knobs. "A fancy piece," says Sam.

It is fancy. Fresh from Dublin and London, Lady
Patrick turns out the bedroom furniture of which Adza
is so proud and brings in the luxurious French bed with
its brass love knots and wreaths, the gilt-legged chairs

with their damask in blue and old rose, the wallpaper striped with tiny roses—peeling now—the gray carpet and white rugs, that match the white curtains embroidered with ferns. The French furniture does not suit the room, nor the house, but it is pretty, the whole room inviting, especially the bed as Lady Patrick first has it, with a pale-blue satin quilt and white muslin pillowcases. Mrs. Quin has a honeycomb counterpane and a Paisley shawl.

There is a narrow space between the cupboard and the wall behind it, not much more than a crack. Stace, as a little boy, pushes marbles into it and cannot get them back. Now Sam finds the marbles and a picture. He dusts it and brings it to Mrs. Quin.

"Who is it?" asks Mrs. Quin. John Henry looks, uncertainly at first, then more certainly, and, "It must be Mother," he says.

"Your mother? Lady Patrick? Did Lady Patrick look like that?" and Mrs. Quin remembers the hard face, the eyes that were icily unfriendly, the mouth that could say such unkind things, even to a little girl. "That brat is not to come into the front of the house." "Who said you could play here?" and, pointing a whip to the groom, "Mason, put that child outside the gate." Mrs. Quin looks at the delicate painting in the gilt frame and it is then that she says what Mr. Fitzgibbon says, "But she's like a wild rose."

The picture is pushed out of sight behind the wardrobe. "I wonder why," says John Henry. "She didn't sleep here. The Porch Room was hers. Ever since I can remember."

"Then what happened?" asks Mrs. Quin. She never knows; it is before Ripsie is born.

"Even on that first morning," says Mr. Fitzgibbon,

"only a day back from their honeymoon, as they were talking to me . . ."

Mr. Fitzgibbon meets them on the drive. Lady Patrick holds Jared's arm; it is as if she does not want to let him go, even for a second. Her dress, Mr. Fitzgibbon remembers, is olive-green, faintly barred with pink; her head, and here he is a little shocked, is bare; she is only walking up to the quarry but no other China Court lady would go out of the house without a bonnet or hat. To make up for this she has a ridiculous rose-colored parasol, "the size of a postage stamp," he teases in the privileged way of an old family manager, and all the time he cannot help seeing the way her hand tightens, loosens, tightens on Jared's arm; the little movement is such a private caress that Mr. Fitzgibbon turns away his eyes.

"You have him under control, my lady."

"Oh no! Not at all! He behaves monstrously!" Her face is so radiant that Mr. Fitzgibbon feels he ought not to look at it in case he intrudes; then, just at that moment, little Dorothy Gann from the village comes down the lane on her way to the laundry or the kitchen; there is not a girl in the village more slatternly than dirty little Dorothy Gann, but as she scurries past them and down the back drive, Mr. Fitzgibbon sees Jared's eyes look after her. "Look, and with *interest*, damned if he didn't," says Mr. Fitzgibbon. He has an insane desire to knock his handsome young employer down.

"You are staying in Rome," said Peter to Tracy as they were finishing breakfast. Warmed and fed he was beginning to feel ashamed of his defensiveness. "It must be a wonderful place. What do you do there?"

"Study." Tracy was noncommittal, but Peter persisted.

"Studying what?" *And I'm curious,* he thought, surprised. That was something he had vowed he would never be again.

"At college I was supposed to be clever," said Tracy as if that were deplorable. "I won a grant."

"But wasn't that something rather splendid?" asked Peter puzzled.

"Yes," said Tracy forlornly.

"Most girls would give their eyes . . ."

"Yes, but for me it—" She broke off. Then, "I didn't know how not to take it," she said.

Peter laughed. "Was it so very dreadful?"

"I had to write and research on literary women travelers of the eighteenth and nineteenth centuries, women like Mary Wollstonecraft and Mary Shelley." She seemed more than ever forlorn.

"And you didn't like that?"

"I don't know." Tracy was evasive then suddenly lucid. "They seemed nothing to do with me," she said. "I wanted something that was mine. I don't like living in books. I like living," she said. "Cooking and doing the flowers and having animals." She slid her arm around August's neck where the big poodle sat beside her. He had attached himself to her almost since Groundsel brought him down. "I expect it's hopelessly ordinary, but I like arranging things and being responsible. There *are* other girls like me," she said as if she were arguing defiantly.

"Not many nowadays." And Peter said, "I should have thought your mother would have moved heaven and earth to keep you at home," but Tracy shook her head.

"People of her age always want you to do things. Besides, we haven't a home, only an apartment. An apartment *can* be a home, but it isn't." She broke off again. "You have a farm. That's a real way to live, but we"— and she drew the checked pattern of the tablecloth with her finger.

"When Gran's letter came," she went on slowly, "I thought I would stay here at China Court with her, as I used to, but for always. I guess I was thinking of myself, not of her. I had forgotten she was so old." She stared at the tablecloth. "Well"—she gave a little shrug and straightened her shoulders—"I must just go back to Rome."

Tracy went through the house. "If I were blindfold," she told Cecily, "I think I should remember my way." For years after Barbara takes her away, Tracy shuts her eyes in bed every night and pretends she is going about China Court, upstairs and downstairs, and out in the garden where she has romped with the lemon-and-white-spangled Sophonisba—"Before you, Bumble," said Tracy now, patting his fatness—pretending she is back in the house with her grandmother and Cecily and Alice, or out in the garden with Groundsel. "Is Groundsel still here?" she asked Cecily, and "He is!" she cried when she found his pasty on the sill.

"But only three days a week," said Cecily. "Mrs. Quin had to let the garden go—almost." That *almost* was visible in the rose trees pruned, delphiniums staked, beds weeded. There were no clipped edges to the grass now, few trimmed hedges, but there were compost heaps carefully made, tools taken care of, boxes of fresh seedlings. Tracy went out, and, with August racing backward and forward in front of her, Bumble trundling behind, wandered up the paths and came on an old basket put down beside a half-weeded bed, and holding a trowel, fork, and Mrs. Quin's gardening gloves. The trowel still had earth clinging to it; Tracy knocked a little of it off and crumbled it in her fingers.

"Mother killed herself in that garden," Bella was to say and if Mrs. Quin could have answered, "That's what I should have chosen to do," she would have said.

On the day that Lady Patrick dies Mrs. Quin comes out on the terrace and takes a deep breath. For five years she has lived in the love of John Henry, but also in the dislike of his mother; still, in Lady Patrick's eye, is the defiance of Ripsie's scarlet tam-o'-shanter, mysteriously an echo of the intrusion of Ann Sly. From the beginning Ripsie is an intruder to Lady Patrick.

"Who said you could play here?"

"Borowis."

"Who asked you to come inside?"

"Borowis."

Ripsie does not mean it to sound impertinent, but it does. Lady Patrick can forget nothing, and even after John Henry has married Ripsie, dreads and dislikes her. "Now you will be able to alter everything," she says to her when she knows she is dying, and Mrs. Quin is glad she finds the grace to reply, "Only in the garden. I shall touch nothing in the house." She keeps her word. The house is as it was, but she begins on the garden that very day.

"The gravel must be moved."

"The *gravel?*"

"Yes."

"But it has always been there," says John Henry.

"Not always," says Mrs. Quin. "There is good earth

underneath—and granite," she says, her eyes lighting up.

"It will cost pounds."

Mrs. Quin does not say he must give her pounds, though she can guess that many, many pounds must be coaxed out of John Henry. "All the money is spent on the garden and the girls," Stace says often and teases, "The girls to get rid of, the garden to keep." Even then Mrs. Quin is wise in the handling of John Henry. *The beds must be moved—not moved, wiped out, she thinks, and these garish flowers burned, and I shall take down the flagpole,* but, with her hand on his arm, she says none of that aloud; she tactfully begins with the gravel.

"McWhirter will never consent," says John Henry, thinking of the bad-tempered Scottish head gardener, and she drops another bombshell. "McWhirter must go."

John Henry is incapable of saying "no"—"fortunately for China Court," says Mrs. Quin. Over and over again in his married life with her he begins by saying, "It's impossible," only to find he has done the impossible thing. Mrs. Quin as a girl and a young woman is not exactly pretty, but she is "like no one else," says John Henry. Borowis is more apt than he knows when he calls her a little blackberry girl; she is not a flower, as most girls are said to be, but unmistakably a bramble; as an old woman she grows prickly and harsh. The Cornish believe in fairies and Ripsie might easily be a changeling she is so small, her skin as white as if she has "green blood," teases Borowis, though her lips are red of themselves—"We had no lipsticks then," says Mrs. Quin. Her eyes have always been compelling and they are greenish too, with dark lashes. Now she looks up at John Henry; though he is not tall, her smallness makes him feel that he is and, though she is now more than well looked after—"cherished," he could have said—for him she always has the waif look that tears his heart, and he knows he is undone.

"McWhirter? Why all these changes suddenly?" he asks, but feebly.

"It isn't suddenly," says Mrs. Quin.

Long ago, when Mrs. Quin is Ripsie, Lady Patrick sees the flash of the tam-o'-shanter and catches Ripsie in the garden where, as it is term time, she has no business to be. Lady Patrick comes right up to her before Ripsie looks up; even then her eyes are unrecognizing, vacant, as if she were somewhere—or someone—else. "What are you thinking about?" asks Lady Patrick, curious in spite of herself.

"Thinking how I should do it," says Ripsie.

"But how did you know about gardens?" Barbara asks Mrs. Quin. "How did you begin?"

Mrs. Quin has to look a long way back before she answers, even beyond that day with Lady Patrick. "It began with the grotto," she says, but she could more truthfully have said, "It began with loneliness."

"I had to have something," says Mrs. Quin.

When the boys have gone to school, Ripsie is a small solitary again and has nothing to do or think about. "It's odd, the garden has always rescued me," says Mrs. Quin. "In times when I didn't want to think, or could not bear to, in any emptiness, there was always the garden. But it began with the grotto," she says.

The grotto is built by Lily, niece of the China Court cook in Lady Patrick's time. Lily has graciously been allowed to come from London to spend a month in the country. She is an unappetizing little girl, even thinner than Ripsie, with sharp elbows and the curiously bleached skin of the London poor; Ripsie avoids her until one day, on the drive, she sees Lily making a curious little erection.

It is made of shells, gray-yellow and fluted, and is being built on a bed of ferns that Lily is edging with pebbles picked out of the gravel. "What is it?" asks Ripsie.

"A grotter," says Lily.

"A—a grotter?"

"Yus."

"What do you do with it?"

"Git coppers," says Lily tersely.

"Coppers?"

"Pennies, stoopid."

Lily does not talk much, she works, "fer sumpin," says Lily, which means for money, but she enlightens Ripsie a little more because she wants Ripsie to help her. "Every year, twenty-fifth 'f July, we mikes grotters—on the pivement, see? Mike 'em pretty, see, and we gits coppers—sime as Guy Fawkes, see."

"The twenty-fifth of July? Why?"

Lily has never heard of Saint James the Great, nor seen a statue or a painting of him carrying his palmer's shell; she does not know why.

Ripsie watches her fitting the shells into place. "Let me help," begs Ripsie, as Lily means her to do.

They work all morning and Ripsie discovers she is better at this than Lily. She does not throw the ferns down carelessly, or mass them, but plants each one, letting every frond show, and sets them off with scarlet pimpernels, lady's-slippers, and clover. "Yer aren't 'alf fussy," says Lily.

"Yes," says Ripsie contentedly and goes on working.

It is almost finished when Lady Patrick comes home on Reynard, her big chestnut hunter.

Ripsie, wary, would have chosen a more private place than the drive for the grotto, but Lily is adamant. "Must be where there's people."

"Why?"

"So's they kin see it. It's fer pennies, stoopid," but Ripsie cannot get it into her head that they are building the grotto for money; by now she is building it for love.

Lady Patrick, coming in at the gate, is not in a good temper, and, though she wants Reynard to walk, she gives him a cut with her whip that makes him plunge. Her face, from anger and the moor wind, looks even more ravaged than usual and Ripsie, experienced, immediately makes herself small and silent, but Lily with cockney aplomb, dances up to Lady Patrick and pipes, "Penny f'r the grotter, milady. Penny f'r the grotter."

"Why are you children playing here?" asks Lady Patrick and reins the snorting Reynard in so that he plunges still more. "Stand, damn you!" she shouts. Then she says, ignoring Ripsie and speaking to Lily, "If I see you here again I shall speak to Cook," and swivels Reynard around so that his hind hoofs catch the grotto, scattering the shells and sending ferns and flowers flying. "Clear that mess away at once," calls Lady Patrick to a garden boy and she rides on up to the house.

Lily puts out her tongue and dances off to the kitchen, but Ripsie has an odd feeling that the small smashed grotto is bleeding, and before the garden boy can move, she has swept it up in her coat, "You are not to touch it," she cries.

Next day she builds another grotto, by the waterfall where nobody can see it, and then another, bigger and better, but with fewer shells, more flowers, "and the grotto grew into the garden," says Mrs. Quin.

"Whoever planned this one was clever," says Barbara.

"I planned it," says Mrs. Quin.

"Then it hasn't always been here?"

"Always," says Mrs. Quin firmly. "This garden was implicit in the house, that other was imposed."

McWhirter is dismissed, a new young gardener comes and he and later Groundsel help to make the garden. "A garden not dictated," says Mrs. Quin, "but growing out of the land itself, with its own contours," not seen all in a moment but a place to explore, and a place not only of flowers but of shape and shades, beauty of foliage, of green and water.

There are, of course, failures, "downright refusals," says Mrs. Quin as with, for instance, gentians. "Four pounds ten shillings, and not a single flower to show for it," explodes John Henry. It is money spent, John Henry protests, "for nothing" but, "Not for nothing," says Mrs. Quin. "To learn." And she says, "You must remember garden catalogs are as big liars as house agents," but fifty years of learning does produce "something," says Mrs. Quin.

At the beginning of spring, in the garden, the flowers are pale, the blossom white, some of it so fragile as to be almost colorless; there are snowdrops, primroses, the first pale daffodils, narcissi. Then the yellow deepens with drifts of daffodils along the drive edges while the tops of the old stone walls are thick with celandines. In May, the real colors come: the strong-colored bluebells and campions in the wood and lanes; gorse among the bracken; buttercups in the fields; and in the garden the brilliance of tulips, primulas, pink apple-blossom buds, and the richness of lilac and irises that have "as many colors as a peacock's tail," quotes Mrs. Quin. It is strange that the irises flourish where the gentians refuse—but they do, though this is a peat garden. Every May on the sloping lawn where the flagstaff has been azaleas flame higher than her head, apricot, pink, and orange, reflecting through the windows onto the walls of the drawing room inside.

In summer the beds are like the flowered stuffs sold in shops, blue, white, and pink. The garden is filled with the scent of lilies that sometimes wins against the clove smell of the pinks, and at night there is the scent of stocks and white tobacco flowers. In late July, the great bushes of hydrangeas, blue and purple, have heads as big as dinner plates and sway across the drive if they are heavy with rain.

Then the mixture of the borders takes a richer color, with marigolds, begonias, and phlox of the red that is found in velvet and stained-glass windows; there are marguerites, high stacks of white flowers, taking the light as the sun moves around.

Perhaps Mrs. Quin loves the garden best in winter; then shapes are seen, shapes of bush and branch and twig, outlines of paths, humps of granite rock, broken by the darkness of the yews. Flowers are few then, doubly precious: the few leftover summer flowers that so distress Minna, a spray of winter jasmines along the walls; Christmas roses, like the breath of winter; and, full and warm, the dark-purple fragrance of daphne and sweeter still of viburnums. Sometimes in January, when the rare snow comes, the waterfall has icicles and Mrs. Quin watches for the first plum blossom; if it comes into flower then, it gives the garden the look of a Japanese print. There is something grotesque in the fringe of the wood, the bare trees have twisted shapes, and the field is straw-colored where the frost has burned the stubble; the plum trees stand up into the gray sky and on the dark branches the still white flowers unfold.

Sometimes Mrs. Quin stands marveling at what she has done. "Where did I get the vision?" she asks.

Now Tracy, with Bumble and August, walked about the tangled garden, avoiding Groundsel by the sound of his clipping. She would have to greet him soon but now she wanted to be by herself, for on these paths, among the flowers, with their scent and the smell of earth and grass and of box hedges and yews, she seemed to step back down the years and was once more a serene and settled Tracy. She could almost see her own small basket and trowel again beside her grandmother's. *I can remember her giving them to me,* thought Tracy, a proper basket, a proper heavy trowel and fork though they were small. *They were not toys,* thought Tracy with dignity, and they must be somewhere in the house still: at China Court, loved things were not thrown away.

She turned back to the house and now the guinea fowls came after her, walking companionably with August and Moses. Bumble had gone in, he soon tired, but August would not leave Tracy, and Moses, who still thought August an interloper, was jealous. The two of them followed her in, but the guinea fowls knew the border of their domain and stayed, pecking, around the doorstep.

Tracy wanted a time alone in the house too before her aunts and uncles came: *Aunt Bella and her Walter,* thought Tracy. She could not remember him, but Cecily had a reserve in her voice when she spoke of him. Aunt Bella and Uncle Walter, and the Aunt Graces and the Graces' husbands, Tom, Dick, and Harry. Were those their real names, or only Mrs. Quin's names for them?

Tracy did not know. *How little I know about my family*, she thought, conscience-stricken.

They were not coming until the afternoon and she was free now to wander through drawing and dining rooms, into the morning room and out again, through the hall, looking, touching, lingering where she wanted to linger, remembering. She knew where Cecily was because Cecily was singing as she put away the clean linen in the hot cupboard upstairs.

"Singin'!" Mrs. Abel would have said shocked, but Cecily had no idea she was singing; she sang as she breathed and, if she had realized, "It's a hymn," she would have said, defending herself. Hymns could not offend death. " 'Rock of Ages, cleft for me, Let me hide myself in Thee,' " sang Cecily.

In the hall, the sunlight lay on flagstone and Persian rugs with their worn deep colors, on oak furniture and copper, not polished now as it once had been; it shone on the big Chinese jar that held the walking sticks and umbrellas, on Great-uncle Mcleod's portrait over the fireplace, and on the watercolors of the sailing clippers, the *Foundling* and the *Mary Bazon*. The sun caught the banisters and struck a spark of light from the grand-father clock.

Tracy paused a moment by that clock. Its face was faded, the gold of the Roman figures turned to brown; "1777, Gorham, Maker to the Royal Family, Kensington," said the gold plate in its dial. It is older than the house, well used to humans, when Eustace buys it, but its pendulum still swung, its ticking filled the hall and could be heard upstairs, and its hands still went around measuring the hours of the day and night, no matter what their happenings, ticking steadily as the people come and go: Eustace, Adza. Adza, Eustace: the Brood:

Mary, Eliza, Anne, Little Eustace, Mcleod the Second, Jared, Damaris. Jared, Lady Patrick, Borowis, John Henry, Ripsie. John Henry, Ripsie: Stace, Bella, Three Little Graces. Tracy and, in the ticking, voices rise, speak, whisper, laugh:

"You will see Rome and Athens!"

"I showed her into the morning room, milady, as I wasn't quite sure."

"It is Papa's place, my dear."

"He shouldn't have touched what didn't belong to him."

"Is Mr. King Lee—Thomas—paying for my clothes?"

"Throw it away. *Burn* it."

"Are you the milk?"

Eustace, Adza: Jared: Borowis: Stace: went the clock, and *Tracy, Tracy, Tracy*, thought Tracy. She had meant this journey through the house and garden to be a leave-taking, but now the ticking seemed to take her one step further, *As if I might have children*, thought Tracy. It did not seem likely, *not for years*, thought Tracy, and certainly her children would not be here; but all the same she began to try names on the clock, names that her friends and her mother's friends' children were called, that were fashionable now: Simon, Christopher, Mark, Sarah, Clare. They did not appear to fit and, *I shall go back to the old names*, she thought. That pleased her; it was as if the clock hands had come around again and she saw a little Adza—but she would have to have blue eyes, and *I couldn't call a son Eustace*, thought Tracy, *but Stace is good, or John Henry, and Damaris is a beautiful name.* Adza, Jared, Stace, Damaris; they seemed so real that they might have been standing around her. Adza seemed to reach to her elbow and Jared had—*red hair?* thought Tracy tingling. Then, *Don't be ridiculous!* and she scolded herself severely: *You are Tracy, with a grant to Rome. You have to study, work, earn your living. You don't belong here now,* but Adza, Jared, Stace, went the clock.

Cecily's steps sounded on the landing overhead. She was coming downstairs and, *I don't want to talk, even to Cecily,* thought Tracy and she slipped down the passage to the arched door of the office where she used to escape when Mrs. Quin had visitors—even then she was hopelessly shy—and sit on a pile of papers and play with the drawers of the old filing cabinet, try and open the safe and sometimes pull out one of the books. *But you couldn't tell which was which,* thought Tracy, *because they all had brown paper covers, and they were so dusty, Alice used to scold me for dirtying my frock.* She remembered a book of martyrs, another with colored plates of flowers, and she saw herself in the armchair with its broken seat, the heavy book on her lap, one leg hanging down—it did not reach the floor and wore a short sock and sandal—the other doubled under her. "Don't hatch," Aunt Bella used to say—surely that was Aunt Bella?—but it was comfortable to sit like that. When visitors came it was peaceful and safe in the office.

As quietly as she used to open the door then, she opened it now, but stopped; standing with his back to her was a man. Tracy knew certainly she had never seen him before; he was standing at a table laden with china—*Our china,* thought Tracy, puzzled—it belonged in the drawing room, she was sure—and he was holding one of Mcleod the Second's plates up to the light; it had a ruby back and on its white ground were cocks and peonies in crimson-rose, faint Chinese pink, green-blue, and deep blue. As she watched, he rang it thoughtfully, turned it over, looked at the bottom, held it to the light again, and thoughtfully put it down. Then he picked up his pipe, knocked it gently in his hand, still thinking, then slowly put his pipe in his mouth and smoked. There was a feeling of quiet and thought in the room and this unknown man fitted in, yet why, it was difficult to say. He was wearing a dark suit—*Don't they call it pepper-and-salt?* thought Tracy—and his bowler hat, odd in the country, lay on a chair; his hair was neat and he wore thick gold-rimmed spectacles. *A city man*, thought Tracy. She was against cities this morning, but she liked the way he touched the plate and she liked the smell of his tobacco. He picked up the plate to look at it again, put it down, sat down himself, and began to write in a long book—*Like a ledger*, thought Tracy. What was he doing? The pipe puffed steadily. Then he put down his pen, his hand went out again, flicked aside a duster, and there, among the plates and bowls and vases, were the Chelsea shepherd and shepherdess—*My Pale Blue Girl and Little Pink Boy*, thought Tracy. She had forgotten them but, *They belong on the fireplace by the clock*, she thought indignantly.

He had picked up the Pale Blue Girl and was serenely looking at the petticoat patterned with roses that Tracy knew so well, at the curly hair and tiny tilted hat, the yellow sleeves, the lamb and flowers in the moss around the china feet, and "W—what are you doing with her?" asked Tracy. "She's mine."

He did not jump, or drop the figure, but carefully put it down beside its pair before he turned, then, "I beg your pardon," he said.

"I mean she was mine. At least, I used to pretend they both belonged to me." August had pushed open the door behind her and she could feel his head under her hand, his solid warmth against her leg. "I used to play with them."

"I beg your pardon again," he said. "I didn't know any of the family had arrived yet."

"I don't expect I count," said Tracy. "I'm only a grand-child—and the youngest one. I'm Tracy Quin."

"Then you count very much," he said. "Mrs. Quin talked of you a great deal."

Tracy's face lit up. "She talked of me—" she began, but Cecily knocked and came in. "Oh, Tracy," she said, "I meant to tell you Mr. Alabaster was here," and, "Your coffee," she said to him putting the cup down on the desk. "Don't you let it get cold now, Mr. Alabaster. Tracy, there's a cup for you if you want one," but, "Mr. Alabaster," Tracy was saying. "What a nice name."

It is not really his name. It is Mrs. Quin who calls him Mr. Alabaster; she is never good at names.

"Mother, can't you be clear?" Bella says often, but Mrs. Quin is too riddled—"muddled," Bella would have said but riddled is more true—riddled with experience; with facts, thoughts, feelings, truths, half-truths, half-lies—"and downright lies," says Mrs. Quin in her harsh-est voice—so riddled that nothing is clear, nor as simple as it seems, "or sounds," says Mrs. Quin.

Mr. Alabaster, in reality, was Mr. Percival Anstruther of Truscott, Alabaster and Grice, Valuers and Assessors, "called in at last," says Walter. For years Walter has been trying to arrange for a valuation to be done at China Court. "Nobody knows what is in this house," says Walter.

"No one." Mrs. Quin would have agreed, except that on principle she never agrees with Walter. "No one will ever know, but you can listen, and think," she could have said, "pick up a fork and spoon, look in a looking glass, study a picture, try on an ivory thimble and think, feel; if you strain all your five wits you may know a little." Mrs. Quin could have said that, but Walter is holding forth. Walter seldom speaks, "he holds forth," says Mrs. Quin. "A reliable firm," booms Walter, "like Truscott, Alabaster and Grice—"

"Couldn't possibly know the value," says Mrs. Quin.

"They are arranging to send their Mr. Anstruther. He—"

"Could not be expected to know the value."

"Mother, you are deliberately trying to annoy Walter."

"If Walter is annoyed by the truth I'm sorry," but Mrs. Quin knows that she is being obstructive, knows too that she is ignorant of names and values and she gives in and Mr. Alabaster comes.

"It's for your benefit, Mother," Bella impresses on her.

"Hmp!" says Mrs. Quin.

She has long ago fathomed why Bella and Walter want Mr. Alabaster—though *fathomed* is the wrong word because, to her, they are quite transparent. "It is so that when I die they will know what they are likely to get," says Mrs. Quin, "and will know what to keep or throw away. Like strangers with a guidebook," says Mrs. Quin.

"But I think you need a guidebook," Mr. Alabaster would have said. "Do you know what this is?" he asks soon after he comes, and he shows Mrs. Quin a certain miniature in a dark frame that has hung by the second drawing-room fireplace for years. "Do you know what this is?"

"It's Richard Loftus Kennedy," says Mrs. Quin. "He was a great-uncle of my mother-in-law, Lady Patrick. She was a Clonfert, her mother a Loftus Kennedy."

Though she is cut off by the Clonferts, Lady Patrick, when she is twenty-one, inherits her mother's property.

"They couldn't prevent that," says Jared, "for all their

bile." She gets the Loftus Kennedy pictures, and the Winterhalter of herself and her brothers as children—"He painted Queen Victoria's children," Mrs. Quin tells Tracy—and as well all the contents of the house in Dublin and a little fortune in money. "But that's all gone," says Mrs. Quin.

"Yes, Richard Loftus Kennedy," she says now quite certainly of the miniature.

"But do you know *what* it *is?*" persists Mr. Alabaster. Mrs. Quin has no idea. "It is an Engleheart," says Mr. Alabaster. Mrs. Quin has never heard of Engleheart.

"But I don't think there is much of what Walter would call 'money' hidden away here," says Mrs. Quin when she has recovered from the Engleheart, "nothing really valuable. Except the Winterhalter perhaps and, of course, the famille rose."

Mr. Alabaster had sat down again at his lists of the china now and Tracy read over his shoulder: "Vase with landscape panels. Ht $14\frac{1}{2}$", copy late 19th century, cracked, 40 guineas. Plate. $D7\frac{7}{8}$", fine copy late 19th century, 110 guineas." "That's an approximate value and there is one . . . another plate. It has the artemisia leaf mark, perhaps it's an original," said Mr. Alabaster. "Perhaps they may fetch more."

"Fetch?" asked Tracy.

"Unfortunately the china, though very nice, is not as valuable as your uncle hoped."

"But he can't sell it," said Tracy, scandalized. "It was Mcleod the Second's, my great-great-uncle's." Mr. Alabaster had picked up the Chelsea shepherd and fondled it as he listened. "I think he bought it after the Opium War," said Tracy. "Didn't it come from the Summer Palace?"

"I don't think it did," said Mr. Alabaster gently. "The Summer Palace was looted in 1861 and, according to the family tree Mrs. Quin showed me when we were trying to trace the date, the young man would have been a schoolboy then. Nor, I'm afraid, except perhaps that one plate, are any of these originals, which are valuable, of course. Your uncle hoped they might be; indeed, he said from the time of Yung Cheng when he wrote. Well, original famille rose *is*, of course." He sighed. "These copies still fox the experts and I know your grand-mother had high hopes of this porcelain, but—"

"Gran had? Gran?" Tracy was aghast. "You don't mean Gran *agreed* with Uncle Walter?"

"By no means," said Mr. Alabaster hastily and then caught himself back. "At least, there sometimes seemed to be some disagreement between them. Colonel Scrym-geour—"

"Is that Uncle Walter's name? Yes, I suppose it is."

"The colonel, I think, wanted a complete sale, while Mrs. Quin"—and Mr. Alabaster's voice softened—"she was a fine old lady—Mrs. Quin had hoped to find per-haps one piece that would have saved the house."

"Saved the house?" whispered Tracy.

"I understand it needs much repairing," said Mr. Ala-baster sadly. "Colonel Scrymgeour showed me a report. These"—and he ran his finger down the list—"could make a nice little sale, but Mrs. Quin hoped for some-thing quite outstanding, shall we say, that she could have sold without damaging the whole. I wish I could have helped her," said Mr. Alabaster.

"And now," whispered Tracy, "Uncle Walter will win?"

"I am afraid he must," said Mr. Alabaster.

* * *

The postman came with a letter from Bella, "telling me to do all the things I have done," said Cecily dryly.

Everything was ready—the baking finished, windows opened in the rooms, flowers arranged: the sweet peas in bowls in the drawing room and hall, roses on the dinner table, and Tracy had put a posy in each aunt's room. Groundsel had brought in vegetables; steaks and kidneys had been delivered; Peter had promised two chickens from the farm; and the shop had sent down groceries. Even Bumble and August had been brushed.

"They have only to come," said Cecily; and the house waited.

Sext

*Qui témperas rerum vices, splendóre mane illûminas, et
ignibus meridiem. . . .*

WHO DOST CHOOSE THE COURSE ALL THINGS SHALL RUN,
DECK THE MORNING WITH BEAUTY BRIGHT AND NOON
WITH THE BLAZING SUN.

HYMN FOR SEXT FROM MRS. QUIN'S *Day Hours*

T *h e* A *d o r a t i o n o f t h e* M *a g i* · The scene
takes place in the stable. The Virgin is seated and holds the
Child on her lap. He stretches forth one of His hands toward
the gift which the first Magus is offering and is crowing with
delight (this expression on the Child's face has been caught
in a masterly manner by the artist). The two other Magi
stand behind the first, waiting to present their gifts. Joseph
stands behind the Virgin in an attitude of protection. A man
(possibly the original owner) is watching the scene through
a window at the side of the stable.

*Full border of conventional flowers and ivy leaves, painted in
colors and heightened with gold. In the right-hand border the
arms of the Bonnefoy family.*

MINIATURE FACING THE OPENING OF SEXT IN THE
HORAE BEATAE VIRGINIS MARIAE, FROM THE HOURS
OF ROBERT BONNEFOY

M r s . Q u i n was buried at eleven o'clock the next morning, simply, and as quietly as the village would allow. "Buried?" Bella had asked in dismay.

"That was her direction," said young Mr. Prendergast, who was not young—*quite as old as Aunt Bella,* thought Tracy, to whom a middle-aged person was old—but had to be distinguished from his father, old Mr. Prendergast. What Mrs. Quin had really said was, "Don't let the girls have me cremated," but young Mr. Prendergast did not tell Bella that. Prendergast and Holtby had been the Quin solicitors since the time of Eustace and young Mr. Prendergast remembered Bella from children's parties. *She used to boss all the games,* thought Mr. Prendergast, *and made us play even when we didn't want to.* "You shall not be cremated," he had told Mrs. Quin and had taken it upon himself to give clear directions to Mr. Hoskins and had driven over to see the family as soon as they arrived.

"Who wants to be buried nowadays?" They were still talking of it after the funeral when they had come back to the house. *They don't let things go,* thought Mr. Prendergast. "Who wants to be buried?" asked Bella.

"I do." It was that mouse of a niece who spoke as if it were jerked out of her. So this was the grandchild Mrs. Quin had loved, thought Mr. Prendergast, loved and sent for again and who had arrived too late. Pity, thought Mr. Prendergast watching her. Tracy shrank back in her corner as soon as she had spoken but did not escape. Attention was riveted on her. "You do?"

"My dear Tracy!"

"I thought in America—"

"But why?"

Tracy blushed, but held her ground and, *Not such a mouse when she blushes*, thought Mr. Prendergast.

"Why?" asked Tracy. "Because I thought Gran's funeral was beautiful."

"Beautiful?"

"Yes. It was homely." As she said that the child seemed to light up, thought Mr. Prendergast. "*Homely.* Oh, not as we use that word," said American-reared Tracy, "but as you do; being at home and carried up the village s-street where she had so often walked." The stutter was overtaking her, but she made herself go on. "Past c-cottages where she knew every person, and then in the ch-church where she was married," said Tracy, "and the churchyard where the f-family were. It wasn't like going away, it was a joining," said Tracy in a rush.

It is a joining; the family dead are up in the windy graveyard, a wide plot of grassed land, filled with wild daffodils in spring and only walled from the moor by piled gray stones; heather and bracken push through the chinks and sometimes wild ponies spring over. "I'm glad they brought Damaris back and let her lie there." Mrs. Quin says that often. Damaris, whose story comes down through Polly, who tells it to Borowis and John Henry, particularly appeals to Mrs. Quin. "I'm glad she is here." There is the same strength of granite as in the house, but the church is far older. "Norman," says Mrs. Quin. Its square tower rises above the churchyard, but the vicarage elms, counterparts of the elms at China Court down the hill, at the opposite end of the village, are higher still.

Though Bella and the Graces would hardly have believed it, cremation is still rare in St. Probus and most of the village dead are here too, with the same names recurring over and over again: Quins, Neots, Tremaynes, and Minvers. The villagers come here often because, contrary to most modern belief, there is comfort in a grave; it can be a quiet place to sit by for a visit, with its ordered grass and still stones, and it brings a sense of nearness. Indeed, a grave can be almost a companion, a visit to it a pilgrimage back to love; but there are some graves in the churchyard with no one to care for them—Jeremy Baxter's for instance. No one remembers now who put up the granite headstone, plain but fine, and the inscription: IMMORTALIA NE SPERES, MONET ANNUS ET ALMUM QUAE RAPIT HORA DIEM,* the only Latin in the churchyard. It is cut in the Quin quarry and the entry for payment is simply "Miss X."

The family grave of the China Court Quins is a little apart, as fits those who have come from outside: EUSTACE QUIN AND ADZA HIS WIFE—with two hands clasped together and the words: WE SHALL MEET AGAIN. Theirs are the largest-cut names, but the earliest dates are Little Eustace's, who dies at thirteen, and two others of the Brood who scarcely live at all: Lucy, three weeks old, and Marion aged one year, both dying in the same diph-

---

"That you hope for nothing to last forever is the lesson of the revolving year and the flight of time that snatches from us the sunny days."—HORACE

theria epidemic. Damaris's inscription is the next: ALSO
OF DAMARIS KING LEE, YOUNGEST DAUGHTER OF THE
ABOVE, AGED EIGHTEEN. Anne is not here, but Eliza is,
and Jared and Lady Patrick with their dates, 1897 and
1904. Borowis is not here either, but John Henry's date
is 1930. Stace's grave is in Italy, but his name is here:
STACE. 1944.

On one side of the big polished granite headstone is
a single name, POLLY. In death as in life she is mingled
with the family but when she dies and her certificate has
to be made out, "What the devil was her surname?" asks
Jared.

Jared and Lady Patrick go through her possessions,
but no one can discover her name. She has not, it appears, had any letters, or if she had she destroys them.
There is only a shabby little prayer book with, written
on the flyleaf, "To my god-daughter, Mary Ann, from
her Aunt, A. Parsons, 1831." But A. Parsons is long ago
forgotten and certainly dead before her niece. "Polly
must have been nearly ninety," and in the end the inscription has to be: "Polly, for fifty-four years faithful
nurse and friend of the Quin family."

Tracy's own little nursemaid Alice once designs a
tombstone for her, Tracy. " 'Here lies a little girl, Tracy,
daughter of Eustace—' "

"His name was Stace," interrupts Tracy, "and he
hasn't a tombstone, but a wooden cross. I have seen it
in a photograph with Mother, in a whole school of little
crosses. They are in a place in Italy."

"Eustace," says Alice firmly. "He must haave all he's
names on a grave. 'Of Eustace and Barbara Quin. Aged
seven years.' "

"And five months," says Tracy jealously.

"Seven years and five months. 'And a little child shall

lead them.' Ow! I likes that!" says Alice and now Tracy said, "I liked the funeral. I didn't expect to. I had dreaded it, but it was yes, a joining, not a going away; and all the people came."

"Sheer impertinence, when they weren't asked," said Bella.

"Impertinence!" cried Tracy, carried away. "But it *wasn't*."

"Really, Tracy. Do you have to contradict like that?"

"B-but it wasn't impertinence," stammered Tracy. "D-don't you see; it didn't occur to them they would n-need to be asked. They t-took it for granted they should come. No one thought of not coming and I thought that was b-beautiful," said Tracy.

"I'm sure Mother would much have preferred it private," said a Grace.

"She would, but she would have seen it couldn't be."

"You were with Mother, how long?" asked Bella, amused and nettled together.

"Three years," muttered Tracy, her head hanging.

"Three years, when you were a child, and you think you know her better than we do?"

Tracy was silent, but her silence seemed to say she was quite sure she did. "Well, really!" said Bella.

"You have come from America," began the third Grace, who was prettier and more gentle than her sisters, "you don't quite understand—" But she was interrupted by the older second Grace. "Americans always set an inordinate value on fusty old customs."

"But it *wasn't* fusty." Tracy could not help herself. Her head came up and she forgot to stammer. "*Fusty* means not used and out of date. This was used, all the time; it was everyday, quiet, homely and that is how I should like mine to be," she flung at them.

"Dear me! I didn't know any young people thought like that."

"They don't," said the second Grace.

"Certainly most of them seem to have no use for homely things," said Tom or Harry—Tracy was not sure which.

"Or for home either."

"Young people over here seem to spend all their time in coffee bars," a Grace explained to Tracy.

"Coffee is the new vice."

"You *are* behind the times, my child."

"We shall have to show you some life."

"We have coffee bars in Rome," said Tracy patiently. "It's where they came from, as a matter of fact and, anyway, I'm too old for them," and she said with what seemed to her aunts a calm rudeness, "Old people are all the same. They read books and newspapers and then think they know all about young ones. You read in the papers about the few interesting ones, what about all the uninteresting ones?" said Tracy. "Why, there are millions of us." She became aware that she was laying down the law and stopped, but she was so much in earnest that she had to try again. "Wouldn't everybody want that f-friendliness? I would. People who had known me, wanting to c-come, p-praying for me," said Tracy blushing again. "Caring, bringing flowers."

"Oh, Tracy. All those dreadful wreaths!"

It is like the pendulum of the grandfather clock, swinging from side to side. Adza is comforted after Little Eustace's death by a beautiful funeral. "There must have been a hundred bunches of flowers."

"Why need we be buried?" asks Eliza after Adza's funeral. "Why can't we be burned like the Hindus? It's far more civilized."

"Don't let the girls have me cremated," says Mrs. Quin, and now Tracy was back to Adza again. "They weren't dreadful wreaths. S-some of them were very beautiful and even those that weren't, were," said Tracy getting tangled, "were because they were meant. It wasn't a shop funeral. You couldn't b-buy it," and a thought struck her. "You have to earn it," said Tracy, but they were not listening.

They were talking again—*And is their talk always criticizing?* wondered Tracy. Now it was criticism of Peter St. Omer.

"You would have thought he could have come in a suit."

"Probably pawned it," said the second Grace, whose tongue was even sharper than Bella's.

"We are only Quins. Why should he bother to dress properly?" said the first sarcastically.

"If he thinks because he's a St. Omer—"

"Always was a casual young blighter," said Walter and even the third Grace said, "I thought he would have had more respect."

"Respect is it?" Cecily was in the middle of them, her eyes snapping with temper. "Peter hasn't a suit. He hasn't spent a penny on himself these last four years."

"Why not?" asked Bella.

"Because he hasn't had it to spend," said Cecily. "Because everything he made went straight back into the farm, he was trying to pull out of the mess *your* gentleman had left it in, Mr. Walter."

"He must have had suits before that," said Bella.

"So he had," said Cecily warmly, "and better ones than any of yours, only he is twice as broad now as when he came. Respect!" said Cecily and she flashed, "You wouldn't have said that, Grace, if you had seen what I did when I went up to tell him about the milk. He was ironing the shirt he had washed *himself*, and his tie and his coat were hung up, pressed by him with his old flatiron. How many of you," she asked rounding on Walter and Tom, Dick, and Harry, "How many of you would do that before you came?"

"It won't do him any good," said Walter, stretching. "He needn't think he will get anything out of us. That young man has finished getting things out of this family."

Cecily was so taken aback that she was silent; then she seemed to swell with anger. "If there's a mean thought, you will have it," said Cecily and her voice was shaking. "If there's a mean thing to do, you will do it."

"Cecily!" cried Bella. "You are speaking to Mr. Walter."

"So I know," said Cecily. "I shall speak as I choose, to Walter and all of you. I may have cooked and cleaned here, but I didn't do it for you. I did it for Mrs. Quin and I shall thank you to remember, I'm not *your* servant," said Cecily and slammed the door as she went out.

For a moment they were nonplussed, then they began to cover it up, thought Tracy. "Cecily gets more and more impossible."

"Of course. Mother spoiled her abominably."

"She has been cock of the walk here far too long."

"Oh, Cecily was always like that," said Bella. "She always did flare up about nothing. Half the time one didn't know what was the matter."

You wouldn't know, thought Tracy. *If one threw a stone at Aunt Bella it wouldn't cut,* she thought, *it would bounce back,* and she had to speak. "The matter is that C-Cecily loved G-Gran," she said far too loudly, her voice stuttering and trembling. "And sh-she knows P—Mr. St.

Omer, l-loved her too, and so did I, while you all
s-seem—" but she choked and had to run out of the
room and upstairs.

Tracy did not go into her own, the White Room; she
had the feeling that one of her aunts, the third Grace
perhaps, might come after her there; instead she took
refuge where she had not been since she came back, in
the old day nursery.

As soon as she pushed open the door, she had again
the sense of life that came to her when she saw Mrs.
Quin's basket standing on the garden path, of life going
on—*never having stopped,* thought Tracy. She ran her
hand up and down a pyramid of painted Russian rings
that stood on the windowsill, then leaned her hot forehead against the window bars and instantly remembered
the feel of those bars, their coolness and the rough
places where the white paint had worn on the iron; and
the way too, that her hair, as limp a gold-brown then as
now, caught on them as it caught now. She used to stand
here and look past the elms, out across the valley to
Penbarrow, *only Pet—Mr. St. Omer,* she corrected herself—*didn't live there then,* she thought. Remembering
the scene downstairs, she tightened her hand on the
pyramid of rings and again that sense of steadiness came
to comfort her.

If the kitchen is the hub of the house, the nursery is
its heart. No other room is like the day nursery with its
gently hissing fire where, on a trivet, Polly, McCann,
and Alice heat milk and warm irons while, on the high
fender, socks and vests are hung to dry.

The varnished yellow wallpaper has never been
changed; its pattern of dancing fiddling mice can still

be faintly discerned. The armchair has a pattern of flowers on scarlet chintz; the table is oak, stained by generations of paint-water; the chairs have battered legs, and one is a highchair with a tray.

The elms are on this side of the house and the rooks sound clearly. Their sound is bound up, for the little Quins, with going to bed on summer evenings, rook caws and a good-night hymn: "Now the Day Is Over." "But it isn't, not nearly," protests Eliza, and Borowis makes the same objection. It is not always that hymn. "There Is a Green Hill Far Away" and "Fight the Good Fight" are both oddly connected in the children's minds with perfect peace, mugs of milk, and the smell of new-mown hay.

On the bookcase was a certain small brassbound case that Tracy remembered too. It was leather over wood and studded with cat's-eyes set in brass and it held three small leatherbound notebooks; it shut with a brass clasp that locked. The child Tracy has often seen it in the White Room and one day, with her usual curiosity—"I was like a little monkey" said Tracy—she finds its key in the davenport. She fits it into the case and then takes it to Mrs. Quin to ask if she may have it.

"It was Aunt Eliza's, John Henry's Aunt Eliza's," says Mrs. Quin, "but I suppose you may."

When the key is turned the clasp springs up. It is a curious small case and, *I must show it to Mr. Alabaster,* thought Tracy now. She had thought, she remembered now, of making a secret tombstone book, like Alice's, but the notebooks were full with figures and writing, and she had put them back and locked the case again and left it here, on the bookcase—*And no one has moved it since, except to dust now and then, not all these twelve years,* thought Tracy marveling, but twelve years is hardly more than a breath for a house.

Children's voices still seem to be here. In those lonely years after Tracy is taken away, Mrs. Quin comes to understand how legends have arisen around toys, for the old toys in the nursury seem to be possessed by a life of their own: The rocking horse is "one of milady's notions," says Polly when Lady Patrick has it sent down from London for the small Borowis. Other children have painted rocking horses, dapple gray with red nostrils, but this one, which Borowis calls Banbury Cross, is of real cow skin, skewbald, with a leather saddle and bridle that can be unbuckled. "Cost more than ten pounds!" says Polly. The rocking horse and the pyramid of Russian rings are still here, a donkey with a tuft for a tail and the old Noah's Ark, while, on the wall, a painting of a faraway little girl, Mary Bazon—destined to be Great-uncle Mcleod's wife and give her name to one of his clippers—looks down from her gilded frame, her cheeks as firmly stuffed as the little rocking-horse's rump. Now, though there was dust on everything, and the armchair was sheeted, and when she patted Banbury Cross a moth came up, Tracy again felt the nursery as living.

China Court has always been a halcyon place for children, but the only one of them who realizes this is Ripsie, because she is shut out.

"Don't let the boys play with her, milady," Polly cautions Lady Patrick.

"Do you think they will get an accent?" asks Lady Patrick. Ripsie can talk like any St. Probus villager but, though Borowis and John Henry tease her to do it, she never will at China Court, yet still, to the end of her life, it sometimes slips out and she will say "daid" for "dead," "braid" for "bread," "knaw" for "know." "Well, I was Cornish born," says Mrs. Quin.

It is not the accent that worries Polly. "Better have tears now than later," she says wisely and does not think of their being Ripsie's tears. It is strange that Mrs. Quin, mistress of China Court, known and respected through the whole county, was once that outcast child.

"Are your father and mother married?" asks Borowis suspiciously.

"What father?" asks Ripsie.

"Your father. You have a father, haven't you, juggins?"

"I don't think so," says Ripsie.

"Then you are a bastard," says John Henry. It is a word he has learned at school, but it conveys nothing to Ripsie and she agrees equably that she is a bastard.

She knows she is different. Her mother never stands at the gate of their cottage gossiping like other village women. When she goes into the village shop a silence falls. The cottage mothers call their children away if Ripsie speaks to them; the children, little imitators, will not play with her. "But I don't want to play with them," says Ripsie. The only place she wants to play is China Court.

"We can't let girls in," says that conservative John Henry.

"We can let girls in," says Borowis.

"Who says so?"

"I say so."

Why Borowis decides to take Ripsie under his protection he does not know; perhaps it is because she amuses him with her smallness and the courage with which she goes about the hostile village. She is quite self-contained and un-self-pitying in her tatterdemalion old blue coat, the shoes with holes in them—in summer she goes bare-foot—and, like a badge of defiance, that scarlet tam-o'-shanter. Perhaps it is the pleading compulsion of her eyes, overbig in her bony small face, or perhaps even then she is attractive; his little blackberry girl he calls her. He takes her under his wing and, as he is the one person who can wheedle Lady Patrick, Ripsie is allowed to stay, but only on sufferance; she is not allowed in the front of the house—Pringle orders her out if she sets foot even in the hall—nor can she play in the front garden, and she has to use the back stairs. She accepts this without resentment—unless Isabel comes to stay.

Isabel is an important little girl. Her father, Borowis's godfather, is Brigadier the Honorable Charles Loftus Kennedy and she will have, Polly says, "Ten thousand a year in her own right."

"Ten thousand what?" asks the ignorant Ripsie.

Isabel has long gold hair like a princess in a fairy tale; the fact that she also has a high nose and pair of merci-less gray eyes escapes most people. "You have a hole in your stocking," she says the first time she meets Ripsie, who does not answer glibly and saucily as she would have done with any child in the village, but tries to twist her foot out of sight. "And another in your shoe!" says Isabel loudly.

She believes in keeping Ripsie in her place. "That's as far as you may come," she commands at the head of the stairs and "You can't use the front door, go around to the back," but Isabel only visits now and then; usually Borowis, John Henry, and Ripsie are three, banded to-gether—*bonded together,* thinks Mrs. Quin—and their domain goes far beyond China Court itself, over the wall to the valley where there are no restrictions because Borowis says it is his.

"It's Lord St. Omer's," says John Henry.

"Jod, I have licensed it," says Borowis with dignity. He means "leased," which of course he has not, but gullible John Henry believes him and from that day is sure he is not trespassing and that the valley is Borowis's.

It does belong to the St. Omers, but none of them ever comes there and it is given over to the beech-woods and the river, the bluebell copse on the island that is not really an island but a peninsula cut off by the stream; given over too, to the marshfields and the herons and the clapper bridge that is six or seven hundred years old.

Ripsie is most useful to the boys. When they build a raft and launch it in the river, they put her on it to see if it will float; it will not and she is very nearly drowned, swept down and only just fished out like a kitten by the scruff of her neck in time. Because she is little and light, they send her up trees higher than they can go, to get birds' eggs. When they concoct a yellow dye, they dip her skimpy linsey-woolsey petticoat in it, and when they brew charms in an old saucepan over a fire between two stones, they make her take their horrible concoctions to see if they have an effect. They do have an effect; once at least she is miserably ill, but she never tells anyone the reason.

In the valley Borowis has his cache for catching ot-ters—he never sees an otter; he has a raft and a harbor built of stones and mud in long hours of toiling in the river—mostly by Ripsie and John Henry—and an ar-mory stocked with food in a hollow tree, though the air gun must not be left there at night; Ripsie carries the air gun. He keeps his egg collection there too; he is an enthusiastic egg collector.

"I put you in charge," he says to Ripsie when these enchanted years are ended by his and John Henry's being sent away to school. "Instead of having lessons with Snoddy," says Borowis contemptuously. Mr. Snodgrass is the last of a line of resented tutors. "Tutors! They treat us like children!" says Borowis.

He should have gone to school long ago, for he is quite out of hand. It begins in small ways when he is not more than nine and breaks into the larder and steals the fruit out of the cherry pies, putting the crust back so that it is innocently carried in to Jared in the dining room. Jared's temper, with the servants, is short these days, and the whole house is upset. This is the first of many stealings and when Jared at last comes upstairs after dinner to beat them, he beats John Henry, but Borowis has wound himself in all the sheets so that by the time Jared has unwound him, they are helpless with laughing and even Jared cannot whip. Borowis and John Henry have perpetual battles with the village boys in which both sides get hurt; they poach with the boy poacher, Jim Neot, trespass and play truant, and the tutors leave almost as soon as they have come.

"You will have to make up your mind to let the boys go to school," Jared tells Lady Patrick.

"And stay here alone with you?" But Jared, humbly, has his way, for it is obvious there is nothing else to be done, and Borowis goes to Rugby, John Henry to a preparatory school for a year before joining him. Borowis is heartlessly pleased, but to shy John Henry, it is agony. On the last night they have dinner downstairs and there is roast duck, Borowis's choice. Ripsie, of course, knows all about it and rejoices, though she will have no chance of eating the duck. John Henry does not eat it either; he chokes on the first mouthful and, slowly, his head sinks down and down until it is on the tablecloth. Jared and Lady Patrick take no notice; she goes on talking—in front of the boys she keeps up appearances—while Borowis kicks John Henry under the table. "Jod, don't be an ass," but for once John Henry does not respond.

"I put you in charge," Borowis tells Ripsie. "Take great care of the egg collection and don't let anyone touch the heron eggs. They are probably worth ten shillings *each*!" Ripsie lifts and dusts them as if they were worth ten pounds.

"It will be the most valuable collection in England, when I get a chough's egg," boasts Borowis.

"I shall get one for you." Ripsie says that quickly before John Henry can. "I shall get you a chough's egg."

"Don't be silly. You are a girl," says Borowis. "It's terribly dangerous. They nest high on the cliffs and you have to hunt because you hardly ever find one. I knew a chap who broke his neck, didn't I, Jod?"

"Yes," says John Henry faintly.

"Both you and John Henry are forbidden near the cliffs," orders Borowis. "I shall get one for myself in the hols," but Ripsie sets her lips.

John Henry often tells the story, known throughout the village, of how Ripsie got the chough's egg. "Jim Neot told it to me. He said he wouldn't have believed it of such a little tacker." Mrs. Quin never mentions it.

"First she had to get to the seaside, miles," John Henry tells, "and remember this was before there were motor cars. She knew where the choughs were supposed to nest, at Pentyre Head, and she got up at four in the morning and walked, and begged a lift in a carrier's cart. All the breakfast she had was some slices of bread; Pentyre Head is almost sheer up from the beach and at high tide the sea comes boiling in; the noise is enough to frighten anyone, let alone the dizziness—and choughs are quite big birds, you know, bigger than crows and she was a bit of a thing. . . ."

"I was twelve," says Mrs. Quin coldly, for this is not until the next summer when the boys have been at school a year.

"You were still tiny," says John Henry, and goes on. "When Jerry Paul, the coast-guard, spotted her, there she was up on the ledge."

"Well, I couldn't get down," says Mrs. Quin.

"Jim Neot says you might have starved there, or turned dizzy and fallen two hundred feet. She was soaked and bleeding," says John Henry, "her fingers and knees half raw. They had to lower a man on a rope to reach her."

"And a good scolding I got," says Mrs. Quin. "From all the Pauls and from my mother when I got home. The doctor from Polzeath brought me in his trap."

"But she had the chough's egg," says John Henry.

The second day of the summer holidays is Borowis's birthday. Birthdays at China Court follow a ritual, of presents after breakfast and, in the afternoon, tea on the dining-room table which is decorated with flowers and has in the center a cake with candles. The cake is on a plate that, when it is lifted, plays a tune. Ripsie knows all this as well as any Quin child, though she, of course, has no birthday kept. Later Mrs. Quin continues the ritual for her own children, then for Tracy; she cannot imagine changing it and on this July day of 1891, Ripsie is completely unaware that the boys have outgrown it.

Two days before, Jared goes up to meet the boys in town; it does not occur to Ripsie that "town" is London—the only town she knows is Bodmin. He has taken them, she hears, to "Lords," which she supposes is a home of the St. Omers. Borowis has had his first suit made to order at Rowes—"no more reach-me-downs," says Borowis—and they are to go to the Haymarket—which she sees as the open-air market at Bodmin, but filled with stooks of hay. They dine at the Criterion and come home next day.

As soon as she judges their breakfast is over, Ripsie is ready, standing at the gate.

She stands there in the lane, waiting for John Henry to remember and fetch her in; her small bare feet feel over the stones; occasionally she scratches the back of her calf with the other foot, but her hands never move; they are holding the chough's egg.

She has blown it, as Borowis taught her, keeping down her disgust with the fishy raw slime she draws out, and has kept the shell in cotton wool in a fuller's-earth box, until the boys come home, "until Boro's birthday," breathes Ripsie.

She always knows when he is coming though he does not write. In all her years of loving Borowis, she never has a letter from him. "No, I had no love letters," Mrs. Quin tells Barbara. With something of Borowis's cruelty, she does not count the gentle shy love letters John Henry writes to her all through his life. "You were abominable to John Henry," says Barbara, but she sounds amused. "Abominable."

"I wasn't," says Mrs. Quin and immediately contradicts herself. "Yes, I was." Then in her harshest voice she says, "He shouldn't have touched what didn't belong to him."

Once again Barbara is quick to understand. "Yes. It was you and Borowis all the time," she says.

"All the time," says Mrs. Quin.

Every holiday Ripsie gets the harbor and raft ready and stocks the armory in the tree, carrying the precious air gun there every morning, taking it home every night. Everything is kept ready, but somehow the holidays seem to be gone and Borowis has not been even to look. He means to—Borowis always means well—but he does not, and the biscuits go moldy and the bull's-eyes consolidate into a sticky lump, the sherbet dries up. John Henry would have eaten them, but Ripsie will not let him. "They are for Boro," she says sternly.

Now the chough's egg, in all its cream-green and flecked beauty has been taken out and polished and laid in a small nest she has found and decorated with moss and flowers. "What? You got it!" Borowis, she knows, will say little more than that, but Ripsie is not used to feeling proud and she expects no more, though it is possible, "just *possible*," whispers Ripsie aloud, that he may give a whistle which will show his astonishment and say, "Jolly good," or, "Good for you." "It will be the most valuable collection in England now, won't it?" Ripsie will say in sublime faith, and she hovers, hoping that John Henry may even fetch her in time to see, through a crack in the door, the birthday presents.

The hope fades as time goes on; endless time, it seems to Ripsie. She begins to wonder what is happening. Breakfast must be over long ago; if she had been less intent she would have heard a commotion around the house; she cannot see through the rhododendrons to the front door, but she could have heard sounds, yet it is as a complete surprise that she sees John Henry and Lady Patrick coming.

First John Henry appears, running to open the gate; then Lady Patrick riding her Reynard. Lady Patrick never looks as hard as when she is riding, nor as beautiful; her black habit fits as if she were cased in it, its low lapels, satin-faced, open to show her wide folded stock, and she gleams, from the tip of her boot which just shows under her heavy skirt, to the bun of her hair in its net under her bowler with its narrow curled brim.

Like the kitchens and what Mr. Alabaster called the "offices," the stables are too big for the house, "and so much more better," as Minna says in surprise when Groundsel takes her over them. In his time there are only two ponies left; the little girls share them and, for a while, there is Stace's hunter. Then the ponies are given away, Stace's hunter is sold, and a solitary Welsh pony is kept for the tubcart; then that is given up and there are none. In 1892 a pair of loose-boxes are turned into a garage for John Henry's first motorcar, a six-and-a-half-horsepower Humberette with one c. gear and three speeds. Greatly daring, he pays one hundred and fifty-seven pounds, ten shillings, for it, and the quarrymen build a cement hut on the edge of the orchard for the petrol, which is delivered in twenty-gallon drums.

In Lady Patrick's younger days the stables are a world in themselves. It is she who floors them with brick, enlarges them by four loose-boxes, makes a new harness room, a flat over them for the coachman and head groom, and adds the gilded weathercock so that all the village can look down and catch its extravagant glitter. There are plenty of horses then: Maxim, Jared's hunter, and Jezebel, his hack, used also for the dogcart; Lady Patrick's Irish hunters, Reynard and Sorrel, her pair of grays for the carriage, Sugar and Spice; a cob for the grooms to ride and, up to now, Basket, the boys' pony.

There is a carriage, the dogcart and the tubcart and a large stable staff, coachman, head groom, two underlings from the village, and a boy. "No wonder her mother's money all went," says Mrs. Quin.

Now as Lady Patrick rides down the drive, looking over her shoulder and reining Reynard to one side, Borowis comes into view around the rhododendrons and Ripsie catches her breath; he is riding a little roan-colored mare, so deep a roan that her coat shines almost blue. She tittups and circles, making a tattoo on the drive with her hoofs as if she were dancing and, "He had her for his birthday," carols John Henry to Ripsie. "She's a real hunter. Her name is Mirabelle. That means beautiful little plum!"

"They are turning that boy into a young pasha," says Mr. Fitzgibbon when he hears. "Bringing a hunter over from Ireland, and he only fifteen," and in John Henry, though he sounds happy and excited now, the memory of Mirabelle always stings: "*I* never had a hunter," he says it again when Stace is given Mrs. Moonlight. Borowis and Stace—John Henry seems caught between them: Mirabelle and Mrs. Moonlight, dark roan and gray dapple. They gradually seem one and the same little mare to Mrs. Quin.

"Bring her along, Boro." Lady Patrick's voice is curt, but even Ripsie can hear the pride in it. Borowis, in his riding clothes, the checked coat and shallow brown bowler, is always a stranger to Ripsie, gone to a world where she cannot follow him; now his face is white under his freckles, and as hard as Lady Patrick's, his eyes a blaze of excitement. Ripsie should have seen he has no scrap of thought to spare for anything but the new mare, but, when he comes to the gate, she cannot help it, she holds up the nest.

The mare plunges and, as if he did not recognize her from any village child, he says curtly, "Get out of the way."

"Boro, she has got something for you. It's—it's—" and John Henry peers nearer. "Gosh, it's—yes it is! Boro, it's a chough's egg. A chough's! Bet you she got it herself." John Henry knows at once what is at stake and he tries hard to catch his brother's attention. "A *chough's* egg for your birthday."

Borowis is not graceless; he tries to pay attention, but Lady Patrick has ridden up the lane and the new mare fidgets and strains. "For my birthday?" Borowis manages to say, but he is watching and feeling the quickness of Mirabelle.

"For your egg collection," Ripsie says it stiffly. She will die rather than show that either he or she is personally involved. "For the egg collection," and she looks far up and over his head, but by now Borowis has remembered. The egg collection in the hollow tree in the valley; it belongs with his armory, an air gun, a harbor—but that is ages ago, thinks Borowis. Collecting eggs? Bird's-nesting? That is for John Henry; for children. He, Borowis, has Mirabelle now and Jared has said he can practice wth the .22 rifle and Lord St. Omer has promised to lend him a shotgun and take him in his butt when pheasant-shooting begins. Borowis has to drag his mind a long long way back to birds' eggs; his mind does not want to be dragged, but even at this distance it can recognize what it means to get a chough's egg and, "Good for you," says Borowis. They are the words Ripsie longed for, but there is something absent-minded in the way he says it and she is not deceived.

For a moment Borowis sees her standing there in the lane in her bare feet and faded cotton frock, holding the carefully flowered nest; for a moment he understands, but Mirabelle tosses her head, her fetlocks dance and he has no more time to see, or even to think and, bending down, he says generously what he thinks will be the best possible thing—only he is not thinking. "Rip, you can have my egg collection," says Borowis.

He has not ridden a yard up the lane when something hits him in the back. It is the nest with the chough's egg.

Jared does not come out riding with them even though it is Borowis's birthday. Maxim and Jezebel stay in the stable. Jared and Lady Patrick still drive to meets together and he puts her up in the saddle—he will not let the groom do it—but they keep apart. He rides out on business, and she often orders a horse out and hacks across the moor, but they never ride together. He will not be at the birthday tea, and will be silent and taciturn at dinner, "if he isn't drunk," says Lady Patrick. She is not silent when the boys are home, she keeps up a pretense, but the more simple Jared finds it difficult to remember. Pringle, who waits on them, has known him go through the whole of dinner without speaking a word. It is fifteen years ago today that Jared begins to hate himself.

A spiral of smoke goes up from the China Court nursery chimney, a spiral that is instantly seen in the village. The nursery fire has been lit.

A stillness is over the house and garden. Its familiars come and go, but quietly; everyone is doing what they have to do, but every now and then they stop and listen, except Cook, who is nervous and has alternate attacks of temper and hysterics. She is, for one thing, upset about the nun who has come over from Ireland. "Why not a good monthly nurse I ask you?" says Cook belligerently.

"Sister Priscilla is a kind of monthly nurse," says the more broadminded Pringle. "She were there when her ladyship were born. Poor lorn thing, it's nice for her to have someone from her own family," but Cook is not to be mollified.

"Nasty creeping things, they rattle." She means Sister Priscilla's beads that click as she walks. "Never thought I should find meself in the same house as *papists*," says Cook darkly.

"We will bear with you, Cook, if you will try and bear with us," says Sister Priscilla's calm voice behind them. "May I have some hot water, please?" She has dared to come into the kitchen herself and Cook is so affronted that she lets an oven ring fall with a loud clang on the stove. It knocks over the kettle which falls in the fender and narrowly escapes scalding the kitchen maid, who screams. Jared shouts, "Stop that infernal clatter in the kitchen," and Cook goes into hysterics again.

One person is working steadily. Polly is radiant as she remembers things afresh, things she has laid by for a long time, laid by but not forgotten, though she is slow. It is as if she had to find her way back, "twenty-three years to Damaris," says Polly. "Damaris was the last."

She moves steadily about the nursery: pieces of muslin are boiled in a bowl "for the eyes and nose" says Polly; olive oil is warming; an apron of old soft toweling, cotton wool for wiping are ready; the bath of white enamel is on its iron stand. China Court babies have new bassinets and baskets, frilled and muslined; Adza, for Damaris, embroiders a whole new set on white over pink, with rosebuds and green leaves, but the bath is always the same. "Vaseline," says Polly, "scissors; needle and cotton, for stitching the binder." Polly never uses a safety pin; they are not safety in her day. Toweling squares and clothes are airing on the fender, the layers of clothes that Polly does not question a baby should wear: binder and diaper, a long wrapover flannel petticoat, a white lawn petticoat, then a robe and short crocheted jacket. When Polly carries one of *her* babies, the robe falls to the hem of her own dress. "All that weight on those poor little legs," exclaims Barbara when she is shown the baby clothes. "It's a wonder they didn't grow up crooked."

"They didn't," says Mrs. Quin. "The Quins have always had straight legs."

Each garment is stitched with minute even stitches— "like a row of tiny pearls," says Adza teaching small Mary, Eliza, and Anne to sew: hemming, herringbone, feather-stitching, buttons so small that fingers can hardly fasten them, smaller loops, infinitesimal tucks, bindings of white silk.

There is an outdoor pelisse of stiff white serge, braided and lined with silk; to match it, is a cap for a boy, a bonnet for a girl. Over these goes a veil and, round and round the baby, like a cocoon, a wide shawl. "If a baby won't stop crying," Polly teaches, "wrap it tightly round in a shawl, and it often will."

There is not one of her charges whom Polly does not know through and through and, "You must behave yourself," she says to Jared this morning, as she says when he is six years old. "Behave." But she knows he will not. "Cocks can't quack," is one of Polly's maxims.

Jared paces through the hall into the drawing room and back through the hall into the dining room and out onto the terrace, then backward and forward over its stones. "I suppose I must stay here," he says. For his little Patrick's sake—and for decency's sake—he knows he must, but he would give worlds to have a horse out and gallop fast up on the moor; or go potting at rabbits—there is nothing else to shoot in July—but speed would be better, or to take out a ferret, anything to get out of the way. "I suppose I can't," says Jared like a rebellious small boy.

He does not like the stillness, and he does not like the sympathy, it makes him feel irritable; nor the expectancy, it makes him feel trapped. I ought to be pleased, but I don't want to settle down yet, thinks Jared. Not start a family. I want to get away with Pat sometimes to town, not rot here. He does not like himself for thinking this, but it is true and he cannot help it and he has a feeling of being throttled by his young wife. "I didn't ask to be loved like this," says Jared to himself and kicks the scraper outside the french doors.

Above all he cannot bear the joy in Lady Patrick's face, joy at being hurt like this, thinks Jared shrinking. Lady Patrick is tall, but she is slender, narrow-hipped, and she has ridden a great deal and in 1876 an old-fashioned doctor does not believe in too much chloroform. Like many big men Jared cannot bear pain; like many thoughtless men he is appalled when he sees pain naked: I did this to her! and his whole being recoils.

"I'm glad you did," pants Lady Patrick. "Be glad."

Glad! Jared sees the sweat break out on her face as her eyes widen in an effort to hold back the screams; he did not know she could look ugly. "Glad," she pants with that dreadful distorted face, the body he has loved spread and swollen on the bed, making curious movements of itself, thinks Jared stunned. "Don't leave me," she cries, "help me," but Jared cannot bear it and, as Sister Priscilla's hands come to her back and hold her, he tears himself loose and stumbles out of the room, "and out of the house," says Polly, as from the landing window she watches him go. She stands for a minute, considering, her hands under her apron, then she goes in to Lady Patrick. "I have sent him away," says Polly.

"Sent him away! How dared you!" It is the imperious Lady Patrick speaking. *No one else must know Jared*, thinks Polly silently, *but at least the young ladyship has been saved from knowing that he has deserted*, thinks Polly, *though he should never have been asked to stay. My goodness, the mistress would never* . . . thinks Polly.

Adza is the one she admires. "Send a message to Mr. Quin," says Adza on each occasion. "Tell him I shall not be down for breakfast—dinner—supper—to make him his tea." When Jared is born, she is in the middle of making marmalade.

"I think you should come upstairs now, ma'am."

"Not just yet, Polly. I think we can finish this batch," and, "He was nearly born in the kitchen," says Polly; but, as Lady Patrick excels Adza in beauty, she excels her in feeling too, "more feeling than sense," says Polly.

Polly would have given Jared a rap: "Grow up. You are married now," but he is gone. From the terrace he goes, stepping lightly by back paths, to reach the drive and disappears toward the stables.

The grandfather clock strikes twelve; the other clocks follow, and Polly runs out on the landing again. "A boy." Her cheeks are pink, her eyes look like a girl's, and she throws her arms around Eliza, who happens to have come upstairs. There is under Eliza's cloak a sharp-edged parcel, but Polly is too elated to feel it.

Eliza stands listening to a cry that fills the landing, a

sound like sparrows chirping or an engine starting up, while below Pringle scurries to the kitchen with the news: "A boy. A boy."

"A boy! and both safe and well, thank God," says Polly.

"Thank Dr. Smollett, I should say," says Eliza crisply, but Polly is not having that behavior. "Certainly thank Dr. Smollett, but none of your talk now, Eliza. You can go and find Jared and tell him. Tell him he can come now," says Polly.

"Jared." Eliza stands on the terrace and calls, "Jared." No answer. She looks around the garden, then goes down the drive and calls again toward the stables. "Surely not gone out?" says Eliza, and goes down to the stables to see.

"Gone out?" Lady Patrick's eyes that have looked so eagerly at the opening door cloud with bewilderment. "Are you *sure*?"

Eliza has none of Polly's mercy. "Quite sure. Trust Jared!" she says.

"We must expect gentlemen to go out and in," says Sister Priscilla.

"He will be back in a few minutes," says Polly, but these are only bandage words, covering up a cut that bleeds through. Lady Patrick will not, as they desire, go to sleep or drink her beef tea. "Something must have happened to him," she insists. It is only toward evening, and then only if they let her hold the baby that, worn out with pain and fretting, she falls into a sleep.

It is both of them asleep that Jared sees, his wife and son, when he comes home late, "with his tail between his legs," says Polly.

"And where have you been?" she asks.

Jared never lies to Polly. It would, in any case, be no

good; Polly knows him through and through. "Meant to go for a quick ride," he says sullenly, "but I met Harry St. Omer."

"And?" says Polly, not letting him off.

"We found a fair, and fooled around." Polly knows his fooling and she asks no more, but drives him sharply into the bedroom.

He stands by the bed, ashamed and miserable, looking at the two heads against the pillow: Lady Patrick's almost child face, still stained by tears and white with tiredness, and the other head, no bigger than a doll's beside her. He stares at that round dark head lying so confidently where no head was before and, as he looks, comprehension of what has been going on here dawns on his mind: *While I was fooling with Harry*, thinks Jared. *I could kick myself!* He groans and goes down on his knees by the bed. Even now she is not properly asleep—every few minues she has wakened fretting, and she wakes now. "Jared!"

"Little Pat. My love, I—" The words choke him. "How could I—"

"No Jeremiahs." Polly's voice comes from behind him and he stops, but kisses Lady Patrick's hand, keeping it against his face, covering it with kisses. "Sweetheart."

Polly does not like these endearments: "Darling," "sweetheart" seem to her extravagant. They won't weather, thinks Polly. The most she ever hears Adza or Eustace allow themselves is "my dear," now and again "my love." Nor does Polly think it wise that Lady Patrick says not one word of reproach. "Jared needs bringing up," Polly could have told her, but Lady Patrick only draws her hand gently away from him and turns the blanket back. "Not me—him," she whispers.

Jared's face as he looks at his baby is so comical that Polly and Sister Priscilla have to turn their faces away, but Lady Patrick draws Jared down to her. "Do you know what his name is?" she whispers.

"His name?" asks Jared stupidly. He has not really taken it in that this is his son, a person.

"He has to have a name," says Lady Patrick and laughs. Jared is so relieved she can laugh that he can almost manage a smile.

"What name, my darling?"

"The dearest name in the world," she whispers. "Your name, Jared."

"No!" cries Jared, stung.

"Why no?" but he is not prepared to confess and he says lamely, "I want him to have another name."

"What name?" asks Lady Patrick.

The only name that comes into Jared's mind is the name of the tightrope walker at that ridiculous fair that afternoon. He and Harry St. Omer have seen a good deal of the tightrope walker for he has a partner, a taking little brunette with plump legs in black mesh stockings. Before he can stop himself, to his horror Jared has said the tightrope walker's name: "Borowis."

"Borowis?"

He tries to take it back. "No, it's too queer." Borowis, the Russian Tightrope Wonder, but, "I like it," says Lady Patrick. "Borowis," she says to the baby.

She is weak and very tired; Sister Priscilla carries away the baby and, with Jared's hand in hers, Lady Patrick has settled down. Polly puts her finger to her lips. "Dear, dear love," murmurs Lady Patrick and is asleep.

Jared kneels there and, in spite of cramp, does not move his hand, "for almost twenty minutes," says Polly.

* * *

"Miss Quin, Miss Damaris Quin for luncheon."

"They mean Eliza and Anne," says Damaris. "They must mean Eliza and Anne."

"Then they wouldn't say 'Damaris,' " snaps Eliza and turns on her sister. "Don't pretend Harry St. Omer doesn't know your name."

"Then why only two of us?" asks Damaris bewildered.

"Because they don't know there are three," says Eliza, "don't know or care."

It is the day after the gale, a day, in the way Cornish weather can change, of sun and calmness, and the note comes soon after breakfast, brought by a groom on horseback, the groom in the buff-and-maroon livery that, though familiar to everyone in St. Probus, has never, so far, been seen at China Court.

In those early days of the house there are not many visitors. The doctor visits, of course, first Dr. Stone and then Dr. Smollett; very often in those days, the stable boy walks Dr. Stone's horse up and down while the doctor is inside with Adza. Dr. Smollett's assistant, courting Mary, comes often; Mrs. Smollett now and then, and there is, of course, the vicar—many vicars, for they change; sometimes there is a vicar's wife, sometimes, as with Miss Preedy, a vicar's sister. There used to be school friends of Mary's or Anne's—Eliza, as has been told, has not the knack of making friends—and presently there will be several of Jared's from Rugby and Oxford—"too young for us," says Eliza—but on the whole, the family lives to itself. "That happens with a big family," says Polly.

"But how do people ever meet people?" asks Eliza in despair, which means, "How do girls ever marry?"

Now the chance is here. The note, borne respectfully on a salver, is brought in to Adza in the morning room. She takes it uncertainly, but Eliza is already trembling, half with eagerness, half with suspicion. Adza reads the note, her lips moving in the way that always irritates Eliza—like a school child, thinks Eliza—and, "She writes as if she knows us," says Adza, puzzled.

"Lady St. Omer?" asks Eliza.

"Yes," and Adza reads aloud: " 'Dear Mrs. Quin, Harry tells me the girls are home. . . .' "

"Home for eight years," says Eliza.

" '. . . so pleased if they may come to an early luncheon with our young people. If you say "yes" as I hope you will, Harry and his friend will drive over—Harry should pay his formal call on you—' "

"When has he ever?" asks Eliza.

" '—and, if they may, the young men will drive them back, cordially, Jane St. Omer.' "

"Cordially! He must be very rich," says Eliza.

"Who?"

"This man, Harry's friend, who wants to see Damaris again."

"He doesn't," cries Damaris, crimson, but Adza looks at the note more thoughtfully still. "There is a post-script: 'I hope you do not object to their driving in a dogcart. I allow Helena.' "

"If Helena does, we can!" says Eliza acridly. She longs for Adza to say no, that she certainly cannot allow her girls . . . but that might seem narrow and provincial. She longs for Adza to refuse the whole invitation and yet . . . It is gratifying to have the St. Omers asking us, thinks Eliza. "A horridly condescending letter," says Eliza aloud to relieve her feelings, but it is not condescending, it is friendly, even if absent-minded. *Why is it so friendly?*

Adza is palpably asking herself that and sits staring at the letter for so long that Eliza loses patience and cries, "Mother, a note is meant to be answered! That groom won't wait all day."

When the answer is gone: "Dear Lady St. Omer . . ." written slowly, for Adza is not much accustomed to notes, she sits on silently at her desk. For once Adza is thinking deeply. "I wish your father were not at the quarry," she says. "I think I shall send for him," and she rings the bell. Meanwhile, behind her, an altercation is going on: "It says Miss Quin. You are Miss Quin, Liz. You must go," says Anne to Eliza.

"Wild horses wouldn't drag me," says Eliza.

"But you are Miss Quin. They will think it odd."

"They won't, because they don't know—or care," says Eliza. "They only know that Damaris has a sister, or sisters. I'm not going in Damaris's train."

Anne does not want to go either. Her reasons are stronger than Eliza's but she is biddable and gentle. "And Anne should go," says Eustace, summoned home. "It may put an end to this chapel nonsense." Anne does not answer, but bends her head over her work.

Two hours later there is the sound of wheels on the gravel, of horses' hooves, men's voices. "They are here already!" Damaris is pale.

"You see, they knew we wouldn't refuse," says Eliza.

Eustace goes out to meet the young men—though Mr. King Lee is not young, nearer middle age—and for a few minutes they stay talking on the step, Eustace admiring Harry's horses. Then their voices sound nearer. Eustace is bringing them in and, "Liz, where are you going?" cries Damaris in panic, but Eliza is gone, slipped out of the drawing room, where a fire has been lit at this unaccustomed hour and the family has gathered. Eliza runs swiftly out of sight down the passage as the men cross the hall to the drawing-room door, and Adza, Anne, and Damaris rise all together; a moment later, "How do you do," Damaris is saying unwillingly.

As soon as she has said it she knows that it is fatal, as fatal as the pink of her dress with its white cuffs and folded white muslin at the neck that shows off her skin and the sheen of her hair. "Can I help it having a sheen?" she wants to ask. "I don't brush it; it's just health and the wind, soft water and air." Mr. King Lee seems to know very well what it is. He looks at it—as if he would like to touch it, thinks Damaris, as frightened as a caught bird. "Don't look at me, look at Anne," she wants to cry.

Harry St. Omer's loud voice, not quite at its ease, praises the room, the flowers, and Eustace's sherry. Mr. King Lee praises nothing but continues to look at Damaris, as if it were wonderful to him to find the Gypsy of yesterday morning turned into a young lady. *Look at Anne*, begs Damaris silently, but he will not look at Anne, so delicate in her summer dress, her skin so fair that the blue veins show, her hair brushed neatly into a pale-gold chignon. The girls' dresses that year are made alike, and in the very newest style taken by Eliza from Paris fashions in the *Illustrated London News*, "though Miss Dawnay's cut is not the same," says Eliza, discontentedly. The dresses are in toile-de-Chine, the upper skirts caught up at the side into panniers, the underskirts plain, but with tabliers, as Eliza calls them, trimmed with a series of flounces, each edged with bands of white muslin and lace. They are dainty and maidenly, with more white muslin and lace edging the neck and sleeves, but Damaris hates them. "Oh Mother, not those sickly sweet-pea colorings. I want scarlet," she has pleaded, "or amber."

"You can't wear a scarlet dress!" says dictatorial Eliza, and Damaris is forced to have the pale pink that matches Anne's pale blue, Eliza's lilac. She hates it, but it appears so to entrance Mr. King Lee that she retreats into the conservatory; she has forgotten, she says, to water the plants. Mr. King Lee follows her there.

Damaris waters Adza's geraniums and begonias, taking extreme care not to knock or bruise the flowers. Although she is so careful, the spout of the small watering can trembles. Presently Mr. King Lee takes it from her and puts it down. "The pots are overflowing," says Mr. King Lee.

There is not a servant in the house who does not now know about Mr. King Lee. Two dogcarts, with yellow wheels, each with a small attendant tiger in buff and maroon, are waiting on the drive. Shy Anne is unwillingly to drive with shyer Harry—"Only shy of girls of his own kind, I hear," says Eustace disapprovingly—but the servants' network of communication is exact and no one wastes a glance on them. It is the sight of Miss Damaris being handed up by the American gentleman that brings all heads to the kitchen window: plain caps and streamers, Cook's ginger hair puffed high with tortoiseshell combs, the kitchen maid, her cap crooked, humbly peeping in a corner. Miss Damaris, they all observe, has a blush. The cook is Cornish in Adza's day and "Her 'ud look purty as a pi'ture in white satin," says Cook.

It is at the time of the kitchen dinner when, always, a peculiarly rich and appetizing smell hangs about the house, "much nicer than ours," declares Jared. China

Court kitchen meals are always good; that day there is soup—"made with bones and trimmin's," grumbles a housemaid—roast leg of mutton, vegetables, and cheese. "Wot? No pudden!" says the knife-boy and gets his ears boxed. Cook sits at the head of the table, Abbie at the bottom; Polly's dinner is carried up to her on a tray and the knife-boy takes his out to the scullery.

There is also, at this time, a smell of hot pasties which have been warmed up for the outside men.

Years later, Groundsel, coming in to fetch his pasty, lingers to catch a glimpse of Minna. One day in late autumn he makes up his mind to speak to her. She is, as is usual at this time, washing up in the scullery from the children's early dinner.

The scullery then, too, has its inconveniently shallow big wooden sinks and an even bigger plate rack; cold water has to be pumped from the hand pump at the side of it but still, to Minna, washing up is a thing of beauty. Plates are scraped clean of scraps and stacked, the knives put aside for the boy to clean in the knife machine, a strange wheel with hollow spokes; spoons and forks are put to soak in a jug of hot water, and the glasses drained. Then Minna gets ready a bowl of soapy hot water, another of hotter water and soda, a third for rinsing, and her deft pink fingers get to work. First the glasses are dried and polished while they are still warm; next the forks and spoons washed, dried, and polished hot; then the small plates, last the large, are sluiced, put in the rack to drip, then carefully dried. Last of all washbowls and sink are emptied and swilled, the mop rinsed and hung by its stick to dry, the draining board scrubbed and dried too. Groundsel, who has seen the other maids throw everything higgledy-piggledy into the sink, is charmed. He stands in the doorway watching with, as it has been raining, his usual rainwear, a sack over his shoulders. Stealing a glance at him, Minna can see raindrops on his dark hair.

"Minna."

"Please?" But Minna feels dull, fatigued, heavy. Groundsel has left the door open so that the wind blows in, but to her the wind feels heavy too, with no life or tang of its own.

Groundsel clears his throat. "Are you liking it here?"

She pauses, her hands on the draining board, then, "No, I don't like—at *all*," she says with energy.

"Well, you must miss your country," says Groundsel reasonably. He comes cautiously closer. "They say it's pretty there. People from this country go there for the snow."

"The snow." Minna looks out of the window to the browns and reds of the bare trees and the bracken on the slope of the field and suddenly she shakes her hands free of water, dries them on her apron and, backing away from Groundsel, runs out of the scullery and up the back stairs.

When Eliza makes her sudden retreat down the passage from Harry St. Omer and his friend, she runs to the office and shuts herself in there, leaning against the door, her eyes closed, her hands clenched. She has no intention of crying, but tears roll out from under her lids. I'm perfectly calm, she tells herself, it's simply that I do not care to meet Harry St. Omer and—the man. Eliza has known from the first that it is the other who is "the man." *I'm not going to be one of the family laid out for him to see when any of the St. Omers choose to lift a little finger,* she thinks fiercely. *Every girl—every woman,* she corrects herself, for she is twenty-six—*every woman is free to choose whom she will, or will not meet,* but that, of course, is a lie. *There isn't any choice,* cries Eliza. It seems as if she cried it out to the housetops, but she has not made a sound; even the door has shut with a small quiet click.

When the others have gone, in the dogcarts in which Helena is permitted to ride, what will she, Eliza, have to do? The same as any other day, thinks Eliza; read, of course—"Liz always has her nose in a book," say the family—but one novel is much like another, the few she loves she knows almost by heart before she is sixteen and she devours the magazines, when they come, in a day. *What else?* thinks Eliza: perhaps write a letter for Mother to Exeter, to complain about defective candles; another to Aunt Emily, Adza's sister, to thank for a birthday present—*a sachet I don't want,* thinks Eliza, *for a birthday about which I don't want to be reminded. Walk up to the village to post the letters; a servant could post them just as well, but I must walk somewhere. Perhaps take old Mrs. Neot a milk jelly, though she must be sick of milk jellies; put a tuck in the right sleeve of my new blouse that Miss Dawnay has made uneven—that will take at least twenty minutes. Go over the pattern book with Mother. . . .* The pattern book is suddenly too much and, *I can't! I can't!* cries Eliza, but silently. If only there were something, she thinks, if the days were not like being a tame mouse or squirrel in a cage, with a wheel to tread round and round, going nowhere. If there were something to think about, to work for!

It isn't that I wanted to go with the others or that I am jealous, cries Eliza passionately, though she does not make a sound. *I know perfectly well that if Harry St. Omer, yes, magnificent Harry St. Omer, fell in love with me*—and she almost has to laugh at the idea, she with her angularities and long nose and colorless hair—*if he did I would be bored in a week. Or in an hour*, thinks Eliza, *if I had to sit through that luncheon.* She despises them, but most of all she despises herself. *Because I don't run away*, thinks Eliza. *Don't do anything. Because I let myself be this—emptiness.* Yet how can she do anything else? She shuts her eyes and tears slide under her lids and trickle down her nose, *tears like gall*, thinks Eliza.

It is then that she is conscious of an even small murmur, as undisturbed by her emotion as a bee:

> *Quaenam discors foedera reum*
> *Causa resoluit? Quis tanta Deus . . .*

It is monotonous. At first she does not know where it comes from; then she traces it to the corner behind the old screen.

She has forgotten that Jeremy Baxter would be in the office, but the old clerk is so much part of its furniture, its muddle of papers and files, that she does not fly out indignantly as she would have done if anyone else had caught her in tears. Besides, he has not caught her; the murmur is steadily oblivious of her. She goes up to the screen and looks around it at his bent back, his face that is the color of parchment and thin almost to emaciation, and at his long, wild-ended white hair.

Eliza knows that Eustace pays Jeremy Baxter twelve pounds a year, less than the wages of a housemaid, to work from eight in the morning until seven or eight at night. She sees nothing wrong with this, in fact she thinks it, like Eustace, a good bargain and now, instinctively, she frowns, for what Jeremy Baxter is engaged in doing is certainly nothing concerned with what he is paid to do—Eustace's letters, accounts, and bills:

nunc membrorum condita nube
non in totum est oblita sui
summamque tenet, singula perdens.
Igitur quisquis uera requirit
neutro est habitu . . .

Is it Latin? Eliza has to ask herself that. It sounds like Latin, but she is not sure. Her ear is quick and her wits and she can remember the boys, Little Eustace for a while, and Mcleod and Jared, groaning over their Latin prose; but this, in the quiet room, sounds like poetry. "I thought Latin was battles"—she hardly knows she has said it aloud—"Roman wars."

"This is Boethius," says Jeremy Baxter not lifting his eyes.

"Both—?"

"Boethius."

"What did he do?"

"Boethius," says Jeremy Baxter and for a moment he looks up from his book. "Boethius?" he says dreamily as if he likes to say it. "I should call him the interpreter of the ancient world and its wisdom; no one has ever superseded him. He goes beyond the Schools to the visionary poets. Yes, you will find his influence in the *Romaunt of the Rose* and in Dante."

Eliza's mouth opens a little. Then she asks: "What is the . . . romance . . . ?"

"Romaunt." He raps it out.

"Romaunt." Eliza is surprised into meekness. "*Romaunt of the Rose*? and Dante?"

"Surely even in *this* house you have heard of Dante."

"I know about Dante," says Eliza, nettled. "He was an Italian poet."

"Really?" says Jeremy Baxter bitingly.

"He was," says Eliza. "There's a painting of him by that new painter in London, new to us," says Eliza, chafing, "because we never see anything until it's *ages* old. The painter is called Dante too: Dante Gabriel Rossetti. *His* people must have cared about things to have called him that. I saw the picture—"

"In that abominable two-color printing," says Jeremy Baxter.

"Was it abominable? I thought it beautiful. Dante and—an angel?" asks Eliza. "I think it was an angel. Dante bends down to look at a girl dead under a pall of flowers—Beatrice—or was it Francesca?"

"You do not know about Dante," says Jeremy Baxter, and Eliza's face, that has been sharp and clear with interest—is she not always the clever one of the family?—falls into sullenness and, *How dare he when he isn't much more than a servant?* she thinks, but she has never heard anyone talk like this and she has to ask, "Did Dante write the *Romaunt of the Rose?*"

"Good God, no!" says Jeremy Baxter.

"Well, how could I tell?" asks Eliza resentfully. Then the resentment gives way to the complaint that corrodes her: "Why don't I know *anything?*"

"Because they sent you to school," says Jeremy Baxter. "A girls' school," he says derisively.

"I couldn't have gone to a boys' school," Eliza points out.

"Then they shouldn't have sent you at all. You didn't learn anything there. Of course not."

"I did," says Eliza.

"Not anything that is anything," says Jeremy Baxter,

"and that's a pity. I used to listen to you when you were small and thought you were more than likely."

"Did you?" Eliza's face is suffused with a blush of sheer pleasure.

"Yes. In this country, at this time, there is only one way to educate a girl," says Jeremy Baxter. "Turn her loose with books, guide her, but let her read. I told your father that but, as he cannot read himself—"

"He can." Eliza is indignant. "We all can."

"Then why don't you?"

"But I do." Eliza's tears almost start again. "I read everything I can lay my hands on. Isn't that something?" she asks.

"It depends what you lay your hands on," says Jeremy Baxter and Eliza blushes, remembering the trashy novels, as Eustace rightly calls them, that she has pored over: *Sylvia* by the author of *Natalie*—many of them are written anonymously—*Drifted and Sifted* by the author of *Until the Shadows Flee Away*; *John* by Mrs. Oliphant—but she writes respectably, thinks Eliza—then has to blush more deeply still when she remembers *On Credit* by Lady Wood, of which one reviewer said: "A blunt and revolting narrative, filled with unnecessary details of married relations between husband and wife. We sincerely hope no husband or father will allow it to contaminate his house." "I shall send for it at once," Eliza says when she reads that, but she is glad now that Jeremy Baxter's small gnat eyes, so sharp and suspicious, cannot see into her mind. "We take the *Illustrated London News*," she says defensively, "and *Punch*, and Mr. Dickens's *All the Year Round*, though that will stop now he has died. I have read his books and Mr. Thackeray's and—"

"Very nice," says Jeremy Baxter, "but that is not reading. Don't waste my time." He goes back to his book but,

"Please, Mr. Baxter," says Eliza and puts out a hand to touch another book that lies open on the table. He makes a quick movement as if he would close it and take it away but she is, after all, grown up—*and a Miss Quin*, thinks Eliza—and he restrains himself but cautions her. "That's a rare book. Touch it carefully."

"What is it?" she asks.

"Among other things, the translation of what I'm reading."

"A translation? Can that be rare?"

"It's the 1532 Chaucer," says Jeremy Baxter dryly.

"But I don't understand," says Eliza. "Chaucer is an English poet. What has he to do with Boethius?"

"He translated *The Consolations of Philosophy* from Latin into English."

"Was that the first translation?"

"The first was by King Alfred."

"King Alfred!" Eliza is almost dumb with surprise. But then could King Alfred read Latin? She has always thought of him as a far-off savage king, but she sees now that he must have been a scholar, *and all I knew of him was that about the cakes!*

"I don't understand Latin and I don't understand English. I don't even know our own history." In her despair Eliza pounds the page she has been reading.

"How do you expect to know if you don't study?" He is quite unsympathetic. "Meanwhile, don't do that to that fine book." Eliza looks at the Chaucer again, then back at the shelves with their rows of shut-away books, and Jeremy Baxter follows her look. "Yes. There are more there," he says. "For instance your father has a *Religio Medici* and Coryat's *Crudities*."

"But are they all religious, serious books?" asks Eliza.

"By no means." The old clerk gets up stiffly and comes

over to the bookcase. "Here is a novel," he says and, putting his hand in beyond the front row of books— the shelves are unexpectedly deep—brings out a book, covered in brown paper, and carries it to the table. "*Moll Flanders* by Daniel Defoe."

"But Defoe wrote *Robinson Crusoe*."

"Does that mean he couldn't write anything else?" Jeremy Baxter can be acrid and she flushes. "It's a first edition too," and he touches it tenderly. "Look at the date: 1722—but you wouldn't know." At that Eliza becomes haughty. "You needn't despise us," she says. "Father paid a high price for these books. He knew they were good."

"But not how good," says Jeremy Baxter and chuckles. "I used to be something of an authority."

"Can you read Greek as well as Latin?" she asks.

"I specialized in Early Christian and Medieval Literature," says Jeremy Baxter. "For that you need Latin and Greek—and Anglo-Saxon and old French. I was a Fellow of Trinity," says Jeremy Baxter, but humbly. Eliza surveys him disbelievingly.

"If you were—all that," she asks, "why are you here?"

"I drink," says Jeremy Baxter. "You know that very well." Then his gnat eyes soften. "No, you are young, you might not dwell on that as most of them do. Perhaps"—and he says it almost longingly—"perhaps you have a mind above scandal. You have a beautiful forehead."

No one has ever called any part of Eliza beautiful and she is strangely touched, which makes her all the more severe. "You might have made a great name for yourself," she scolds. "Been successful."

"People don't know the consolations of being unsuccessful," says Jeremy Baxter. "If I had been successful I should have had no peace or time."

"What time do you have now?" retorts Eliza. "Papa is not a philanthropist."

"I take an hour," says Jeremy Baxter and she knows he is trusting her with a secret. "I allow myself that each morning and evening. He owes me that for treasuring his books. I make covers for them and dust them, though nobody knows. Sometimes I take a book home."

"But you bring it back," says Eliza, sharp at once.

"I bring it back," says Jeremy Baxter regretfully, "though why I should when he doesn't know . . ."

The Romaunt of the Rose; *Dante*; *Boethius*; *visionary*—the words seem to have fallen into Eliza and, as if she were fertile ground, they stir. "Mr. Baxter." Her voice is hesitant, humble, eager, not at all like Eliza's. "Mr. Baxter."

"Yes," asks Jeremy Baxter absently, and though he is talking to his employer's daughter, he keeps his finger in his place. *Well, I would too, if I could read Latin and somebody interrupted me*, thinks Eliza. She notices that his cuff is frayed and dirty though his manner is regal. "Yes?" he says, but is obviously not prepared to let her waste his time. Eliza has never imagined that time could be precious and she gathers herself together to speak quickly and to the point. "Mr. Baxter, would you do what you said should be done with girls—though I am not a girl now? Would you do what you said, guide me and turn me loose with books?"

"Tracy! Tracy!" It was Aunt Bella's voice; she was upstairs, had opened the White Room door, found nobody there, and was searching, coming nearer. "Tracy, where are you? We are having a drink before luncheon. Dr. Taft and the vicar are here and Mr. Prendergast. You must come down. Tracy! Tracy!"

I can't go down like this! Tracy hastily looked at herself in the mirror that hung over the toy cupboard; her eyes were red, her face marked from crying. Why did she cry? *Because they criticized,* thought Tracy, *criticized Gran and me and everything, especially Peter—Mr. St. Omer. I suppose I'm too prickly, perhaps I was upset before, but it was suddenly too much,* she thought, her eyes flooding again. She could not face them like this—*and let them see that I mind,* thought Tracy.

"Tra-cy!"

Aunt Bella was coming nearer. Desperately Tracy looked around and her eyes fell on the brass-bound case that had belonged to Eliza. She snatched it up and went to the door. "Coming, Aunt Bella," she called down the passage. "J-just coming, but I promised to take something to show Mr. Alabaster," and she ran down the back stairs.

None

Rerum, Deus, tenax vigor, immótus in te pérmanens.
Lucis diurnae tempora successibus detérminans.

O GOD UNCHANGING, BY THY POWER ALL THINGS IN
BEING ARE MAINTAINED.
AT THY COMMAND HOUR FOLLOWS HOUR, AND TIME'S
FULL CYCLE IS ORDAINED.

HYMN FOR NONE FROM MRS. QUIN'S
Day Hours

T h e   P r e s e n t a t i o n   i n   t h e   T e m p l e ·
The scene takes place in a Gothic church. Very fine architectural details. The Virgin presents the Infant Christ to the High Priest, who wears rich vestments. Joseph and a few attendants stand by.

Full border of conventional flowers and ivy leaves, painted in
colors and heightened with gold. Grotesque of a serpent with a
woman's head (symbolical of the Fall of Man).

MINIATURE FACING THE OPENING OF NONE
IN THE HORAE BEATAE VIRGINIS MARIAE,
FROM THE HOURS OF ROBERT BONNEFOY

A *f t e r   l u n c h e o n*, when the vicar and doctor had gone, the family gathered in the drawing room for the reading of the will. "Dear Mother's will," said the third Grace, wiping her eyes.

The clock struck three as Mr. Prendergast opened his briefcase on the table that Cecily had set and cleared for him.

"This is just a formality," Bella was saying. "We have decided how we shall divide it all." Mr. Prendergast made no comment.

Tracy had been present at some of that deciding— unwillingly present, she would have said; *but I couldn't get up and go away from the table*, she thought, *I'm so much the youngest and it would have looked . . .*

It had begun quite pleasantly at dinner the night before; Cecily had cleared the table, carried out the tray, and shut the door, when a Grace said thoughtfully, "Mother will have looked after Cecily, I suppose."

"Cecily and Groundsel, possibly Minna," said Bella. "I expect there will be several bequests."

"I hope not too many," said Walter. "The estate won't fetch very much as it is."

"The farm more than the house, I should guess," said Tom.

"There isn't much in the way of securities." Walter had settled down in his chair. *He likes talking about money,* thought Tracy. In fact, all the voices had quickened.

"I could have doubled her capital if she had let me," Walter was saying.

"But she would hang on to her consols and three percents." That was Bella.

"And there are some unfortunate South American railway holdings. She never would take my advice," said Walter.

"If we had known there would be this fantastic rise in cosmetics we should never have let her sell the works," said Bella.

"Is china clay used in cosmetics?" asked Tracy. She would have liked to hear much more about the family business, but Walter swept her question out of the way.

"You must remember Canverisk was out-of-date, and we should have been up against big concerns like the Associated Clay Works," he said. "It would have meant sinking a new shaft, and making a new pumping station. There was only an old-type Cornish pump," he explained. "I don't want to criticize your father," he said to Bella and the Graces, "but it should have been modernized long ago, while as for your mother! She just used to say, 'Plenty of works manage as they are.'"

"And I gather she wanted to get money, not spend it," said Dick.

"Get it for us girls," said the third Grace softly.

"But we should have had *more,*" said Bella.

"Anyway, let's hope, there's enough cash to pay duty," said Harry. Dick had sent around a decanter of port and Harry poured himself another glass and pushed the decanter across to Tom, as if they were settling down for a comfortable talk, thought Tracy. "Pay duty and allow a clear sum from the sale."

"If she had seven hundred a year, I shall be surprised," said Tom.

"No, the old lady won't cut up very well."

"Harry, what a horrible expression!" *But that is just what they are doing,* thought Tracy, *cutting her up, and Gran is still lying upstairs!* Tracy's cheeks burned and she gripped the edge of the table so hard that the polish showed slurred marks.

"If the whole could have been left to one daughter—" Walter began again.

"Meaning Bella?" The second Grace's voice was high, but Tom, the peacemaker, quickly interposed.

"Of course Walter didn't mean that. It's only fair you girls should share."

"If I were asked, I should like the pink tea set," said the youngest Grace—*and that started them off,* thought Tracy.

"Who will have the piano?"

"Does anybody want an old square piano like that?"

"It won't bring much," said Walter.

"I could do with these dining-room chairs."

"They match the table, and none of us has room for that."

"It will spoil the price if they are not sold together."

"The silver must be divided."

"But most must be sold."

"I agree. Who wants silver dish covers, and teapots, and who would clean those silver trays?"

"It must be worth a good deal."

"No, too old-fashioned."

"There's that little Queen Anne coffee service. I always called it mine."

"But it *wasn't* yours."

It seemed almost as if there might be a quarrel and Tracy quickly asked the question that was tormenting her.

"What will happen to the animals? Moses and Bumble and—and August?" She could hardly trust herself to say his name.

"Yes, we shall have to think of that," said Bella and a silence fell.

"Moses is easy," said Bella at last. "Cecily will have him, I'm sure, or Groundsel and Minna."

"And anyone could have Trill," said the youngest Grace. "He's the sweetest canary."

"But the dogs?"

There was an uneasy pause; then, "Let's face it," said Bella, "none of us could undertake old Bumble. He's old, old and smelly. We shall have to let him be put to sleep."

Bumble, hearing his name, thumped his tail, while August's anxious face looked from one to another of them.

"And—August?" whispered Tracy.

"I couldn't have August in a flat," said a Grace. "He's far too rampageous."

"I couldn't have him either, not in London," said the second.

"He's still young. He could be sold to a good home," said Tom.

"We paid enough for him," said Walter.

"He's worth more now he's over his puppy troubles."

"Yes. Poodles get more and more fashionable every year."

"They were the most popular breed at Crufts."

August's big body trembled; he crept closer to Tracy and under the table put his head with its black peruke on her knee.

"W-wouldn't one of you have him?" asked Tracy, stammering with misery. "I mean, he would hate to be sold. Oh, I would have him at once, but I wouldn't be allowed him in Rome. Oh please."

"They are dogs, Tracy," said Bella, but kindly. "We mustn't be sentimental. If we had bigger homes . . ."

It was no good protesting. It was all being settled—irrevocably, thought Tracy. Already the talk had swept on.

"What shall we do with the paintings?" the second Grace asked. "Share them out or sell them?" and the talk broke out again.

"They should be kept together. Perhaps Bella as eldest . . ."

"Bella can't expect to have everything."

"Who said I expected it?" Bella was belligerent but, "Of course not," Tom said quickly. "If, in her will, your mother doesn't specify, we should perhaps draw lots," but most of them preferred a sale.

"I love the Winterhalter, but I wouldn't like the responsibility," said the first Grace.

"No, imagine having to insure!"

"We have no room to hang it, or any of them."

"Better sell," said Walter. "Paintings are fetching fantastic prices."

"Yes. Surely with them and the silver and china, especially the famille rose—"

"Alabaster says those are copies."

"Copies are worth quite a lot."

"Yes. We should have quite a noteworthy sale."

And Gran is upstairs, thought Tracy again. *She is here still, but they are wiping her out.* It was then that the third Grace, mistaking the stiff unhappiness on her face, asked, "What would you like, Tracy?" and the others, perhaps ashamed of those almost avid moments, had joined in. "Yes. We mustn't forget you, Tracy."

Now, as Mr. Prendergast settled his papers, Bella turned to her and said, "Tracy, you never told us what it was you particularly wanted."

"I—couldn't choose," said Tracy.

"Of course you can. You are Stace's daughter."

"And he was the only son."

"Didn't you like the Chelsea figures?" asked the third Grace. "I seem to remember . . ."

"Or anything else you like."

"Not, of course, the most valuable pictures."

"And excepting the porcelain and best silver."

"Of course. Well, Tracy, what would you like?"

"I would rather wait and see what Gran says."

It fell into the middle of them so like a rebuke that Tracy hurriedly said, floundering, "I m-mean anything she put down that I should have, w-wanted me to have, I should love, but I c-couldn't choose. I couldn't!"

"Tracy," said Bella. "You are not by any chance a little prig."

"I'm not a prig," and Tracy burst out in sudden anger, "I'm sorry but"—and it flared out—"I hated to hear you adding up and dividing Gran's things." Then she floundered again. "I m-mean, it isn't f-for us to divide—"

"Do you think," Bella's voice cut across at Tracy, "do you think I hadn't Mother's fullest confidence? Why, your Uncle Walter arranged all her affairs as Mr. Prendergast can tell you." But Mr. Prendergast stayed silent and Bella's eyes narrowed as they did when she was displeased. "You are ready, Mr. Prendergast," she said. "Then what are we waiting for?"

"For Mr. St. Omer," said Mr. Prendergast.

"For *Peter*?" and like dismayed echoes: "For Peter! Peter? St. Omer? Why St. Omer?" came from all parts of the room.

"How can this possibly concern him?" asked Walter.

"It does concern him, Colonel Scrymgeour." Mr. Prendergast spoke steadily and quietly as if, thought Tracy, he was prepared for everyone at once to turn on him.

"Concerns Peter! Whew!" said Tom.

"We might have known it," said Walter and, "You don't mean to say Mother has been so foolish—" Bella had begun when Cecily came in.

"Peter, Mr. St. Omer, is sorry, sir," she said to Mr. Prendergast. "I sent Groundsel up, as you asked, but he brought back a message. Mr. St. Omer can't come until he has finished milking."

"Well!" said Bella. *"Well!"*

"Cows have to be milked," said Mr. Prendergast mildly, but they were not appeased.

"Disgracefully rude," said Bella.

"That is certainly a very cool young man," said Tom.

"I thought cows were milked at four o'clock," objected Walter.

"Not with daylight saving," said Cecily. "He has no one to help, and he wasn't expecting to be needed," she said with emphasis and at Bella, but Bella was too indignant to be fair.

"Not only is he to be here," she cried, "here, on a very private occasion, in the middle of our *intimate* affairs, but we are to wait. To wait!" said Bella, the indignation growing. "We certainly shan't do that. Mr. Prendergast, you will please start to read the will at once."

"I'm afraid I can't." Mr. Prendergast's voice, thought Tracy, was very pleasant after Bella's rising tones. "Your mother expressly laid it down that her will was to be read in the presence of you all—of course she did not know about Miss Tracy, but I'm very glad that she is here—of you all, and Miss Cecily Morgan and Mr. Peter St. Omer."

It was a long and difficult hour. "An hour!" cried Bella and she said, "Surely, no cows can take as long as this?"

"He has six, seven with the calf." Tracy could have bitten her tongue for saying that, but Cecily's calm voice came across hers and saved her from being noticed. "He has to milk by hand," said Cecily. "There are no machines at Penbarrow."

"Good thing when that farm is brought up to date," said Walter, who was restlessly pacing the room. *Funny,* thought Tracy, *when they knew what was in the will it didn't matter when they heard it; now that they don't know, it's urgent.* She had an idea that Mr. Prendergast was enjoying himself. *I wonder if Gran has left Peter all her money,* thought Tracy with a thrill of amusement and she settled down in her straightbacked chair, the most insignificant in the room, to wait, not listening to the talk, shutting her ears to it, looking around the room.

She loved this drawing room with its length and twin windows back and front looking over the rhododendron island and across the garden to the woods, a restful quiet room that had grown into its own beauty, by accident, as it were; it might equally well have been ugly, thought Tracy; but for Lady Patrick it would have been, as neither Adza nor Mrs. Quin has any taste.

Lady Patrick removes Adza's horsehair sofa and chairs with their white crocheted "protectors" as Adza calls them; her Turkey carpet goes into the servants' sitting room, her red curtains are laid away in the attic. Lady Patrick brings over her own mother's furniture from Dublin; it is mahogany, dark and plain, while the wood of the chairs and sofas is inlaid with gilt that is still gold, though the striped damask of their upholstery has split so that the stuffing is coming through.

The wallpaper is French, faded to faint silver-green, its stripes long lost, but the carpet still has its true moss-green and its pattern of roses and white ribbons. "Early nineteenth-century French," said Mr. Alabaster. In Mrs. Quin's day there is never any money for furnishings and when the curtains rot she searches through the attic and discovers Adza's red ones; Lady Patrick is right when she says in dismay that they will never wear out; their silk twill is perfectly good and the room receives them back and fits them in, *for it is a living room,* thought Tracy—it takes and contains the new as it contains the old: the miniatures of the Three Little Graces are added to the Loftus Kennedy paintings, the "Boy with a Hoop" by Benjamin West, and the companion "Girl with a Muff," who are Lady Patrick's uncle and aunt. A daub of Eliza wearing a blue dress, the painting set in a wide golden frame, hangs next to the exquisite Engleheart; there is a framed watercolor of surprised-looking clematis, painted by Anne, a photograph of kittens given to Mrs. Quin by Tracy, and the most famous painting of all, Lady Patrick herself as a little girl with her brothers and sister, in the Winterhalter over the fireplace.

The whole room is full of things, old and new, cheap and valuable.

The cabinets along the wall are bought to hold Mcleod the Second's famille rose with its crimson and pinks, blue-greens and dark blues on white glaze, but now Mr. Alabaster had all its pieces in the library; only a few figures in ivory were left and some jade cups, set out with Stace's running cups, won at school, and with cheap eggcups and ashtrays in Staffordshire china, presents from the seaside bought for Mrs. Quin by Bella and her sisters long ago on summer holidays. There is a collection of shells and a broken silver punch ladle, its handle mended with sticking-plaster. On the chimney shelf over the farther fireplace, the French clock was alone. The Pale Blue Girl and the Little Pink Boy were with Mr. Alabaster too. Tracy missed them.

There are few books in the room, only some bound volumes of *Punch* and old albums in the bottom shelves of the bureau, a shelf of what the family call "drawing-room books" in bindings of white and gold and, on a table, a miniature set of Shakespeare in scarlet leather in its own small bookcase.

On the windowsills were saucers of seeds put to ripen in the sun; August's ball was on the writing table. *It's all very shabby*, thought Tracy, not only the split damask, and marked mahogany, but the paint was yellow and cracked, while the window catches were rusty and one grate was broken. Tracy saw this with a pang and, damping her handkerchief with a little spit, tried to rub away a mark on the table near her. "Must you fidget?" asked the irritated Bella and Tracy guiltily put the handkerchief away and sank back into her private remembering.

There is a square piano in mahogany with a wide panel of pleated brown silk. On each side of the keyboard a bracket pulls out to hold a candlestick. As a child Tracy thinks its inscription the height of romance: "J. Broadwood. Maker to Her Majesty and the Princesses. Poulteney Street, Golden Square, London."

The room smelled of lilies. Someone, *perhaps a neighbor who grew them*, thought Tracy, had brought an armful of arums too late for the funeral and Cecily had put them in a jar in the empty fireplace. They made the afternoon air heavy, drowsy, as did the sound of a bee going up and down the windowpane, but no one was sleepy. They were all waiting, alert—*and their voices still hostile*, thought Tracy.

Thoughtfully she got up and let the bee out. "I asked you not to fidget," said Bella sharply and broke off. Steps had sounded in the hall.

It was a man's step, firm and decided—*what the house needs*, thought Tracy—*and if a man had been here, all those last years with Gran*, she thought suddenly, *it wouldn't have grown so shabby. The paint would not have been allowed to crack and yellow, the catches to rust, the grate not to be mended. I wish* . . . thought Tracy, but it was no use wishing. Peter—*Mr. St. Omer*, Tracy corrected herself—was in the doorway; in a minute Mr. Prendergast would start to read the will.

"I'm sorry I kept you," said Peter. "I had to finish up there, and, as I guessed you would be in the drawing room, I had to change."

"What I should have done myself," said Mr. Prendergast but no one else spoke and Peter's face took on its "flint look," as Cecily called it. "May I sit here?" he asked curtly and sat down in an empty chair by Mr. Prendergast's table and next to Tracy. She gave him a fleeting smile; it was fleet only because she was shy before all the relations, but his look grew more flintlike still and Tracy, absurdly, felt rebuffed. *Oh well!* she thought, *I'm only a spectator, I came to see Gran, no one else. I can go back to Rome tomorrow.*

" 'THIS IS THE LAST WILL AND TESTAMENT OF DEBORAH QUIN of China Court, St. Probus in the County of Cornwall,' " and Mr. Prendergast began to read, " 'I HEREBY REVOKE all former Wills and testamentary dispositions made by me and declare this to be my last Will and Testament.' "

The exact legal language soothed Tracy and filled the room.

" 'I give to Cecily Morgan the sum of £500, and an annuity of £150 and also my personal clothing in appreciation of the many years of devoted service she has given to me.' "

Cecily did not cry, but her dark eyes grew very bright as she sat looking far over their heads.

" 'I give to Maurice Edward Groundsel the sum of £200 and my late husband's gold watch free of duty.' "

One or two small gifts followed and then, "There are certain sums of money invested in securities," said Mr. Prendergast "and of these Mrs. Quin says:

"I have kept these securities unchanged in spite of Walter's advice [Walter gave an indignant snort] in the hope that these securities will realize a sufficient sum to pay all death duties and my debts and testamentary expenses leaving my estate free and unencumbered for the benefit of those who become entitled under this my Will."

Then Mr. Prendergast cleared his throat.

"Having made suitable provision for my daughters at
the time of the sale of Canverisk China Clay Co. and my
son Eustace John having predeceased me I GIVE DEVISE
AND BEQUEATH my freehold property known as "China
Court" together with all messuages, tenements, heredi-
taments, and appurtenances thereto belonging (except
Penbarrow Farm) but including all the contents and effects thereunto belonging and, subject to the payment
of my debts funeral and testamentary expenses, all securities investments stocks and shares belonging to me at
the time of my death, to my granddaughter Stacia Deborah Quin absolutely."

There was a moment of stunned silence before the
voices broke out.

"To Tracy?"

"Tracy?"

"The whole estate!"

"Everything!"

The room had seemed to lift and sway away from
Tracy; now the voices beat around her head as she
pressed herself down on her chair, trying to hold on to
something real. It can't be true, it can't, thought Tracy,
dizzily.

"The whole estate!"

"Not the whole estate." It was Walter's voice and Tracy
could tell at once that her Uncle Walter was angry. "Not
the whole." Tracy rather welcomed that anger. It made
it begin to be true, she thought, though still dizzily.

"Penbarrow is excepted," said Walter. "Let us hear
what your mother"—and he said the words as if he
wished they could have reached Mrs. Quin and hurt

her—"let us hear what *your mother* has chosen to do with Penbarrow. Please go on, Mr. Prendergast."

" 'And I GIVE DEVISE AND BEQUEATH,' " read Mr. Prendergast, his voice unshaken, " 'my freehold farm known as Penbarrow together with all messuages, tenements and appurtenances, contents and effects thereunto belonging more particularly delineated and described in the County Map No. 156 to The Honourable Peter Alex—' "

"I knew it!" cried Bella.

"Scallywag!"

"It's a scandal!"

" 'Peter Alexander Hugh Barry St. Omer,' " said Mr. Prendergast, raising his voice, " 'at present tenant thereof, together with all the contents thereof including any live and dead farming stock in which I have any share.' "

"So she *did* pay for those cows!"

"She *was* helping."

"I always said he had bewitched her."

"He got round her—"

"Please! Ladies!" called Mr. Prendergast. "*Please.* I must continue," but Walter had risen to his feet.

"We shall contest," said Walter.

"On what grounds, Colonel?" asked Mr. Prendergast.

"What grounds? Undue influence, of course," said Walter, glaring at Peter.

Peter looked levelly at Walter and did not speak, but Tracy could see the pulse below the red hair visibly beating and the hand on his knee was held so tightly that the knuckles were white.

"I think you would find it difficult to prove," said Mr. Prendergast quietly. "I am satisfied that Mr. St. Omer had not the slightest inkling or expectation of any sort of a bequest, which can be borne out by Miss Morgan and others who knew both him and Mrs. Quin."

"He hadn't the slightest idea," said Cecily. "Nobody had."

"Not you?" asked Bella disbelievingly.

"Mrs. Quin wasn't one for talking, Bella, and I'm not one for asking," said Cecily.

"She was subject to likes and dislikes," said Walter.

"We all are," said Mr. Prendergast.

"Hers were extraordinarily violent ones," said Walter. "I think we could reasonably contest that she was not of sound mind."

"She anticipated you would say that, Colonel Scrymgeour, and took the precaution of asking Dr. Taft, who had been her doctor for very many years, to be one of the witnesses and certify she was sane."

"And did he?"

"He wrote, 'Very much in her right mind,' " said Mr. Pendergast dryly. "No, I do not think there are grounds for contestation, but perhaps you had better let me finish reading."

"*Is* there anymore?" asked Bella dramatically.

"Yes," said Mr. Prendergast. "For these bequests there is a condition. . . ."

"A condition?" Their faces altered at once, from anger—*to a gleam of hope*, thought Tracy. Then did they dislike her so much? *And Peter—Mr. St. Omer?* thought Tracy. The room still seemed to shimmer and sway in front of her, but now she could see Cecily's eyes, beaming at her, with a pleased excited look lighting up her whole face; she could feel August's head pressed beside her, she had not known it but she was kneading his curls with her fingers, and she was very conscious of Peter sitting beside her. Peter was stiff and white but, in Tracy, it felt as if a bell had begun to swing, a bell of joy, such joy as she had never felt before.

"There is a condition," said Bella. "Mother wasn't quite mad," and, "Any condition, any," swung the bell inside Tracy.

"I must tell you," said Mr. Prendergast, "as I warned Mrs. Quin I should have to tell you—as a lawyer I would not insert this condition in the Will proper, because the proviso is bad in law." A tinge of humor had come into his voice as he remembered telling Mrs. Quin this.

"Bad law or good law, I want it in," says Mrs. Quin.

"It is contrary to public policy," Mr. Prendergast explains.

"This isn't public, it's private," says Mrs. Quin. "Put it in."

"At last I persuaded her," said Mr. Prendergast now, "to let me state this proviso in the form of a letter, but I must say frankly that you, Mr. St. Omer, and you, Miss Tracy, would, in my view, be able in law to take these gifts free from this condition."

"I would rather take mine as Mrs. Quin wished," said Peter, through set lips, "or not at all."

"And I," said Tracy.

"You had better hear the condition first," said Bella.

"Then if you will allow me," and Mr. Prendergast read out: " 'To my solicitor and all who should have, or think they should have' "—he could not forgo a glance at Bella and Walter—" 'an interest in the disposal of my property: I especially desire that this letter should be read to all parties who may be concerned, immediately after the reading of my last Will and Testament. The bequests of the freehold property of China Court with all its messuages, tenements . . .' " carefully Mr. Prendergast went through them again—" 'to Stacia Deborah Quin,

and of my freehold farm known as Penbarrow with all
. . .' " and the list was read—" 'to the Honourable Peter
Alexander Hugh Barry St. Omer, are on condition that
the said Stacia Quin and Peter St. Omer shall meet as
soon as conveniently can be arranged after my death,
and shall marry each other within six months of such
meeting—' "

"Marry!" Neither Peter nor Tracy knew from which
one of them the word escaped, but it sounded like a
gasp.

" 'Marry, and further, that they shall make China
Court their home. I have imposed this condition because
it is my belief that it will make for the happiness and
mutual satisfaction of them both, and because it is my
earnest wish.' This letter," said Prendergast, looking up
into their shocked faces, "is signed by Mrs. Quin and
witnessed by the same parties who witnessed the will
itself."

If Mr. Prendergast had exploded a bomb in the drawing room, Tracy could hardly have been more surprised.
The bell stopped instantly, and a strange cold tingling
ran over her. *Don't let me blush*, prayed Tracy silently.
Once more the room seemed to sway and Peter beside
her, though she tried not to look at him, seemed to come
alarmingly close, then to swing far away. *I am blushing*,
thought Tracy agonized, and pressed herself down even
more tightly in her chair, keeping her eyes fixed on the
carpet while she waited for the storm of protest to break
around their ears.

It did not come; instead, "Poor old lady!" said Tom
at last.

"Yes, poor dear Mother. What would she have
thought of next?"

"It was pathetic the way she loved this house."

"Fantastic."

"She must have been more senile than we thought."

"Poor Mother."

"Poor old lady!"

Tracy lifted her eyes. Amusement, pity, tolerance were on all their faces, and Walter had sat down.

" 'As I do not want,' " Mr. Prendergast went on reading, " 'to risk the house being shut up and empty, pending their decision, and also feel it unfair to keep the family in a state of suspense—and because I believe in such matters swift decisions are best—the said Peter St. Omer and Stacia Quin must make up their minds and decide within a week of their meeting.' She then adds that if you decide not to fulfil the condition," said Mr. Prendergast to Tracy and Peter, "then the whole estate is to be sold, and of the proceeds four hundred pounds go to Mr. St. Omer, and the residue is to be divided: one half to you, Miss Tracy, and of the other half, a quarter to each of your aunts."

"Then except that most of us are poorer we are as we were before," said Bella briskly.

"Why are we?"

Tracy hardly knew she had spoken, but even while she felt the dreaded blush coming up her neck to her face, the bell of joy began to swing again, and steadily, as if it were not at all upset. "Wh-why are we?" asked Tracy.

"Don't be silly, Tracy," but Tracy made herself be calm.

"Why *silly*?"

"Naturally, my dear child, you can't accept."

"I m-might." It sounded bold as Tracy said it, but her stammer betrayed her and her heart had begun to beat so painfully that she almost choked; her cheeks were burning while her hands and knees felt damply cold. "I might accept."

Now she had let loose a real clamor. "Tracy, don't be absurd."

"One doesn't marry like that."

"This is the twentieth century."

"An old lady's whim."

"A whim! It's quite evident that Mother *was* out of her mind."

"It's like a fairy tale," said the third Grace.

"A fairy tale! Sheer novelette!"

"And about as probable."

"You will have the money, Tracy."

"Most of the money."

"But I don't want the money," said Tracy.

The amusement and tolerance left their faces. "Tracy, you are not *serious?*" cried Bella, and, "You couldn't possibly consider . . ." said a Grace.

"W-why n-not?" stammered Tracy. "Gran was the dearest wisest—" She could not go on. Though she had begun loudly, her voice tailed away, she was beginning to feel as if she were being driven back to the wall, and then there was a wall behind her. Peter had laid his arm on the back of her chair, not touching her, but near enough for her to feel it there, "And as you heard," said Peter, "it was Mrs. Quin's earnest wish."

"Then she was quite mad."

"She was not. She was wise and sane." Peter's voice was trembling too, *but not because he's afraid*, thought Tracy, *because he's thinking of Gran*. "We may not be able to accept," said Peter, "but we shall certainly consider—"

"*You* will naturally. You want Penbarrow."

"I want Penbarrow but I have to consider the price."

"Well really!" said a Grace and Walter's face seemed to swell with indignation but Peter went straight on. "Tracy—may I say Tracy?—Tracy, I'm sure, wants the house and it would be fitting for her to have it—"

"Fitting!" said Walter.

"Yes, fitting." There was an edge in Peter's voice. *He would fight for me*, thought Tracy with a thrill of pride. "Tracy loves it, as none of you do," said Peter, "and she's a Quin, but she has to think of the price too. Neither of us would like to take anything except as Mrs. Quin wished and the price is higher for Tracy than for me, I know that very well." For a moment he looked down at Tracy, and, "I'm not pretty," said Peter and he gave her the smile she had seen in that first moment yesterday, so warm and approving that her heart seemed to quiet. "I think, if you don't mind," he said standing up and facing them all again, "we should like to go away separately and be by ourselves to think it over. Shouldn't we, Tracy?"

She nodded and he drew her to her feet.

"Very sensible," said Mr. Prendergast and he stood up too and, opening his wallet, gave Tracy a card. "Here are my home and office telephone numbers. I can be with you in an hour if you want me."

"But Walter, she mustn't. She mustn't be alone with Peter," cried Bella. "Think how he got round Mother."

"I didn't get round Mrs. Quin," said Peter. "She got round me, thank God."

"Tracy, don't be silly."

"He's a professional charmer."

"Tracy dear, listen to me—"

"Walter, stop her."

"Tracy, how old are you?" asked Peter.

"Almost twenty-two." Tracy did not know how she found the courage to step forward and stand with what seemed like calm and dignity, thought Cecily, in front of them all. "I am t-twenty-one, even though I don't s-seem like it," said Tracy. "That's of age and P-Peter is right. I should like to be by myself for a while. I have to think."

"You had better think," said Walter. "I'm your uncle, Tracy, and I have something to say. This is all very dazzling for you, but I think you need some advice."

"I'm not sure I'm open to advice, Uncle Walter."

"That is simply being obstinate."

"It's only by being obstinate that anything is got, or done." Tracy might have said that but she refrained. "Very well, go on," she said to Walter.

Walter stood up—to pronounce, thought Tracy, as Mrs. Quin so often thinks. "Peter speaks as if you could keep the house," said Walter, "but you couldn't, Tracy. As Aunt Bella told you, I know its affairs. You would be getting a white elephant, my dear. It's in a bad state of repair. The roof is leaking and there's dry rot. Everything is old-fashioned and neglected. There's no electric light except that obsolete old engine, the plumbing needs redoing, the garden is overgrown. It takes a great deal of upkeep and where is the money for that? Your grandmother was at her wits' end, I don't mind telling you that."

"Gran was old and frail," said Tracy with a catch in her voice. "We are young."

"True, but very inexperienced. Peter hasn't made Penbarrow pay."

"It will pay next year," said Peter.

"Next year is always an excuse for this."

"That isn't fair," said Peter. "I had to pull it round and without capital."

"There's no capital now," said Walter. "Don't make a mistake about that. There will be death duties to swallow up any securities Mrs. Quin had left. As you heard, even she anticipated that," and he boomed on. "I had fortunately persuaded Mrs. Quin to call in Alabaster, Truscott and Grice, to make a valuation and see what we could sell. It was fortunate because it helps us to assess now where we all are. A few things are quite valuable, but it's obvious that nothing short of a complete sale would help, and you can't have that, my dear; to fulfill the conditions of that ridiculous will, you have to live in the house. No, Tracy, it needs too much spent on it to be of any use."

It was quiet in the drawing room when Walter stopped. Peter did not speak, nor anyone else. Mr. Prendergast, who had sat down again, scratched with his pen as he drew circles on an envelope. Cecily fanned herself with her handkerchief and her stays creaked. Outside in the garden, a guinea fowl screamed. Tracy looked around the green lily-smelling room; at the familiar chairs and tables: at the pictures, the "Boy with the Hoop," the "Girl with the Muff," the sashed children in the Winterhalter; the china cabinets, the ivory and jade, the chimney shelf where her shepherd and shepherdess should stand—and *mine*, insisted Tracy, *mine*. She lifted her head to face Uncle Walter, but her bell had stopped swinging; it hung lifelessly inside her.

"Not a possible proposition, I'm afraid," said Walter. "A dear house, but it has had its day."

The bell seemed to give a vibration and deep in Tracy stirred a memory, something that her grandmother had told her long ago; a memory dredged up, thought

Tracy, from deep down, away back in her mind to save her: a story about Uncle Walter, Walter and Bella. "It has had its day," said Walter and sighed and, "Uncle Walter," said Tracy, "I think you should remember the apricot tree."

Vespers

Jam sol recédit igneus . . .
THE SETTING SUN NOW TURNS OUR GAZE TO THEE.

HYMN FOR VESPERS OF SATURDAY FROM
MRS. QUIN'S *Day Hours*

T h e   F l i g h t   i n t o   E g y p t · The Virgin is seated on an ass and holds the Child to her bosom. He is asleep. Joseph walks behind supporting his steps with a long staff. Bleak, rocky landscape. In the distance a lion searching for prey and two robbers beating their victim with cudgels.

Full border of conventional flowers, fruit, and ivy leaves painted in colors and heightened with gold. Figure of a cat playing with a mouse (satire on the robbers and their victim).

MINIATURE FACING THE OPENING OF VESPERS
IN THE HORAE BEATAE VIRGINIS MARIAE,
FROM THE HOURS OF ROBERT BONNEFOY

I *t w a s t h e* next afternoon and the hands of the grandfather clock in the hall were slowly moving toward teatime "of this *interminable* day," groaned Bella. "Here we are," she said, angrily pacing the drawing room, "all of us, hanging about waiting for a chit of a girl."

"We may have to wait a week," the second Grace reminded her gloomily. "We have only had twenty-four hours."

They had gathered because the news had spread that, an hour ago, a boy had brought a letter for Tracy from Peter. "A letter and a bunch of clover," the youngest Grace had reported, since when speculation had filled the house.

"I didn't think Mother would have done this to us," said the eldest Grace.

"If you ask me, she delighted in being contrary," said the second.

"I think Tracy will see reason," said Walter. "I have talked to her."

"As a matter of fact, so have I," said Harry.

"It's a pity you did that, Harry," said Walter put out. "Too many cooks, you know."

"Well, I had a word with her myself," said Tom.

"I don't think it matters who talks to her," said Bella. "I don't believe she listens."

"She certainly isn't very responsive," said the second Grace. "When Dick and I—"

"Who would have believed that such a timid manner could hide such a stone wall!"

"It isn't that she's rude—" began the youngest Grace.

"The reverse," said Bella in an access of irritation. "She's *bafflingly* polite."

"The child ought to play poker," said Dick.

"It isn't funny, Dick."

"I asked her what her mother would think," said a Grace, "and all she said was '*Mother* can't talk to me about marrying!'"

"Nor Barbara can."

"All the same, she shouldn't talk of her mother like that."

"Tracy didn't say it until we pressed her." The youngest Grace was fair.

"I knew you would take her part," said Bella. "You are far too soft."

"But I like her," said the youngest Grace.

"We all like her," said Bella angrily. "Isn't she in the family?"

"Of course," said the first Grace, "I told her we were only thinking of her good."

"Naturally. One just couldn't let her be saddled . . ."

"At her age."

"Yes, she's so young."

"She has no idea what she would be letting herself in for."

"A house can persecute you."

"She wouldn't have a moment to call her own the rest of her life."

"Did you tell her that?"

"Yes, and she said, 'A moment to do what?' "

"Why, all sorts of things," cried Bella now, "take an interest; taste life; travel," but it seemed Tracy had not responded to this. "She said she had done all that," said the second Grace.

"Well, she has traveled a great deal," began the youngest, but Bella cut across her again and, having the softest voice of them all, the youngest Grace had to yield.

"I tried to advise her," said Bella. "I pointed out that when *we* were young we broke away from this tyranny of domesticity," said Bella, her color high. "She said why? and I told her we wanted to live for bigger things: movements, ideas, causes."

"What did she say to that?"

"She said, 'That's just it. You had causes. You didn't live.' The child is obsessed with living, *daily* living, that's all you can call it," said Bella, more than ever incensed.

"She has no idea what she would be letting herself in for," said a Grace again.

"And, like all young people, she won't be told."

"C-could I speak, p-please Aunt Bella."

Tracy, with her shadow August, was standing in the middle of them. As if all these criticisms had been buffets, her skin showed hectic patches; *nerve patches,* thought the youngest Grace. Tracy was so tense that it looked as if any moment her stillness might crack, and she stammered more badly than ever as she said "I h-have had a l-l-letter from Peter. I should l-like to read it to you, p-please, Aunt B-Bella."

"You could have heard a pin drop," Cecily told Mrs.

Abel afterward, for Tracy had gone into the kitchen first and called Cecily in. "You too, C-Cecily. Everyone."

"And not one of them said a word," said Cecily. "Oh, no! I could have burst out laughing they were all so anxious."

" 'Dear Tracy,' " read Tracy and as she read her stammering calmed. " 'I think you are probably in your room now, as I am in mine, as I have been all day when I was not working about the farm, while perhaps you were out too in the garden, but both of us thinking. I hope they have left you alone to have your own thoughts.' "

"I'm sorry," said Tracy, breaking off, "but I am going to read it all," and she went on.

" 'I know the round and round, in which our thoughts must go: if you say "no," you make me lose Penbarrow: if I say "no," you lose China Court and we both of us love these places, so I have been trying to think differently and, being older, for both of us.

" 'It was a beautiful idea of your grandmother's,' " read Tracy, " 'full of imagination and generosity, as she always was, but she did not choose one of her people well, because, you see, we don't start evenly: you are fresh and clean while I should be bringing you someone stained and once a bit disgraceful. (I hate to agree with your Aunt Bella and her Walter but I have to over this.) It would be easy for me: Penbarrow is my world and I could never hope to marry such a girl as you—I shall never forget you that first morning . . .' "

"Ah, so he *had* met you," began Bella, but Tracy gave her a glance so unexpectedly severe that she stopped.

" '. . . that first morning,' " read Tracy, " 'but if you don't have China Court there is still the whole world waiting for you, with every chance, and I think that solves it; and that is why, dear, I am going to refuse.

" 'In an hour I shall have to wash and change and come up the valley path because I have telephoned Mr. Prendergast and asked him to come—no need to keep everyone on tenterhooks—but I wanted you to know this first. When he comes, I hope you and I shall take hands—to show them we are friends—and firmly and gently say "no." Then we shall go our separate ways. May yours be as splendid as possible—and don't worry about mine. Peter.

" 'The clover is from Clover. Come and see her calf all the same.' "

There was silence until Cecily took out her large white handkerchief and blew her nose.

"Well! Well! Well!" said Bella. "Who would have thought it?"

"I wouldn't," said Walter, as if there were a catch somewhere.

"I could almost take off my hat to the boy," said Tom reluctantly.

"It's a sweet, sweet letter," said the youngest Grace; it was the first breach in the wall of opposition, but Tracy turned on her.

"It isn't sweet. It's silly," said Tracy.

They all stared at her.

"But Tracy, what he says about not starting evenly— so brave and sensible."

"It's morbid," flashed Tracy. Her eyes were brilliant with temper. They had never seen her look as pretty. "Gran believed in him. What more does he want? Didn't he think she would take all that into account? And how does he know I'm fresh and clean?" asked Tracy, furious. "I might have led a terrible life for all he knows. Of course we shan't refuse. We shall accept."

"But Tracy, if he doesn't want you, you can hardly—" began Bella.

"He does want me," said Tracy roundly. "He came up twice today and stood by the wall. I saw him. I hoped and hoped he would come to me. Well, he will have to now. I'm going down to meet him, with Uncle Walter."

"With *me?*" asked Walter.

"I can't ask him to marry me," said Tracy. "You heard Aunt Bella. I can't ask him and he must be asked before Mr. Prendergast gets here. Peter has told him to come and he will be here any minute. You can see Peter won't ask me. Oh, I need somebody," said Tracy, almost wringing her hands.

"A go-between," said the second Grace but she did not say it mockingly. "A go-between. Well, Walter, will you?"

"Certainly not," said Walter.

"Why ask Uncle Walter when you know he doesn't approve?"

"Approve!" said Walter and snorted.

"I don't ask you to approve," said Tracy, "but you are the eldest and so I ask you to do it."

"In the teeth of your whole family's opposition?"

"Yes," said Tracy and she pleaded, "You are the head of the family, Uncle Walter. You s-said so."

"As a matter of fact, he isn't." The usually silent Dick suddenly spoke, making the second breach. "He isn't."

"Then who is?"

"You," said Dick, and before the others could break in, he went on, "If Mrs. Quin had been the queen, her son, your father, Stace, would have succeeded her but, as he died before she did and left a daughter, that daughter would be queen."

"Isn't that rather far-fetched?" asked the second Grace, his wife.

"Legitimate succession," said Dick blandly.

"Over her uncles and aunts?" asked Tracy looking at the ring of her powerful elders.

"Over her uncles and aunts."

"Then what should they do if she asks something of them?"

"They would doubtless advise her," said Dick dryly.

"Yes, but if she still chose her own way, they should do as she says?"

"She could command them—I think," said Dick and he added, "If Walter won't do this, I will."

They all, including Dick, knew that Walter particularly disliked this brother-in-law, so much more detached than the rest of them. "He hasn't had time to be attached," says Bella, which is true; he is the second Grace's third husband—"Not even a gentleman," says Bella when the family first meets him. "Bounder. Dresses like a bookie," says Walter and, "I wasn't going to have Mr. Dick poking his nose in," Walter said to Bella afterward.

From the window, they waited for Walter and Tracy, with the dogs, to come out from the hidden path behind the yews and go down past the sweet peas, until they disappeared again into the kitchen garden, then came back into view as they walked across the field, Walter's shape, large and ambling, and Tracy, looking slim and small, her hair touched to green-gold by the light. In the drawing room they heard August's excited welcoming bark. "Peter must be coming," said Bella. Then they saw

Tracy stationing herself under a tree, while Walter went up to the wall.

"Tom proposed to me," said the youngest Grace softly, "on the front stairs."

"Harry asked me in the garden."

"Walter asked me at breakfast," said Bella. "We were both down early. I remember the smell of sausages."

The second Grace who, like Barbara, had had "a Tom, a Harry, and now a Dick," as Mrs. Quin says, did not speak.

"Miss Quin. Mary," says the doctor's young assistant. "I have come to regard you . . ." and Mary, the long-forgotten eldest daughter of the Brood, says, very simply, "Yes."

"Miss Damaris, you know that I am going to marry you."

"Oh no!" cries Damaris, her eyes like a startled hare's. "Please no!" but "Yes," says Mr. King Lee.

There is, in the house, an exquisite valentine—exquisite because it is expensive, lace on white satin with rosebuds, from Bond Street—sent by Harry St. Omer to Anne in a moment of passing fancy. "Very passing," says Anne, but it causes Eustace and Adza to look at one another.

"You are probably the only girl he ever met who didn't angle for him," says Eliza astutely, and Eustace that night says to Adza, "Mother, I believe we should ask the St. Omers to dinner."

Borowis proposes to Isabel, exactly as planned, at her—and John Henry's—joint birthday dance, the only dance ever given at China Court. John Henry never asks Ripsie to marry him; he announces their engagement, "because it was the only thing to do," while Ripsie, white-lipped, does not stop him.

Groundsel asks Minna in the dell.

In Minna's second winter at China Court, it snows and the snow lies.

When she steps out of bed in the morning, a quick exhilaration that she has not felt here before is in her limbs. She dresses joyfully, her feet and fingers fly and she is halfway through her work before the other maids come down. Her steps are light and crisp and every now and then she steps outside in her felt slippers, to powder the snow in her fingers.

There is sun and frost in the trees with a Switzerland sky, and, round the house, a continual attendance of birds. The snow hushes all the outside domestic noises: the turning of barrow wheels, the sweepings, and sluicings, the digging and the comings and goings between the house and the stables.

Groundsel comes to sweep the snow off the back steps and Minna smiles at him, her face awake with a sparkling firmness; he stands up straight and looks at her with a grave particular attention. "More like your home?" he asks.

"Please? Yes. Yes." Minna smiles and nods. "It is fine. Yes."

He watches her, then says, in his slow Cornish voice, "Be 'ee goin' down the wood in the afternoon, Minna? Be thick down in the woods."

There is a sudden pause in Minna, then a deep inward trembling as if she has to step across a dangerous gulf. The moment hangs in space, then "Yes. Yes," she says, "I shall go. . . . Yes."

Groundsel waits in the dell and toward four o'clock, when the sun is low and red behind the wood, he sees her coming down the field; the curiously patterned foreign apron she wears under her short coat shows, as she moves toward him, a patch of yellow on it fluttering like a star between her legs. Her hair shines and her face is touched by the sun as if she wears a halo.

"Minna," he calls, "Minna."

Minna runs down the field and through the wicket gate to him and he puts his arms around her and kisses her. He is warm and so is she. The crisp cold air comes up about them; their breaths are warm together on the air. She turns in the circle of his arms and puts her own round his neck and kisses him too. Their lips are warm, hot against one another in the cold.

"I love 'ee, Minna. Do 'ee love me?"

"I love. *Ach* yes! *Ich liebe.*"

"Will 'ee marry me, Minna?"

"Miss Quin. Mary. I have come to regard you . . ."

"Bella, before you begin your coffee I . . ."

"And I have to tell you all, too, that I am engaged to Miss Russell."

"Miss Russell? Who is Miss Russell?" The whispers run through the guests.

"That little dark-haired girl with the strange eyes."

"Who is she? Doesn't anybody know?"

"Who is Miss Russell?"

On the afternoon of one of China Court's luncheon parties Lady Patrick asks that question herself. The parlormaid—Paget, successor to Pringle—has come into the drawing room with a card on a salver. "I had a card *printed*," says Ripsie as if it were a talisman and, "I showed the young pers—lady into the morning room, milady, as I wasn't quite sure," says Paget.

"A young lady? Alone?"

"Yes, milady." Paget's voice is so carefully expressionless that it expresses—*everything*, thinks John Henry. Lady Patrick looks at the card. "Miss Deborah Russell," she reads and asks, "Boys, do I know anyone called Deborah Russell?"

There are several people in the room, "leftovers," as John Henry calls them, from the luncheon party. In the brief budding-out that is the habit of county families when sons and daughters reach a marriageable age, Lady Patrick this summer has been systematically entertaining. It is the year 1899, so that it is John Henry who comes of age this season, "but I don't count," says John Henry. He says it without resentment for it seems completely natural to him. Borowis's coming of age was unmarked because he was in India, on special absence from his regiment to go with a second cousin, General Francis Brandan, to the frontier, "and had my first taste of blood," says Borowis, but he is on long leave now before he goes to Egypt with Isabel's father. "Boro specializes in special absences," says John Henry. Everything for Borowis is coming to fruition, fruition because the seeds were sown long ago and the plant has been carefully watched and grown. Isabel's father, now General Loftus Kennedy, is on a mission, "and if Boro . . ." says Lady Patrick. She need say no more; Borowis knows quite well it all depends on him and what he does now. He means to do it, but at times he can be rebellious. "To get anywhere you must do some time on the staff. The Clonferts have always been brilliant soldiers."

"I'm not a Clonfert, I'm a Quin, and is being old Charles's aide brilliant?"

"It's a step."

"Handing cups of tea when I ought to be subduing the natives," Borowis banters but John Henry can tell he is serious.

"It isn't a question of cups of tea," says Lady Patrick. "It's your career."

"There happens to be a war on," says Borowis, "and I happen to belong to a regiment. It's going out and I shall go with it, I warn you."

"But Boro—"

"Mother, you are talking about what you cannot understand."

Lady Patrick looks at his face and is diplomatically silent.

John Henry is not on leave or even on holiday. From school he is delivered over to Mr. Fitzgibbon to put into the works and the quarry. With the pattern of Eustace, long ago, and the warning of Jared, old Mr. Fitzgibbon works him hard. The quarry, it is decided, shall be sold—Jared leaves a load of debts behind him and Lady Patrick's money is all spent—but fortunately the works are growing and John Henry has plenty to do learning all the processes of winning and treating china clay: the washing, the removal of waste, "sand, stone, and stent," says John Henry; the pumping of the slurry, wet clay, to the surface; refining it again and drying it. Mr. Fitzgibbon makes him go in with the men and then keeps him long after they have gone home, working over figures and ledgers, so that it is only once in a while, "A while! A blue moon!" says John Henry, that he gets an hour or two off. He is tired and now has eaten too much—he is greedy—and is drowsing in an armchair. Borowis, bored, is on the far windowsill catching flies while Isabel is whispering by the piano with her pretty friend Margaret. "Pretty! Hair like straw and eyes like china beads," says John Henry derisively. "Intended for you," drawls Borowis. Isabel's mother is on the sofa talking to Lady St. Omer, who has driven over from Tremellen. The other guests have gone, and Lady Patrick is making plans for the afternoon as Paget brings in the card.

"Deborah Russell?" asks John Henry lazily. "No. I have no idea who she is."

"Probably one of Isabel's innumerable cousins," says Borowis who has had a sickener of eligible girls.

"My cousins don't call on people alone," says Isabel smartly.

"But who can she be?" asks Lady Patrick.

"Have her in and you will see," says Borowis. He is tired of luncheon parties, all parties, tired of Isabel too; he feels she has been rammed down his throat. She has not; Lady Patrick has been most skillful, but Borowis knows so well what is expected of him that the least mention of Isabel makes him fume. A new girl, he thinks, will at least be more entertaining than catching flies and, "Have her in," he suggests.

"Very well, Paget," says Lady Patrick.

"This way, miss."

"I knaw the way," says a clear young voice with a trace of a Cornish accent, but Paget's voice says with icy correctness, "*If* you please, miss," and they can hear the rustle of her starched skirts on the flags of the hall. "Miss Russell," announces Paget as she might have announced "Miss Upstart," and holds open the door.

The girl on the threshold flinches; clearly she did not expect a room full of people, and formidable people, for they are no more welcoming than Paget. "Miss Russell." Small and slight, she is as different from the other girls as cheese from chalk and John Henry sits up and rubs the sleep out of his eyes. She is a small girl, so little and slightly built that she makes the others look clumsy; her hair is dark and curls in rings below her hat and above the nape of her neck—"It would never grow evenly after the village and I had ringworm," says Mrs. Quin— a neck that, as she bends her head, nervously fidgeting with her card case, looks to John Henry as small and white and vulnerable as the necks of the little girls at prayers long ago seem to Eustace; small and vulnerable but, "when she wanted anything, she would always go straight in and burn herself," says John Henry.

Now, though she has flinched, she walks past Paget into the room and straight up to Lady Patrick, but the hand holding the card case clutches it so tightly that her glove splits.

"Miss Russell? I'm afraid I don't—" says Lady Patrick, but in her nervousness, the girl interrupts. "Excuse my coming like this, but I felt I had to, as soon as I was back and heard you were all here. . . ." It trails off. She has seen, too late, that she should not have interrupted; all the conventional phrases die and, "I wanted to see the boys so badly," she says honestly, "that I had to come."

"The boys!" Coming from a grown-up girl it sounds— *like a housemaid,* thinks John Henry wryly and, as she lifts her eyes to smile at Lady Patrick, he is not surprised there is no answering smile but, "Don't you remember me?" asks the girl.

It is John Henry who cries, "By God! It's Ripsie!"

There is no mistaking the warmth and welcome in that. "Boro! It's Ripsie!" and John Henry jumps up and takes Ripsie's hands, shaking them up and down. "How perfectly splendid!" says John Henry beaming.

A little color comes into the small face that has been tense and set under the overloaded hat, and Ripsie's eyes smile gratefully up at John Henry; it is only gratitude, as he is to find out a moment later, when the color and smile deepen to a true warmth as Borowis unwinds him-

self from the window seat and comes over. "Great Jehoshaphat!" says Borowis. "It is Ripsie."

John Henry is the same kind young man as he was
the kind small boy, pale, too fat, with Quin mouse hair
and pale-blue eyes. *Not changed at all,* thinks Ripsie but,
as she answers his questions, she cannot help her eyes
stealing to Borowis, dazzled by the height of him, the
swagger he has inherited from Jared, his mother's hair
and brilliant brown eyes, though his are good-hu-
mored—and indifferent, John Henry could have told
Ripsie. Ripsie does not see the indifference; she only
knows that her heart seems to be beating very strangely
under her turquoise-blue bodice. Bright turquoise in
the daytime! Isabel's glance has already said that to Margaret, but Ripsie is oblivious of the two girls; she can
only see Borowis while, "Little Ripsie, grown up!" says
Borowis. For the first time that afternoon he sounds
amused.

Lady Patrick and Mrs. Loftus Kennedy begin, at once,
to talk, but Lady St. Omer sits upright, a patch like
scarlet rouge on each of her cheeks, though of course
she wears no rouge. Then there is a sound, quickly
suppressed but still suspiciously like a titter from the
piano; Ripsie looks across and recognizes Isabel; instantly, with that uncanny instinct girls have, thinks John
Henry, and without Isabel's saying a word, Ripsie knows
that her clothes are wrong.

Isabel and Margaret are in tailored skirts, a little
shabby but of fine tweed; their blouses are impeccably
laundered and belted and they wear matching pale-blue
ties—it is their latest notion to dress as far as possible
alike. Margaret's tie has a gold pin, Isabel's a small pret-
tily set opal brooch. They look charming, but Ripsie has
mistakenly plumped for what she thinks is style and

a pretty color, "in the country, in the daytime!" Now, suddenly, she can imagine Isabel saying that.

She sees their eyes taking in the fussiness of the lace on her turquoise poplin skirt; there is more lace frilled on the sleeves and again, she knows it is a mistake. "It looked all right in the shop," she says to John Henry afterward.

"What shop?" John Henry is withering.

"I never did know how to dress," says Mrs. Quin. Mrs. Quin does not mind, but this afternoon Ripsie feels that the whole room is looking, even at her shoes, and she flinches as she sees Isabel lift a significant eyebrow at Margaret. Are colored shoes not all right then? Finally they look at her hat and it is too much for them. In a spasm of giggles Margaret turns to the piano and Isabel quickly pretends to change the music, but Ripsie can see their shoulders shaking. "Well, was it a *whole* pheasant on top?" asks John Henry.

Lady Patrick does not ask Ripsie to sit down nor does she introduce her, but John Henry resolutely takes her elbow and breaks in on the talk. "Have you met Isabel's mother? Aunt Vera, this is a friend we knew when we were children. Lady St. Omer—" but Lady St. Omer rises.

"Pat, I have to go," she says as if she were stifling. "Will you ring? No, I will find my own things." Lady Patrick flashes a warning at John Henry, but he goes on resolutely. "Isa, you remember Ripsie."

"I remember you," says Isabel with a sweet smile. "I was always so sorry for you, having to use the back stairs."

"But where have you been?" asks John Henry coming between this and Ripsie and, "Yes, where have you been all this time?" asks Borowis. "Where did you go?"

"To school," says Ripsie innocently, and Lady St. Omer stops by the door.

When Ripsie disappears from St. Probus, seven years ago, there is village gossip; her mother has died, the vicar's sister takes her in, and the vicar brings certain pressures to bear; the gossip spreads and speedily reaches China Court, traveling the usual way through the kitchen, the servants' sitting room, and upstairs to Polly. It is Polly who tells Lady Patrick.

"Why is Harry St. Omer paying for that child's schooling?" Lady Patrick asks Jared.

Jared shrugs sulkily. "Has to, I expect," and Lady Patrick looks white.

"He too?" she whispers.

"Don't be silly," says Jared brusquely. "Harry has a reputation all over the county," but it is as if a darkening has shadowed the room and, "Men are hideous! Hideous!" says Lady Patrick.

"But it isn't Ripsie's fault," John Henry argues when his mother tells him this.

"No, but you can see how outrageous it was for her to come when guests were here."

"Our guests will have to get used to her," says Borowis.

"No, Boro," says Lady Patrick.

"Yes," says Borowis, looking his mother straight in the eye, but this is to come and now Mrs. Loftus Kennedy rises and, going to the two girls at the piano, quietly takes them by the arms, propelling them toward the conservatory. Isabel does not want to go—*enjoying the fun*, thinks John Henry fiercely; *there is no cruelty like the cruelty of girls to girls*, he thinks. Lady St. Omer has gone and Lady Patrick stands in glacial silence by the fireplace. John Henry racks his brains for something to say, but the silence nonplusses him. Borowis, he can see, is highly amused. The silence goes on until, "I think I should go now," says Ripsie.

Lady Patrick inclines her head. "John Henry, please ring," but suddenly Borowis has had enough. Lordly in his height, he looks down at Ripsie and smiles, that peculiarly brilliant and genuinely sweet smile that, as John Henry knows, undoes everyone. "Rip, do you still ride?" asks Borowis.

"No. No, I don't."

"Remember how you fell off Basket? We didn't think anybody could, she was so wide. Never mind. I can teach you properly now. I have a new little mare."

"Like Mirabelle?" She is Ripsie once more, unafraid and independent.

"Come and see," and he holds out a hand.

"Borowis, you have to drive Isabel—"

"Oh, Isa's all right," says Borowis easily. "Jod can take her or I will come back," and it is Borowis, not Paget, who holds open the door for Ripsie.

"You shouldn't have come," says John Henry.

He has followed Ripsie and Borowis, "like a burr" he says despising himself, but he knows he must not leave Borowis alone with Ripsie. "Hasn't the conscience of a tinker," says John Henry. Under Borowis's easy warmth is the same inability of his father, Jared, to love loyally, the untouchedness, perhaps of Damaris, and perhaps of that legendary sailor who begot Great-uncle Mcleod and sailed away; it is like breaking oneself against a stone wall or catching at mist and it is a streak not found in the other Quins who, unimaginative though they may be, are always kind, always loving. John Henry knows this in his very bones, but Ripsie has no eyes or ears for

him. She is chattering to Borowis, the hurt in the drawing room might never have been and Borowis, John
Henry can see, is charmed. He can smell trouble and,
moodily, he kicks the side of the loose-box.

They do not notice him at all. Borowis is showing
Ripsie how to hold her hand while she offers the mare
some sugar.

"Don't curl your fingers round, you will get them
nipped," he says and protects them with his hand.
"Tiny," says Borowis, looking down at them.

It is not for long. "Mr. Borowis, her ladyship would
like you to go to her in the morning room," but Ripsie
does not care. *He came with me,* he left Isabel for me, and
she puts her cheek against the new mare's neck, against
the sheen of the close hairs, and sings a little tune. It
sounds so happy that John Henry becomes extraordinarily cross. "You shouldn't have come," he says.

"I know," says Ripsie and shuts her eyes contentedly.
John Henry watches the shadow that her eyelashes make
on the whiteness of her skin, and such a lump comes in
his throat that he has to be unkind to her or choke.

"Boro is going to marry Isabel," he says.

"They are not engaged."

"They will be. Her father's in Egypt now. Boro is
going out as his A.D.C. She will have at least ten thousand a year," he says, repeating what he has heard steadily since his nursery days with Polly.

"She's ugly," says Ripsie. "Boro won't marry anyone
ugly."

"And you think you are pretty," says John Henry and
baits her as he would have done as a schoolboy. "Girls
don't make calls on their own."

"I know," says Ripsie again. "Miss Porter, where I was
at school, once wrote a book of etiquette, and every girl

was given a copy when she left. It was called *The Ladies'
Science of Etiquette*." She has opened her eyes and is
laughing. " 'Young ladies, of course, do not call,' " she
quotes " 'unless accompanied by an older person.'
Well?" and her chin comes up again. "I have no older
person. I'm earning my living," says Ripsie. "Helping
here in the school. That's disgraceful, isn't it? 'A married
sister, a brother, or mother or father,' " she mocks. "My
mother has been dead for years, and I haven't a father.
We all know that."

"Shut up," says John Henry as the old pity stirs.

"A book of etiquette is very useful," says Ripsie, strok-
ing the mare's neck. "It lets you know exactly how you
are treated and it tells you when to leave before you
have the shame of being asked to, before you are thrown
out," and in misery she flings at him, "What was I to do?
I couldn't hang round the gate as I used to, could I?"

"So you walked straight into the lion's den. You little
fool."

"I would have walked into twenty dens to see him."
She does not say it, but John Henry knows that without
being told; he remembers the chough's cliff; but now
his taunts have gone home; tears steal down her cheeks
that are very wan and tired under the ridiculous hat that
has slipped to one side as she leans against the mare.
John Henry holds out for perhaps a minute, the longest
he can ever bring himself to be unkind to Ripsie, then
he sighs and gathers her to sob against his solid and
comfortable chest—*and she doesn't even know it is me*,
thinks John Henry.

"Then, is being young wanting what you haven't?"
asks old Mrs. Quin. "And being old, accepting what you
haven't? Oh, just for once," she cries, "I should like to
make it come true for somebody young, while they are

young," but, "Crying for the moon," Polly would have said and, almost always, "Want must be your master," says Polly.

"Going to Italy!" Eliza puts down the hated sewing, hemming sheets, turning sides to middle, while Anne looks up startled. "Italy, before you both sail for New York!"

A gulf is separating Damaris from her sisters. When she turns her head there is a glitter; she is wearing a pair of diamond earrings that Mr. King Lee calls "earbobs," while her ring is an emerald clasped with two golden hands. Mr. King Lee sends down from London a set of luggage with a white jewel box and white leather writing case—"for Damaris who doesn't care for jewels and who never writes a letter," mocks Eliza. They are all initialed in gold: D.K.L. and Damaris looks at those initials in terror. There is an enameled traveling clock, a gold pen and pencil, besides hampers from Fortnum and Mason's, a case of wine; and Damaris is to go up to London with Adza to be dressed.

"I am dressed," says Damaris.

"This is your trousseau."

"Can't Miss Dawnay make it?"

Miss Dawnay comes each year, since the Brood are children, to make the girls dresses; the dummy she uses frightens Tracy up in the attic nearly ninety years later. "Why can't Miss Dawnay . . ."

"It wouldn't be fit."

A thought strikes Damaris. "Mother, is Mr. King Lee paying for my clothes?"

"He has made an arrangement with your father. Mr. King Lee is a very rich man, Damaris. We could not compete . . ."

Damaris grows paler and more silent.

"It is a heaven-sent match for you, my dear."

"Yes, Mother."

"You have made your father very happy."

"Yes, Mother."

Once, Damaris tries to end it. "I shan't be able to bear it, Mother, I shan't. I shall run away," but, "Think of your sisters," urges Adza. "Think what you can do for them. What chance have they here, and you know Eliza . . ." Damaris submits and, as in a bad dream, is taken up to London and comes back even more silent, a look of strained paleness under her tan. "She has lost her glow. Isn't she well?" Mr. King Lee fusses, and asks Adza to give her iron and make her drink a glass of claret after her lunch and dinner. Damaris, with a trapped look in her eyes, takes the iron, drinks the claret, and a basket of white roses comes down from London and is driven over to St. Probus by the railway carrier.

She tries the citadel itself. She comes to Mr. King Lee in the conservatory. "Mr. King Lee—"

"Thomas."

"Thomas," she corrects herself. "Thomas . . ." but he is not listening, he is looking at her. That look of his is probably in the house still, it is so passionately in love, and, meeting it, Damaris knows that it must overpower her.

Still she tries. "Thomas . . ." and she blurts out, "I do not love you, Mr. King Lee." It sounds like a line from a stilted novel and she says it again, earnestly, "I don't love you, Thomas."

"I know you don't," says Mr. King Lee, quite undisturbed.

"Then?"

"I love you. That will do for the present. Kiss me," says Mr. King Lee.

"Italy!" says Eliza now.

"Yes," says Damaris hopelessly. "We were going through France, but because of the war we can't." The Siege of Paris is taking its terrible course, but this is as far as it affects St. Probus. "We go by sea to Genoa." Damaris sounds more hopeless still. "He wants me to see Rome," she says, tears in her voice, "perhaps even Athens before we go—home." Damaris says that word as if it appalled her but, "Rome! Athens! And I have to stay here in St. Probus," says Eliza.

Once Eliza thinks she sees a way of escape. Great-Uncle Mcleod dies; Mcleod the Second, then, must be alone in Canton and, "Can't I go out and keep house for him?" asks Eliza.

"Certainly not!" The shocked tone in Adza's voice rivets Eliza's attention at once. Adza has no intention of telling anything more, but she is no match for Eliza. There are persistent and skillful questions, until at last Adza is betrayed into saying, "He has not been with your uncle for years."

"Why?"

"They had a—disagreement."

"Why?"

"Hush, dear," but Eliza soon ferrets it out: Mcleod the Second, their own brother, is living with a Chinese woman, not a wife but—Adza can hardly bring herself to whisper it—"a concubine."

"I thought they were only in the Bible," says Eliza.

She is amused, but Anne has dropped her sewing. "Poor soul! Poor woman!" says Anne and she sits looking far out of the morning room, all the way to China. "Those poor ignorant teeming millions. Think of their plight, Liz. Just think!" But Eliza is thinking of Eliza. "I would willingly be a concubine to get to China," she says and now Damaris is to go to Rome, Athens, America. "I didn't know I could be so unhappy," says Eliza.

"I didn't know I could," says Damaris.

Damaris's wedding dress, wrapped in blue paper, is in the oak chest in the Porch Room. Made by Worth it is, as Cook predicted, of satin. "Windsor satin!" Adza has not heard of that before, cream-white Windsor satin draped over a lace underskirt, the overskirt with crenellated edges, softened by frilled lace, with twisted cords and tassels where the fullness begins at the back of the skirt. The veil is Brussels lace; "She wore it draped over the skirt of a white ball dress when she went to the Embassy Ball," Adza tells everyone when a letter comes from Mr. King Lee in Rome. Damaris herself never writes.

The wedding is in London—Eustace and Adza seem to be like pigeons on a chalk line. Eliza refuses to be bridesmaid so that the only sister who attends Damaris up the aisle is Anne in pale-blue silk with cream cords and a fashionable Watteau hat of blue, pink, and cream flowers. She walks back down the aisle with Harry St. Omer, who is best man, while Jared, an usher, has the first of the two child bridesmaids, a beautiful little second cousin of Mr. King Lee's from a branch of his only relations in England, the Loftus Kennedys. The small bridesmaid is just thirteen, brought over from Clonfert in Ireland for the wedding; this is her first visit to London and she is wild with excitement. Under the pale-blue tilted hat, a miniature copy of Anne's with its insipid pink and cream-colored wreath, a pair of golden-brown eyes steal such long and meaningful glances up at Jared that he is first amused, then intrigued.

"I'm glad you were intrigued because there was nothing amusing about it," she tells him afterward, and she says with dignity, "I may have been only thirteen, but I had fallen in love." She seems to Jared not a child as much as an exquisite little belle, fallen into the rather dull wedding. She has a waist, the beginnings, quite clearly, of high small breasts and, when she smiles, beguiling dimples. Her name is Lady Mary Teresa Claire Brandan and she is only allowed to be at the wedding because her father, the tenth earl of Clonfert, has business deals in the newly expanding Western States with Mr. King Lee. "Money can do anything," says Eliza when they hear that, as the Clonferts are Roman Catholics, a dispensation has to be granted to allow the little Lady Mary to be a bridesmaid. All this makes the Quins look at her as if she were a curiosity, though Adza is inclined to be offended. "A dispensation to attend our church!" Damaris, who is now a second cousin, is too overawed to speak to any Clonfert or Loftus Kennedy, but Jared teases Lady Mary and calls her Lady Patrick.

It is a strange wedding for a Quin; they are all, except Jared, out of their element, "but if we had had it at St. Probus," says Eustace, "Damaris might have jumped out of the church window and run away on the moor."

He says it in joke, but a year later, Mr. King Lee sends them a little package. "She always carried it in her purse," he writes. Inside are some sprigs of dried heather, wrapped in paper and falling to bits, a feather, and a small granite pebble.

Adza does not recover. She becomes what she calls "a little unwell." This is an understatement; she has cancer and it is now that Eliza takes over the housekeeping.

"If I am to be the housekeeper," says Eliza, "I ought to be paid."

Eustace has never heard of such a thing. "Pay my own daughter, in her own home!"

"Yes," says Eliza.

"But why?" He is a little put out.

"Because I need money."

"For what?" but now Eustace is tickled. "A proper Quin," he tells Mr. Fitzgibbon and, "Don't I give you enough dresses and fallals?" he demands, but with an indulgent twinkle. "I give you money at Christmas and Easter."

"And threepence to put in the plate on Sundays," says Eliza.

Eustace ceases to be tickled and indulgent. "Yes, I do," he says, "I give you everything. What else do you want?"

"Money that I have earned," says Eliza and then— "Yes, like a chip of the old block," says Mr. Fitzgibbon when he hears—she makes Eustace an offer: "A housekeeper would cost you at least sixty pounds a year. I will do it for you, for fifty."

If Jared had said this Eustace would have been amused and cheered, but Jared is unlikely to say any such thing—"a young prodigal if ever I saw one," says Mr. Fitzgibbon. Coming from a daughter, it profoundly displeases Eustace. "You will do it when I tell you, miss, and mend your manners."

To Eustace a daughter is an appendage, not a person, but on reflection he gives Eliza a pocket allowance of ten pounds a year. He never gives Adza an allowance and it makes him feel up to date, almost daringly modern, but, "Ten pounds!" says Eliza to Jeremy Baxter in despair.

She has marked Tarrant's catalog for him to see:

"Tarrant's of Exeter. Dealers in fine and antique books.

"The *Opera omnia* of Erasmus, ten volumes in eleven, folio, Leyden, 1703–06, calf, (rather shabby).

"Johnson (Samuel) *A Journey to the Western Islands of Scotland*, First Edition, contemporary calf 8vo, 1775.

"Byron's *Waltz*, published under the name of Horace Hornem, Esq.

"Congreve (William) *The Works*, 3 vols., portrait, 5 plates, contemporary red morocco, spines gilt, yellow edges, 8vo, Birmingham, Baskerville, 1761."

Jeremy Baxter's eyebrows push his spectacles farther up on his forehead—he has always to push his spectacles up when he wishes to look at anyone. "These are books with high prices. You haven't the money, Miss Eliza. You must put such things quite out of your mind."

"I shall, for the present," and a look comes on Eliza's face that is quite new there, the look, with narrowed scheming eyes, of a cat that has marked a bird; in the days to come it will often be on Eliza's face, and will sometimes give way to the look of a cat that has been at the cream. Eliza is quite as astute as Eustace.

"I shouldn't buy them at Tarrant's," says Eliza, "but I like to know they are there; that they are obtainable," she says dreamily.

"This will grow on you," prophesies Jeremy Baxter. "One gets like a miser."

"I think misers must be very happy people," says Eliza and, as always when Jeremy Baxter is pleased, he grows crabbed.

"The Johnson alone would cost you . . ."

"I shall get it."

"How?" He says it sharply, but there is a gleam in his eyes.

"Somehow." There is also a gleam in Eliza's, and it is from then that she begins her "practices," as Jared calls them, flabbergasted when he finds out. "I should never have believed it," says Jared, "not even of Eliza."

Eliza keeps house for Eustace for the ten pounds pocket allowance; she will not do that for Jared when he is master of the house. "But Liz, you must," says Jared.

Jared brings his Lady Patrick home in 1875, the happiest of happy brides; a bare three years later she hands him the household keys. "I will live in your house," she says, "because of Borowis."

"And because of the new baby, Pat," pleads Jared.

"The new baby," says Lady Patrick with disgust. "Because I can't help it," and she says, her head held high, "I don't want them to grow up under a scandal, and I can't go home." She is very young still, only twenty-one, and a quiver breaks her voice. Jared steps forward but she turns on him and says like a lash, "Although I'm their mother I'm no longer your wife, nor will I be, in *any* way," and she gives him back the keys.

It is earlier in that third year that she engages a second housemaid to help Hester, who has so much to do. "Will you see the young person in here, milady?" Pringle asks at the morning-room door.

Lady Patrick is standing at the window to watch Jared go down the drive and she ignores Pringle. Had the parlormaid been a minute earlier she would have seen her mistress kissing her hand to him—"Yes, I was as silly as that," says Lady Patrick scornfully—but, as usual to Lady Patrick, a servant is so much furniture and she would not have cared. Now without answering she looks again down the drive where she can see a tall back in a tobacco-brown coat going through the gate, two setters loping after; one is new, bought to train, and she can hear Jared whistling to it as he goes up the lane. He is on his way to put in an appearance at the quarry, "for once," says Mr. Fitzgibbon.

Poor Jared! He does so hate it, but I suppose he must go in, thinks Lady Patrick, and reluctantly comes back to the morning room. "Well, Pringle?"

"The young person, where will you see her, milady?"

"In here, with Hester. Tell them to come in."

When they are standing in front of her, Lady Patrick cannot help looking doubtfully at the new girl; even to her inexperienced eyes she does not look at all like a servant of the kind to whom Lady Patrick is accustomed, and this makes Lady Patrick notice the fussy, cut-about brown dress with its dusty black braid, its over-frilled underskirt and too large bow, and Lady Patrick's eyes go immediately to Hester's immaculate sprigged gingham, with its collar band of white and her clean bibbed apron. Lady Patrick looks, too, at the curled hair under a bonnet of tattered feathers and flowers, and then at Hester's center parting and modest chignon under the white cap, shaped like a jelly bag—only Lady Patrick has never seen a jelly bag. There is a smell of cheap scent—servants' scent, thinks Lady Patrick wrinkling her nose distastefully—and the girl has a pair of black eyes that even now, when she is trying to keep them expressionless, seem bold while her cheeks are—brassy, thinks Lady Patrick. Can cheeks be brassy when they are red? Lady Patrick decides they can and at once thinks she is unfair; *just because the girl's color is high,* she thinks, and turns resolutely to the household books that Eliza has made over to her—and rewritten, though Lady Patrick does not know that—an account book and Adza's book of recipes and a thick tome, her *Book of Household Management.*

Until she marries, Lady Patrick barely knows that

household books or household management exist. "You shouldn't know," Jared declares. "We shall have a house-keeper," but, much as she loves him, Lady Patrick knows by now that they cannot have all he grandiloquently promises, not even with her mother's money to come. "And that is all you will have," her father says when she runs away with "this Tom," as he calls Jared. "You have married him, now you can live on him. You won't have a penny of mine."

She defiantly says she does not want a penny. "I shall manage." Then she corrects herself. "*We* shall manage," but, "No more idea than a babe unborn," says Cook and, "A change from Miss Eliza, I must say," says Pringle.

It is a change from everything: China Court is made over again, its furnishings, its habits, its friends. It becomes suddenly fashionable, "county" says Eliza, mocking now because this that she has longed for has come, for her, too late; county and expensive. Lady Patrick does not understand Mr. Fitzgibbon's warnings. She knows no other way to live and sincerely believes she is practicing strict economy. "But we have only one groom to two horses," she says, opening her brown eyes wide at Mr. Fitzgibbon. "My father would never have dreamed of such a thing. I have no personal maid. We haven't even a butler. I only go to London now and then."

"Mrs. Eustace never went at all," says Mr. Fitzgibbon.

Butler or no, the staff mysteriously grows bigger. "Why? The house is the same size as before?" says Mr. Fitzgibbon. It is the same house, but it seems doubled in position and importance, and now the new London cook needs help in the kitchen and Hester cannot manage upstairs.

"All nonsense," says Polly. "The mistress would never

have allowed it." To Polly, Adza is always "the mistress."
"And we were nine in family then," says Polly.

"But you didn't have the company," says Pringle condescendingly.

A girl is engaged to come daily from the village to
help Cook, and Hester has produced this girl—*a relation
got into trouble?* wonders Lady Patrick. "Do you want to
do this work?" she asks her. She cannot imagine that
anyone could want to. " 'Her first duty, after the fire is
lighted,' " Lady Patrick reads out from *Household Management*, where she has marked the relevant pages, " 'is
to sweep and clean kitchen and offices.' " *Where, and
what, are offices?* wonders Lady Patrick. " 'The stone steps
at the entrance, and all the passages leading to the
kitchen, must be thoroughly washed and scrubbed,' "
she reads out impressively, and then knits her beautiful
brows over: " 'Scrubbing out of shelves—cupboards,
kitchen tables, scullery boards' "—*what is a scullery
board?*—" 'nursery and servants' dinner; prepare fish,
poultry, vegetables.' That seems a great deal for one
person to do?" she asks Hester frowning.

"No, milady, it is as it should be but I think you have
the kitchenmaid, milady," says Hester in reproof.

Lady Patrick closes *Household Management* and, to re-
coup her dignity, begins to ask the sort of questions she
thinks Eliza would ask.

"What is your name?"

"Ann, ma'am. Ann Sly. I'm twenty-six."

Older than I am, thinks Lady Patrick. She has a feeling
Ann Sly guesses this, which seems to her impertinent,
and she becomes very cold.

"Hester will tell you what your duties are."

"Yes ma'am."

"Milady," Hester prompts.

"Yes, milady."

The girl is respectful and yet Lady Patrick knows that those black eyes have explored everything in the room with an inquisitiveness that is an intrusion. She is sure, for instance, that Ann Sly has made an inventory of everything she, Lady Patrick, is wearing: her morning dress with its lapels, cascading lace jabot, and wide satin ribbon trimming, her ring with its diamond and she has a curious instinct to cover the ring with her hand; it is her engagement ring and Jared paid too much for it. "I couldn't give you anything less," says Jared.

"The wages are fourteen pounds," she says, as instructed by Eliza and to close the interview, "fourteen pounds a year."

"With sugar, milady, tea, and beer," Hester reminds her.

Fourteen pounds a year. The diamond must have cost perhaps four hundred, but it never occurs to Lady Patrick that this is too much of a contrast and she is happy, too happy to be wary. She has not told Jared yet there will be another baby: *It isn't till autumn*, thinks Lady Patrick, *no need to tell him yet*. She wants the new baby, of course, as she wanted Borowis, a dozen of Jared's sons, *but there is no need to interrupt—anything*, thinks Lady Patrick: sleeping together in the big bed, their private world and warmth, turning, when the lamp is put out, into Jared's arms and now, forgetting Ann Sly and Hester, Lady Patrick falls into a dream, her chin on her hand, her fingers curving against her cheek, while her other hand plays with her ring, forgetting she wanted to cover it. Then Hester gives a cough and Lady Patrick wakes.

"Hester will show you the different rooms."

"Yes, milady."

"Your master is particular," which is not true, for Jared never notices anything about the house. Lady Patrick says it because it is what she likes to say, but the girl does not hear it; the black eyes, that have been looking so respectfully at Lady Patrick, have lifted. Ann Sly has heard what Lady Patrick for once has missed: a step in the hall.

Jared steps lightly because he is a little ashamed of what he has decided to do: give up the quarry for today and take out the new young dog. "He will be ruined if he isn't trained. It won't be very long," says Jared, "or if it is, I can go in tomorrow." He has come back for the check lead and the crop that he left in the morning room. Very quietly he opens the door.

Lady Patrick is talking, sitting with her back to him. Her back is slender and straight—she always sits as if she were on a horse, he tells her teasingly; the curls that have escaped from her hair shine on her neck as the light catches them, but Jared is not looking at his wife. His eyes have gone straight to the girl standing before her, *a prize of a girl,* thinks Jared, with cheeks like red apples, black eyes, large curves, ripe; Jared looks at the brown bodice strained too tightly over big soft mounds and his hand goes up to play with his narrow tie. Then, over Lady Patrick's head, his eyes and the black eyes meet.

"Pat will come round," Jared tells Eliza. "She must come round," but he still does not know the Clonfert pride. "I don't compromise," she tells Father Blackwell, chaplain at Dozemary Abbey and her confessor, whom Jared has begged to ride over and talk to her. "We never compromise," says Lady Patrick, once again Lady Mary Teresa Claire Brandan.

"You say that as if it were a virtue," says Father Blackwell. "It isn't. It's pride."

"Very well, it's pride," says Lady Patrick.

"Pride and impetuosity. That's a difficult mixture," says Father Blackwell thoughtfully.

"I didn't ask you to bother with it, Father," says Lady Patrick.

"I meant difficult for you, not for me," says Father Blackwell. At that she gets up and rings the bell for Pringle to show him out and then gives orders that when Father Blackwell calls she is not at home. "He would make her forgive Jared, and forgive—with them— *means* forgive," says Polly. Lady Patrick refuses to see the father, she stops going to mass and Borowis is not, as promised, brought up as a Catholic. "She is afraid the father would work on her through the child," says Polly. As Lady Patrick shuts her heart to love, she shuts it too on faith—and on hope, Father Blackwell would have told her but, "I won't compromise," says Lady Patrick. That shows in small things as well as big. Hester, for instance, learns it bitterly.

When Ann Sly comes Hester is promoted to upper housemaid and attends Lady Patrick—until the day of the scent and the summer dressing gown.

She calls it a dressing gown, but to Lady Patrick it is a negligée, a remainder of the London Season she never finishes. It is a luxurious clinging gown in cream lace and chiffon with blue ribbons and she wears it to rest in, sometimes for breakfast and sometimes slips into it on the nights when she sleeps without a nightgown— though Hester does not know that.

The day begins badly: Lady Patrick has breakfast in

bed and after it Hester comes in to dress her and, as she kneels meekly by the bed to put on her mistress's slippers for her, Lady Patrick draws sharply back. "Hester, you are wearing scent."

Hester lifts a startled face. "Oh no, milady!"

"Don't lie." Lady Patrick stands up, still drawing herself away. "Go and wash yourself and change," and she says coldly, "Get my bath ready and go."

Hester turns to proffer the summer dressing gown, but, "Don't touch it," commands Lady Patrick and, picking up her afghan, winds it around her and takes herself to the bathroom.

As Hester obediently goes to her attic bedroom she realizes that Lady Patrick is right.

At the servants' breakfast that morning, Ann Sly shows the other maids her new scent spray. "And we know where *that* comes from," says Cook. Hester knows too; it is from Thomas, the head groom, who, like his master, knows a tempting girl when he sees one, "and I should guess she paid for it," says Hester and purses her lips, but Ann Sly is getting bolder and, though Hester is a senior servant, she dares to retaliate by squirting her with scent. " 'Tis called 'Flowers of 'eaven,' " says Ann Sly laughing. Hester ducks, but a few drops fall on her collar.

No wonder Lady Patrick objects. The scent has such a strong cloying smell that when Hester takes off her collar and plunges it into the water jug, the water is permeated. " 'Flowers of Heaven.' Nasty cheap heaven, if you ask me," says Hester.

She washes in fresh water, puts on a clean collar and apron, sniffs herself carefully, and goes downstairs. Lady Patrick is still in the bathroom and Hester sets about tidying the room and putting out Lady Patrick's riding habit and boots. The summer dressing gown is on the bed exactly where it was before; Hester notices that because she has always and so particularly admired it.

When Lady Patrick is dressed she stands a moment and smiles at herself in the glass. She cannot help smiling—she knows she never looks better than in a habit: the heavy skirt and tailored bodice of dark-gray cloth, the velvet collar show off her figure: it is a little fuller, but Jared still has not noticed that—she has not told him yet about the baby, and she smiles again, a secret smile; *fuller, but still slender,* thinks Lady Patrick. She does not wear a bun for riding on the moor and the thick chestnut hair is in a doorknocker plait with a bow. The severe white stock shows off her skin and her chin, with the dimples that caught Jared's attention in the little bridesmaid. Her eyes, this morning, look like—*topazes,* she thinks, and no wonder; in the glass, she can see the bed behind her, tumbled now, and across it the dressing gown. Her nightgown, put on in the morning for Hester's sake, is left in the bathroom. As she looks at the dressing gown, Lady Patrick blushes—but a blush can be happy as well as shy—and quickly she turns to snatch up the dressing gown and hold it close, close, closer— and as quickly holds it away.

"Hester!"

"Milady?"

"You have put this on."

"*On,* milady?" Hester's voice is so incredulous that if Lady Patrick had been less angry even she would have noticed. "I?" says Hester dazed. "Of course not, milady." But Lady Patrick is not listening.

"Take it and throw it away, burn it," she says, her eyes

blazing in a way that makes Hester afraid to speak. "No wait, I will see to that myself. You can pack," says Lady Patrick. "Then you may come to the morning room for your money. You will leave today."

Polly is bold enough to interfere. "It wasn't Hester, milady."

"Who was it then?"

"I don't know, but I can guess. Hester would never do such a thing."

"It was Hester's scent," says Lady Patrick and adds, "Hester is here to look after my room and my clothes. They are her responsibility and this happened. She must go."

There is real indignation among the servants; none of them dare approach Lady Patrick, but Pringle appeals to Jared, who lazily says, "If I were you, Pat, I should give the woman a second chance." Lady Patrick answers with the hard directness they learn later to expect, "I don't give second chances."

They all think her hard; they do not know that she has an instinct so strong that it amounts to panic; something precious has been—*desecrated*, thinks Lady Patrick. How right that instinct is she finds out, not many weeks later.

"Pat won't hold out against me." Jared swears that to Eliza but the days, weeks, months go by. John Henry is born in the small room they call the Porch Room. "At least keep your own room," says Jared, "I can sleep anywhere. It's your room, Pat."

"You could have remembered that," she says. Jared can hardly recognize this white hard face. "I shall never go into that bedroom again," says Lady Patrick and keeps her word.

The house settles into its new regime. Eliza has to be housekeeper again, but this time she does not object. She has discovered, in her years with Eustace, what housekeeping as done by clever Eliza can mean.

It begins, ironically enough, with her own honesty and exactness. Food has never been stinted at China Court and, in Adza's time, the house is stored as if for a siege; it has its own fruit and vegetables—"garden vegetables, with seasons," Tracy was to say contentedly. Grown up in cities and in an era of deep freeze, she had forgotten the delights of the first peas, of fresh-picked lettuce and asparagus. "Even cabbages are beautiful," said Tracy. When Eustace adds Penbarrow to the estate, the farmer and his wife are expected to send down milk, cream, butter, and eggs in quantity, as well as supplying chickens and bacon. The butcher from Canverisk calls every day, fish is sent by carrier from Port Quin, and groceries come from Exeter every three months, ordered in bulk from Cutler and Barr, Provision Merchants, who send their catalog and whose traveler calls personally at Christmas.

The day the stores come is a great day for the Brood. All of them help to unpack, check, and put away, and the smell of blue paper, packing cases, straw bottle covers, shavings, soap, boot polish, and candles is part of their lives for, every day, one child is allowed to help Adza give out the day's stores after breakfast. The servants come with their trays: Cook with a mighty black japanned one, covered in saucers and pudding bowls; Abbie takes mustard for the pantry, hartshorn powder for the silver; a housemaid may ask for soap or sweet oil, or emery paper for the steel fireplaces; the knifeboy wants dubbin for Eustace's gaiters and Polly has a perpetual demand for soft soap. It is a busy time with the dark-blue, pink, and lilac print dresses, the white aprons and green baize ones going to and fro.

In Cutler and Barr's catalog the prices are clearly quoted, but Adza is never good at figures and, as she grows older, relies more and more upon Abbie. Abbie becomes Miss Abbott to everyone round; and all the village knows that she wears a sealskin coat and muff on her Sunday in the month. She is unchallenged in the storeroom until, "That can't be eight pounds of candles," says new-broom Eliza and, "That looks very little for a pound of tea." "Is there a *whole* two pounds of sugar in that bag?" she asks. She weighs it and, too, weighs the tea and candles. There are six and a half pounds of candles, only twelve ounces of tea, one pound, ten ounces of sugar. *Is each of the two-pound bags the same?* wonders Eliza, looking at the shelves. She takes the trouble to weigh them all and, "Cutler and Barr, sending short weight!" Eliza, stupefied, says it aloud. "Cutler and Barr! Why, we have dealt with them for years," and in her innocence she says to Abbie, "There must be a mistake. Father is going to Exeter soon. I will go with him and see them."

"Better let me do that for you, Miss Liz," says Abbie— Abbie who has been with them all as children. "It wouldn't be pleasant for a young lady like you." It sounds faithful, but something in Abbie's tone makes Eliza, always astute, look at her squarely. Abbie's eyes flicker, there is a curious flush on her sallow cheeks and neck and, "No, Abbie," says Eliza, "this is my responsibility now. I shall go myself." Next day Abbie gives in her notice.

Eliza goes to Exeter with Eustace, driving to Bodmin Road station to catch the morning train. "And what happened?" asks Jeremy Baxter.

"I was wearing my brown cloak," says Eliza. She should be in mourning for Adza, but Eliza always refuses to do as others do and, "My brown cloak and the old straw bonnet," says Eliza slowly. It seems an irrelevant answer, but Jeremy Baxter waits.

"I should have said who I was," says Eliza, and for a moment she buries her face in her hands.

"Go on," says Jeremy Baxter.

"It didn't occur to me. I just went into the shop and said, 'I am calling on behalf of Mr. Quin of China Court and I want to speak to Mr. Cutler.' Insufferable little man!" says Eliza hotly.

"Go on."

"He asked if Abbie were ill. I said she had left. I was housekeeper now and he said, 'Ah,' and looked at the tips of his fingers. Then I complained about the weights. He said, 'Shall I take it off the bill?' and looked up straight at me. I didn't know then what he meant and—well, it might have been Abbie alone though I don't see how—I felt I had to be *sure* it was Cutler and Barr's fault—and so I said, 'Perhaps not this time,' and . . ."

"And?"

"My purse was on the table, I had put it down with my gloves and . . ."

"And?"

"He reached across, picked it up, opened it, and dropped in—five sovereigns." Eliza chokes.

"Five!" says Jeremy Baxter. "Whew! You must have a big grocery bill!"

"Yes. He said, 'Thank you, Miss . . . ?' and I said, 'Miss Quin.' He could have dropped through the floor. Then—I don't know how it happened, but I found I had got up and was walking to the door with my purse— it was habit, of course. I picked it up quite naturally," says Eliza, "but when I remembered—I—I didn't return the five sovereigns. Oh, how could I not?" says Eliza.

"Because you wanted them," snapped Jeremy Baxter.

"Yes," says Eliza in a small voice. "Mr. Cutler said, 'We shall see you at Christmas, I hope. Miss Abbott's order for Christmas was always very large.' He's a horrid oily little man, but—I nodded." Her voice sinks away with shame.

"Perhaps we shall be able to buy the Johnson after all," says Jeremy, and Eliza's head comes up. "I must have something," she says. "If Mother was so stupid and Father so blind . . ." and then she says breathlessly, "But not the Johnson. Today I went rummaging," her eyes light up with pride. "In a little shop at the back of the Cathedral I found . . . this," says Eliza.

It is a folio, the binding shabby but: William Borlase. *Observations on the Antiquities of Cornwall*, 1769. "Humph!" says Jeremy Baxter, but his hands go out to take it and he opens it at once.

"The first edition is listed in Tarrant's catalog at fifteen pounds," says Eliza, "but this isn't the first edition."

"It's the second," says Jeremy Baxter. "The second edition is better; it's a little worn, but still! How much did you pay?"

"All my five pounds," says Eliza, but there is no regret, in fact unmistakable triumph, in her voice.

"Books are not meant to be bargains." Jeremy Baxter is triumphant, too, though a part of him disapproves. "Buy books for what is in them, Miss Eliza"—to the very end he keeps his punctilious way of addressing her— "for what is in them."

"Yes, but I like bargains," says obstinate Eliza.

From that day, except for the three years' interlude of Lady Patrick's housekeeping, Eliza unpacks the stores herself, and only Eliza gives them out. No one is allowed to help her, "with good reason," says Jared afterward. "She got seventy pounds a year salary out of me—seventy pounds, my own sister! And on top of that . . ."

She has a simple method of overordering and returning the things, personally and for cash, then not removing them from the bills until after she has presented these to Jared. "Give me the money to pay them directly and we shall get a discount," she says and the simple Jared does not ask who "we" are.

Now and again he wonders and complains, "The bills go up and up."

"Your wife keeps a lot of servants," says Eliza. She knows she has only to say "your wife" and Jared is silenced. Once he is driven to real protest. "Twelve pounds of tapioca. *Twelve* pounds! It's impossible."

"That was for St. Thomas's Day," says Eliza glibly.

On St. Thomas's Day, December the twenty-second, the poor people, in Adza's time, come from miles around to the servants' hall, which is decorated for the occasion. Old men and old married women are given twopence each, widows threepence, and each person has a bowl of soup from gallons made in the washday cauldron—soup and a slice of homemade bread and tapioca pudding. They are waited on by the children, and as each comes to the door, he or she says, "Please to remember St. Thomas's Day." "But I didn't know we kept that up *now*," says Jared. Eliza does not say that they do keep it up; she simply says, "You were in London."

Jared is very often in London. More and more he removes himself from the reproach that is in his home. Mr. Fitzgibbon is worried; he is getting old and wants to retire and, at last, he suggests to Lady Patrick that

Borowis should be taken away from school and put straight into the business.

"Borowis!" Lady Patrick stares at Mr. Fitzgibbon in horror.

"Before he gets ideas," says Mr. Fitzgibbon. "I warn you, we can't stand another Jared."

"Boro is not another Jared," says Lady Patrick, "and he won't be going into the works."

"Not going! But he's the eldest son."

"Borowis is not going into the works," says Lady Patrick. "He will go into the army, like all the Clonferts. The army to begin with, then later . . ." She stops and Mr. Fitzgibbon knows that he cannot follow her or Borowis where they mean to go. "You can have John Henry," says Lady Patrick.

"John Henry is a good boy," says Mr. Fitzgibbon discontentedly, "but Borowis has the brains."

So has his Aunt Eliza. "Show a cat the way to the dairy!" chuckles Jeremy Baxter. In her housekeeping for Jared, Eliza pushes down, once and for all, the troublesome spear of conscience Adza—and, more successfully, Polly—has planted in her; from a spear it dwindles to a prick, and then to nothing. "Wasn't she ashamed?" asks Jared.

"Not in the least," Eliza would have said. She is only amazed at her own cleverness, and the deviousness of her ways. For instance, she drives herself in the tubcart over to Canverisk to read to the old people in the almshouses there, "and take them a few comforts," she says.

"Precious little comforts if you ask me," says Cook. Eliza goes once a week, "and it isn't like her," says Jared. She takes a large bag and on the way she stops at the tumbledown little shop kept by Jacob Hinty at the crossroads, where she buys some tobacco and peppermints, which is not like Eliza either. "She never spends a penny if she can help it," says Jared, "and why Jacob Hinty's? Why not our shop?" There is one at St. Probus. "Hinty is a first-rate villain," says Jared.

"Oh, Eliza likes disreputable old men," says Lady Patrick.

It seems she does. When drunken old Jeremy Baxter dies, falling down the disused tin-mine shaft, "in broad daylight," say the villagers, only one person goes to his funeral. He has been dismissed from China Court long ago, "drunk even at nine in the morning," says Jared, yet the one person is Miss Eliza Quin, sitting very upright in the front pew, walking out into the churchyard after the coffin, "and not a pauper's coffin," the village remarks. Someone has paid for a good oakwood one with brass handles, all the village knows who it is, and, looking over the wall, knows too that, as she stands by the grave while the coffin is lowered into it, tears roll down Eliza's cheeks. Jared will not believe it; no one at China Court, or out of it, has ever seen Eliza cry. Nor does she say one word about it; she does not, nowadays, say many words at any time. What has happened to the talkative little girl, the opinionated young woman? "A cross between a cat and an oyster," says Jared and, now and then, "Is something going on here?" he asks.

Long ago, as Ripsie, Mrs. Quin sees something she is not meant to see. In term time she is forbidden to come inside the front gate or over the wall, but she still comes; like a ghost presence, an invisible child, she haunts the house and garden. Someone catches sight of the end of a coat, or a pair of legs in black stockings—"with holes in them," says Mrs. Quin—or a flash of scarlet from her tam-o'-shanter and, perhaps, the print of a dirty small hand; no one exactly sees Ripsie, but Ripsie is there and it is she who watches Borowis's Aunt Eliza go down to the cellar and bring up the wine.

With Eustace and Adza the wines are simple: claret and port, cider in the cask, or perry, that wonderful clean white English pear wine. When the Brood grow up there is also sherry, served sometimes in the morning with a slice of Madeira cake. Adza, too, makes cowslip wine and every spring there is a picnic in a wagonette to the cliffs at Mother Medlar's Bay where the best cowslips grow. Next day, the Brood help to strip the pips, or flowers, from the stalks, throwing them into a tub that gradually fills with a heap of spring-pale green and gold. Wine is used in puddings, too—in the famous recipe of Adza's for velvet cream: "Rub twenty lumps of sugar with the rind of ripe lemon; put in a silver pan with the lemon juice, a breakfast cup of raisin wine and four leaves of gelatine; stir until all is dissolved, cool, and when exactly cool enough, stir in a pint of thick cream." Like all Adza's recipes it is simple and excellent though "exactly cool enough" takes experience to gauge; Bella is too impatient and never fails to curdle it. There is, too, brandy butter each year for the plum pudding and brandy to light it; more brandy for setting fire to the Snapdragon played afterward, when the mysterious spirit-smelling blue flames dance over the raisins. There is also ratafia, pink and smelling of almonds; on any-body's birthday, each of the Brood is allowed a thimble-sized glass at dessert.

Two children at China Court never come down for dessert: Tracy, because in her day there is no formal dinner—Mrs. Quin has a tray in the drawing room—and Ripsie because she is outcast.

To come down for dessert. To Ripsie that is like the

stars, moon, sun, and crown jewels all in one, and equally unobtainable. She thinks dinner is a feast and would not have believed that, night after night, Jared, Lady Patrick, and Eliza sit in silence while the boring panoply of food goes on. When Pringle has carried out the last tray of plates she goes in again and, by an occasional quiet chink and gentle swishing, the children can tell she is taking off the silver, sweeping away the crumbs.

Then she draws off the slips and, in front of each person, sets a dessert plate on which is a fine gauze doily, pen-painted long ago by Anne with Scottish mountain scenes; on the doily is a green glass finger bowl holding warmed water and a flower petal or two; fruit and nuts, dishes of ginger and a few sweets are put on; for special occasions there is crystallized fruit as well, and Chinese figs or Carlsbad plums. The Madeira and port decanters are set in front of Jared, the decanters in Sheffield-plate coasters scalloped at the edges and wooden-bottomed. Then Pringle comes out, but holds the door open. "You can go in now," she calls to the children on the stairs.

When Isabel is there she wears for these evenings white embroidered muslin dresses with sashes in blue or old-rose silk ending in fringes so rich and long they touch the backs of her knees. Her hair, released from its daytime pigtails, is brushed until it floats; Ripsie's hair is cropped disgracefully because she catches ringworm in the village school to which she is sent for a time. It makes her feel like a little shorn black lamb.

While the others go down she stands looking proudly out of the landing window, over the garden which, at this time, seems to swim in the sunset light, or perhaps it is the curiously hot shine in her own eyes. The light lies on the lawn, and on the rooks' wings as they peck for insects; a scent of roses and cut grass comes in at the window. It is a peaceful happy scene, but when the dining-room door closes, Ripsie sits down on the top step of the stairs and sinks her face on her knees. Now and then, defying Isabel, she goes down a step or two ready to wriggle back if Polly or Isabel's Fräulein should appear, but no, they are too busy talking in the nursery at the end of the passage.

Before the others come back, Ripsie goes. If the boys had been alone she would have waited; John Henry never fails to bring her something, but, even if he brought her that prize of prizes, a bit of red crystallized pear, not even if Borowis brought it would she have taken it in front of Isabel.

The boys are taught to take their wine, starting at ten years old with a little in water. Under Jared and Lady Patrick, the cellar becomes more sophisticated; theirs is the peak. Now there are clarets: Lafite, Château La Tour, St. Julien, Pauillac; and burgundies: Beaune, Chambertin; there are hocks and sauternes, for Lady Patrick who likes a sweet wine. Jared lays down a pipe of port for Borowis; Borowis never drinks it and at last John Henry sells it and at a handsome profit. When Lady Patrick grows so thin after John Henry's birth, the doctor advises porter, which she does not take, then egg-flips beaten with brandy and two glasses of claret at dinner. Lady Patrick disregards them all; she does not care if she is thin.

With John Henry and Mrs. Quin in charge, the cellar falls off again; wine is out of fashion; the dining room goes back to cider, perry, and beer and John Henry begins to like a whisky and soda before he goes to bed or when he comes in tired from work. Nobody quite remembers when drinks before dinner are started; first it is sherry, then cocktails. It is Barbara who mixes the first martini; there is a silver cocktail shaker that she leaves behind. After Tracy goes there is little drink in the house except brandy for accidents, and South African sherry kept in the sideboard. "I can't drink alone," says Mrs. Quin.

She can remember the time when the cellar seems an awesome place to her. It has a grating level with the garden, not unlike the grating over the zeal by the gate, but on this one Ripsie can lie full length and look in. In the cellar are only stillness, gloom, cobwebs, with a gleam where the light catches a bottle, but one day, as Ripsie looks in, Miss Quin, Eliza, comes down the steps with a candle and Ripsie flattens herself on the grating and hardly dares to breathe. Eliza lifts her full skirts a little from the floor with one hand. She is wearing a shawl and an apron and behind her comes Pringle with a basket. Now the candle has been brought in, Ripsie can see flagstone, barrels, a long-bristled broom, a stool, and all along the walls, racks of bottles. Eliza holds the candle to the racks, passing along them, looking, and then, carefully, she takes out a bottle of wine here and there, and hands it to Pringle, who holding it with care too, dusts it and sets it upright in the basket.

"That will do I think, Pringle," says Eliza when they have six or seven. "Take them up while I enter them," and she goes to a book with mottled covers hanging from a peg on the wall; but instead of writing, the moment Pringle is gone, Eliza sets down the candle and, undoing her cuff, from her sleeve she pulls out some pieces of material—not handkerchiefs, they look too large and thick to be handkerchiefs, they are flannel, decides Ripsie—and, so quickly that she can hardly believe what she sees, from a separate rack Eliza takes two bottles more and wraps them in the flannel, *so that they won't chink,* thinks Ripsie instantly. She has been trained in piracy by Borowis, yet she catches her breath and nearly chokes with amazement at what she sees next: Eliza whips up her skirt and there, underneath, are two bags; swiftly she opens first one, then the other, sliding the bottles in, draws the strings, and drops her skirt. A moment later, with the candle, she goes up the steps and walks out, calm, efficient Miss Eliza. "Great Jehoshaphat!" says Ripsie.

She does not tell the boys in the letters, one or two a term, that she manages to write; such momentous news is kept for Borowis when he comes home, but he is not as scandalized as she hopes. "Poor old Aunt Liz," he says. "She doesn't have much and I don't suppose she got away with much either," but he underestimates his aunt, as Mr. Alabaster might have told him if he could have spoken down the years.

Mr. Alabaster had opened the brass-clasped case Tracy had brought him; now he sat at his table with the three small books he had taken out of it. They were account books, as Tracy had found, but very strange ones, thought Mr. Alabaster. "Eliza Adza Quin. Private," was written in a firm hand at the beginning of each. The entries began in 1872 with a hiatus for the years from 1875 until April 1878. Eliza had headed the left-hand pages "per"—for credits, thought Mr. Alabaster—the right-hand ones "to," but both the entries were of equal oddness: "per Christmas boxes, halved, £1.1.0." Mr. Alabaster could make nothing of that.

At Christmas the tradesmen call formally on their customers; Mr. Theobald, the butcher, for instance, wears his straw hat, Cutler and Barr's traveler a frock coat and lavender gloves. They are asked into the servants' sitting room, where Adza herself brings them a glass of port, while their delivery boys, all the days of Christmas, can draw themselves a pint of beer from the barrel that is set up on trestles outside the back door and, on Boxing Day, for every boy there is a florin. Eliza stops the beer, though she still charges Jared for it, halves the florins, and asks the tradesmen into the office where, when he leaves, she inherits Jeremy Baxter's desk. They get their glass of port, "and do we pay for it!" says Mr. Theobold. "We get away with our skins, just," says Cutler and Barr's traveler, and not only at Christmas; the entries run all through the year:

per Theobald, quarterly bill	£1.10.0
Cutler and Barr	£5. 0.0
Farm eggs and milk 10%	14.0

The tradesmen paying her? Mr. Alabaster was growing more and more mystified. That he was in the correct column was shown by the yearly entry: "From Father, allowance £10:"—"(mean)" Eliza had written in brackets after it. Mr. Alabaster thought so too. There was no allowance for the years 1875 until 1878 and then it appeared again but, Mr. Alabaster was glad to see, it had risen: "per Jared," "allowance" was crossed out and corrected to "salary," "(quarter) £17.10.0." She was getting seventy pounds a year, better, thought Mr. Alabaster, but he puzzled again over those recurring entries: "per Theobald, £2.13.0" "£3.0.0." "£1.4.0."

"Theobald," says Eliza every quarter. "My brother would like me to pay your bill. You delivered a saddle of mutton on the twelfth of November," and she reads: " 'Two pounds best rump steak.' 'Breast of veal, three pounds four ounces.' 'Saddle of mutton, ten pounds.' It was nine pounds, six ounces," says Eliza.

"Miss Eliza, it—"

"I weighed it." Eliza cuts the butcher short. "On November the twentieth, 'twelve chops.' There were eleven, and you can hand me the difference," says Eliza.

Every month too there was a list of names and figures:

per Cook	£0.10.0
Pringle	£0. 50
1st Housemd	2.6
2nd Housemd	1.6

—right down to "kn.by"—*knife-boy?* wondered Mr. Alabaster—"kn.by—5d." *She took a percentage of their wages,* thought Mr. Alabaster, but "kn.by—5d!" "This is becoming a mania," said Mr. Alabaster severely. It was so real to him that he said it aloud. Recurring all the way through was a pair of initials, "J.H.," followed by: "2 @ 4/6 = 9/–." "Two at four shillings and sixpence, nine shillings?" Mr. Alabaster did not dream that in Eliza's day the best Scotch whisky sells at sixty shillings a dozen. Eliza lets Jacob Hinty have it at sixpence under cost.

"But what did she do with the money?" asks Jared when Eliza dies. "She has practically nothing in the bank, no jewelry or clothes worth a penny. She certainly did not give it away. It must be hidden in the house." They cannot find it, but he is right.

The second little book was an account book too, but an account of—"Books?" asked Mr. Alabaster, puzzled. Most of the entries were on the right-hand page: "To Lot 52 at Witcombe Rectory sale £2.0.0." and in brackets "(Worthless. Disposed)." "To Parr's Book Shop, Truro: Goldsmith (Oliver) *The Vicar of Wakefield*, 2 vol, First Edition, 12mo, Printed at Salisbury, 1766 £21.0.0" and "(had to bargain)" was written after it. "To Lot 5, nine books. Pierce and Peltzer, auction, Penzance, including Johnson (Samuel) *A Journey to the Western Islands of Scotland*, First Edition, 12 line errata, calf, covers slightly scratched, 23/." "To Hailey's Auction Rooms, Plymouth. In lot of five books, Spenser (Edmund) *The Faerie Queene*, vol. 1, First Edition, 1590, 8/-." "Eight shillings!" Mr. Alabaster could not help exclaiming that aloud, and dated nine years later he found another entry for *The Faerie Queene* but for vol. 2. This time the price was forty pounds—*must have attracted someone else's attention,* thought Mr. Alabaster, *but if it really is the first edition . . . And she waited nine years for it,* he thought. Something of Eliza's determination seemed to reach him; forty pounds was a big sum to set beside the others, those careful shillings, and nearly double that other large flutter up to twenty-one pounds for *The Vicar of Wakefield. She had courage,* thought Mr. Alabaster. Courage, in fact, was in every line of those account books; courage to face tradesmen at their own game—*and she did that, even if she had meannesses,* thought Mr. Alabaster; *courage to travel— and how she traveled!* he thought, looking at the entries: Penzance, Liskeard, Exeter, *and in all seasons,* thought Mr. Alabaster, looking at the dates, *in all weathers* and he remembered the moor wind, even now in summer, as he had walked down that morning from the village; the day was suddenly cold and blowy as it could be in a Cornish summer and he had thought then of what it must be like in winter.

Eliza driving the tubcart to the station is a familiar sight. "Nobody cares what I do," she complains once to Jeremy Baxter and, "Then you are lucky," he answers. "You are free." Quite free to get up in the dark and make herself a breakfast of bread and milk in the empty kitchen, to put on her old brown cloak and ludicrously old-fashioned bonnet—both becoming familiar in the sale rooms—to take a lantern to the stables, harness Kitty, and, as the first light breaks, drive over to the moor—that bleakest of moors—with her purse tucked in her muff and a feed for Kitty under her feet. There is no station at St. Probus, she has to drive to Canverisk or Bodmin Road, put up the pony at an inn and give the ostler sixpence to rub her down and feed her, while she, Eliza, catches her train. She has in her muff, too, a piece of cold pie or pudding; Eliza does not spend money on her own food.

On her way home she stops mysteriously at Jacob Hinty's; sometimes Kitty is kept standing outside his derelict shop and cottage for an hour or more; sometimes she is even put up beside the bony white horse he keeps for his carrier's cart. Eliza uses the room behind the shop—Jacob's junk room—as a clearing house. It pays the old man to have her; if people had watched what Jacob did they would have been amazed at the strange old books he peddles, selling them on market days or from door to door at anything from a penny to a shilling. He keeps those with the brightest covers and gets a good profit; the rest he uses as fuel. It is only what she calls her "prizes," and the books that are worth her own selling, that Eliza takes home.

It is often dark when she comes in. Sometimes the servants are having their nine-o'clock supper, sometimes it is even too late for that. If Jared is at home a light will be burning in the morning room; another light is in the drawing room where Lady Patrick, alone too, sits with her embroidery frame, stitching, her needle making an even small plock-plock sound as it goes through the silk. At ten o'clock she will cover the frame and go to bed—alone. Sometimes, everyone has gone to bed and Eliza lets herself into a sleeping house, takes the soup or stew Cook has left for her on the range, and goes upstairs.

If it has been a blank day she blows out her candle at once, but if she has found something then, sitting up in bed, her red shawl huddled around her, the light of the candle throwing her shadow huge onto the walls, she will read and brood until the early hours of the morning. " 'Too late have I loved thee, O Thou beauty of ancient days . . .' " croons Eliza or " 'Man is a reed, but a thinking reed,' " or " 'I have seen the thorn frown all winter long; bears yet in spring a rosebud on its top,' " or, because she is, as all single women are, deeply romantic,

> *Take him and cut him out in little stars,*
> *And he will make the face of heaven so fine*
> *That all the world will be in love with night . . .*

—and, as she grows older, what truly comes to pass, " 'My mind to me a Kingdom is . . .' "

She keeps these lines and many others in her mind all day, remembering them as if they were a nosegay and every now and then she could sniff their fragrance. No one seeing her going about the house, in her brown house frock and apron, silent or tart, fault-finding, would have guessed what beauty was in her mind. "Poor old Aunt Liz. She doesn't have much," and Mr. Alabaster opened the last book.

It was not an account book but a catalog of books: "The Permanent Collection of E.A.Q." Each book was carefully—*lovingly*, thought Mr. Alabaster—listed with its description and the circumstances in which it was found, each entry separated by a ruled red line from the next. There was a footnote on the first page: a neat asterisk, "to signify of value to me," had written Eliza, while two asterisks meant "of worth."

To Mr. Alabaster that quiet understatement was typical of the Eliza he was beginning to know.

Among the two-asterisk entries were:

The Book of Hawking, Hunting and Blasing of Arms, known as the Book of St. Albans, attributed to Dame Juliana Berners or Barnes, folio, printed at St. Albans by the so-called Schoolmaster Printer in 1486. First Edition, lacking 23 leaves.

Meres (Francis) *Palladis Tamia: Wits Treasury*, small 8vo, 1598.

Richardson (Samuel) *Pamela*, 4 vols., First Edition, 8vo, 1741–42.

His eyebrows rose as he read. Was she imagining this?—these, he felt sure, were old rare books—but there were the two ledgers to support it, the accounts, the twenty years of hoarding, saving, traveling, and suddenly Mr. Alabaster's gaze went to the deep bookcase behind him, filled with books covered in brown paper. He got up and opened the glass doors. The shelves were deep in dust and when he pulled a book out, the brown paper split and he could shred it off; there were books behind these books, *two deep,* thought Mr. Alabaster. He put his hand in farther and pulled out one of the back books and "Cessolis (Jacobus) *The Game and Playe of the Chesse*, translated by William Caxton, folio. Printed at Westminster by William Caxton about 1483, second edition," read Mr. Alabaster. He took out the two next to it and his hands trembled as he took them both back to the table. The first edition of *The Faerie Queene* and, as far as he could see, complete and almost unblemished. *What can they be worth?* thought Mr. Alabaster. He had no real idea but, *Surely a great deal,* he thought giddily.

Next to them in the bookcase was a smaller, thinner book, "Sir Thomas Browne's *Religio Medici.*" He found it in the catalog: "First Edition, small 8vo, 1642," with the note, "bought by Father with the books in bookcase."

"This is quite beyond my scope," Mr. Alabaster began to mutter, "quite beyond my scope." He kept on saying that aloud, but still he could not keep from reading Eliza's catalog, going to the bookcase, coming back to the catalog. He found he was sweating with excitement and haste and getting so covered in dust that he took off his coat, hung it on the chair, and rolled up his sleeves. Then, coming back to the catalog, he had begun to read again when he stopped, his finger on a page.

"Are we to wait for them any longer?" asked Bella.

Cecily had brought in tea; they were all gathered in the drawing room and Mr. Prendergast had arrived. "What can they be doing?" asked Bella.

"They must have a great deal to talk about," said the youngest Grace in fairness to Tracy and Peter.

"They should talk about it afterward, not now, at tea-time."

"They have to persuade Peter."

"He won't need much persuading." Bella was beginning to recover from the letter. "It's inconsiderate. Mr. Prendergast hasn't the whole afternoon."

"I'm in no hurry," said Mr. Prendergast.

"And they are coming," said the youngest Grace who had not ceased to watch from the window. "Yes, here they come with Walter. What a good couple they make!"

"No need to get sentimental," said Bella. "This is a marriage of pure convenience. Look at them!" Bella had come to the window too, and now the sight of Peter provoked her afresh. "Look at them coming up to take possession of our house."

"Their house by now, I expect," said the second Grace.

"So calm and cool!" said Bella.

"Well, would you expect them to show they are anything else?" Mr. Prendergast, who was watching too, would have liked to say that; in the way Tracy and Peter walked apart, careful not to touch one another, they reminded him of a stiff young couple he had seen at a Spanish wedding, arranged too, of course; and indeed, when they came into the room, Tracy's mask of fright made her seem like some cold little infanta while Peter, in his nervousness, behaved like a young grandee, staying just inside the door and inclining his head to them instead of speaking.

"Well?" asked Bella. "Well?"

"We sh-shall accept," said Tracy to Mr. Prendergast. She had meant to speak evenly and with dignity, but it came out so jerkily that it sounded defiant. "There is no need to keep anyone waiting any longer. We have decided we sh-shall accept."

"And we hope it will be well," said Peter pleasantly. He genuinely meant it to be pleasant but—*If I hadn't spoken lightly I should have wept*, he thought, and after Tracy's seeming defiance it sounded mocking. The youngest Grace, who had got up to go to Tracy, sat down again; Tom cleared his throat uneasily and Bella looked Tracy up and down.

"We shall accept." There was a long silence into which came the sound of the kettle just beginning to boil on its tripod over the methylated flame. "Very well," said Bella and shrugged. "Mr. Prendergast is staying to tea," she said. "Since it is to be your house now, Tracy, I suggest you pour out."

Tea at China Court was a ritual: "an absurd anachronism," Bella said often.

"But a delightful one," said Tom.

Cecily had carried in the silver tray and lit the spirit-lamp under the kettle. The table now had a lace-edged embroidered cloth and on it was the pink tea set the third Grace had envied, with its shallow cups, its cream jug, a bowl for rinsing the cups, and its matching gold and pink enameled spoons. Two teapots stood ready and warmed; the cups had to be warmed too for, "If the tea touches anything cold it loses the aroma." Mrs. Quin impresses Tracy with that. "Only vandals," says Mrs. Quin, "put in the milk first." The caddy had two compartments, for China and Indian tea; its small silver scoop was dented where the little boy Stace, in a temper, throws it on the floor and deliberately stamps on it. The sugar tongs were Georgian and shaped like scissors; there were small plates with silver knives and small, lace-edged napkins. "And the food! What food! What work!" Bella groaned, though Tom's and Dick's and Harry's and, yes, her own Walter's, eyes glistened. "We have a cup of tea with a biscuit at home," said Walter yearningly. Now Cecily brought in saffron cake, buttered scones hot in a silver dish, brown bread and butter cut thin as wafers, quince jelly and strawberry jam from the China Court quinces and strawberries; she had made shortbread, fruit cake, and, because Tracy likes them as a child, jumbles, thin rolled ginger snaps filled with cream. Of course in the days when Mrs. Quin is alone there is not all this food, but all the same, "What work!" said Bella and from the first afternoon she had declared,

"Nowhere, nowhere in the world, except in England, does this slavery persist."

"We had tea often in New York," Tracy had said, though timidly, "and sometimes in Rome and it's getting fashionable in France." She seemed fated to nettle her Aunt Bella and now she quailed. "P-pour out the tea?"

She could see herself sitting on a straight-backed chair, her legs dangling because they cannot reach the floor, her clean dress spread around her—a child does not have tea with Mrs. Quin in dungarees—while she watches her grandmother's hand move over the tray, preparing, rinsing, measuring, and then dispensing. They are ugly mottled old hands stained with gardening and knotted with rheumatism, but they look graceful as they do this—*because it is a graceful occupation*, thought Tracy now, *dignified, like a ceremony; and I shall disgrace it under all their eyes.* Her aunts, trained by Mrs. Quin, must, Tracy knew, be expert, no matter what they said, *And they are so sure I shall make a mess of it,* thought Tracy in panic and, "Please no, Aunt Bella. You pour," she was just going to say, when Peter stepped past her and pulled out her chair.

Peter had been a working farmer for nearly five years now, but drawing rooms were in his blood and suddenly he was not a defensive young man, nor a nonchalant grandee leaning in the doorway, he was—*a host*, thought Mr. Prendergast. He pulled up chairs for Bella and the Graces, took cups from Tracy and carried them to small tables, offered sugar and milk, handed plates—*and talked,* thought Mr. Prendergast, *easily and naturally covering up Tracy's confusion.*

The youngest Grace and Mr. Prendergast helped him; then Tom joined in, then Harry.

"... a by-election, that's certain. Old Ramsbottom's announced he will retire."

"Who will the government put in?"

"Tarrington's a local man."

"Or Drayton. He was born in Canverisk."

"I expect Ramsbottom will get his baronetcy."

"Pity he ever stood. Too old."

"I had heard that Tom Dezvery—"

"The Newquay Dezverys?"

As the tension in the room eased, Tracy's hands grew steady. She had been blindly copying her grandmother, seeing only those old mottled hands, but now she sat straighter as she put more hot water in the teapots— and was able to join in without a stammer or a blush, thought Tracy.

"Peter, Aunt Bella hasn't any jam."

"I think Uncle Tom would like a scone."

"Shall I cut you some cake?"

"More tea, Aunt Bella?"

They will do, thought Mr. Prendergast. *They will do*, but when the last cup had been drunk, the last jumble eaten—"There wasn't one left," said Cecily, pleased— the tension was back. *Yes, they will have to face hostility*, thought Mr. Prendergast.

The youngest Grace unwittingly began it.

"You will be living here," she said. "Then what will you do with the house at Penbarrow?"

"A farmer should live where his stock is," said Harry.

"But we must live here," said Tracy.

"In part of the house?"

"In all of it," said Tracy and the obstinate look they were beginning to know came on her face; *but I have to be obstinate*, thought Tracy.

"You won't be able to keep it up."

"We shall try. We shall make it a little more modern, but I want to keep the house almost exactly as it is."

"How?" asked Bella.

"S-somehow." Tracy was beginning to stammer again.

"We haven't really discussed it," said Peter. "We haven't had time. As Tracy says, we must modernize—and repair. I think I might move the dairy over to the stables here—we hope to electrify of course—and pull down those old ramshackle Penbarrow buildings. The house there could convert into two farm cottages."

"Very nice if you had the money," said Tom.

"You won't have the money. I have told you," said Walter, "when duty is paid . . ."

A savagery seemed to possess Walter at the sight of those two hopeful young faces. *Well, he had arranged to sell the Winterhalter and, I suspect, other things*, thought Mr. Prendergast.

"These grandiose plans!" said Walter.

"They are not very grandiose," said Peter. "Only practical."

"Practical! I tell you, you are dreaming. Yes, your capital will be almost nil," said Walter with relish. "You will be up to your neck in debt before you have time to turn round."

"Excuse me," said a voice and, "Walter. It's Mr. ?" said Bella but Walter was in spate.

"I have warned you," he was saying, "but you wouldn't listen to me. Oh no! Of course not. It's Mrs. Quin over again. Well, I can tell you, you will have to think again. Keep the house as it is! You will have to strip it."

"I won't," cried Tracy in pain, and the other voices joined in.

"You will find you will have to."

"Don't live in dreamland."

"The house isn't sacred, my dear."

"You will have to sell most of . . ."

"I won't," said Tracy. "I won't."

"Excuse me, Colonel," said the voice.

"I shall keep it as it is," cried Tracy.

"Penbarrow—" began Peter, coming to her rescue.

"Penbarrow!" said Walter and snorted.

"Penbarrow will do very well," said Peter trying not to lose his temper this time. "Very well, given a chance."

"And how will you give it a chance? Money doesn't grow on Christmas trees," said Walter.

"Colonel Scrymgeour—" the voice persisted.

"I could raise a mortgage on Penbarrow if I owned it," said Peter.

"Contrary to St. Omer belief," said Walter acidly, "mortgages have to be paid."

"That's damned offensive," said Peter.

"I didn't think you would like it," said Walter. His face was mottled with temper and triumph, while white patches were showing round Peter's nostrils. *In a moment,* thought Tracy, *he will really lose his temper—a red-haired temper—and there will be a fight*—but, "Colonel Scrymgeour, you *must* excuse me. . . ." The voice was almost shouting now and, "Walter!" Bella really shouted. "Walter! It's Mr.—" In the strain of the moment Bella still could not think of the right name. "Walter! It's Mr.—Mr. *Alabaster.*"

It was Mr. Alabaster, but not the quiet withdrawn Mr. Alabaster they knew, in the brushed London suit, black tie worn in deference to Mrs. Quin, neat hair and gold spectacles. Mr. Alabaster was in his shirt sleeves, his hair on end, his spectacles pushed up on his forehead, while his hands were filthy and he had smudges on his face where he had mopped his forehead with a handkerchief he had used as a duster.

"Forgive me, but of importance, I think," said Mr. Alabaster but he did not talk, he babbled. "If what I think I have found is what I think. But it *is*," he burst out, "I feel sure but all the same, it's quite beyond my scope. With your permission I shall telephone, go up to the village and ring up. This will have to be for Mr. Truscott himself. I am not sure, of course, but I strongly suspect. There is one I haven't found, possibly worth most of all," said Mr. Alabaster. "I happen to have some little knowledge of Horae—"

"What is the man talking about?" asked Walter.

"You must excuse me. I happen to have a little knowledge of Horae. A Book of Hours. 'The Hours of Robert Bonnefoy.' By its description it would seem to be of great quality, but she may not be reliable, of course, though what I have found as evidence . . . Yes, if we could find it I might be able to tell Mr. Truscott with a little more certainty. I really feel quite shaken. I suppose none of you has ever looked, or thought of looking in that bookcase? Perhaps if you did you would not know . . . and more in the boxes, and under the papers. It all needs confirmation, of course. We will get Mr. Truscott, or he will nominate . . . if I may telephone. . . . It's not my field but if I could find . . ." And here Mr. Alabaster became clear. "Can you tell me," said Mr. Alabaster, "are there any other books in the house?"

It was getting late when Cecily came down the hill. "I knew," said Cecily, "as soon as I saw Peter and Tracy walking up together from the garden. I didn't wait for the village to get the news, I went straight up to Groundsel and Minna," but now she was aware she ought to hurry—*or dinner will be late,* she thought—but it was such a fine clear evening that she had to linger. *Mild and sweet and the wind has dropped; more fine weather on the way,* thought Cecily. It seemed to her a good omen.

The sky over Penbarrow was a clear luminous primrose, but behind the hill and village it had the colors, Cecily thought, of some old-fashioned party dresses that the girls once had—Mrs. Quin's choices were always a little dowdy—dove-colored chiffon with that faint blue satin that is backed with heliotrope. The grass under the last yellow light had turned to olive-green, the color of grass in Victorian oleographs, and on the drive the rhododendrons were dark.

The windows all along the house were dark, too, except for one flickering square in the office: *Mr. Alabaster using a candle?* thought Cecily in surprise and, *Why haven't they lit the lamps?* she wondered. *I left them all ready*—but the whole house seemed to be in twilight. "We were too busy to stop," said Tracy afterward. Bumble came to meet Cecily as she went in by the front door; there was no sign of August. "He never was one for servants," Cecily says often and without rancor. Moses would be in his armchair in the kitchen—*and wanting his fish,* thought Cecily. Trill was silent, gone to sleep in the darkness. *Where is everyone?* she wondered as she stood on a chair, the oak-seated chair she always used, to light the hanging lamps in the hall, and, as the wicks caught and the lamps threw a golden circle on the flags, by contrast the rooms, through their open doorways, the stairs and passages, only dusk-shadowed till then, grew darker. Wondering at their emptiness, Cecily went into the drawing room where twilight glimmered through the windows. *They might have taken the tea out for me*, thought Cecily, a little hurt. She picked up the tray, then, as she went down the passage to the kitchen wing, she heard babel coming from the office; Tracy came running down the front stairs, a Grace came down the back. More feet sounded overhead. "Are you playing hide and seek?" asked Cecily.

They were. From the White Room Tracy brought down a row of books: Dante's *Vita Nuova* and a three-volume *Divine Comedy*; a Chaucer, a small Shakespeare, the *Confessions* of Saint Augustine, the *Philobiblion* of Richard de Bury. "They were on the bottom shelf of the cupboard, behind the 'What Katy Did' books, behind them and some Penguins. Do you suppose," she asked awed, "these were Great-aunt Eliza's?"

"They look like hers," said Mr. Alabaster. "This is a very old Chaucer." He was studying it reverently. "1532. It might be the first edition."

"Of *Chaucer*! But wouldn't that be worth a tremendous amount?"

"I should guess that it is fairly rare."

"And I wrote all over it!" said Bella appalled. "I remember finding it when I was doing *The Canterbury Tales* for my Senior Cambridge."

"At least you wrote in pencil," said Mr. Alabaster.

There was a bookcase on the landing but, "Nothing. Nothing," said Mr. Alabaster, waving its books aside. "These must have belonged to the house." He said that too of all the drawing-room books: the red leather set of Shakespeare; the bound volumes of *Punch* and *Illustrated London News;* and the shelf of tooled white-and-gold editions of *Sesame and Lilies*, Ella Wheeler Wilcox, and Ouida's *Two Little Wooden Shoes.*

"I remember they were for Sundays," said the youngest Grace, "and for looking at when we came in to the drawing room at five o'clock, with the Kate Greenaway books and Caldecott and the *Just So Stories*." The nursery yielded all the Coloured Fairy Books: the Orange, the Green, the Blue, and the Violet, as well as *The Princess and the Goblin, Tanglewood Tales*, and tattered copies of *Little Women, Good Wives*, and *Jo's Boys*. "*Little Women!*" cried the youngest Grace and took it into a corner. In the White Room cupboard too were a few Victorian books for girls on which Bella pounced with glee. "*Fern Leaves from Fanny's Portfolio,*" she read out, "*Stories of Courage and Principle, or Fit to Be a Duchess*. How delicious! *Aunt Jane's Hero, or Stepping Heavenwards*, and *look* at the prices!" cried Bella. "The Lily Series, one shilling each. The Girls' Favourite Library, three and six."

In the attic, where Tom and Harry had taken a torch, they discovered among tied piles of papers a box of *Chatterbox, The Coral Island*. Henty. Jules Verne. "They were Stace's, I expect," said Bella, but some of them are Borowis's and John Henry's, kept and handed down. In the attic too were more *Punches*, unbound but tied together with string, copies of *The Landowners Gazette, Ceramic and Pottery Dealers* and *Blackwood's Magazine*.

Cecily, going to the lamp room to fetch the rest of the lamps, almost collided with Tom carrying a collection of family prayerbooks, from the shelf where they had always been kept in the morning room. "What in the world is happening?" asked Cecily. Tom did not answer. He had pushed open the office door with his shoulder and gone in.

The office floor was littered with brown paper covers where Mr. Alabaster had stripped them off. The china had been hurriedly transferred to the dining room, the books had been taken out of the bookcase and piled on the table; now Walter was reading out Eliza's list while Mr. Alabaster tried to identify each item and Mr. Prendergast put them, one by one, carefully aside, separating them "from the dross," said Peter.

"Whew! They are dirty," said Tom, and picking up one, gave the boards a brisk clap.

"It would be better not to handle them like that," suggested Mr. Alabaster. "They are old, you know."

"The Anatomy of Melancholy," Tom read out the title, puzzled by it as Eliza herself is puzzled years before. "Would anyone be interested in that?" he asked.

"I seem to remember a copy being sold in London last year," said Mr. Prendergast, "for about a hundred and fifty pounds." Tom put the book down as quickly as if it scorched him.

"You were right. This must be quite a hoard," he said to Mr. Alabaster.

"A hoard! She was in business!" said Mr. Alabaster.

"It will make quite a sale after all," said Walter, as the piles grew.

"I should say good but not outstanding," said Mr. Alabaster.

"Great Jupiter! What do you call outstanding?" asked Tom.

"I hoped, if we could have found the Bonnefoy *Hours* . . ."

"Would this be it?" asked Bella, who had gone upstairs again to ferret around. "It was in the bottom of the chest in the Porch Room."

"A Victorian missal," said Mr. Alabaster turning it over. It is Lady Patrick's "and not valuable?" asked Bella so disappointed that she argues, "It's written in Latin, half of it at any rate, and it has pictures. Are you sure?"

"An ordinary Victorian missal," said Mr. Alabaster

again. "What we are looking for is this," and he said patiently, "I will read you the description again." Even in Eliza's flymark writing it took eight of the little notebook's pages, "But I will read you the general description," he said.

THE HOURS OF ROBERT BONNEFOY.

HORAE BEATAE VIRGINIS MARIAE (USE OF PARIS) WITH CALENDAR, ILLUMINATED MANUSCRIPT ON VELLUM, written in a very clear and regular *gothic* script in red and black. 13 HALF-PAGE MINIATURES IN ARCHED COMPARTMENTS, MINIATURES OF THE 4 EVANGELISTS AND 11 SMALLER MINIATURES OF SAINTS, all the pages containing the large miniatures surrounded by full borders decorated with flowers, leaves, fruit, grotesques, animals and birds, each page of the calendar surrounded by a full decorated border containing a small painting of the appropriate occupation of the month, 25 illuminated and historical initials with three-quarter borders painted with flowers, leaves and fruit, numerous smaller illuminated initials and line-terminals, faded red velvet binding of later date with silver clasp and catch.——*small quarto (8 ins by 6 ins approx.)*

(Paris, early 15th century.)

"Someone must have taught her to describe it," said Mr. Alabaster. "Well, she must have had many bookseller friends." Instead of the double asterisk "of worth" Eliza had written at the foot of the last page "of great worth," with a note: "found wrapped in a piece of calico in the bottom of a workbox in the sale of Eileine Manor (gave workbox as a Christmas present to Polly) Paid 12/–."

"And nobody knew it was there, I suppose," breathed Bella.

"Twelve shillings," said Walter. "Are you sure?"

"I'm not at all sure," said Mr. Alabaster, "but one thing I have learned this afternoon, and that is to trust this Miss Eliza; besides, as you see, there is another note: 'Showed privately to Tarrant. Offered two hundred pounds. Refused.' "

"Did she offer it at two hundred pounds or was she offered that? It isn't clear," said Mr. Prendergast.

"Nothing is clear," said Mr. Alabaster, "but there are descriptions of the larger miniatures," and he read out: " 'Matins. The Annunciation. The Virgin kneels in her bedchamber with her hands crossed on her breast in an attitude of the deepest humility. She has a charming childlike face expressive of sublime innocence. The Angel stands before her with his right hand raised. The Holy Ghost descends on golden beams shining through an open arched window. . . .' "

"Golden beams through a window." Tracy could not hold herself back any longer. "I have seen that," she said.

"Seen it?"

"Yes, often with Gran. We used to look at it almost every morning. Yes, I'm sure. It was a little book, only about that big." She measured with her hands. "The pictures were in the middle of the pages, with an edge of flowers and patterns round the writing. You could look and look. The more you looked the more you saw," said Tracy.

"Where did she show it to you?"

"Where did she keep it?"

"Where?"

"Where?" but, "I don't know," said Tracy, "I think—"
But she broke off. "No, I can't remember."

"You don't think Mother sold it?" said a Grace horrified, but Walter shook his head.

"She wouldn't have known that it was worth so much."

"She might have lost it," said Bella. "You know how
careless she was. She often left a book out in the garden
all night."

"Ouch!" said Mr. Alabaster but Tracy protested, "She
had great r-respect for anything old and beautiful, and
it was very beautiful."

"It must have been," said Mr. Alabaster.

"Ring for Cecily," said Walter. "We must have more
light and if the book is here she ought to know. Ring,"
but at that moment Cecily knocked, bringing in the lamp
and, "Good gracious me!" said Cecily, inside the door.

"Cecily," began Walter, unfailingly pompous. "We are
looking for a book—"

"So I see," said Cecily and as she set down the lamp
her eyes looked distressed. "Oh, I'm sorry they are so
dirty."

"They might have been *dusted*," began Bella but, "Cecily was alone," cried Tracy, "alone where there used to
be four, five, six servants," and she put her arms round
Cecily. "Don't mind them," she whispered.

"Hush, Bella. Hush, Tracy," said Walter. "This is a
book like a Bible, Cecily," and he said testily, "Let Cecily
pay attention, Tracy. A Bible with pictures." He spoke
slowly and carefully, *as if Cecily were an idiot child*, thought
Tracy. "They would be small pictures?" he asked, turning to Mr. Alabaster who nodded, "small on thick paper
with writing in Latin, foreign writing that you wouldn't
be able to read."

"And handwritten," said Mr. Alabaster.

"But when I say *Bible*, Cecily," said Walter kindly, "I don't want you to think of an English Bible bound in black; this one is red, red velvet."

"It isn't," said Cecily. "It's pink."

"Red velvet," said Walter, holding up his hand to stem the others.

"You may call it red," said Cecily unmoved. "I call it pink."

Walter still held up his hand but now the questions came tumbling.

"You have seen it?"

"You have?"

"When?"

"Where?"

"Where?"

"Every day," said Cecily, "when I *dusted*," she said with a thrust at Bella. "Mrs. Quin used to look at that book a lot. So did I. Latin and all," she said to Walter.

"But she couldn't have known the value," said Walter.

"No, she just liked it," said Cecily.

"But where is it?" cried Bella.

"Where it has always been. In her bedroom. She kept it on the table by her bed."

"The book by her bed? We might have known," said Bella and her excitement abruptly ebbed away. "Cecily is thinking of those *Day Hours*, you know the one Mother kept a peacock feather in it though we said it was unlucky, and she used to read it every day," said Bella.

"Bound in black without pictures. I'm not a zany," said Cecily.

"But I looked—" and Bella went quickly out of the room. They heard her running upstairs, but in a few moments she came back hot and indignant. "There's nothing on the table by her bed but this." She held up the detective paperback. "It was nearly dark but I'm positive—"

"You come with me," said Cecily and picked up the lamp.

"I will wait for you," said Mr. Alabaster but, "No, we may need you," said Walter. "Please come."

"But I will wait in the drawing room," said Mr. Prendergast. "I must collect my papers."

At the head of the stairs, and on the landing, they paused. Except Bella, they flinched from going into Mrs. Quin's room; a quietness fell on them and they filed silently in at the door, but it was singularly as usual, the windows open to the dusk, the bed glimmering under its white sheet, the roses, dropping now in the vase. "I haven't had time to tidy up," said Cecily. As she set down the lamp, its globe and flame were reflected in mahogany surfaces, in looking glasses and in the windowpanes. The curtains shivered in the draft, but nothing else stirred. Even the clock had stopped.

No one spoke as Cecily went to the bed, drew off the sheet, and turned back the pillow. "She had the *Day Hours* book under her pillow when she died. I put it back and the other with it. Here you are," said Cecily. Standing round the bed they all stared at the black book on one side where the pillow had been and a shape, wrapped in yellowed silk, on the other. "Is that it?" whispered Bella.

Cecily handed it to her and Bella took it and carried it to the lamp, the others crowding round her. Only Tracy held back, standing with Peter and Cecily on one side.

"Be careful, my dear," said Walter.

"Careful! when it's been under Mother's pillow!" said Bella with a strangely throttled little laugh. "The silk's nearly rotten." The intrepid Bella sounded almost afraid and, "You open it," she said and gave it to Mr. Alabaster.

As they watched, Mr. Alabaster unwound the old silk revealing a thick, rather clumsy book with a clasp. In the soft lamplight its velvet was faded to a brown rose. "It is pink," said Tracy.

"But—is *that* the book?" asked Bella.

"It may very well be," said Mr. Alabaster.

"But *I* remember it," said a Grace and, "Can it be worth much? We used to touch it," said another.

"Look at it on Sundays with Father."

"It *can't* be the one."

Mr. Alabaster had laid it on the table; now he lifted the clasp. The book opened easily, as if it were accustomed; he turned over a page as it lay on the table and came to a half-page miniature with borders and colors, "Like jewels," whispered Tracy. Mr. Alabaster bent over it, then, "Yes!" he said like a proud showman. "It's the Annunciation. I read its description to you."

"Then it is it!" said a Grace incredulously, and the chorus ran around, "It is it," "It's the book," "It really is."

"There's a greasy mark on it," said Bella.

"Children's fingers," said Walter in agony.

"Will it clean?"

"Does it detract from the value, if the book has been used?"

"At least she kept it wrapped up."

"If we had dreamed . . ."

As their anxious faces crowded around Mr. Alabaster and the anxious voices rose, Tracy slipped in between Bella and Tom and pressed near the table to look. Peter edged in beside her. "That's the window I remember," she told him, touching the golden rays. "Look, there's her bed and look at the shelf, with her books, and there's a table with her jug and basin, even a half-folded towel." She lifted the book and pored over the tiny painting, her face as unconscious as a child's. "Beautiful!" said Tracy like a breath.

"Tracy. Are you *touching* it?" Bella would have snatched it, but Tracy put it back on the table and spread her hands on it.

"Not your dirty hands!" cried Bella in a shriek and at once, all the pent-up excitement of Tracy's elders broke out in scolding.

"When we have all just been told . . ."

"Have you no respect . . ."

"Even your Aunt Bella didn't open it. She gave it to Mr. Alabaster."

"No one," declared Walter, "should touch it at all. Wrap it up and leave it to the experts," but Tracy still kept her hands on the book.

"I th-think," said Tracy and, though she stammered and her voice was small, it was perfectly clear, "I think you have all forgotten s-something. The b-book is mine."

Compline

Noctem quiétam et finem perféctum concédat nobis. . . .
MAY HE GRANT US A QUIET NIGHT AND A PERFECT END.

BLESSING FOR COMPLINE FROM MRS. QUIN'S
Day Hours

T h e   C o r o n a t i o n   o f   t h e   V i r g i n ·
Christ places a rich golden crown on the Virgin's head. They
are surrounded by a host of angels singing and playing
musical instruments (long trumpets, harps, regals, i.e. small
portable organs and timbrels, i.e. small drums played by
beating with the hand). The haloes, robes, and instruments
are lavishly gilded.

*Full border of conventional flowers, fruit and ivy leaves, painted
in colors and heightened with gold. Figure of a sheep playing
the bagpipes (satire on the angel musicians).*

MINIATURE FACING THE OPENING OF COMPLINE
IN THE HORAE BEATAE VIRGINIS MARIAE,
FROM THE HOURS OF ROBERT BONNEFOY

"A *q u i e t* night and a perfect end," but it had seemed as if China Court would never be quiet again; as Tracy said to Peter, "You know in the Bible where it says 'The evening and the morning were the first day' and there was a whole span of creation in between? This feels like that."

"It has been three days," Peter reminded her.

"And such days," said Tracy. They did not suit China Court. *It doesn't like surprises and excitements,* thought Tracy, *only the ordinary dramas of death and birth and*—but she shied away from the third word—*love* was not to be thought of between her and Peter—yet. But she liked to remember how they had stood shoulder to shoulder when, downstairs in the drawing room, they had faced the family, "in the fight," said Peter and grimaced.

It had, Tracy had to admit, been a fight and not a pleasant one. "Gran would have turned in her grave."

"I don't believe she would," said Peter. "I believe she would have quite enjoyed it."

"The b-book is mine," Tracy had said, with her hands on it. "Mine."

There had been a moment's amazed consternation

into which Dick's detached, rather amused voice had spoken: "The child is right."

"Right?" Then Bella seemed to choke and had run out on the landing, calling over the banisters and as she ran downstairs, "Mr. Prendergast! Mr. Prendergast!"

Immediately the others began.

"Tracy's?"

"Do you mean to say all those books . . . ?"

"The books as well?"

"Look, we can't wrangle here," Peter had said and the third Grace chimed in, "No, not in Mother's room," and, "M-Mr. Alabaster," said Tracy, her voice stammering and shivering with nerves, "p-please do as Uncle Walter s-said and look after the b-book." Then she had turned, trying to brace herself. "I had better g-go to Aunt Bella."

"I will come with you," said Peter and the rest trooped after them, gathering around as Tracy and Peter stood facing them, *shoulder to shoulder*, thought Tracy; *though her shoulder only comes halfway up mine*, thought Peter. Tracy stood her ground with every appearance of being calm and dignified, but he could feel how she was quivering. He would have liked to put his arm around her— *but not in front of them*, thought Peter.

"I-if I was wrong, Aunt Bella, I'm s-sorry," said Tracy.

"You were not wrong," said Bella shortly.

Mr. Prendergast tried to smooth the shortness away. "We must look on this find as a windfall for these young people—as I hope it will be."

"And we have no share in this windfall?" That acidity could only be the second Grace and the others broke in.

"Why should it all be Tracy's?"

"Do you mean Mother left her *everything*?"

"Everything that's in the house is hers," said Bella.

"But *all* the books?"

"The books as *well*?"

"But Mother didn't know they were in the house."

"That makes no difference."

"*None* of it for us?"

"No share at all?"

"No," said Tracy baldly. Then she flushed and said, "I'm s-sorry but it's for China C-Court."

"Is that quite fair?"

"Quite fair," said Tracy passionately. "We need it, you don't. You would like to have it, of course, but we need it."

"There are more than a hundred books. It may run into four or five thousand pounds," said Walter.

"We need all of it. You said so. There is the roof and the pipes and the dry rot. We need electricity and there's the farm to put in order and the garden."

"Don't count your chickens before they are hatched," said Walter, "and you must remember, if this is as valuable as we suspect, it will make a considerable difference in the death duties. A considerable difference," he said, brightening so visibly that Mr. Prendergast had to suppress a smile.

"Still, we hope it will be a windfall," said Mr. Prendergast, "and I'm sure Miss Tracy and Mr. St. Omer have far too much sense to think that anything can be estimated until we have expert advice."

Mr. Alabaster's Mr. Truscott did not come. "He does not feel competent," Mr. Alabaster reported solemnly. He was solemn, for this confirmed him in what he thought he had found. "If it suits you he will arrange for a Mr. Robin Bellamy of Sotheby's to come down tomorrow."

"Sotheby's!" said Bella giddily. "Sotheby's!" and the exclamations ran around while Walter began explaining what Sotheby's salesrooms were.

"They will charge a stiff percentage," he warned.

"Well, how do you think they live?" said Dick. Only Peter stayed calm. "If he could catch the Cornish Express I will meet him in Exeter," he said, but objections broke out.

"Exeter? He can come to Bodmin Road."

"I have to go to Exeter. On business," said Peter.

"Business? *Now?*"

"Yes. Business," said Peter.

"Why don't the aunts and uncles go home?" Peter had asked Tracy that three days ago.

"They want to see what happens."

"Even when it's nothing to do with them?"

"It is to do with them. They are relatives."

Peter groaned, but Tracy was firm. "A proper family has relatives."

Mr. Bellamy was not at all as any of them had imagined an expert on books to be. "I thought he would be old," said a Grace.

"Yes, old and vague."

"Like a professor, rather dusty and shabby."

On the contrary, he was a suave, dark young man, well brushed and groomed; "probably with a wife and young children living somewhere like Weybridge," said a Grace disappointed. "He might be a young stockbroker," she complained.

"Not when he talks," said Bella and certainly his talking was brief, smooth, and curiously enigmatical.

"More as I imagine a diplomat," said Tracy.

"Do you think someone like that can really know about books?" they asked, but Tracy, peeping into the office thought, as she watched his hands examining the books, it was as if even his fingertips could read.

The commercial hotel at Canverisk where Mr. Alabaster was staying, and the old village taxi that drove him over every day, did not seem adequate for Sotheby's, but Mr. Bellamy did not appear to mind. Mr. Alabaster and Peter had taken him Eliza's catalog and account books to study overnight and next day he came to China Court. "To work in the office?" asked Bella doubtfully. "Shouldn't we give up the dining room?" but again, he did not appear to mind and was closed in the office all day. He was chary of giving an opinion about possible prices of individual books, but, "We should, of course, be pleased to offer at auction all the books I have selected," he said.

"That is an opinion," said Peter and Mr. Bellamy smiled, but still he said, "It's very difficult to estimate the value of rare books until one has examined them closely. This could only be done at Sotheby's, for instance, where we have a large bibliographical reference library."

"But the Book of Hours. Surely you can tell us what you think?" said Bella.

"Is it as good as Mr. Alabaster hoped?"

"At least tell us that." The aunts were crowding round him.

"The Bonnefoy Hours is a manuscript of the finest Parisian workmanship," he admitted, "and in an excellent state of preservation. The expressions on the faces, in particular, are masterly. Masterly!" said Mr. Bellamy.

"Then it is rare and valuable?"

"Decidedly."

"How valuable?"

Mr. Bellamy plainly preferred not to commit himself—*but he doesn't know the aunts,* thought Tracy.

"Valuable might be anything from a hundred to a thousand pounds," complained Bella.

"If that old *Anatomy of Melancholy* book sold for a hundred and fifty . . ." said a Grace.

"Mr. Prendergast wasn't sure."

"No, but this one ought—"

"Eliza was offered two hundred pounds all those years ago," said the third Grace.

"Or asked two hundred. We don't know."

"It should get more than that now."

"Five hundred perhaps," said a Grace, and, "Could it fetch five hundred?" they asked.

"Yes, could it?"

"Or even a thousand?"

"A thousand for a book!" They pressed Mr. Bellamy until he was driven to say, "It wouldn't be unreasonable to put a reserve on it."

"Of what?" asked the aunts.

"Of a thousand pounds?" said one boldly.

"Perhaps six thousand," said Mr. Bellamy.

"Six thousand!"

Tracy had put herself next to Dick—she found this silent and sometimes unexpected uncle soothing—and now he said softly and privately to her, "They usually estimate a reserve at about two thirds of the price they expect to get."

Six thousand pounds, two thirds! thought Tracy. She was suddenly giddy. "But that's—that's nine thousand," she whispered to Dick, who nodded. *Nine thousand!* She had to put her hands on his arm to steady herself. *Nine thousand pounds! Why that would be enough . . .* and once again she felt as if she had a bell of excitement and joy swinging in her.

"The market has never been as high"—Mr. Bellamy was trying to be truthful and at the same time extricate himself—"and rare books are getting rarer, but naturally copies of the same book vary greatly in value. So much depends on condition, 'points,' as one calls them, binding, provenance, and so on." Then he seemed to give up and turned to Walter. "You have other books, you know, perhaps even more interesting. There is the Cessolis."

"That's the one on chess," said Bella.

"Can a book on *chess* be worth much?"

"It was translated and printed by Caxton," said Mr. Bellamy dryly.

Tracy felt giddier still. Even more rare than nine thousand pounds; and there are the Spenser and Chaucer too and at least a hundred other books. *Oh, if I could talk to Peter*, thought Tracy. She longed to talk it over with him, to try and estimate—*though of course we don't really know yet, not until they get to London*, she thought. *They may not be worth all this. Mr. Bellamy might be mistaken*—yet, as she thought that, he leaned across the office table and picked up a small thin calf-bound book. "Now if you want a real sensation . . ." and he showed it to them.

"*Ralph Roister Doister*," read Bella. Their faces were blank; the sensation had not reached them.

"The earliest English comedy attributed to Nicholas Udall," said Mr. Bellamy, "about 1566."

"And is that very valuable?"

"Only one copy, *one copy*, is known and that's in the library at Eton College—and it lacks the title page. This has the title page," said Mr. Bellamy.

"You mean that ordinary-looking little book is worth more than the beauty of the Book of Hours?" said Dick.

"It is far more rare," said Mr. Bellamy, and for once there was silence, complete silence, among the aunts.

Mr. Bellamy left, shaking hands at the front door; he had decided to go straight up to London from Canverisk in the morning and had consented to take the books. "I should like them out of the house," said Walter. "Your mother, of course, had not insured them." Mr. Bellamy had rung up Sotheby's and had the books insured, "And what a figure," said Bella. And he and Mr. Alabaster had packed them in two leather suitcases brought down by Tom and Peter from the attics.

As the sound of the taxi grew faint up the lane the family wandered back into the drawing room. "It's too late to change for dinner," said a Grace.

"But still time for a drink," said Harry and Peter went to fetch glasses from the pantry.

Mrs. Quin's sherry had been left in the sideboard undisturbed. "South African," Dick had said briefly, and had gone into Canverisk to buy some Tio Pepe; he had brought gin and whisky down with him. "Walter hates my guts," he had told his Grace, "but he will drink my gin."

"I could use a gin," said Bella now. They were all a little irritable and on edge and, as they waited for Peter, Bella began on Tracy again. "And when will this famous housekeeping begin? We all have to make plans, you know."

"Bella shouldn't keep on pressing," said Tom to Dick, who was setting out the bottles.

"She could save her breath," said Dick.

"Yes, that young man's a lone wolf," said Tom, "if ever I saw one, and Tracy was brought up in America; shy, good manners and all that, but independent. They won't let Bella or any of us arrange their lives, but listen."

Before Tracy had had a chance to answer, the others had "clocked in" as Dick said, and, "I must say that child is patient," he said.

"We ought to know where we are," a Grace was saying. "We must plan . . ."

"But won't we have to wait for probate?"

"I imagine not. The terms of the will—"

"Yes. Don't wills have to be proved?"

"They don't even listen to their own answers," murmured Dick.

"We came for a night," complained a Grace. "We have been here five days!"

"And I ought to have been in town long ago."

"We were supposed to be leaving for Italy."

"Walter had started apple-picking, Beauty of Bath and Irish Peach. We must go back."

"But we can't all go now, there is Tracy."

"She could be married from our house."

"But her mother . . ."

"Barbara will come over, of course."

"Tracy had a cable today."

"A quiet wedding . . ."

"Quiet! There are about a thousand St. Omers."

"Then in London perhaps . . ."

"That's such an expense for us all."

"I suppose they should wait three months, after Mother . . ."

"It would be nice at Christmas . . . velvet . . . the bridesmaids could have little muffs."

"Do you remember Amanda's wedding? Ivory wild silk . . ."

"Absolutely simple . . ."

"Tracy could come home with me."

"Surely she will need to go back to Rome and collect her things."

"Or are they in America?"

"She would be wise to get her trousseau in America. They have such pretty things. Their underclothes . . ."

"You can get to New York and back now, for about two hundred pounds."

"My dear Harry. Money doesn't matter to Tracy now!"

"I don't know what Barbara will want to do about linen, but I have a little woman . . ."

"My dear girl, brides don't have house linen nowadays."

"Surely it should be announced in the *Times* and the *Telegraph*."

"Oh no! They will be flooded with advertisements. I can't tell you what it was like with Amanda. All those leaflets and photographers."

"The telephone rang incessantly."

"There isn't a telephone here," said Tracy who had been waiting for a pause, "and we have announced it."

"You have!"

"*Already!*"

"Yes. Mr. Prendergast thought we sh-should, as we plan to marry s—"

"You mean be married soon?"

"Yes. In f-fact—" but a Grace wailed, "Soon! Then we shall all have to come back when we have just gone."

"We can't go on and on upsetting everything."

"First Mother, now . . ."

". . . take leave again so soon . . ."

"Change all our plans *again* . . ."

"I don't think so, Bella." Peter had come in with a salver of glasses. "Bella and all of you. You needn't change anything; that is if you plan to stay here tonight as I think you must now. We shan't detain you," said Peter. He put the salver on the table. "I got a special license in Exeter yesterday. That was my business there," he said to Bella. "Tracy has had a cable from her mother and we should like to ask you all to our wedding tomorrow."

"In St. Probus, very quietly owing to a recent bereavement . . ."

"Quietly!" said Peter and groaned again.

"But in a way it was quiet," said Tracy and that was true: antagonism, rivalry, even criticism had stopped, "melted away at the word 'wedding.' I shouldn't have believed it," said Peter.

"Tomorrow!" There had been consternation, "but not at the *fact* of the wedding," said Peter in astonishment. "Suddenly that was accepted."

"Well, it had gone beyond argument," said Mr. Prendergast. No, it was consternation over one question and one question only: "What will Tracy wear?"

"A frock," Tracy had said.

"A cotton frock. But you can't."

"Or the suit I came in, or jeans."

"*Jeans!*"

"It's all I have. I have a lovely shantung suit in Rome."

"A shantung suit! Don't you want a proper wedding? I thought every girl—"

"I can't have one," said Tracy reasonably. "There isn't

time. It's to be at eleven o'clock tomorrow morning. There are no wedding dresses in St. Probus."

"But there are," said Cecily, "in the chest."

"The chest? With the baby clothes?"

"Yes. I put moth balls in this very year. The veils are there too and some beautiful lace."

"The Limerick! Grandmother's family veil!"

"Of course!"

"The one we all wore."

"I can't be married in just a veil," said Tracy.

"And the dresses are too old."

"But are they?" asked a Grace. "They may be so old that they have come round again," and the aunts took Tracy upstairs to open the chest in the Porch Room. The baby clothes have been put away since the youngest Grace wore them. The long robes and nightgowns are unhealthy, Bella says when her children are born, and the other girls follow her. "No baby wears flannel petticoats now, or cambric vests," but they use the christening robes. There are two: one made by Adza in lawn with a tucked front and lace ruffles; the other, handed down from Lady Patrick's mother, is entirely of Irish lace. "Gran said I wore that and it's an heirloom," said Tracy reverently. Under them, wrapped in blue paper, were the dresses.

"Mother would never let us dress up in these," said Bella, "not even for the Christmas charades."

Lady Patrick, of course, has no wedding dress; she is married just as she is in her street dress when she walks out of her father's town house after breakfast, taking her maid as witness, and meets Jared at the small Catholic church on the corner; but Damaris's, sent back with all her possessions by Mr. King Lee, is in the chest, all its richness still fresh. "I had forgotten it was so lovely," breathed a Grace. "Feel the satin. It would be exquisite with the Limerick veil."

"But I couldn't wear it in a little country church in the morning," protested Tracy, "and it's far too big for me, and Damaris died."

"Perhaps it would be unlucky."

"Whose was this?"

Bella had taken out a dress of limp lawn, full-skirted and tucked, tight-sleeved and lined with white silk. It had cuffs and a narrow collar frilled with lace. "Whose was this?"

"It must have been . . . Great-grandmother's?"

"Adza's?" Tracy was startled. "Could it have lasted all that time?" but her aunts were in full cry, as Peter would have said.

"Would it look queer?"

"It's too simple to be queer."

"It would get up beautifully."

"We could take it up to Minna. You know how clever she is."

"Try it on, Tracy."

Adza is plumper than Tracy but, "We could take it in here," said Bella, "and here."

"With darts," said a Grace.

"It wouldn't matter if the yoke were full."

"The hem is ripped here."

"That's nothing—a stitch."

"It looks really rather charming."

"With a simple veil, not the lace."

"I know. The confirmation veil. Thank goodness we refused to wear the thick ones they had at school."

"Like mosquito netting, I remember . . ."

"This is as fine as tulle."

"What about shoes?"

"White sandals, or we could borrow in the village."

"For her head there's the circle of pearls."

"Or flowers."

"Real flowers!"

"That would be pretty, to match her bouquet."

"Thank goodness we live in a flower-growing place."

"Would Sir Gervase's arums be over?"

"Arums? For a headdress?"

"Goose, I meant for the bouquet."

"What about Major Bruce? He might have violets. They would suit this."

"If he has any of his double white ones . . ."

Tracy was twisted and turned and, while her aunts chattered and Bella pinned in the darts and Cecily stitched at the hem, she stood, not in a dream—*the reverse*, thought Tracy—in a new reality in which she herself seemed to grow indistinct, *lose my edges*, thought Tracy—*to dwindle, or was it to grow? and merge with all the young girls who had stood here in their wedding dresses, their hearts beating faster because of tomorrow, the tomorrow for each one of us*, thought Tracy.

The largest wedding is Groundsel and Minna's, at which Minna rends Groundsel by crying throughout.

She cries, but she keeps her word. "Will 'ee marry me, Minna?"

"*Ach*, yes!" She says that in the happiness of that day of the first snow, but two days later the snow is gone.

The thaw is sudden and complete; no trace of snow is left. The sun shines and soon even the slush is dried.

Minna does not see Groundsel in the morning; altogether there is no color in the day; the sun goes in; the wind comes over the field rough and warm from the Atlantic; it roars in the lane, but the wood, when she wanders to it, in the afternoon, is still and dank, smelling of earth and wet holly. There is no Groundsel to meet her there either; he has had to take over the stable work because the groom has gone with the children to the Meet.

Cook has told Minna to bring in some mint on her way back through the kitchen garden. "If there's any escaped the frost," says Cook and, in the patch of mint, Minna finds a purple head of stock where the snow had been. "Fonny!" says Minna. The little frostbitten flower seems to stab her. She walks slowly back to the house, her apron blowing against her legs. Instead of mint she has picked the bitter purple flowers.

After tea Groundsel comes to the kitchen to fetch kettles of hot water to make the ponies' mash. Minna will not look at him, she goes on with the washing up, but she has given her promise.

"I love 'ee Minna. Do 'ee love me?"

"I love. *Ach*, yes! I love," and a tear slips down her cheek into the washing-up bowl.

Their wedding in 1913 is the largest because the whole village comes to it. The quietest is Ripsie's about which no one hears until it is all over. Damaris's is the most expensive, the youngest Grace has the prettiest, but one seems to merge into another until they are all the same: *I*, thought Tracy, *and these aunts humming round me, and Gran and before Gran, right back to Adza; I and them all.*

"It is Papa's place, my dear."

"A considerable difference in the death duties."

"I wanted to see the boys so badly that I had to come."

"Would you do what you said, guide me and turn me loose with books?"

"*Ach*, yes. *Ach*, yes! I love."

"I shall never go into that bedroom again."

"Christen her in the *font*?"

Adza often unwraps the white lawn dress and looks at it, "though I don't know why I keep it," she says. Mary, that eldest of the Brood who marries the young doctor, has her own ideas about a wedding dress; white lawn is not grand enough for Damaris; every year makes it increasingly clear that Eliza will never marry, and Anne . . . Adza's soft plump face grows almost hard when she thinks about Anne. "She was such a gentle biddable little girl and to think," says Adza, "we need never have given the Dinner Party." It has capital letters forever in all their minds.

After Damaris's wedding, while she and Mr. King Lee are still on their way to New York, Harry St. Omer sends Anne some flowers; then at Christmas a box of chocolates; and in February comes the valentine. "He does it to dozens of girls," says Anne, but, "My dear," says Eustace to Adza, "I think we should give a little dinner and ask the St. Omers."

In February the St. Omers are safely in London and Adza does not pay much heed, but that year they come down to Tremellen early for the whole summer and Eustace says it again.

"But we have dinner in the middle of the day," says Adza trying to escape.

"Perhaps we should alter." Eustace is unperturbed. "Ask them for seven o'clock."

"But who can we ask with them?"

"Not many, perhaps two or three couples."

"Two or three couples!" Adza and Eliza look at one another.

"Mr. Preedy," says Eliza—Mr. Preedy is still the present vicar—"but then Miss Preedy will have to come and she clacks her false teeth."

"I will ask Sir Philip Ware," says Eustace. "After all, he is our M.P."

"But won't he be surprised?"

"The Tunstalls," suggests Adza.

"No, Mother!"

"Mr. Fitzgibbon," but even Adza is doubtful about that and Eliza confirms the doubt.

"Mr. Fitzgibbon and hear him eat his soup! We don't know the sort of people who go out to dinner," says Eliza cuttingly.

"There is no reason why we shouldn't," says Eustace. "If we ask Sir Philip in the right way he will come. We are getting on, you know. The works are enlarging every year and Damaris's marriage did us good. We don't know what it will lead to," says Eustace with a glance at Anne. "It may change everything here and perhaps it's time we began having dinner company," but there were other and burning questions.

"Will Abbie be able to manage the waiting?"

"I hope so. Sarah must help her."

"Sarah hasn't a black dress."

"You must get her one, and what about us? Father will have to get some evening clothes."

"Nonsense. We shall tell them we don't dress."

"The St. Omers!" and Eliza cries, "Better not to ask them at all."

In the end Eustace does go to Exeter and orders a set of tails, a watered-silk waistcoat—though he is a little doubtful about that—a shirt with its front panel discreetly frilled, a turned-up collar, and soft white bow tie. "You look splendid, Papa," says Eliza when they come home and he puts them all on to show them, pacing up and down the morning room as pleased as a small boy. "Splendid. But what about us?" asks Eliza.

"We have our dresses from Damaris's wedding," says Adza.

"Lady St. Omer will recognize them."

"She must if she must and surely it's no shame. It's better than ostentation. We have only worn them once and Anne's is so very pretty." Eliza agrees reluctantly, but Anne is silent.

"And the food," says Adza. "What can I give them?"

"What you give us," says Eustace. "Couldn't be better."

"But this is a *dinner*," and Adza goes to *Household Management*, but the very beginning dismays her: "It is usual now," says *Household Management*, "to precede the soup with little appetizers: caviar, oysters, crevettes . . ." "Crevettes?" asks Adza.

They none of them know until Eliza looks it up in Larousse—she has guessed it to be French and, "I don't trust prawns in May," says Adza promptly.

"Of course, you can, Mother, if they say so." Eliza is impatient. "It is recipe twenty eighty-six. See what it says."

Adza looks it up and the bewilderment deepens. "Crevettes. These may be served with the heads stuck into a lemon, neatly and evenly, so that they make a pretty little dish." "*How* would you stick a prawn's head into a lemon?" asks Adza. "Lemons are hard, prawns are soft."

Eliza draws up a menu. As this dinner, they all know, is for Anne's benefit, Eliza is obliging. "Come out of her books for once," says Adza, but, "Liz, dear, don't," begs Anne.

"Don't what?"

"Don't encourage this dinner, for I won't come," says Anne.

"Of course you will come."

"I will not." Those three words, firmly spoken, are so unlike Anne that Eliza should have paid attention, "but she always did go bull-headed for an idea," says Polly and against her sister's quick tongue Anne has no chance. Eliza throws herself into planning the dinner, food, wine, table decorations, and guests. Sir Philip accepts, "and with him and the Preedys it shouldn't be too bad—though why Mother wants to ask the Tunstalls! Still," says Eliza, and it is not without hope that she copies out what seems to her the best menu from *Household Management*:

Potage à la reine

* *

Fried soles
melted butter

* *

Lobster cream
Salmi of wild duck
Fillet of beef

* *

Hare

* *

Snow eggs
Marbled jelly

* *

Vegetables with beef
Potatoes
New peas . . .

"Cook can't make all that," says Adza.

"She can if you are firm," and, "It's all perfectly simple," Eliza tells Cook and reads her the recipe for the *potage à la reine*. Cook listens with an adamantine face.

"Almonds in chicken zoup!" she says when Eliza has finished, "I never heard tell o't, and 'rub through a tammy.' What's a tammy, I should like to knaw? If you wants chicken zoup," says Cook dangerously, "I shall make me own."

Eliza has no more success with the salmi. "Wild duck?" asks Cook scornfully. "Where will 'ee get that, Miss Eliza, to this time o' year? Wild duck, my foot!" says Cook, who does not mince words when she is angry, Miss Eliza or not.

"If a salmi is too difficult—" Adza tries to interpose.

"Difficult, it's 'ash," says Cook with scorn after she has read the recipe. "Will 'ee give an 'ash at a dinner party, m'm? It don't 'ardly seem fitty. An' I can't do lobsters," says Cook, "I can't bear to hear 'em scream so don't 'ee ask me to."

"Why all this?" asks Eustace when he hears. "Give them spring lamb and why not have asparagus? Ours should just be ready."

"We can't have asparagus," says Eliza. "We have no asparagus tongs."

She sends to Truro, but there are no asparagus tongs there either. Adza has never heard of them, nor of grape scissors and other things Eliza says they must have, and, "Do you think we can *ever* teach Abbie to fold the dinner napkins properly?" Eliza studies these in the chapter on "The Dinner Table": there is the Fan, "and the Palm Leaf, the Sachet," says Eliza, "all perfectly simple," but Abbie's hands are large and inclined to be hot and her

Fan and Palm Leaf look bunched, while the Sachet gets grubby edges. "Better have them folded flat on the bread plates," says Adza.

"But you don't have bread plates at a dinner party."

"What do you do with your bread then?"

"Crumble it on the tablecloth, I think."

"*And* the butter?" Eustace is on the verge of being sarcastic, unbelievable for him, but these dinner-party discussions have gone on for days, "and all day," says Eustace. "*And* the butter?"

"You don't have butter."

"That would be a funny kind of meal. Of course we shall have butter."

"Then yours will be a funny kind of dinner party," says Eliza pertly.

"We shall do as we have always done. They can take it or leave it."

"Then why ask the St. Omers?"

As the time grows near Adza lies awake at night with worry, Eliza is bright-eyed and avid and Eustace almost cross, for Adza keeps him awake too, while Cook has nerves over the marbled jelly. "Do we have to have this stuff every day?" asks Eustace disgusted.

"Hasn't she to practice?" asks Adza almost sharply.

Sarah weeps and asks to be allowed to go back home to her mother because "Miss Eliza says I breathe so heavy when I serves." At that Adza snaps Eliza's head off, Adza who never snaps. "You will please leave the servants *alone*," and all the while, quietly insistent, Anne says she will not come.

"But I'm doing it for you," Eliza points out.

"And I asked you not to." It is a rebuke, gentle, but decided. This is a new Anne, one whom Eliza has not met.

"I have told you, Eliza, and you, Mother, I can't meet Harry St. Omer like this."

"There's no harm in a dinner, my dear."

"There is an insinuation," says Anne.

"Well, and why not?" cries Eliza.

"I don't like him."

"Not like Harry St. Omer!" To Adza, Anne might almost as well have said she did not like God, but the answer comes back unbending. "I don't like him. I don't approve of his principles."

"He hasn't any principles," says Eliza.

"That is what I mean. I thought you, Father, did not approve of him either?" but Eustace evades that question.

"Oh, Anne, don't be so narrow-minded!" cried Eliza.

"I am narrow-minded over this."

"It's this chapel of yours."

"Certainly it's the chapel. I will not meet him."

"Papa will make you," says Eliza cruelly.

In spite of these worries, on the day of the dinner Eliza cannot help being elated; the St. Omers, Sir Philip, are coming to China Court, the whole village knows it and, too, she is gratified by the look of the table. Under its central hanging lamp it gleams with silver and glass; fresh rolls are in the folded napkins—she has listened to Adza there. The cloth is plain damask, but Eliza has made an oval center of golden-yellow velvet and on it put three miniature palms—palms grow well in Cornwall—the center one a little higher than the others, each standing in moss with lilac flowers and ferns. On each side, between the palms, are tall white china vases holding yellow and mauve tulips, while in front of each place in a smaller matching vase—Eustace bought the set at a sale—is a single tulip and ferns. The menu cards are written in mauve and gold—Eliza sends to Exeter for the inks—and stand upon miniature easels that she has cut from cardboard and painted in gilt. As a final touch there are four pedestal white china fruit dishes of apples and grapes, yellow apples and purple grapes.

The servants gather in the doorway to look; even Cook takes a moment from the kitchen. "Never seed nort like it," says Cook.

"Could be the West End," says Abbie, who has once been to London but, "Eight bunches!" Eustace explodes when he sees the grapes and, "I don't like serving foreign fruit," says Adza, but Eliza has her way. "Cost two shillin's a pound!" says little Sarah. "*Sixteen* shillin's for they!" Sarah earns five shillings a week.

The wine is set out. The maids are ready in their new aprons and caps, Sarah in her new black dress. Eliza goes upstairs to change.

It is a typical moor May evening, chilly, with wind and rain—every windy rainy evening after Eliza is reminded of it, but now, as she goes upstairs, her mind is too busy to think of Anne; all her thoughts are still in the dining room, hovering over the table. "A work of art!" She can almost hear Lady St. Omer saying it, and she wonders if she ought to tell Abbie to light the fire. *If I do she will build it up fit to roast an ox and some of us have to sit with our backs to it*, she thinks. She is so preoccupied with this problem that it is only when she comes to the landing and sees her and Anne's dresses hanging there ready, that she remembers that this dinner is for Anne.

Now she comes to think of it, she has not seen Anne all afternoon. *Anne might at least have come and looked*, she thinks. *After all, I did it all for her.*

"I asked you not to." That still sounds in her inner ear, but she shuts her mind to it. *Anne will think differently when she sees the table,* thinks Eliza, *and when she sees herself dressed.*

Polly has ironed and freshened their dresses: Eliza's plain olive-green faye seems inconspicuous by the Worth bridesmaid's dress with its exquisite pale-blue silk, the overdress crenellated to match Damaris's wedding dress and tied with the same cream silk cords. Polly has cut off the train, "though it's small, it's too much for a country dinner," and she has taken the cream, blue, and pink flowers from the hat and made them into a wreath. Eliza has never taken such pleasure in a dress since her own faraway salmon silk ball gown—and that was silly, says Eliza candidly now.

She takes the pale-blue dress from its hanger and opens the White Room door. "I will help you first, Anne," she says generously and stops.

In the middle of the floor is a small trunk, shut and strapped. On the trunk is a note, with her name in Anne's firm writing. Eliza takes two dazed steps into the room, but it is empty.

In one of the volumes of Dante that Tracy found in the White Room, was a tress of hair, long, and pale gold. It is Anne's that she sends to Eliza before she sails: "I thought you might like to have this. I am cutting my hair short because of the lice."

"Lice!" cries Adza recoiling but the letter goes on: "We have been warned we may get them in Szechuan."

"Anne, who couldn't say 'boo' to a goose!" Eustace is dumbfounded. "Anne, going out to China as a missionary!" he says over and over again.

"A Baptist missionary!" wails Adza. "Not even C.M.S."

"Well I am damned!" says Eustace.

"You might at least have warned Father and Mother," Eliza writes back.

"They would have said 'no,' and it is painful to argue." Anne's second letter is quite clear, quite calm. *Painful to argue! She has often sat by, often, while I . . .* thinks Eliza. It seems to her deceitful and wounds her in a strange deep way that she cannot get over, though the end of the letter is warm: "Forgive me, Liz. You would if you knew how happy and useful I am," but "useful" seems like another reproach. *I shall never be of use to anyone,* thinks Eliza. She does not feel forgiving; or unforgiving either; she feels only a dull empty ache.

"You wasted a fortnight over those fallals," scolds Jeremy Baxter.

"Yes."

"Your sister knew better than that."

"Yes." Knew enough to leave without a word. "It is painful to argue." Anne is taking a training; soon she will be gone. "I shall never love anyone again," says Eliza and she wastes no more time but learns, reads, scrapes pennies into shillings, shillings into pounds, makes her pilgrimages to sales, and becomes avid.

Though she has decided not to love anyone, when Eustace and later Jeremy Baxter die she is very much alone. She lives in the house, ostensibly with her brother and sister-in-law and her two young nephews, but in reality lives with nobody, except Polly, who still in a way understands. With the rest she is armed, shut as in a keep and, as the years go on, strange stories begin to be told about Miss Eliza Quin, "privately and publicly," says Jared with distaste.

Eliza, in the inevitable brown cloak and bonnet that from being a shabby economy have become an eccentricity, is known now in the West Country, and recognized and respected by the dealers. At first she does not understand. "I was bid right out," she comes back from sale after sale and tells Jeremy Baxter; then, slowly, through Tarrant's, she gets to know their "tricks" as she calls them, a childish word for the ring, but she tries to avoid the big sales and, setting out even earlier, goes farther and into even more out-of-the-way places.

It begins to be said in the village that she travels on a broomstick; no one is surprised because the village has long known she is a witch. Lights have been seen in the churchyard at night. Jim Neot saw her go into the steeple and a great white owl fly out. People have heard voices—" 'Tis a witch."

As usual the talk comes down from the village into China Court and filters to Polly. "Miss Eliza is a witch. She talks in the churchyard. The butcher boy said so."

"Talks? Who to?"

Polly catches the butcher boy and holds him. She is a good deal smaller than he is, but far fiercer. "Who does she talk to?"

"I den knaw."

"You tell me, or else," says Polly shaking him.

"I tell 'ee I den knaw."

"You tell me or I shall tell Mr. Theobald you dropped those sweetbreads off the pony into the dust. He will make you pay for them! Miss Eliza talks to who?"

"Daiders," says the butcher boy with a howl.

"Daiders? Dead people? You go inside, miss," says Polly turning on a housemaid who has stolen up to listen. "You go in and don't let me catch you hanging around here." She gives the butcher boy another shake. "You can't talk to dead people."

" 'Er does, ma'am. 'Er talks to th' daid."

"Who heard her?"

"Us 'ave all yurd 'er," and certainly the boy is tense with fear. "There's lights up to th' churchyard," he whispers, "and they says . . ."

"What do they say?"

"For 'er they baint daid. They gets up."

Polly watches and when, next time at dusk, Eliza puts on her outdoor things and quietly leaves the house, Polly follows her. She is still nimble, but the hill gives her a stitch—*and I used to push them up it in that great pram*—but she manages to keep near enough to Eliza to see what happens in the village street and, "My poor lamb!" says Polly, "My poor lamb!"

"You must listen to me. You must," says Polly to Lady Patrick. She knows Jared's wife is the only person who can stir him and, "You listen," says Polly fiercely. She stands over Lady Patrick, knotting and unknotting her old hands in her apron, the tears streaming down her cheeks that are still pink, though they are wrinkled. "To think that Eliza—our Eliza! All the way up the street they were staring at her, children running out to twitch her cloak, nip her and run away, daring each other as if she was Old Nick hisself," says Polly. "Some of them made as if they would throw stones. Oh it was daredevil, just the big boys, but soon they will throw them. She took no notice, she went straight on up as if they wasn't there, to the churchyard. It was pitch dark there and they dursen't come, though they play there enough in the daytime."

The churchyard at night is dark, high, and remote above the village, with a soughing from the elms and the moor wind whistling in the grasses and around the headstones. Mr. Preedy, long gone, has at that time no successor and for years the curate at Canverisk rides over to take a service on Sundays; the vicarage windows are nailed up, the churchyard wall of loose stones is nearly tumbled down, and there are nettles in the corners.

"I could just see the stones and the crosses," says Polly. "But eh! it was eerie. There was a stone angel I nearly bumped into, I thought it was something walking, and I don't like the churchyard smell. I know it's only earth and wet stones, but it seems—and then there *was* a light, like they says."

"Had they seen a light then?"

"Ask anyone," says Polly.

"But what light?"

"They says, like a will-o'-the-wisp, but it was her, striking matches. She had a lantern under her cloak. She didn't light it before she went through the village because I guess she thought she could slip through without notice. She lit it under her cloak, but it looked—eerie," says Polly again and shivers. "With the matches spluttering and dying it was fitful, might have been the will-o'-the-wisp, and then when it steadied I saw she was . . ." Polly's voice died too.

"Was . . . ?"

"Kneeling by a grave," whispers Polly. "She had set the lantern down, her cloak round it to hide it, and was undoing a little bundle. Oh! I don't know what I thought it was," says Polly, "but it was books."

"Books?" Lady Patrick is incredulous.

"Yes. She held them up one by one, so he could see," says Polly in a gasp of horror.

"Who could see?"

"Jeremy Baxter."

"Who is Jeremy Baxter?"

"Old Mr. Baxter, who worked for the master. Him who died. You know."

"How could I know?"

"He was clerk to the master. He died of the drink, and she was kneeling by his grave, and holding them for him, and showing them to him, as if he was alive!"

"Showing them to a grave?" says Lady Patrick.

"Yes," says Polly certainly. "Oh milady, it made my blood turn cold, but I crept up and hid behind one of the big headstones." And Polly breaks into fresh sobs. "Showing them to him in his grave, and all the way back those boys followed her. Do you wonder?"

"Perhaps Jared will interfere," says Lady Patrick.

"They say she has been peddling things to Jacob Hinty."

"Hinty. That old drunkard at the crossroads shop? Nonsense."

"They say she put the Eye on Mrs. Morren who had that idiot child."

"That was inbreeding," says Lady Patrick, who is not delicate.

"They say they have seen Kitty fly, tubcart and all."

"Oh, Polly! Don't be absurd."

"Absurd or not, when that starts it's like a bonfire. They will mob her and hurt her. What can I do?"

"I will tell Jared to talk to Eliza." Lady Patrick is bored.

"Jared can't talk to Eliza. It's like talking to a stone wall," says Polly and lazy Jared agrees.

"It's probably only old wives' tales," says Jared. "Liz has always been queer. Leave her alone and it will all die down," but Lady Patrick has lived in an Irish village and uneasiness stirs; she pushes it down. "It's nothing to do with me. They, none of them, are anything to do with me."

Four months later, early one morning, the men come down from the quarry to fetch Jared. A granite cutter who lives out on the moor has brought the news in. Kitty has been found placidly grazing, but with her reins tangled round her knees, the broken shafts behind her and, farther on by the bridge, is the tubcart, overturned and smashed against the granite bridge wall. Eliza is lying on the sward.

"If she was thrown on the grass, how did she get that bruise on her forehead?" It is a bruise with a gash on it, as if from a stone; Lady Patrick's words die away, and, "Kitty wouldn' bolt," say the men in the stables. " 'Er was a brave old mare, steady's a rock. Kitty wouldn' 'less somethin' 'ad frightened 'er."

A resentful silence hangs over the village and it is many years before there is any more friendliness between it and China Court. "And it was a scandal," says Jared still scalding. "Smashed whisky bottles all over the bridge. What was she *doing*?" cried Jared.

"Taking them to Jacob Hinty. Your whisky." Lady Patrick is amused, but to Jared this is a further humiliation, a final endorsement of inferiority.

They are advised to bury Eliza at Canverisk, or better still, in Bodmin, "where no one knows."

"Everyone knows," says Jared. "The whole county. Well, let them know," and a stiffness comes in him, something of the backbone of Eustace and Great-uncle Mcleod. "She was my sister, my mother and father's daughter, she will be buried where she belongs in the family grave," and, as when she was small, the family protects her. No one scrawls rude words about Eliza on the polished granite; a few people even put flowers on the grave and, after a while, the children come back to play in the churchyard.

Then Jared discovers the bills, his bills and Eliza's; there is such a difference between the totals that even

Jared cannot help seeing it. Shops send in demands, "shops I had paid," and Jacob Hinty comes drunk one day, roaring for his whisky. "It must have been hundreds of pounds," says Jared, "but what did she do with it?"

There seems no answer to that.

He and Polly search the White Room and find not as much as five pounds. Eliza's purse has been flung far into the heather where it moulders and turns back to earth; it is the only money she has ever wasted.

Jared finds the key of the brass-bound case, unlocks it, and flips through the notebooks "but only more petty figures, more cheating," he says. He bestows no more than a glance on the list of books. "There isn't a trace," says Jared. He cannot get over the whole strange affair. "Showing books to Jeremy Baxter. She was mad."

"She wasn't mad," says Lady Patrick. "She was lonely."

Homes must know a certain loneliness because all humans are lonely, shut away from one another, even in the act of talking, of loving. Adza cannot follow Eustace in his business deals and preoccupations as she cannot follow Mcleod the Second or Anne or Jared—no one can follow Eliza. Mr. King Lee, kissing Damaris, has no inkling of the desolation he has brought her, just as Groundsel only half guesses Minna's; Jared hides himself from Lady Patrick, and John Henry and Ripsie, in their long years together, are always separated by Borowis. The children especially are secret; Adza, Lady Patrick, Mrs. Quin have to learn, each in her turn, that it is no use asking where they have been, though they come back from their adventures, their brows thick with what has happened to them. It is better not to ask questions. "It's like sticking pins into me," protests Eliza dramatically to Adza, while Borowis parries Lady Patrick's wistful probings with the skill of an accustomed diplomat and, "Even if they told you," says Mrs. Quin, "you would never really know."

Loneliness can be good. Mrs. Quin learns that in the long companionship of the years after Tracy goes, when she and Cecily are alone in the house; companionship of rooms and stairs, of windows and colors; in the gentle ticking away of the hours, the swinging pendulum of the grandfather clock. "I was happy," Mrs. Quin could have said. Contented loneliness is rich because it takes the imprint of each thing it sees and hears and tastes. "There's time if one is alone," says Mrs. Quin. She is, of course, conditioned to it, Ripsie is the most solitary of children, but there is another kind of loneliness that sears and, "Poor silly tragic exaggerated Lady Patrick," says Mrs. Quin.

Bursts of laughter sometimes come through the baize door at the end of the passage, bursts instantly hushed; they cannot quite be hushed because the kitchen wing teems with a heady life of talk, gossips, quarrels, laughter. On the house side of the door is silence.

No one is comfortable then in China Court. It is quiet; few guests come in those middle years and the boys have their own haunts; the nursery has become the schoolroom and they have their lessons there, or else they are away in their hide-holes in the garden or the valley. Jared sleeps alone in the dressing room next to the shut big bedroom, Lady Patrick in the Porch Room. He sits in the morning room where Adza and the girls used to sit. The drawing room they keep for state occasions is Lady Patrick's natural habitat; its space does not daunt her; she fills it with flowers, and her embroidery frame is by one of the fireplaces in winter, in the garden window in summer. When she is not hunting or riding she sits there all day, and every evening she waits there for the clock to chime ten and another day be done.

At the beginning Jared besieges her. "Sweetheart. Pat. Sweetheart."

"My heart is not sweet," says this new stony-eyed young Lady Patrick. It is not sweet; it is like the heart in those statues of Christ in the convent, a heart pierced and bleeding, "only His is so great it consents to go on bleeding, mine is dried up," says Lady Patrick.

Harry St. Omer, red and embarrassed, comes to speak for Jared. "Men do things like that," he says miserably. "You must forgive him, Pat."

"It isn't Jared I can't forgive. It's myself." Harry has not imagined she could be as haughty. "My father was right," says Lady Patrick. "Clonferts shouldn't marry persons like this." She speaks with infinite disdain. "I don't know how I could have so forgotten myself. There is no more to say."

There is no more. The house is full of whispers, the whole county gossips, but Lady Patrick says not a word. "She has her pride, that one," says Polly. Polly, privileged, tries to talk to her; Mr. Fitzgibbon's honest old eyes look anguished, but Lady Patrick lets the pride make a shell that fits more and more closely around her.

Harry St. Omer attacks her. "It was your fault for going away. Jared missed you."

"I was away two days."

"And another thing," says Harry. "Jared was always— well, er—he liked them a bit low," says Harry. "He adores you, Pat, but sometimes—I mean nice women are—well, perhaps—you might be, er—too nice a woman, too delicate for him."

She bends her head over her embroidery because a blush that she cannot stop is burning her body, from her thighs up to her forehead; she longs to cry out, "I'm not a nice woman. If ever a man should have been satisfied, it was Jared. I was mad about him. I threw myself at his head. I behaved—that bed with the brass lover's knots was my world, no it was my heaven. That's why I came stealing back. . . ."

There is an owl then in the China Court garden at night. It sits on the flagpole giving its melancholy cry, high above the house and the elms, the glimmering slope of the hill. It sounds lost and lonely out there in the night and moonlight makes it cry more. Now when there is moonlight, Lady Patrick tells Pringle to draw the curtains.

"They are drawn, milady."

"Then shut the windows," but she can feel the moonlight through the closed glass and velvet. "It was moonlight when I came back, cruel white moonlight, showing everything so that it was clear, beyond a doubt. Oh, why did I come back?" She asks that question again and again.

The paradox is that Jared does not wish her to go. "Why do you want to?" he asks.

"I don't want to," she says, "but, all my life, every year, since I was a little girl at school—"

"So many years!" teases Jared.

"Every year, I have made my retreat."

"Retreat from what?" He is still teasing.

"Too much world," says Lady Patrick slowly.

"But what do you do?"

"Listen. Think. Pray. Get clean."

"Are you so dirty, my little love?"

"Yes," says Lady Patrick. She is thinking of a conversation she has with Father Blackwell last time she sees him. "You can spare four days," says the Father.

"For the God who made me?" she says flippantly.

"Yes," says Father Blackwell, not flippant.

"He made Jared too. He shouldn't have made him so well if He didn't want me to love him." She tilts her chin at the priest. "Now go on, Father. Tell me I love him too much," but Father Blackwell can surprise her.

"Too much and too little," says Father Blackwell.

"Too *little?*"

"I should like to see you love Jared enough to hurt him when it's necessary," says Father Blackwell, "and"— he pauses—"to let him hurt you."

She says certainly, confidently, "Jared would never hurt me."

Jared himself decides her going. "Let the old father boil his head," says Jared disrespectfully. "You don't need him. I'm your religion now."

"Ssh!" She puts her hand over his mouth, but it is true. She has no religion now but Jared, and, on her second night, she comes back, stealing in—"Like a little vixen in season," she says, catching her lip in her teeth each time she remembers—but it is not only that; she is homesick.

The convent gives her a feeling of chill. It is not austere. Dozemary Abbey is adequately furnished in every way, but it is plain almost to bareness and Lady Patrick feels there like an overfeathered bird. She takes off her jewelry and gives it to Hester's successor to keep for her—even to a convent Lady Patrick does not go without a maid—but she still feels overdressed. The plain neat bedroom, the refectory table severely laid and served, the recreation room with its one round table and chairs against the walls, the women making their retreat with her, the silence, all depress her. "You don't want to be thinking of friends and furnishings here," says the Guest

Mistress, but Lady Patrick longs for talk and laughter, for China Court's rooms of color and softness, flowers, firelight. The silence seems to her only an empty one; she does not want to think serious thoughts, or any thoughts at all; she wants to live, to be. There is the emphasis on pain, poverty, struggle, and death; the bleeding heart; the cross; they seem to her, who has accepted them all her life, morbid now. She is seeing with Jared's eyes: the cross, forgetting the figure on it, the heart's wound and not that it lives. "I don't want to see," cries Lady Patrick, "see or hear." She only wants to bury her head on Jared's shoulder and shut out the whole world.

"Jared! Jared!" and that night she comes, almost running up the drive, leaving the disgruntled groom at the stables. "Fetched from Dozemary village at nearly ten o'clock at night, made to saddle two drowsy horses, ride nine damned eerie miles across the moor at night!" He grumbles under his breath all the way. The maid is left behind to be fetched in the morning; the Mother Superior is icily disappointed, the Guest Mistress nearly in tears, all the nuns shocked and hurt. "I don't care," says Lady Patrick now. "I'm at home."

She has not thought of how she can get in; she does not want to ring the bell, send it pealing through the house to startle everyone; she wants to surprise, to come like a thief upstairs, shed her clothes and slip into the warm bed beside Jared, though he may be sleeping in the dressing room of course. She walks around the house, leaving footprints in the heavy dew, trying the garden door, the back door, while the moonlight watches. The dogs bay in the kennel, but they always bay when there is a moon.

One window is open a crack, a slit of a window below

the pantry. "So that's how they close the house." She does not know that the knife-boy sleeps here in what was built as a cupboard. The open window is against all his mother taught him, but the cupboard is so small and airless that he would stifle if it did not leave a crack.

A crack is enough for Lady Patrick. She pushes the window up. She is slim and agile, and, even in the heavy skirts of her habit, can swing herself up on the sill. She turns on it, brings her legs through and, feeling with a cautious toe in the darkness, finds the knife-boy in his truckle bed. They scream together, her scream stifled, his loud, and, "Ssh!" says Lady Patrick peremptorily, tumbling on the bed. "Ssh! Don't move. Stay where you are. It's her ladyship."

"Her ladyship!" Not really awake, confused with fright, astonishment, and a certain amount of pain, for she has tumbled straight on top of him, he does stay where he is and in a moment cannot believe what he has felt and seen and heard, for Lady Patrick's eyes have lost the first shock of gloom and she has found the door and vanished.

The knife-boy stays, propped up on one elbow look-ing at the door where it has closed. He looks, his mouth open, then he rubs his sticky nose on his hand and goes back to sleep.

The stale smell of him, though, stays on Lady Patrick as she sits down on a hall chair to shed her riding boots. It is a struggle—she is not used to taking them off her-self; a maid usually bends over, her back to her mistress, the foot with the boot between her legs, and Lady Patrick puts her other foot on the print-skirted rump, pushes, when the maid is propelled in a run across the room and the boot comes off. Now Lady Patrick thinks she will have to wake the knife-boy again to help her, but at last she gets the boots off and, in Lady Patrick's fashion, leaves them lying on the hall floor. She goes up the stairs in her stockinged feet, her skirt trailing on the steps; her cheeks are hot after her struggle with the boots, and her heart is so eager that she cannot get her breath and she has to pause and lean against the banisters at the top of the stairs.

"Jared. Jared," she will whisper, and he, half waking, will open his eyes, confused, unable to believe. "What? Where?" and then, as through sleep he understands, in happiness like her own, his arms will reach out for her, gather her in. "Sweetheart. Little Pat. Sweetheart."

Outside the dressing-room door she stops and listens, then very carefully turns the handle. He is not there. The single bed is smooth; his clothes are on the chair. Quickly she tosses her hat on the bed and undresses, letting her clothes fall round her on the floor, pulling the pins out of her hair impatiently, feeling its weight drop against her skin. She takes Jared's comb and runs it through the long strands until they are silky. Then, her hair in a cloak round her, her eyes bright with mischief, very quietly she opens the bedroom door—and the owl seems to be calling in her ear, the moonlight is ice cold.

It floods the room so that there can be no illusion, no mistake: Jared is asleep in the wide bed and beside him, in her space, is a mound under the bedclothes; on her should-be-empty pillow lies a black head, asleep too and turned where she had wanted to hide from all pain, on Jared's shoulder.

"And they were married and lived happily ever after." That is the ending in fairy tales, Perrault, the Orange, Green, or Violet Fairy Books, and the children believe it.

Weddings and Fathers and Mothers are the two favorite games. "What do you want to be when you are grown up?" people ask John Henry and he always answers, "A father."

"Don't be stupid. A man must be a soldier, or a sailor, or an engineer."

"I'm going to be a father," says John Henry.

Adza, when the Brood are all small, meets Anne, dressed in a white sheet trailing down the stairs. "What are you doing?"

"Hush, I'm the angel, bringing the baby."

"The doctor," says the ruthless sense of Eliza. Stace, Bella, and the Graces are brought up to echo that, but Tracy goes back—or further on perhaps. "In a way it is the doctor *and* the angel," says Tracy.

As a child she has a secret game that she plays, a game called Children; in it she has three, Big Boy, Big Girl, and Little A. Sometimes she adds the Chelsea shepherd and shepherdess on the drawing-room chimney shelf: the Little Pink Boy and the Pale Blue Girl. They are all her children and they are not left to be blown about by any wind; they are kept safe and, "firm," says Tracy. That is the nearest she can put it. "Is it a firm promise?" says her grandmother, which means it will not be broken.

"Where are your mother and father?" The real children who come to tea with Tracy at China Court usually ask her that. "Where are they?"

"Gone," says Tracy evasively.

"Gone where?"

"Well, I think Mother is changing over," says Tracy.

"Changing over?"

"Oh, grown-ups marry," says Tracy. "Then they get

tired of each other and they all change over." She is not as airy as she sounds. Often, when she first arrives at China Court, she cries in the night.

Alice, the little nursemaid, tries to get up and comfort her. Alice sits on the edge of the bed, her bare feet on the floor and the moonlight falls through the night-nursery window in a shaft of light that seems to cut her in half; her feet and white nightgown shine on the floor rug, but above she is all in shadow, only her eyes gleam at Tracy.

It is cold and Alice's green eiderdown is warm; the pillow is still impressed with her sleep; sleep weighs down her eyelids, fills her mouth and makes her yawn. No words will come to help Tracy's crying. Alice hears, but her sleep is heavy. She heaves herself off her bed and blunders into the day nursery and goes to the biscuit tin on the red dresser and takes out a biscuit, comes back, and thrusts it into Tracy's hand. "Eat that," she says and falls back into bed. Tracy sits crying with the biscuit in her hand, the cold creeps around her, but Alice is asleep.

A light falls through the door and Mrs. Quin comes in, her Paisley shawl around her shoulders, her hair in an unfamiliar gray plait down her back. She removes the biscuit from Tracy, takes her hand and helps her out of bed, then under the shawl walks her down the passage to her own room with its big bed.

She says nothing, asks no questions, but as Tracy lies against her, the sobs cease to be real and soon she lies abandoned to the warm bed, her arms cast out, her mouth heavy and contented; but Mrs. Quin lies awake, staring into the dark. Why couldn't they, Barbara and Stace, think of the child? Like a little fly Tracy is brushed out of the way, blindly. Is it a wonder if she is maimed?

"At least, Stace, I thought about you," cries Mrs. Quin in the night. "I thought about you." Nobody knew about Stace, least of all Stace himself. Nobody at all. "I didn't harm you. Miraculously I was able to avoid that. If I hadn't held my tongue you might have been hurt; there could have been an uproar, but I told no one. No one!" but once again, as she says that, she feels as if John Henry smiles.

"You little ostrich," John Henry would have said, only he never speaks of it. "There were always the three of us in everything, Boro and me and you. That was why I did what I had to do at the dance."

There has never been another at China Court. The dances for Stace, Bella, and her sisters are shared in London with friends. "Never another here," says Mrs. Quin and John Henry does not press it.

It is the height of China Court's entertaining. Adza and Eliza would not have believed it; there are house parties for it over half Cornwall, even a small one at China Court itself. The dinner, though, is held at Tremellen—China Court cannot rise to a dinner and dance at once—as it is, most of the furniture of the downstairs rooms has to be taken out and stored, "over to Bodmin," says the village. The whole house becomes unfamiliar: A marquee is built along the terrace; the french doors of the dining room, and the wide door from the hall to the drawing room, are taken off their hinges; a platform for the band is built below the stairs—it has a gilded railing, palms, and hydrangeas. More hydrangeas and marguerites—"from the newfangled glass-house nurseries over to St. Austell," the village reports—are set in tubs along the marquee with marguerites, cornflowers, and ferns in vases on the long tables, which have silver candelabra lent from Tremellen. "Are candles safe under canvas?" asks cautious John Henry, but it is uncommonly warm and windless weather, which holds for the dance.

A chef and waiters take over the kitchen; Cook and the kitchenmaids and Paget do not know whether they are on their heads or their heels. The housemaids are on all-night duty upstairs in the big bedroom, which has been opened for the occasion and turned into a ladies' cloakroom. There is a tent behind the marquee for the men's cloakroom; the morning room is a card room, the dining room a champagne buffet for the gentlemen. Even the garden is changed with sitting-out places, each with two gilt chairs and a palm, while fairy lamps are strung in the trees and along the paths and among the roses. "Fairy lamps! Roses! It sounds like *Maud*," says Bella.

"It was all a little like *Maud*," says Mrs. Quin calmly, "but then I think *Maud* is romantic and exciting," and painful she could have said. "And you must remember," she says aloud, "dances were far more of occasions then than they are now."

Bella and the girls laugh gently at those occasions as quaint; the chaperons, the music—"either treacly waltzes or polkas, jig jig jig jig"—and at the programs; they would call sentimental the heartbreak those programs could cause, "and of which no girl would ever give an inkling, because the hallmark of those days was politeness," says Mrs. Quin.

"A false politeness," says Bella.

"At least it was tidy," retorts Mrs. Quin. It is an odd word to use, but people and things, then, kept their faces—"and I kept mine," says Mrs. Quin, but she does not say it aloud. Nor does she tell Bella that the sight of the peculiar kind of silver lettering used on those programs, or a pale-pink pencil with a fluff of tassel, or a long glove in white kid, even the smell of those gloves, even those little bedizens of fairy lamps, can make her flinch yet.

The village gathers at the top of the hill to watch the carriages come down, and the big field at the bottom is borrowed from Penbarrow and strewn with cinders for the carriages to turn around and wait, with another small marquee with refreshments for the coachmen and footmen. From midnight until dawn, carriage lamps shine along the village street, taking people home.

Tremellen is lent for the dinner, but the St. Omers, Lady St. Omer and Harry, do not come down for it from London. "Odd," says the county, "when it is almost their dance," but St. Probus knows it is not at all odd. Outrageous though it is, Ripsie, Deborah Russell, has been invited. Why? The whole village is agog to know, but Lady Patrick says nothing about it. Since the day of Ripsie's call, on the matter of Ripsie she is silent.

Lady Patrick, in these years, has grown wise. In 1897 Jared dies of a heart attack. "What a strange thing for him to die of," says Lady Patrick icily, but when she sees him in his coffin, she has such an attack of weeping that even Borowis, called down from Sandhurst, cannot calm her. After that a spring seems to fail in Lady Patrick. She is no longer the mixture that alarmed Father Blackwell, but though the impetuosity is gone, she is still proud. John Henry knows that very well and, "What is Mother up to?" he asks uneasily.

Ripsie herself is surprised at the invitation—then not surprised. "It's because Boro and I . . . ." She does not go on but John Henry knows what she is thinking.

"Wake up, Rip," he says and warns her, "They were not very kind to you when you called. You may be ostracized."

"I don't care if I am," says Ripsie. "I have Boro."

"You know you can't count on Boro," but she flares up.

"You have always been jealous of Borowis. Ever since I have known you," and John Henry says no more.

Lady Patrick even manages to hold Isabel in check, which is not easy.

"Boro has done his best, consistently, from the very beginning, to spoil this dance," cries Isabel.

Her dress arrives from London, a Paquin dress of net over embroidered satin, its frills threaded with waved ribbon in palest pink-gold, a shade deeper than the net's pink-ivory.

"Exquisite," says Lady Patrick.

"And it will go with Boro's mess dress *perfectly*," says Isabel. It has been designed for that, but, "It won't, because I shall be wearing tails," says Borowis.

"Tails!"

"Yes."

"But—the Eleventh have the best mess dress of all," wails Isabel. She is almost in tears. The cherry-colored overalls, the dark-blue-and-gold jacket have been in her eye for weeks. "You must wear it. I want you to," she cries.

"Hush, Isa," says Lady Patrick and, "I have never seen you in mess dress, Boro," she says pleadingly.

"My dear Mother, you don't wear mess dress to a small country dance."

"This isn't small," says Isabel hotly.

"I can wear blues if you like," says Borowis.

"Blues! When everyone else will be in tails."

"Then I shall wear tails too," says Borowis.

Lady Patrick does not pursue this as she pursues "nothing," says John Henry puzzled. Borowis appears to be free to go his own way, yet, as the night of the dance draws near, he grows more and more quiet. Even Ripsie, enraptured, has to notice his silence. "Don't you *want* the dance?" she asks amazed.

"Dances are three a penny in the season," he says, but they are not three a penny to Ripsie. He can see that by one look at her face and he makes a sound that is very like a groan.

Ripsie is not, of course, at the dinner. Even in this new acceptance that so puzzles John Henry, it has not been suggested that Ripsie can be asked to Tremellen, and he calls for her on his way from the dinner to the dance. "I guessed it would be me," he says.

"You? Not Boro?" He knows that will be his welcome as, with a sinking reluctance, he drives the dogcart, the only available carriage, over the moor roads. The reluctance is not only jealousy—*though I suppose I am jealous*, thinks John Henry—Ripsie has been invited, and strangely nobody has opposed this, but he knows quite well that he is taking a lamb to the slaughter and he is extraordinarily bad-tempered when he gets to the farm.

She is waiting in the kitchen. "Why?" snaps John Henry.

"Because I was cold."

Cold with excitement, not apprehension, as she should be, he thinks. In the dingy kitchen her dress looks unbelievably pretty and fresh, her bare shoulders and arms gleamingly exposed and, "I'm not going to drive you through the village like that," says John Henry.

"Is it too low, Jod?" she whispers coming nearer. "In the shop it didn't look as bare as this."

"It did." John Henry does not tell her what that first sight of her bare shoulders and arms in the shop set up in him, such a tingling in his fingers—*and thighs*, thinks John Henry shocked—that, all the way home from Exeter, he has to be surly and bury himself in his newspaper. *We were alone in the railway carriage, but I might have been a seat cushion*, thinks John Henry. Nor does he ever tell her what it feels like to have her brought to him in the showroom in all those different dresses, as if she were his own. "They thought I was going to be *your* wife," says Ripsie amused.

"Naturally as I was paying," says John Henry disagreeably.

It is odd that, while it is Borowis she loves, it is to John Henry that Ripsie is able to go to about her dress. "I haven't one, Jod. Nothing that will do. You see I have never been to a dance."

"And you want to come to this?"

"Want."

John Henry knows her face when its thinness seems to grow even thinner with longing, her eyes translucent with what she sees, "or she thinks she sees," says John Henry and weakly he plays truant from Mr. Fitzgibbon and takes her to Exeter and buys her a dress.

As a matter of fact it is not he who buys it; it is Lady Patrick, though Ripsie does not dream of that. "John Henry," his mother has said, "has that girl anything presentable to wear?"

"Ripsie?"

"Who else?" Lady Patrick is impatient.

"I haven't the faintest idea," he says coldly. "See to it," says Lady Patrick, "even if you have to buy her one," and she gives him the money—John Henry has not then bullied her and Mr. Fitzgibbon into giving him a proper salary. "See it's possible," orders Lady Patrick and, *What is Mother up to?* thinks John Henry.

Lady Patrick's idea of the cost of clothes is governed by the couturiers she knows in Paris and London; there is nothing to come near that in Exeter and John Henry worries about the dress.

"It's too cheap."

"Cheap! It was wickedly expensive," says Ripsie.

"Isabel's cost eighty guineas," he says. "And then the real world did come crashing in on me," says Mrs. Quin afterward. "I had a moment of reality." "Eighty guineas! That's twice as much as I earn in a year," says Ripsie in a small humble voice, but when John Henry is worried he can be insensitive. "Too cheap and too pretty," he says. "Can a dress be too pretty?" She has to learn that it can; meanwhile he goes gloomily on. "It's not expensive enough and it should have been white." The dress is in pale green *mousseline de soie* caught with apple blossom, that matches a spray to wear in the puffs of her dark hair. Now in the lamplight the foam of green is so becoming that John Henry has to look away and he sees that the farmer's wife has her lips set thin, while her husband and sons are greedily staring. "Put on your cloak, Rip," says John Henry.

She has no evening cloak. John Henry is beginning to fathom the scantiness of Ripsie's possessions, and the dreaded tenderness, the instant protection sweeps over him again. "Your dress isn't too low," he says, speaking slowly and distinctly for the farmer's wife. "Not for a dance. You should see Isabel and Margaret," and, "Put on my cloak," he says.

It is his first, sumptuously lined with white watered silk.

"I didn't know you had this, Jod."

She is impressed, as he had meant her to be, which is why he is wearing it on this warm night, but now, "God knows why I bought it," he says. "I suppose because Boro had one. I shall hardly ever wear it."

It suits Ripsie far better than it does him. "I look like a cabby," he says when he first puts it on, while she looks like a young cadet. "But they will say I arrived in a man's cloak."

"Do you mind?"

"I expect I shall make every possible gaffe," she says, but she takes his arm and squeezes it. "Jod, don't let's be late," and he can feel her shivering with anticipation.

When Ripsie comes downstairs from the big bedroom, it is the first time at China Court she has ever used the front stairs—she makes John Henry take her up the back way to avoid anyone's seeing her in his cloak—and she cannot help pausing to take in the wonder. *But they will say I'm afraid to come down*, she thinks, and makes herself go down the flight and cross the hall where she has to pass the formidable barrier of Lady Patrick, Mrs. Loftus Kennedy, and Isabel, who are receiving with John Henry at the drawing-room door. "Miss Russell." The Tremellen butler, lent for the evening, has a penetrating voice—"Well, it was meant to be penetrating," says John Henry—"Miss Russell." Suddenly she feels alone and conspicuous; no other girl, she is sure, has come without a chaperon; she sees several heads turn and unmistakably look as, her own head high but her cheeks as pink as her apple blossom, she goes forward.

I have an invitation, she is telling herself, *they will* have *to recognize me*, but she will get, she is sure, no more than the slightest inclination of the head from Lady Patrick, perhaps the tips of two fingers from Mrs. Loftus Kennedy, a stare up and down from Isabel and she braces herself but, "Ah, Ripsie! Good evening," and Lady Patrick holds out her black-gloved hand. "I'm glad to see John Henry brought you safely," says Mrs. Loftus Kennedy in those ringing tones that can be heard in every corner of the room. "What a pretty dress!" says Isabel, and suddenly, piercingly, Ripsie is afraid.

John Henry is next and he catches her hands, holding them and beaming with relief. *Then does he think everything is to be all right?* she thinks, in wonder. "Jod, what are they doing?" she wants to cry, but she cannot even ask him in a whisper—a man and girl are close behind her—she has to pass on into the transformed and beflowered drawing room.

The girls are gathered all together near the window at the far end, the rhododendron window; cocksure girls, all, Ripsie is certain, possessing evening cloaks, all impeccably chaperoned. They are talking, laughing, careful not to give the least glance to where the men are standing around the Winterhalter fireplace and the garden window. Then as Ripsie stands uncertainly there, as if at a given signal, the men pull down their waistcoats, finger their ties—those not in mess dress—and go skimming across the room to the girls. Once again Ripsie is conspicuously alone; the man and girl who were behind her pass her and join the others, and she catches her breath, then Margaret, in pale-blue satin, forget-me-nots in her hair, is beside her, a Margaret as transformed as the drawing room, and smiling. "Hello, Ripsie, Isa asked me to watch for you. Look, here's a program." She puts the pink-and-silver card with its tiny pencil into Ripsie's hand. "Come along," and Ripsie, bewilderingly, is shepherded in among the girls. "Ursula, this is Deborah Russell, Isa's little friend from the country. She doesn't know anyone. Be nice to her, girls.

Ripsie, this is Terence. Terence, this is Miss Russell. Yes, she wants lots of dances. Introduce her to Jimmy. Iris, this is Isa's little friend."

What's happening? thinks Ripsie in fresh panic. She is introduced, handed round. Young men appear in front of her; are led up by other girls. "Deborah Russell." Her program collects scribble after scribble. It is filling up and she is helpless until suddenly she sees Borowis standing by John Henry in the doorway, and, like a fish escaping from a net, she flies across the room to him. "Boro! Boro!"

Borowis is in mess dress. "Well, half the regiment is here," he defends himself from John Henry's comments. "Practically the whole mess from Bodmin." Then he gives up the pretense of that. "What does it matter?" he says.

Isabel is right; the cherry-colored overalls, the waistcoat and dark-blue gold-braided jacket are almost theatrical in their effect. They make Borowis look tall, tall but not heavy, for he is very slim; no one has noticed yet that John Henry's shoulders are broader, but then he does not take the eye as Borowis does. "Boro looks a young prince," Mrs. Loftus Kennedy has said and she is not given to gushing; Isabel is pleased and proud, but Ripsie does not care what he is wearing, she only sees Borowis himself. "Boro!" yet as soon as she touches him, she knows he is a stranger—*and strange,* thinks Ripsie, more than ever terrified.

His hair is not combed, one lock is falling over his eye, the tight neck of his jacket, with its frogging, is undone; he has a redness, like painted patches over his cheekbones, while his eyes seem to glitter. *Has he been drinking?* wonders Ripsie.

"Boro, you are going to ask me to dance."

"No."

"No?" She cannot believe it. As if there were nobody else in the room, she puts both hands on his arm and shakes him. "Boro, it's Ripsie. Look at me," but he will not look, he whose look has been only for her, and private and unmistakable. Now he looks over her head.

Then the music begins. It is the silly catching tune from *Floradora*: "If you're in love with somebody, Happy and lucky somebody . . ."

It filters in from the band in the hall, slowly filling every corner. As this is for their joint birthdays, Isabel and John Henry are to open the dance and he has to leave Borowis and Ripsie and go to Isabel. In a moment the first couples begin circling down the long room and past them into the hall. A red-haired young man in tails, his large hands in white kid gloves, appears before Ripsie. "Miss Russell . . ."

She ignores him.

"Boro."

"Rip, you are to dance." It is an order, given as he would order her in the old valley days. "Dance, and for God's sake, don't come near me." Abruptly, he walks away.

She would have run after him, leaving the red-haired young man, but Borowis does what is wise if he wants to be impregnable, goes to his mother and bows. Lady Patrick looks at him, and Ripsie sees the sudden look of dismay on her face. It is gone as soon as Ripsie sees it; almost in a caress Lady Patrick smooths back the lock of hair, fastens his jacket; he puts his arm around her and, holding her—as a shield? asks Ripsie, quivering with the hurt—takes her onto the floor, as the red-haired young man takes Ripsie, and Borowis does not dance again all night—"until," says Mrs. Quin long afterward, "until . . ."

"One of the most successful and brilliant dances ever given in the county," the fashion magazines and papers report and, "Enjoying it, Ripsie?" asks Isabel. No one but Isabel and Ripsie herself could suspect the barb in that. The strange solicitude goes on. "Miss Russell, are they looking after you?" "Ripsie, have you any dances left? Geoffrey Mafor is dying to be introduced to you." "Abominably clever of you," says Mrs. Loftus Kennedy, "with your white skin to find that color green." "So that is the little Russell girl," Ripsie hears more than one chaperon say, "the mysterious little Russell," and she hears Lady Patrick's smooth answer. "Yes. *We* have known her since she was a child, of course."

One dowager is more direct. "Yes, I have heard she and Borowis were friends."

"Of course they are friends." Lady Patrick's voice is unruffled, "I told you, the boys have known her since they were children."

"It was the first time," says Mrs. Quin, "that I felt the force of a family, banded together. They made me into a pawn. As a pawn I was quite a success," she says.

When she dances she is so light that in the Lancers she is swung too high and Mrs. Loftus Kennedy has to protest, though laughingly but, "She wasn't really laughing," says Ripsie. To waltz with her, say the young men, is like waltzing with a feather. Girls sitting out, taking refuge in the cloakroom, would have changed with her a dozen times over, "though I'm not hallmarked as they are," she says. There is a photograph of her afterward in the *Sketch*: "Miss Deborah Russell dancing with the Hon. Tommy Lampson," and,

"Tommy Lampson, Captain Helford, Bunny Porches-
ter, John Philips: I danced with dozens of them," says
Ripsie, wearily.

The dances she longed to dance are there:
"Polka Botschaft"
"Waltz Breezes" from Vienna
"Lancers," from *Floradora*
"Barn Dance," *Dusky Dinah*
"Waltz," from *San Toy*
"Galop," *Tivoli Bazaar.*

Tinkly sentimental dances. "Bella is right," says Mrs.
Quin and all the while the hurt and bewilderment gather
in Ripsie's eyes, for Borowis does not come near her.
He only looks whiter and whiter, except for that strange
red on his cheeks. "He didn't just do it." Mrs. Quin
holds that to herself over and over again. "He minded,
cruelly."

He does not dance again, though several times he sits
out a dance with Isabel. For the rest of the time he is at
the buffet—"Boro, you are drinking too much," says
John Henry again and again—or else he stands against
the wall watching the room with that glitter in his eyes,
the lock of hair falling over his eye again and the red
flushes that make him look like a wooden soldier.

Ripsie longs to get away, to be by herself, but she
cannot go back to the farm unless she walks through the
village street and suddenly she shrinks from the village;
besides, in satin shoes she cannot walk over the moor
and she cannot take John Henry who, because of Borowis's behavior, has to act as China Court's host. He is
not only the host, he is a host of strength, genial and
popular and it is then, for the first time, that Ripsie sees
John Henry as himself; John Henry Quin, not Jod, an
appendage to Borowis.

John Henry takes her in to supper and they say not a word until he removes her third glass of champagne and then gives it back to her. "Drink it," he says briefly. After it, the long marquee, the candles, marguerites, and cornflowers on the long tables, the hydrangeas in their tubs, the crowd of people all seem to melt a little and swim in a haze; the smell of scent, French chalk, hot canvas, wilting ferns, and salmon mayonnaise grows overpowering, and Ripsie feels frighteningly giddy.

She cannot go upstairs; she feels the maids there would be agog over her and Borowis. She cannot disappear in the garden as she used to do in her old camouflage clothes, the pale-green dress is too conspicuous; when she tries to hide in one of the far sitting-out places, Tommy Lampson follows her there and tries to kiss her. "He seemed to think he might," she tells John Henry, who rescues her. "I suppose it is my reputation. My reputation that your mother and all of you are trying to save me from," she might have said. "Oh, not for my sake, I know that very well." It is for the family and she does not care a farthing for the family then. "Why did I let them? Perhaps I was stunned," says Mrs. Quin, but she knows the answer to that, and it is like a cry. "I let you because Borowis, my Boro, consented."

The night drags on, down to the last dance before the extras, and John Henry comes to Ripsie where she is dancing. "Let me dance with Miss Russell, that's a good chap," he says to her partner and when she is relinquished, he says, "Boro is going to make an announcement."

"No," whispers Ripsie, "no," and very gently John Henry answers, "Yes."

It is an inexorable "Yes." Borowis is on the stairs. He has, John Henry tells Ripsie, been very sick and he looks pallid now and miserably young, years younger than John Henry. He stands a step below Isabel and though Isabel is flushed, her eyes are their usual cold gray, and hard as they were when she was a little girl. She lifts her hand commandingly and the band comes to a stop. "Tell them, Boro," says Isabel clearly and Borowis is obedient.

"Sorry to interrupt and all that," he says. His voice is hoarse and a little blurred, but it is mercilessly clear to Ripsie. She is below, at the foot of the steps, where John Henry has brought her. She wishes he would not stand so near her; she cannot bear anyone, not even John Henry. "We, Isabel, John Henry, and I," says Borowis, "want to thank you all for coming." *Putting it off*, thinks John Henry, wise in the ways of his brother, but Borowis has to go on. "As you know," he begins, "this dance is nothing to do with me, it isn't my birthday," when Isabel steps down one step farther so that she is close behind him. "Isabel and I have something to tell you," says Borowis, as swiftly as if she had pricked him, and Ripsie gives a little gasp as the words sound through the hall. " 'Smatter of fact," says Borowis, "we are engaged," and John Henry catches Ripsie's hand and holds it down against his side, crushing it so that the gasp is cut short as she sways and leans against him, faint with the pain. "I hope you are all pleased." It sounds like a taunt and Borowis's gaze sweeps over them, brilliantly deliberately blind. "Isabel and I are engaged." The band breaks out into "They are jolly good fellows," everyone claps, but there is no morsel of sound from Ripsie; only the hand, crushed in John Henry's, grows cold and colder and her head, with the puffs of dark hair and the apple-blossom sprays, sinks.

John Henry can bear no more. His soft heart seems suddenly to swell and almost before he knows what he is doing, he has stepped forward to the stairs taking Ripsie with him. He holds up his hand against the clapping and the band, which stops again. "And I have something to tell you," cries John Henry more loudly and clearly than he has ever spoken in his life. "I have never let my brother beat me yet." There is laughter and clapping. By now in the county, John Henry is a beloved buffoon, but he is serious now and a silence falls. "*I am engaged*," says John Henry. "*We* are engaged. I and Miss Russell."

The laughing and congratulations are all around them, a glow of real approval, and the music starts again. Borowis is still on the stairs with Isabel, Ripsie at the bottom with John Henry, when over the heads of the others, they look at one another. "I expect we were very theatrical," says Mrs. Quin, but still cannot help her voice trembling.

Slowly, as if in a dream, Borowis comes down the stairs and, as if John Henry were a footman, he brushes him aside, puts his arm round Ripsie and begins to dance with her. His arm is trembling and she can feel his heat, in his dry hands and under the braided jacket. It is as familiar to her as her own skin.

"It began in April," Mrs. Quin tells Barbara in that strange confidence they have together, "April and went on through May."

May in Cornwall is more beautiful than anywhere else in the world, Mrs. Quin thinks often. It is, too, more heady and lush, with its froth of campions, bluebells, and lady's lace in the lanes, the apple-blossom buds deep pink in the orchards and, in the China Court garden, even the ugly garden of those days, the vivid strong

colors of tulips, forget-me-nots, primulas, the smell of
early stocks. It is hot that year for May, and Ripsie often
appears in the garden after dinner and she and Borowis
walk there until it is late.

Mrs. Quin never ceases to see them—only she will not
look. They are up on the knoll by the flagpole; Eustace's
flagpole is still there then and, later, on the night of the
dance, it is to glimmer and be struck by the reflections
of the fairy lights, blue, dark pink, and emerald. Ripsie
and Borowis go down the hidden path behind the yews
or to the low wall where the sweet peas are now, or
through the kitchen garden and the field to the dell and
the valley path. "I had a dress," says Mrs. Quin. She
does not say, as most old women do, "What ridiculous
clothes we wore then," she says, "How pretty they were,"
and remembers them with love and pain, that dress and
the green one of the dance. This, that she wears in those
evenings, is white, patterned with roses, "but so old, so
washed thin, that they were only outlines of pale pink;
but I liked it, it was soft and it fluttered and it had,
I remember, a patent-leather belt—my waist was tiny
then—and a high turn-down collar." She knows the collar sets off her dark head that, even though it is dressed
with puffs and combs, still looks almost as small as when
her hair is cropped. Mrs. Quin can see herself, but she
cannot see Borowis: the young man, the tall young offi-
cer, the tall young man, each description seems to cloak
him with fresh anonymity, yet she can feel him, "unmistakably and forever," says Mrs. Quin. She has only to
shut her eyes to remember his hands, sure because they
know so well what they want, not to be gainsaid, but
gentle. "I never had a chance against you, Boro, because
I was with you," says Mrs. Quin. When his arm is around
her, she knows its curve as she knows the hardness of

his shoulder and its surprising size; his lips are cold to feel at first—"and possessive," says Ripsie with a gasp.

He disappears with Ripsie for whole days on the moor. The sky there is wider than anywhere else, the gorse is a flush of gold, the grass full of infinitesimal moor flowers, and there are larks; the wild mares have foals, the river pools are churned to froth bubbles. To Ripsie it feels as if she were caught up in that immensity, in the gold and singing, the nuzzling warm tenderness and bubbling life; and all that month John Henry is tethered by Mr. Fitzgibbon, laboring all day at the works, riding to Canverisk and back across the moor, spending his evenings "swotting," says John Henry.

"Swotting what?" asks Ripsie.

"Chemistry," says John Henry. "Statistics, prices, costs, wages, all that and learning about mechanization—things are changing even in our works," he says and regretfully, because John Henry is conservative. "Stick-in-the-mud, I fear," says Mr. Fitzgibbon. "There's not much in the way of brains, but the boy is steady." That is such a welcome relief after Jared that the old manager decides to be satisfied. "Yes, machines," says John Henry, who dislikes them. "Problems about transport, distribution, marketing." John Henry sounds weary, but he is satisfied too, deeply satisfied, and as he works at this man's work, the last traces of the schoolboy fall from him. Coming up in him is something new: responsibility. "I followed Boro like a blind sheep. Now I can't."

Because of the hours she spends with Borowis, Ripsie has not only to leave the vicarage, she has lost her post. The schoolmaster will not keep her, though the vicar has promised to talk to her again. "But he won't," says Ripsie. "I shan't let him."

"What can you do to prevent him?" asks John Henry.

"Not listen," says Ripsie again.

"But you must listen. Listen and think. What will you do without any work?"

"I don't know," says Ripsie dreamily. She has a flower between her fingers and is twirling it.

"You have to eat, keep a room."

The flower is a small Dutch iris imported by McWhirter. Ripsie has just found it and is looking at the brown mottling, velvet on the paper-thin petals, each so pale a mauve that she would hardly have said it was colored at all until she holds it against her white dress, when it is unmistakably mauve. The brown is overlaid with a dust of brilliant pollen; it comes off on her finger. Even in those days a flower can blot out the whole world for her but, "You have to eat," says John Henry, and takes the iris away.

He worries, but he is powerless. Borowis and Ripsie are like sleepwalkers, except when they are together. "Haven't you any regard for other people?" scolds John Henry.

"What people?" asks Ripsie.

For her, all that month there are no people; no eyes looking from doorways, faces peering behind the lace curtains that make the tiny cottage windows tinier still, but are screens to see through without being seen. There are no whispers in the China Court kitchen, or talk in the county drawing rooms, no kind friends to warn Lady Patrick: "I met them on the moor, my dear, not riding, walking—their horses behind them, the reins positively trailing."

"Borowis, these days, seems to have disappeared. Where is he, Pat?"

"My dear, I don't want to repeat scandal but . . ."

Lady Patrick still says nothing, but one breakfast time at the end of May, the post brings Borowis's orders; the mission, it seems, is to start earlier than they had expected. He is to join it the day after the dance. "That's a little too neat," says Borowis. "That's Mother." There is also an unpleasant note from Mr. Fitzgibbon. "This is the list of the outstanding accounts you gave me to be settled by your mother. She refers them back to you, and asks me to ask you what you propose to do about them." Afterward in the morning room Borowis stands by the window, his fingers drumming a tattoo on the sill. He has had too, John Henry is sure, an ultimatum from Isabel. "You have, haven't you?" "Shut up," says Borowis, but he does not leave the morning room to go up on the moor as usual and John Henry, with a clarity that is new to him—because, he thinks, the hero-worship is gone at last—John Henry watches to see what his brother will do.

"Look, Jod," says Borowis at last, "I believe Mother was right. It would be better not to ask Rip to the dance."

"You have asked her."

"I know, but look, Jod, if you explain to her . . ."

"You can do your own explaining," but it seems Borowis cannot, and—"What the hell can I do?" he asks John Henry, over and over again, in those last days before the dance.

"Tell Isabel. Tell her the truth."

"I can't. You don't understand. I'm in debt."

"On that whacking great allowance?"

"It isn't whacking. Most of our chaps have a thousand a year at least," says Borowis aggrieved.

"Doesn't anyone live on their pay?" says John Henry.

"They couldn't. You don't understand, Jod. It's all very well for you."

Mysteriously, it is. John Henry has only an allowance—"like a schoolboy," he says. It is ridiculously small, but it is all he needs, though sometimes he feels he ought to rebel against this taking for granted. "What if I won't?" asks John Henry. "Won't stay here? Suppose I say *I* want to go into the army, or the navy, or be a doctor?"—but he knows he does not. The St. Probus and Canverisk businesses suit him exactly, as they suit his grandfather, and it is a soothing thought that in the quarry and the works he, not Borowis, is the king pin. "If it came to a showdown," John Henry tells Ripsie—and sometimes he longs for it to come to a showdown—"they would have to give me everything I want, because there's no one else to carry on. No one." This gives him a respectability and a decency that Borowis with all his mangificence has not. "I haven't any debts." John Henry says this without smugness; he says it gratefully. "No debts; no ambitions, but I don't have to marry Isabel."

"What can I do?" groans Borowis.

"Change to a less expensive regiment. Marry Ripsie and be happy and ordinary," but John Henry does not say it and it never crosses Borowis's mind. *Well, some people are like show animals*, thinks John Henry, *born to take the limelight, live in it, be ambitious. Perhaps Mother is right*, he thinks, *and it is something to do with pedigree. Well it has missed me*, and John Henry thinks of his squareness and thick-set arms and legs, his Quin hair and pale-blue eyes; *but*, he thinks, *Ripsie has blood too. Of course, St. Omer*, and he thinks of her small erect head, her almost Chinese command of face, the sublime disregard of people that is so like Lady Patrick herself, and the glacial edge she can put in her voice. *She would be a better wife for Boro than Isabel*, thinks John Henry often, but Borowis cannot see it. He is following the laid-down conventional pattern and a surprising thought comes in these May evenings to John Henry: it is that his glamorous wonderful brother is dull. *Duller than I am?* asks John Henry, but that is heresy and he cannot believe it.

All that month he has been in torture. "Boro, you will do something about Ripsie."

"I shall take care of her."

"How?"

"I shall take care of her," but, as the days before the dance go on, John Henry learns this is as much fantasy as the boy Borowis's leasing of the valley and that Borowis's promises are quicksand.

Now the fairy lamps have burned all night on the paths in the garden; a few are beginning to flicker; some have gone out, and the sky behind the stars is beginning to pale. The music plays heartlessly on, playing that first tune again, the *Floradora* song, that is bound up with this night forever: "If you're in love with somebody, Happy and lucky somebody . . ." and Borowis dances with Ripsie at last.

She says not a word, neither does he, but holds her close and closer. Ripsie does not mistake that closeness; it is her knell and she makes no protest, not the smallest struggle; only as they dance, she grows colder, while the pain from her fingers that John Henry has crushed in his seems to run up her arm into her heart.

They dance and as the music ends, Borowis makes a few last turns to the stairs, where the furious Isabel is waiting. He passes her, stops, and very gently gives Ripsie to John Henry.

Matins

Domini est terra et quae replent eam orbis terrarum et qui habitant in eo.

THE LORD OWNS EARTH AND ALL EARTH'S FULLNESS, THE ROUND WORLD, AND ALL ITS INHABITANTS.

PSALM FOR MATINS. LITTLE OFFICE OF THE VIRGIN MARY, FROM MRS. QUIN'S *Day Hours*

T h e   A n n u n c i a t i o n · The Virgin kneels in her bedroom with her hands crossed on her breast in an attitude of the deepest humility. She has a charming childlike face expressive of sublime innocence. The Angel stands before her with his right hand raised. The Holy Ghost descends on golden beams shining through an open arched window. In the background is the Virgin's bed with a shelf at the head containing a few leatherbound books fastened by clasps. In the corner of the room behind the Virgin is a table on which stand a jug and basin and a half-folded towel.

Full border of conventional flowers, fruit, and ivy leaves, with three birds painted in colors and heightened with gold.

MINIATURE FACING THE OPENING OF MATINS
IN THE HORAE BEATAE VIRGINIS MARIAE,
FROM THE HOURS OF ROBERT BONNEFOY

A *d z a , a l l* her life, worries about the house and gives it continual care; then she has to relinquish the reins, and the house runs perfectly well without her. Lady Patrick turns her face away from faith and love, but when she is dying she asks for a priest, then a nun to nurse her, "and they came at once," says Mrs. Quin, "after all those years." Lady Patrick asks, too, if she can be moved into the big bedroom. Perhaps she goes back to those first nights in it because, at the last, "So happy," she murmurs, turns with a sigh to the other pillow, and, "falls asleep," says Mrs. Quin; a death is not usually like falling asleep, but this one is. Borowis marries Isabel, but the Eleventh has been ordered to South Africa and he throws up the mission to join it. "I warned you I would," says Borowis. He is killed at Paardeberg in February 1900. "She didn't have him for long," says Ripsie and finds she can say, "Poor Isabel," and when Bella is born, asks Isabel to be godmother. Ripsie's heart bleeds away at that dance—and she lives happily on with John Henry and makes the garden. "Then what was all the pother about?" asks Mrs. Quin.

* * *

"No more voices!" said Peter sinking into a chair. The chorus had died away in a crescendo of good-byes; Walter's boom, Bella's commands had faded; the last car had gone up the lane and Peter had come back from the gate to find quiet; only the sound of birds, of the rooks and guinea fowls in the garden and, in the house, of water running, footsteps, the clicking of August's nails on the hall flagstones and Tracy humming as she helped Cecily to wash up the tea things; ordinary everyday sounds of evening quiet.

He had to go up to the farm. "Yes, even on my wedding day," said Peter. "I must know that Ern Neot has looked after the calf." He had been up after the wedding luncheon to change and bring his suitcases down, but, "I haven't seen Ern about the animals," said Peter.

"What will Peter wear for the wedding?" That had provoked a panic.

"A lounge suit, I suppose."

"He hasn't a suit, don't you remember at the funeral . . ."

"He *can't* wear a jacket and trousers."

"He simply can't."

"I suppose he must," and a wail. "He will spoil the wedding."

"Ruin it completely," but, when they got to the church, there was Peter with his brother Harold, both in morning dress with pearl-gray waistcoats, identical gray-and-black ties, carnations, and gray top hats.

"Harold brought them down on the train last night," said Peter. "Remnants of glory," but he could say that without bitterness now.

"But *how*?"

"How did he know?"

"I telephoned," said Peter. "There is a telephone in St. Probus, you know. I couldn't get near my own old things, but Harold was resourceful and borrowed Father's. We had to take a fold in the trousers, but my chest is as broad as his, as you can see."

Tracy, too, had changed from the lawn wedding dress which Cecily had laid carefully on the White Room bed. "I will wash it to take the starch out and put it in blue paper."

"Is that what you do to keep muslin?"

"To keep" had become for Tracy the most important verb in the English language. "And it isn't only possessive," she had defended herself against Bella. "It means to watch over, take care of, maintain."

"*Maintain*, that's an odd sort of word," said Tom.

"Is it odd? To hold in one's hand?" asked Tracy. She liked it and, "The house will not change hands yet," said Tracy. It seemed to her a miracle. There world still be hands to direct, write letters, sign checks; to bolt the doors and close the windows at night; turn keys in cupboard locks and desks and in the ignition switches of cars. Hands that do household chores, use vacuum cleaners and washing machines—"if we are lucky," said Tracy, "if the books bring"—but it seemed they would. Hands that dial and pick up the receiver of the telephone, switch on lights; *and there may be fresh small hands,* thought Tracy and, *I hope, hands to help—if we are luckier still—but all belonging, all our hands.* "It's beginning," said Tracy.

She walked up to Penbarrow with Peter to see the calf and waited for him there. When they came back, up the valley path and over the wall, it was late, nearly nine o'clock.

The garden had changed in a week. "Is it only a week?" asked Peter. The sweet peas were almost over and though stocks and marigolds still flowered, the Michaelmas daisies were beginning. There were Japanese anemones, black-eyed susans, roses. A sting of cold was in the air—*The dew will be heavy*, thought Peter—and there was a smell of woodsmoke, Groundsel had been having a bonfire.

"Autumn is so melancholy," says Barbara once to Mrs. Quin. "Dead leaves, dead bracken, withered stalks of flowers, bonfires, mists. Melancholy," says Barbara with a shiver.

"That's a town convention," says Mrs. Quin. "If you lived in the country you would know better than that. Autumn is not just ash," she says stirring the bonfire.

"What is it then?" asks Barbara.

"Potash," says Mrs. Quin.

"Potash," the commonsense word breaks through the mists and the fading colors and, "Those must go on the bonfire," said Peter now, looking at the withering sweet peas. In the dusk by the wall Tracy found an autumn crocus where last year's holly leaves were dead; as she knelt down to look at it, brushing the still prickly holly aside, Peter knelt too and, with an almost unbearable happiness, she looked up past his red head and saw a new moon. The sky was still light and the moon's crescent had a flaky whiteness, almost transparent in the luminous sky. "We ought to wish," said Tracy and her wish was so strong that she had to take refuge—*in antics*, thought Tracy. "I must curtsy seven times, but you have to bow, Peter," and she commanded, "turn your money."

"Turn your ring," retorted Peter, and there was a sudden silence.

It is the latest ring at China Court, that is all, thought
Tracy. Adza's is heavy gold, a plain wide band; Lady
Patrick's narrower, chased and engraved inside. "Forever." "Jared always did have fancy ideas," says Polly.
Mrs. Quin's is a thin circle of platinum; Tracy's is gold
again but still thin; only the latest wedding ring, but
both Peter and Tracy were suddenly so conscious of it
that they had to change the subject and, "I'm cold and
hungry," said Tracy. "Let's go in."

Lamplight fell from the house windows and as they
came up the garden they could see firelight on the drawing-room walls. The room was waiting for them, ready,
dusted, and polished, the flowers freshened. Mr. Alabaster had finished with the famille rose and it was back,
ranged in its cabinets, and the Little Pink Boy, the Pale
Blue Girl were back too with the clock and its cupid on
the far chimney shelf. A table was laid for two and drawn
up to the fire, but as Tracy and Peter walked in, the
house was empty. On the hall table was a note from
Cecily: "Chicken in the oven. Mr. Walter left you the
wine. I have gone up to Minna and Groundsel for the
night. Your room is ready," and a question fell between
them like a plummet. What room?

"If you will open the wine," said Tracy a little breathlessly, "I will go and see what is in the kitchen," but the
moment Peter went into the drawing room, she ran
upstairs. The White Room was empty except for the
wedding dress laid on the counterpaned bed; all her
things had been moved. Slowly, her nerves tingling,
Tracy walked out onto the landing and saw Peter's suitcases in the dressing room. *Then?* thought Tracy and
tiptoed in.

The door to the big bedroom was open; the fire was
lit here too, a lamp was turned low on the dressing table

where her brush and comb, looking curiously childish, were put out beside a bowl of double white violets, *my bouquet*, thought Tracy. The curtains were drawn, the bed turned down, but Tracy's eyes hastily looked away from the bed. In the same moment she turned and saw Peter in the doorway.

"I thought you were opening the wine."

"I thought you were in the kitchen."

Were these the same two who, not an hour ago, had been leaning in perfect companionship on the cow shed half-door to watch the week-old calf?

The calf, completely at home in the world now, had turned its unalarmed, deep-lashed eyes, wide in its mole-colored face, to look at them, then, with a heave of its flanks had yawned, and Tracy had laughed with delight. "I have never seen a calf yawn."

"Haven't you?" Then Peter stopped. He had never seen one yawn either. "Wait. You will see . . ." and it was as if a long glimpse had been unfolded from immortality when he thought of all Tracy should see through him. *Was that us?* thought Peter. *And did we find the autumn crocus, and wish on the new moon?*

"W-we can't s-sleep here," stuttered Tracy. "It's G-Gran's room."

"The biggest bedroom, my dear"—Peter tried to be airy but only succeeded in sounding mocking—"is where the master and mistress usually sleep. We are the master and mistress."

Tracy fled downstairs to the kitchen. In the dressing room Peter began opening the unfamiliar drawers and cupboards. He opened them briskly merely to deflect his thoughts, but it sounded in the kitchen as if he were slamming them and Tracy's face set into its mask as she put the dogs' plates down for them, filled their water bowl, then took Cecily's carefully cooked chicken out of the oven. *Cooked with love*, thought Tracy miserably, with love, but eaten—she could not predict how it would be eaten, but her hands were shaking as she slid it onto its dish.

They had finished dinner long ago and cleared away, *hours ago*, thought Tracy. "Don't wash up," said a notice from Cecily on the sink. "Cecily seems to be in charge," said Peter.

They came back to the drawing room and lit cigarettes. Tracy sat on the ugly old hassock near the fire, smoothing August's ears as his head lay on her knee. Every now and then she pushed him away and knelt down to take up the poker and stir the fire. Moses, seeing there was no more chicken, had loped away to the kitchen. Bumble had gone to his basket, but August sat wearily between them looking from one to the other, clearly asking why they did not all go to bed. Tracy got up, peered between the curtains and came back.

"The moon has gone d-down."

"It would by now. It's new."

"Yes," said Tracy. She poked the fire again and asked, "Do you need to go up to P-Penbarrow again?"

"No. Ern is sleeping there."

"Did C-Cecily arrange that too?"

"No, I did," said Peter.

His face, on the other side of the fire, looked bony and closed and Tracy knew that her own was just as stiff; self-consciousness was on them like a straitjacket. *Of course, there have been couples who left each other on their wedding night*, she thought and, *I don't know him*, she thought in panic.

She was very tired. The taste of the wine was in her mouth and her head felt swimming. *I shouldn't have drunk all that*, thought Tracy. The lamps seemed to be burning on and on, but with a double flame. *Have I drunk as much as that?* she thought.

Peter made up the fire, but a moment later she picked up the poker and stirred it again. Then August ran to the door and whined. "He w-wants to go out," said Tracy. "He always g-goes out before he goes to—" She broke off sharply. It was long past his bedtime, but she did not say that either. Peter got up and stretched and went with August into the garden. He called Bumble too, but it seemed only a moment before they were back. Tracy heard him lock the front door; heard a creak as Bumble got back into his basket, then August scratched at the drawing-room door and Peter came in with him, shut the door, put another and unnecessary log on the fire and sat down. *Are we going to sit here all night, as far away from each other as we can get?* wondered Tracy.

Silence settled on the room. Tracy hunched herself on the hassock, her feet together, her elbows on her knees as she looked at the fire, but Peter sat upright in his chair, one leg crossed over the other.

He's handsome, thought Tracy grudgingly.

She's pretty, thought Peter.

Handsome and my husband, thought Tracy, cold with dread. *This stranger!* and she longed, as she had not longed all these years, to be home again, *not here that I thought was home, but back in New York, in the world I know.* She longed for New York and for Barbara, her gay, light, yes light, mother who would never have dreamed of falling into such depths as this. *This comes of being serious, why am I serious?* moaned Tracy, but without a sign. *What have I done now?* In this moment she would have given China Court, and all England, to be back in America again.

Pretty and utterly baffling, thought Peter. *A little fish, or a block of ice. I should have known she couldn't like me*—and he would have given Penbarrow to be back at Penbarrow again; not to be here, tied to this silence, with the inscrutable face opposite him, its eyelids sealed. *Prim and ridiculous*, thought Peter.

I ought to have remembered who I was, cried the silent Tracy.

I should have kept myself to myself as I swore I would, said the silent Peter.

Tracy was afraid she would cry and, to hide her face, picked up the poker and suddenly Peter said between his teeth, "Tracy, if you poke that fire again I swear I shall hit you."

She looked at him in cold surprise, turned and poked the fire. Peter leaned forward and gave her a stinging slap on the cheek.

Never in her life had anyone hit Tracy. She jumped; the poker fell into the grate with a clatter as, astonished and hurt, she stared at Peter, the mark reddening on her cheek, tears welling in her eyes. "I'm sorry," said Peter, "but I warned you. Perhaps another time you will believe me."

"An-noth-ther!" Blind with tears, Tracy stumbled over the hassock as she sprang up. Rage and misery made her more incoherent than ever. "You great b-b-beast! If you think I shall st-stay here an-other m-m-minute—"

"And where will you go this time of night? America? Rome?" sneered Peter.

She said what she knew would goad him most. "I shall go to Aunt Bella tomorrow."

"You little cat!" Peter was up too and coming nearer. Seen through tears he looked so big and menacing that Tracy backed away down the room, around chairs and tables, until a smell of arums warned her she was near the other fireplace.

"Don't touch me," she cried in panic but, "Little cat!" said Peter again. He was white with temper and Tracy hastily tried to step sideways, but in her blindness and hurry, she stumbled over the curb; to save herself she clutched at the mantel, narrowly missing the Little Pink Boy and the French clock; then there was a rattle and a crash as her hand swept the Pale Blue Girl into the fender.

Tracy and Peter stood appalled, looking down at the mess of pale-blue china with its gilt and roses. A piece of yellow petticoat and a china hand in a blue sleeve had fallen on the hearth rug; a bit of curly head with a sliver of straw hat lay by the lilies; a shoe had rolled away under the grate. Slowly Tracy knelt down, shivering with nerves as she tried to pick up the pieces. "Look what you have made me do," she whispered. "What I . . ." She gave a sob and Peter knelt beside her.

"That's how we keep things." She had begun to cry in earnest now, the stiffness gone. "I loved her ever since I was a little girl. She was ours now and I smashed her."

"Yes, thank God."

"*Th-thank* God?" She turned an amazed face to look up at him.

Peter pulled her handkerchief out of her sleeve and gave it to her. "Yes, because we were nearly smashing everything. Don't try and pick up the pieces now." He drew her to her feet. "Leave them. I can explain to Cecily in the morning. Just now, I want you."

"Yes," said Tracy. She dabbed at her eyes and blew

her nose and sat down again. "Yes," she said. "Let's sit and talk as we have been doing all these days, talk about our plans."

"Not now, my darling."

Darling. Tracy's stomach seemed to give a small independent leap of itself. "But . . ."

"There's one thing we have to do first," said Peter.

"First?"

"Yes. We have to be married," said Peter. "Get up, Tracy." Tracy stood up. "Come here."

"I have never touched you," said Peter, "except for that slap." He laid his hand against the hot mark. "Never touched you, not because I didn't want to, but because it wasn't time. Now . . ." Peter's voice was suddenly husky. He put his other hand on Tracy's shoulder and gently ran it up her neck so that her hair fell over his hand. "Your hair's like silk," said Peter, and picked up again what he had been saying. "Now I am going to touch you. Pay attention, Tracy. You are my wife and I am going to kiss you." His arms went round her. "Stand up straight," said Peter, "and stop dreaming."

Startled, Tracy stood in his arms. For a moment she fought against him, but he only held her more tightly, forcing her lips up to his, shutting out the room and the firelight, his face warm and close to hers, as her mouth softened under his kiss. She could feel the hardness of his body pressed to hers, hard where she was soft. *Then we are the two halves of a whole*, thought Tracy and her heart began to beat as if it were clamoring.

"Go upstairs," said Peter, "and get into bed and wait for me."

At dawn a breeze comes ruffling the trees. The dew, as Peter said it would be, is heavy. The doors are locked; the windows dark with the curtains drawn. The lamps are out, the fires only handfuls of red embers; the dogs are in their baskets while the cats, Minerva, Cuckoo, Moses, curl in the kitchen armchair. A baby cries; a child dreams, somebody snores; someone lies awake, staring at the wall, but the voices hush because the house is asleep, "and now the stories seem like tales," says old Mrs. Quin when she is very old. "Perhaps they don't matter," she says, for she is also very tired, "except to the people who lived through them. The stories are all different—of course, each has its time and place—yet they are all alike in that, as with every day, they must be lived through from sunrise to sunset, all the hours of the day; and as the day ends, it begins," says Mrs. Quin.

The Hours of the Day

[*in the early usage*]

MATINS and LAUDS	*are night prayers according to the early custom of reciting them after midnight*

In Those Days:

PRIME	*was said at the first hour of the day, i.e. six o'clock*
TIERCE	*or the third hour, at nine o'clock*
SEXT	*the sixth hour, corresponds to noon*
NONE	*the ninth hour, three o'clock*
VESPERS	*at the close of day (when dusk falls)*
COMPLINE	*the evening hour, which terminates the day*

Makeup of a Typical Book of Hours of the Late Fifteenth Century:

1. Calendar
2. Extracts from the Gospels

John	I	1–14
Luke	I	26–28
Matthew	II	1–12
Mark	XVI	14–20

3. Hours of the Blessed Virgin Mary
4. Hours of the Cross

5. Hours of the Holy Ghost
6. Seven penitential Psalms and Litany
7. Offices of the dead
8. Memorials to various saints and frequently
two long prayers to the Virgin

Acknowledgments

My thanks are due to Messrs. Sotheby and Co. for help over the rare books found in China Court and for the descriptions from the Bonnefoy Book of Hours; to Charles Causley and the Reverend W. A. Kneebone of Atarnum for checking of Cornish dialect and terms; to Mrs. Mary Oliver for the loan of books; and especially to Mrs. E. M. Taylor for endless and patient research.

The translations of the Latin quotations from the Book of Hours are taken from *The Little Breviary*, edited by the Benedictine nuns of Stanbrook Abbey, Worcester, England.